Helmuth Moltke

Letters of Field-Marshal Count Helmuth von Moltke

to his mother and his brothers

Helmuth Moltke

Letters of Field-Marshal Count Helmuth von Moltke
to his mother and his brothers

ISBN/EAN: 9783337383602

Printed in Europe, USA, Canada, Australia, Japan

Cover: Foto ©Andreas Hilbeck / pixelio.de

More available books at **www.hansebooks.com**

LETTERS

OF

FIELD-MARSHAL

COUNT HELMUTH von MOLTKE

TO

HIS MOTHER AND HIS BROTHERS

TRANSLATED BY

CLARA BELL AND HENRY W. FISCHER

WITH ILLUSTRATIONS

NEW YORK

HARPER & BROTHERS, FRANKLIN SQUARE

1892

CONTENTS.

I.

COUNT VON MOLTKE'S LETTERS TO HIS MOTHER
(1823 TO 1837).

II.

COUNT VON MOLTKE'S LETTERS TO HIS BROTHER ADOLF
(1839 TO 1871).

III.

COUNT VON MOLTKE'S LETTERS TO HIS BROTHER LUDWIG
(1828 TO 1888).

CONTENTS.

TABLE SHOWING THE NEAREST RELATIONS OF FIELD-MARSHAL COUNT HELMUTH VON MOLTKE.

ILLUSTRATIONS.

This sketch was made by the Field-Marshal at the time when he and his brother were living together at Berlin, Adolf as a law student, and Helmuth as a lieutenant. Helmuth, whose military position took him a great deal into the society of the capital, had the greatest regard for his reserved, laborious brother, to whom he was affectionately attached. He took advantage of a quiet hour to sketch him absorbed in his studies, sitting a little way behind him. To the end of his life the Field-Marshal would ask to see this drawing from time to time, and contemplate it with smiling interest.

I.

LETTERS TO HIS MOTHER.

1823 to 1837.

HENRIETTE VON MOLTKE.

HENRIETTE VON MOLTKE.

FRAU HENRIETTE VON MOLTKE, the Field-Marshal's mother, was the daughter of Finanzrath Paschen, and born at Lübeck, on February 5th, 1777. Her father, belonging to one of the first families of that Hanseatic town, was a merchant of importance, with extensive connections, by which he and his family gained a larger and broader view of life. Henriette was admirably brought up by her step-mother, and was a charming and highly educated girl of twenty when she made the acquaintance of Friedrich Philipp Victor von Moltke, at that time a remarkably handsome young lieutenant, and immediately fell in love with him. Her prudent father was opposed to the marriage; but what Henriette had once made up her mind to, her determined nature clung to for life; and after a short engagement she married the husband of her choice, in May, 1797.

Frau von Moltke is described as a woman of medium height, a good figure and proud, repellent manners. Large, intelligent eyes, an acquiline nose, firmly set lips, and waving, powdered hair, gave her face an unusually marked individuality. But though she was reserved and grave, almost stern, she had a passionate nature and a tender, faithful heart. Her understanding was excellent; she was mistress of several languages, and expressed herself in writing, even in moments of the deepest agitation, with equal clearness and brevity. Her soul was animated by deep Christian feeling. This is evident in a letter to her son Adolf, of January 14th, 1830: "May you ever more and more acknowledge the hand of God, even if He lay it on you in trial. A pure faith and firm confidence give courage and strength in every situation in life. What if we lack honors and temporal blessings?

They are all perishable, and there is no permanent good but the consciousness of duty fulfilled.   This may God grant you!"

Gifted with a fine voice, she loved music and poetry, and a life of sunshine, such as was her lot for but a short time.

After the first happy years of her married life, misfortunes, loss of money, and anxieties began.   Her husband, who was in the Danish Army, was constantly absent, and the house and buildings on an estate he had purchased in Holstein were burnt to the ground.   At that time Frau von Moltke had the strength of mind and body to nurse the child of her bailiff as well as her own for three months, the infant's mother having fallen sick with alarm at the fire, soon after its birth.   He is now an old man of eighty-six.

Her whole being was greatly affected by the fact that, as time went on, she and her husband understood each other less and less, and lived apart.   But her energy only gained fresh impetus to devote herself with increased conscientiousness and fidelity to her eight children.   Though accustomed from her youth to wealth and comfort, no sacrifice was too great for her; she gave up everything to give her children the best possible education.   And she was so happy as to see them all develop nobly, and to be venerated by them with an affection which kept her memory alive in transfigured beauty long after her death.   She lived at Preetz till 1832; then, her youngest daughter Augusta having married Herr Burt, she removed to Schleswig.

She died as she had lived, heroically.   She concealed her malady, which was complicated with symptoms of dropsy, with unfailing determination from all her children.   On the last evening of her life, her daughter Helene (Frau Pröpstin Bröker), on returning from a party, found her at her writing-table in a room where the fire had gone out.   She silenced an affectionate remonstrance as to taking better care of herself with a good-night kiss, and next morning her daughter found her on the floor, dying of an apoplectic stroke.   Thus she departed, May 27th, 1837; while her son Helmuth, whose character in many important points resembled hers, was on the distant shores of the Bosphorus.

COUNT VON MOLTKE'S
LETTERS TO HIS MOTHER.

Frankfort-on-the-Oder,* June 5th, 1823.

Dear Mother:

As Ludwig is setting off on the journey which he so ardently desires, and to which I look back with so much pleasure, I give him these lines for you. I can vividly imagine the joy which his presence in Preetz will cause, and he will be no less happy to be there. Your pretty little garden must produce a quantity of strawberries and peas: here the season is over and I have had but few. If I can get it finished, I will enclose a little sketch of a mill not far from Frankfort to which I sometimes walk; I only beg, in exchange, for the unfinished sketch of Preetz which I left behind. Also you will do me a great pleasure by sending me a little lock of your hair, and of Lena's, Gusta's and Vips'.† I have a locket in which I shall wear them. I look forward to Ludwig's return for much news of you all. Whether I shall get into the Staff-college in

* Helmuth von Moltke was at this time lieutenant in the Fusilier battalion of the 8th (Life) Infantry; the 1st battalion was at Lübben, the 2nd at Guben.

† The different members of the family alluded to in these letters may be identified by a reference to the pedigree attached to this volume. *Vips*, is Victor.

the autumn is still uncertain; it depends on whether my work places me among the best fifty out of sixty-eight men. We exercise at least once every day. In the evening I go to bathe with some of the others. The best swimmers can swim across the Oder, which is now much swollen by the rains, and has overflowed the meadows on the banks. Then we go to the Kirschberge, and eat cherries or sour milk, and sometimes both. Have you any cherries yet in your garden? On the 24th of this month the other two battalions are to come here, and then we shall exercise in earnest; and on the 12th August three more battalions arrive, with artillery and Jägers. Then we shall have to march a mile [four English miles] out to the exercising ground. Finally, on September 2nd, we go to Berlin, where about 30,000 men will be quartered. Best love to my sisters and Vips. Forgive this hastily written letter: often think of your

HELMUTH.

OBER-SALZBRUNN, August 15th, 1825.

DEAR MOTHER:

Although it is not long since I last wrote, I will no longer deprive myself of the pleasure of beginning another letter. I yesterday received by Ludwig your welcome letter of July 23rd. How glad I always am to get a peep into your quiet home, so utterly unlike my life here. You are certainly right in saying that the peace of mind you now so deservedly enjoy is the only true happiness for which we need strive. And how often has my sore heart longed for it, when disappointed hopes, sickness, or enmity have crushed all my vital courage. But this is a malady of my youth. It is only after going through storms that peace is precious, nor may we have it before. Here I am collecting fresh strength for life. Fate has given me so little cause for complaint that it would be really unpardonable in me to complain, were it not that physical peculiarities make me particularly susceptible to melancholy impressions. However, from my former experience I have reason to hope that the waters will do me good service. And then I will set out with new courage on the thorny race-course on which I am striving after fortune, alone, and so far from you all. May I attain it for you all!

There is a young girl here worthy to be your daughter-in-law. She is a Gräfin Reichenbach. She is lovely and well educated; you would take her to your heart. But unluckily she has no fortune. The very antipodes may be found among some Polish acquaintance, very grand folks and very rich. I do not know whether you have ever had much to do with Poles; nothing can be pleasanter; you are made at home at once, at once a friend and an intimate. They load you with such kindness and courtesy as Germans would call importunate. They are all alike in this, and highly educated, entertaining and gay; and yet I should not like to give you a Polish daughter-in-law.

I have had a pressing invitation to visit Poland, from a Starostin Obrocziewska.* This lady brings her own man-cook with her; you dine off silver at her table; she speaks French perfectly, has very pretty daughters, and is the gayest old lady I have ever seen. But my finances, which are sadly reduced by my journey to Dresden, and above all by paying off my Berlin bills, require the strictest economy. I am lucky in having a harbor of refuge with my friend Von Frobel at Glatz, where I may stay for a time at no

* Thus spelled in the letter; but whether this is the correct spelling is uncertain.

cost. I am afraid that I can only afford the expense of this month at the baths, at most; for I must keep enough for the return journey.

It is long since I have liked any place so well as this, and that may be doing me as much good as the waters. I have wine and a carriage almost for nothing, for Colonel Count Wartensleben, my father's friend, who has twice been to see me, has taken quite a fancy to me, which is unlike him as a rule. I drive out almost every day in his elegant droschky to one of the beautiful old forts or castles, of which one can never see enough here. Lately we made an excursion by water underground, which is perhaps unique in the world. Imagine a vault one thousand fathoms in length, partly blasted out of the rock, but only four feet in width and scarcely more in height, winding for hundreds of feet, beneath hills, villages, and brooks. The bottom is covered, to a depth of about three feet, with water which is fed by subterranean springs, and kept up by a sluice. The boat in which you navigate this Styx is almost as wide as the channel. The light of day soon disappears, and in spite of the numerous lamps in the boat, total darkness reigns, till the eye becomes accustomed to it. Then the black anthracite, blocks of granite and trickling streams become visible, and from time to time a little dock or bay to enable boats to pass. The air is chill but pure. Summer and winter are unknown; even thunder is inaudible. On the return, the first sight of the opening in the distance is particularly beautiful. The semicircular arch looks exactly like the setting sun, and is mirrored all along the smooth track of water. On emerging one is quite blinded. We went the other day to Adersbach. What struck me as most beautiful in this strangely shaped hill of sandstone was a high water-fall, tumbling down a narrow rift into a deep, dark cave, to be entered only through one cleft in the rock.

I received your welcome letter of the 23rd the day before yesterday, and read it all with the greatest delight.

September 6th.—The delightful time I have spent here in Salzbrunn is now a thing of the past, and to my great grief I must leave. I shall never regret having been here. The trip has done me great good and I have made several pleasant acquaintances, some of whom I shall continue to see in Berlin. I tear myself with regret from such a lovely neighborhood and so many kind people, who have made me so welcome. As there is still a month to spare before the Staff-college opens, my plan is as follows: I go to Breslau on the 14th; whether I shall before that ascend Schnee-koppe * with Count Reichenbach is uncertain. In Breslau I shall stay with a Count Wartensleben, an uncle of my friend, with whom I am going to drive in his carriage, on the 17th, to Rusko, not far from Krotochin in Poland, to spend a few days with Frau von Obrocziewska. At the end of the month we return to Breslau. From thence I go to Glatz to stay for a fortnight with my friend Von Frobel, and with him I return to Berlin on October 15th.

September 13th.—I set out for Breslau to-morrow morning. I have made the excursion to the Riesengebirge. It began under bad auspices, but was brought to a happy issue. The state of my finances was as low as the barometer; however, all turned out well. At six in the morning I started with young Reichenbach for Waldenburg. There a vehicle was waiting to carry us to Landeshut, and hence we proceeded by the

* The highest peak of the Riesengebirge. Murray gives the height as 5250 feet.

mail to Schmiedeberg. Just before entering this town the road zig-zags for about half a mile [two English miles] down a high, steep hill. The view meanwhile is beyond description. At your feet flows the Lomnitz, along which the pretty little town lies for about half a mile; behind it rises the enormous mass of the Riesengebirge, Schneekoppe crowning the whole with its little chapel. To the right stretches a long valley, where Warmbrunn, Hirschberg, the castle of Kynast, and various other forts and castles are seen.

We arrived at about one o'clock. Reichenbach went to his brother-in-law, Prince Reusz, who owns the old castle of Heinhof. The Prince, whose acquaintance I had made here, came at once to beg me to stay with him, as I did till next morning, and it was like being in a fairy palace. Nothing can be compared to the sunrise and sunset in this paradise. I could hardly tear myself away the morning after at about three to ascend Schneekoppe. By ten o'clock I was on Austrian ground, where I refreshed myself with a draught of Hungarian wine. Then, quite alone—for Reichenbach dared not climb for fear of his chest—and even without a guide, till one o'clock I made my way with great difficulty but steadily up hill; however, though the climb was really very stiff, I was amply rewarded by the glorious view over an extent of above twenty miles [93 English miles] towards Prague and Breslau, from the topmost peak of this range, which is crowned with a chapel to the Virgin. I could get no higher than this for hundreds of miles round; I stood where no tree will grow, on the highest ground in all Germany, 4900 feet above your heads. Below me, snow was lying in the hollows; two streams flow from the steep wall of rock in opposite directions. Lower down come the pine forests, looking like a field of cresses, and beyond lie the endless plains with numberless villages, pools, woods, and bleaching-grounds. But it is impossible to give any idea of it. Then I turned to the northward and looked out towards where you dwell, and wrote a few words to you in my note-book. I then left, and after a tremendous walk, found myself back in Schmiedeberg by six o'clock. There I found a coach on the point of starting for Landeshut, so I got in and arrived at eight. From thence I returned the same evening to Salzbrunn, a distance of three miles, getting in at about midnight. The excursion did me great good, it did not cost me a thaler, and I shall never forget it. I have now been seven weeks in Salzbrunn, much longer than I at first intended. It has, however, cost me more than I had expected. I am setting out for Poland with eight thalers, and five thalers more which I have borrowed. However much I may have to pinch in Berlin, I can never regret having seen so much for such a relatively small outlay. And if I may only hope to keep as well and hearty as I now am, I have not paid too dear for it. So I am in the best spirits, and only wish that you all may be as flourishing as I am; excepting only in the matter of money. My next letter will reach you from Berlin, where I must positively be by the 15th. If either of the brothers is at home, I shall beg him to give my father news of my journey and my stay here; I will write to him as soon as I get to Berlin. But it is not worth while to send another letter from home, the postage is so enormously dear. The moss and violets I enclose, grow only on the very summit of Schneekoppe, where all other vegetation ceases to exist.

Now farewell, dear mother. Keep well and think of me often. I will let you hear at once of my return to

Berlin. Best love to the dear sisters. Once more
good-bye, and always love your   HELMUTH.

FRANKFORT, March 25th, 1828.

DEAR MOTHER:

Nothing but the fear lest our letters should cross,
has kept me so long from writing, so it is all the pleasanter to be able to do so now and to tell you that my
health is perfectly good, and that I hope in the course
of the summer to have a few weeks' bathing at Swine-
münde, and so prevent any relapse.

The news you send me of my father grieves me
greatly, though it was not wholly unexpected. Six
weeks ago I wrote to him, and tried to dissuade him
from the notion of retiring from military life—the
only sphere of occupation for him, and giving up his
only hope when he was really so near being made Colonel of his Regiment. I offered him my salary of
sixty to eighty thalers if he should be in need of ready
money for the first outfit. But the idea had taken too
deep root; he thought himself too unlucky in his military career to reflect that any other promised even less
success, with less opportunity for work and smaller
pay. However, it is done, and we must hope that he
may not rue it; at any rate, we will not let him see
that we blame him. The king will surely do something for him.

If only my father could rent and manage a farm.
But the worst of it is that the mischief is not so much
in his ill-luck as in himself. We must wait and see
what comes of it.

I am heartily glad that I can give you the good
news of myself that some weeks since, as a result of

my personal application and of the reports sent in to the Court of Directors of the Military Students, the chief of the General Staff promised unconditionally that I should be appointed to the work of the General Staff in May or July; and this, with the present restricted numbers of the General Staff, is wonderfully good luck, for it would not have come to me in turn for the next six or seven years. I shall then for nine months in the year draw from twenty to twenty-five thalers a month, and need no further help. Thus, in time, your position, too, will be improved, and till then the only thing, especially for me, is to be as wide-awake as possible.

For the present, and apparently till I am appointed to the office, I shall retain my place in the Staff-college of the division. As I have now taken up surveying and drawing, I have no lack of work; I have fourteen lectures and eight inspections a week, as well as the surveillance of thirty-one youngsters, who, however, like me, and whom I keep in proper respect and good order. But I owe my promised appointment to the very favorable report from the Division.

During the last few months I have been compiling a compendium for my pupils on military map-making, which is now in the press. The remuneration will amount to at least a hundred thalers, which, however, I must to some extent anticipate, since I no longer give private teaching; and I have also lost my mess allowance, for I am no longer attached to the battalion, which has been moved to Stettin.

My position here is very pleasant, and brings with it many advantages, among which I include the capital riding-lessons, for which I pay nothing, and which I have been having for the last five months. They are

now at an end; to-day we are to ride a grand qua-
drille in all the various paces.

I have lately made the acquaintance of Countess
Blumenthal and her family, who have been to Guts-
nachbar in the Liebethal, and say they recognized me
by my family likeness. You tell me nothing about
Adolf. I hope that he and Ludwig will decide on not
trying to make a career in Denmark. I see here with
envy so many young fellows of my own age, councillors (*Räthe*) and assessors, with incomes of from six
hundred to one thousand thalers a year. I shall never
regret having given up the comforts of home, and so
having secured prospects of advancement, little as
may have come of it hitherto.

How is your sweet little garden looking? You
must by this time be very busy. How I should like
to go there for a half an hour now and then, if only I
had not to work there with you.

Here it is quite spring-like; the Oder already over-
flows its banks, and as soon as it has got rid of its
sheet of ice, the boats will be skimming over the
meadows with wide, shining sails, like large swans.

If I am not obliged to spend most of my profits in
advance, I should enjoy nothing so much as to make
an excursion through the mountains, to dear Silesia
or Saxony; when once I am in the office there will be
an end of that, and this summer is, perhaps, the last
of my freedom. I shall get a short leave of absence in
winter, I dare say, and as money will soon be easier,
it is to be hoped, I shall drop in on you for Christmas
some day, when you least expect me.

Now adieu, dear mother; a thousand loves to all the
dear ones. Take care of yourself, and think sometimes of your

HELMUTH.

My dear Lena:

There is still room for a few words to you; how are you, that you never write to me? How have you got through the winter? I hope you are well. Keep that little limb, Vips, in good order, that's all. My health is wonderful. I often lie unconscious for eight or ten hours—at night; I have no appetite after meals; towards evening such convulsive yawning and stretching, and all day utter sleeplessness, and restlessness in all my body,—I only hope you do not suffer so. I draw diligently, and yesterday finished off a grand Turk's head; I will soon begin the landscape for you. As I write I get a letter from Berlin which is charged one thaler four groschen for postage. There are surveying instruments with it for the school. I am glad to think that I shall soon have done with surveying.

Does old Schmidt still pull your hair? Remember me to all who ask for me, and write soon to your loving and faithful brother

HELMUTH.

You say nothing about my novellette, "The Friends."* Oh! to think of the things which flowed from this immortal pen during my illness, and the publisher did me out of my honorarium!

FRANKFORT-ON-THE-ODER, May 9th, 1828.

DEAR MOTHER:

Your dear letter, which I have just received, transported me in an instant from all my maps, reports, examination papers, and the other things with which I am inundated, to your cloister-like home. I see the coffee-machine sputtering on the table, the sisters stitching, Vips with a counting-board, and quinine-

* This is the only known effort by the Field-Marshal in the domain of *belles-lettres.*

powders, and you with a pair of fearfully ragged stockings—in your hand—shaking your head as you settle your spectacles to repair the leak in this Danaid's sieve. And I can hear my friend the cow lowing for some fresh grass; and there is something stamping and shouting overhead, probably one of my respected brothers, announcing his late *levée*. You are all so busy that you do not see that I, or my spirit—look round, Lena—am standing in your midst. As far as my body is concerned, it is sitting here, at this very writing-table strewn with an amazing chaos of maps, letters, instruments, plane-tables, calculations, and what not, and there lies a long money-bag of goodly proportions—but not a bag of money. The facts are these. I have been quite unexpectedly appointed, since the beginning of the year, to the Survey Office, and by June 1st I must be at Namslau, in Upper Silesia. As you may suppose, it was a delightful surprise to me. But now such a mass of business crowds on me all at once, that I hardly know how I am ever to get through it.

May 26th.—As I am off to Silesia the day after tomorrow, I hasten to finish this letter, which, in consequence of an unexpected duty, has been set aside for a fortnight. I was sent off with my Division-students to survey four-and-a-half square miles [about 21 English square miles] of ground on the right bank of the Oder for the Lieutenant-General. We were in the field every day for ten or eleven hours. In the evening we all assembled outside my quarters, which were commonly very good, since I might take them wherever I would in any village. There we would sing; we had taken a guitar; we ate and drank whatever was to be had, and last evening, in the most lovely moonlight, we crossed the Oder and came home. As soon as I am at the quarters of my survey I will write again. I am very unwilling to leave my Division-students and they too are not best pleased at the change. Now adieu, dear mother, I only wish you may all be as well and happy as I am. Best love to the dear sisters; keep me in your affectionate remembrance.

HELMUTH.

GRUTTENBERG, NEAR OELS, July 6th, 1828.

DEAR MOTHER:

It is long since you have heard from me, and let that always be a sign to you that all is well with me. I wish I could be sure of the same with regard to you, for the thought of home is to me always mingled with fears and regrets.

Of myself I have nothing to tell but what is pleasant. In the last four or five weeks I have been living here on the estate of one Herr von Kleist, who makes me as much at home as a child of his own, so that I have surveyed almost half of my section from this as headquarters. At half-past four in the morning a coffee-pot is brought in to me, with two plates on which slices of bread and butter and cakes are piled up to a considerable height, irresistibly suggesting the hospitalities of a Highland chieftain. Then I sally forth attired in unbleached gaiters, a gray dust cloak, white foraging cap, and gloves without finger-tips, armed with an instrument case and a good Ramsden telescope. Behind me my servant with the plane-table. So I go across fields and gardens, relying on my general pass, which I always carry in my pocket, and which affords extraordinary facilities; for instance, one of my colleagues had all the bells removed from a tower because they were in his way. Every mayor is enjoined to provide us with horses, quarters, and two men every day. As soon as I get in we sit down to dinner, when my only anxiety is how to manage to eat some of each dish, there are so many. At supper again from three to four dishes are served, and between whiles there is breakfast, luncheon, afternoon coffee, and what not, and good Hungary wine in plenty; added to which I am perfectly well, and so, perfectly content.

As I now really get four times as much as Fritz and Wilhelm, I deduct from it five thalers every month; this, during the nine months for which I draw this pay—and for three years—makes 45 thalers, which I place at your service.

My finances are, of course, in a flourishing condition. All the profits are gone, to be sure, in paying my debts, for I never had so little money as last year, and I have had to procure a complete civilian outfit, that being necessary in my present employment; but now, with the very good pay of 45 thalers, I have very few expenses. In Berlin, indeed, I shall not be so well off. I am taking advantage of a favorable opportunity, to start to-morrow for three weeks in the mountains, which, at a distance of twenty miles, show their blue peaks quite on the horizon. I shall go first to Schweidnitz to visit Wartensleben, who is now married; and from thence to Salzbrunn, where I shall take the waters. I am rejoicing at the thought of seeing incomparable Fürstenstein again, only the day after to-morrow.

If only I could give you a peep from the Riesengrab and through the deep, dark Feldschlucht to the old and new castles!

Your next letter, which I look for with impatience, I will beg you to send during the next fortnight to Schweidnitz, and after that to Oels, where I will send

SCHÖN-BRIESE CASTLE, FROM THE PARK.

for it. After my return I shall be staying at Ludwigs-
dorf near Oels, with his Excellency General von P.
The parting here to-day will be quite a sad one; the
children have got quite used to their lodger. I have
been obliged to promise that I will return for the
harvest-home.

Adieu, dear mother, keep well and strong, and write
soon to your loving son

HELMUTH.

Again much love to the sisters. Augusta's slippers
are still extant, and the barège scarf, like Lena's dress,
still excites much admiration and envy.

SCHON-BRIESE, August 18th, 1828.

DEAR MOTHER:

I found your letter of July 20th on coming in, and
had the comfort of learning that you are well and
sound. Tell Adolf, who no doubt was known to
Walter Scott when he invented the character of Alan
Fairford in "Red Gauntlet," that I wish him all success,
and some impudence in his examination. It is really
a melancholy thing that, with you, even the most solid
learning must be subject to the chances of a single
throw, and that even if the dice fall right, it is hardly
regarded as a well-founded claim to a brilliant career.
Loui must look forward to this break-neck examination with two-fold agitation. I really believe he would
rather set a whole law book to music than learn it by
heart, and if it came to fetching the blind goddess out
of hell—as Proserpina * was once fetched by another
musician—he would do it without looking round at
her once. Give my best love to the dear, good little
sisters. We really must dance a galop together again
some day, and they must overhaul my cuffs and neck-

* Eurydice ?

erchiefs. I hope that Lena keeps Victor in as good
order as of yore, when he only occasionally gave vent
to his feelings by a few thumps and a mild curse if his
cap was not brushed or his frill not soft enough.

The failure of the fruit crops, and the storms and
rain, you suffer in common with us, far and wide
throughout the country; still, the summer has been
fine, and the corn harvest here extremely abundant.
I had to limit my journey to a fortnight, so could stay
only six days at Salzbrunn; however, I drank ninety
glasses of the water. I was unfortunately obliged to
make my tour in the mountains alone. So I hurried
through it; in fact, I made the long excursion from
Schmiedeberg, over the whole range to Schreiberhau,
in one day, and did not ascend Schneekoppe, knowing
it already. In one of the high villages I provided myself with a guide, and climbed literally up into the
clouds which soon enwrapped us closely. We got up
the Seiffenlehne by one of the most fatiguing paths, a
staircase of great boulders, which took us up to 4000
feet above your heads. Here we walked among tall
pine-trees above a rushing streamlet, and then over
a green and always wet meadow, on which the herds
were wandering with their bells. At the top it began
to rain smartly. But the view, when the wind blew
the masses of cloud among the dark pine-forests, and
swept through the deep ravines, is indescribable.
Now a wide valley—houses, hamlets, and towns, with
the open country for miles beyond and villages innumerable; then suddenly everything hidden again in
gray clouds, wreathing the peaks with a majestic roar.
I saw the same spectacle again on the Schneegruben,
and I prefer it infinitely to a quite clear sky. You
can hardly believe your eyes when the vast curtain of
cloud parts on the wings of the storm, worthy of the

stage of perhaps ten thousand square miles on which you look down. The longer you gaze the more you discern—a streak, a speck; and the speck is a town, a hill, or a wood, over which the clouds are driving, far beneath your feet. Especially lovely are the great bleaching grounds which stretch in regular, snow-white fields between the blue mirrors of tiny lakes among the black woods. The roads meander like fine wandering threads over the hills, which, though it made you pant to climb them, from hence look quite flat. Along them for a mile or so stretch the villages and towns with their clean white walls and shining, silver-gray shingle roofs. Immediately at my feet was a precipice of perhaps nine hundred feet of perpendicular cliff.

In the evening I descended with some difficulty into the ominous-looking valley through which the Elbe tumbles in little cascades over numberless ridges and boulders, presenting a grand spectacle as a whole. My favorite spot too, the falls of the Zacken, I saw in the twilight from the Teufelsthal, and I spent the night in a glass house by the foaming Zacken. On the following morning I visited the Kocher Fall and the castle of Kynast, of which you know the romantic legend. Certainly only a very cruel heart could require a man to ride out of the high window and round the top of the wall, where it would be impossible to turn, or even to come down. The precipice beneath the walls is deeper at every step, the points of the highest peaks are dizzy before the horseman's eyes, and close to the entrance to the castle a gulf yawns which, like a serpent, seems to draw the unhappy wretch to his destruction from sheer horror. What a terrific fall must it have been of the armed Knight and horse from that peak of rock. The sight of the ruins of these great fortresses, such as Bolkenburg, Schweinhaus, Nimmersatt, and others, makes a peculiarly melancholy impression. I visited these on my way, and Adolf and Ludwig will have seen others yet finer. A certain unsatisfied curiosity enhances the feeling; the neighbors and inhabitants of such places know nothing about them but that they have furnished the stones for building their hovels. (As the commandant of Pilsen asserts that the murder of Wallenstein, if it ever took place at all, must have happened long before his time.) And still the half-effaced trace of a saint's effigy on a wall, or the ruts in the rocky soil rouse a whole flood of hypotheses and reflections.

However, it is time to return from these ruined strongholds to the beautiful castle where I am at present staying. You go through a finely-painted domed hall, where the walls are prettily decorated with stucco, excepting where they are covered with coats of arms, cherubs, festoons, and the like. It leads into a suite of rooms which constitute my lodgings. These lofty rooms are fitted with large mirrors, damask sofas, panelled walls, elaborately inlaid floors, and marble chimney shelves; the walls are covered with a collection of choice pictures, the work of such painters as Titian, Rubens, Van Dyck, Wouvermans, and other masters. Here, after my work is done, I loiter round undisturbed, a catalogue in my hand, in delicious *far niente*, sometimes gazing, sometimes copying, sometimes wondering how I have become possessed of so much splendor. For he who enjoys possesses; and can the owner do more, or be secure of possessing them longer than I? Though I wish he may, and indeed have no reason to doubt it. Before my eyes spreads the park, enclosed within walls and graced with stone statues and urns filled with a luxuriant growth of pink and blue hydrangeas, which I might

SCHÖN-BRIESE CASTLE : THE DRAWING ROOM.

call an aristocratic flower—as Scott calls the peacock
an aristocratic bird—and with trailing creepers looking
as if they had overflowed from them. Fountains, terraces, arbors, and all the devices of a Lenôtre are to
be seen within these walls, but the whole is very fit to
be the hereditary estate of the Imperial Counts of Kos-
poth and gives an idea of wealth and power. And it
is not unpleasant to transfer the finest oranges from
the tree to one's own mouth. My host and his handsome wife, the very ideal of a lady of rank, are as good
and kind to me as strict etiquette allows them to be.
The young ladies at first treated me with icy coldness;
but we know each other better now; and though I
have been here no more than a week, in that time I
have learnt, however tired I may come in, always to
appear in full dress at dinner. An elegant black evening suit, which my profession has shed, has therefore
come in very usefully. How long I shall remain I
cannot say, for here, where it has long since ceased to
be customary to say all you think, only tact can tell
me how long I shall be welcome. But I beg you still
to address your letters to Oels, where I will have them
called for. Adieu, dear mother—space—and postage!
Yours,

HELMUTH.

BERLIN, November 15th, 1828.

DEAR MOTHER:

I have delayed replying to your dear letter of the
24th ult. because I wanted to tell you something of
my new position, and since I arrived here the bustle
of business, settling and dissipation, have till now
prevented my telling you that I reached Berlin safe
and sound on November 1st, and have established myself here for the next four months. It was with the

greatest interest that I read, at a distance, all that was going on within your quiet—or rather, at that time, noisy cloister-walls. My stay at Briese was prolonged to ten weeks, and I might have stayed on for two years if it had not occurred to me that I must give in my drawings. Torn young from my parental home and your loving care, you know how early I was forced to find myself a stranger wherever I went, and to earn from others the affection, friendship, and esteem which comes to most men from the ties of relationship or friendly intercourse. Never, unless I except the good Stemanns, have I been so kindly received, nowhere have I been so content and so thoroughly at home as at the Kospoths. It is a fine thing for a poor devil like me, perpetually beset by want of money, superior officers, the service, obedience to orders, and all the other evils which flew out of Pandora's box, to find himself in a berth where all the minor annoyances of life, which, in combination, may make it wretched, have ceased to exist; where everything is beautiful, pleasing, rich, and noble; where pleasure may be the end of effort because work is in itself a pleasure; where art is not the stinted spice of life, but is life itself, and where, by pleasing himself he pleases others. Briese was a warm gleam of sunshine in a dark autumn day. Really, I could have fancied myself at the Court of Ferrara; and if I were not absolutely lacking in everything Tasso-like, I could have believed myself the much-honored poet.

When I am perfectly happy—and I think at once of the ass—I write verses, but only then. So posterity has every reason to wish me happy! If you could see that beautiful castle with the splendid picture-gallery, the great orangery—the largest in Silesia—the truth of my comparison would strike you.

(Here follows a parody on Mignon's song in Goethe's "Wilhelm Meister" * adapted to the circumstances of Von Moltke's visit to Briese.)

> * Kennst bu die Flur, wo die Citronen blüh'n,
> Im dunkeln Laub die Golborangen glüh'n,
> Ein sanfter Wind burch hohe Pappeln weht,
> In langen Reih'n die golb'ne Rebe steht?
> Dahin, bahin — lenkt die Erinnerung gern ben Sinn.
>
> Kennst bu das Schloß, es leuchtet fern sein Dach,
> Hell glänzt der Saal, es schimmert bas Gemach,
> Die Bilber seh'n von allen Wänden brein,
> Als fragten sie: ist hier nicht herrlich sein?
> Dahin, bahin so gerne die Gebanken zieh'n.
>
> Wohl kenne ich bas Schloß mit hohem Dach,
> Den schönen Park, bas schimmernbe Gemach.
> Was nun ber „Drachen alte Brut" anbelangt, so änberte ich bas ab in:
> Unb ber Bewohner Liebenswürdigkeit,
> Die Allem erst ben rechten Werth verleiht,
> Es waltet brin — für Schönes unb für Gutes ebler Sinn.

How greatly I now miss the friendly intercourse of such cultivated people. Now, when I get home at about two o'clock—for I work till then, from eight in the morning, at the General Staff Office—I find, to begin with, a considerable difference between my dinners here and there. The cook at Briese has evidently thoroughly studied his branch of chemistry, and uses superior matter. The capital Hungarian wine, too, is lacking. However, I shall get used to all that. But when six o'clock strikes I always feel as though I ought to cast all my books and papers to the winds and go down into the red damask drawing-room to stretch myself comfortably in the delicious arm-chair into which I fitted like the yolk in an egg, like a snail in its shell. That incomparable piece of furniture was so much my own that even the Countess herself would have given it up, I am sure, as soon as I appeared. Then, while the young Count divagated on the piano, in fugues, chorales, and contrapuntal variations, I patiently awaited the advent of the ladies with their embroidery, and the old Count with a book out of which he read aloud while I drew, or sometimes set stitches in a row at the embroidery frame, which the young countess no less industriously picked out again. —But I wait in vain; not even old Cadeau comes in, a good beast who had lost all his senses from sheer old age—excepting smell; for he did smell sometimes very perceptibly. The Kospoths interest themselves in everything that is fashionable and *distingué* in Silesia, so we often went out on little excursions, or hunting. The time slipped by most agreeably and improvingly, and our parting was sad and not without tears. I had hardly arrived here when I found a case of pine-apples, without any name, but enclosing a file which I had left at Briese.

My stay there has also been highly advantageous to my finances, or rather to my creditors. During this last lean year, when I depended solely on my pay, they have been so sympathetic that I can only be grateful to them; the greater part of my debts are paid, and I hope to be quite free in the course of next year. With this view I gave up returning by Dresden. I have had the opportunity of copying many pretty pictures, but have left most of them behind. I brought with me a Holy Family by Rubens; it is the largest thing I have yet done, and includes four heads of life-size, of the greatest beauty—not counting the head of the Dove. I was delighted when the Countess herself pronounced that I had quite caught the resemblance; they framed it and hung it.

I have not much to tell of my life here. I am like a man lying on an uncomfortable sofa, who changes his attitude every moment. I have hitherto been constantly to the play, oftener than I ought in the future; but it is a great temptation to me. I also go often to the picture exhibition in the Academy gallery. All the best painters send their works there from the remotest ends of the kingdom, that they may be seen, criticised, and sold. Besides the many fine painted pictures, you there see a crowd of living ones; and if you have any acquaintance you are sure to meet them.

I heard with joy from my father that Adolf has got through his examination, and well. I fancy the added words, " with distinction," mean something very good; is he himself satisfied? Write to me, dear mother, what prospects now lie before him; and when he gets home give him my hearty congratulations. Best love to all the others who may be with you. I hope to hear before long how they are going on. To-day I can only write to Ludwig to answer his letter. He is, so far, the one who knows most of my surroundings here, so we have more interests in common on which to enlarge than I have with either of the others. My father writes that he may perhaps pay a visit to Berlin this winter, and I have advised him to do so; it will be a change for him.

We have had a fearful September and October, with much rain, which hinders my work; the poor troops are almost drowned in camp.

Farewell, dear mother; let me hear what are Fritz's prospects of promotion; he is the most luckless of us all. Take care of yourself, dear mother, and always love your most affectionate

HELMUTH.

BERLIN, December 25th, 1828.

Address: Grosse Friedrichstrasse, No. 66, c.

DEAR MOTHER:

That I am still in the land of the living you will be fully assured by the accompanying document, in which will you be good enough to fill in the blank spaces? Besides this I feel bound to tell you that I am perfectly well and very happy. I account for this in the first place by the fact that I am very busy, so that sometimes, when I go out at eight in the morning I put the door key in my pocket. Work at the office goes on till two, drawing, reducing plans or taking problems from the Staff-officers of the General Staff, as well as reading the newspapers and going out for breakfast. The hours are rather long, no doubt, but not without interest. We relate our experience while on survey, discuss the newspapers, criticise the theatre or plan battles against one another. As there are some very clever heads among my new associates, and all have had the sort of education which alone makes social intercourse a pleasure, the talk is as various as it is lively. Nor are we in the smallest degree on ceremony from the highest downwards. Those who have no relations in the city have organized a sort of mess where we dine well and cheaply. We are always very jolly over this meal; we often sit over a glass of wine afterwards till nearly four o'clock. Then come our private studies. I am attending, gratis, a course on French literature, one of Modern History at the office, and one on Goethe at the University. Almost a third of the class is military, and at an English course we number more than the students. My other lessons, besides these, cost me thirteen thalers, sixteen silver groschen a month; namely Russian, riding, and dancing. This last is only for the sake of the Mazurka, which I must know in case I go to Poland next summer. The riding, to my great delight, is in a very large new riding-school, lighted with gas. The teaching is excellent, and irrespective of the capital exercise,

I fancy I am making good progress. In time I shall no doubt have a mount, and then this constant practice will stand me in good stead. Russian I consider of the first importance. Russia is to Prussia of the first consequence, and very few are familiar with its language; I work at it with great zeal. In the good conduct lists for officers there is a special heading for the languages they know: this will be my fifth. Thus we come to six or seven o'clock, and if I am going to the theatre the day is at an end. This mode of life is of course only possible under the favorable conditions which I now enjoy, and which, besides the year's expenses, have placed me in a position to pay away more than 150 thalers in bills which had accumulated during hard times.

That my thoughts yesterday, on Christmas Eve, were with you in the yellow room* in the convent you may easily imagine. I ended dinner cheerfully over a bowl with my comrades, and spent the evening with the Ballhorns. I was delightfully surprised when the postman this morning brought me an anonymous letter and a box with the Oels post-mark. On opening it, I first took a large taper out of the cotton wool, then a beautiful pocket-book. When I opened it, I found first a charming little picture of the room where we used to sit together at Briese, with everything just as I left it. My chair is by the table, old Cadeau snoring in his basket by the stove, the oranges and wine are on the table, the pictures, the vine outside the window, all exactly shown. In short, as I look at it by candle-light, I could fancy myself there. Even prettier if possible is a second picture; a view of the house from the park, from a point which I had once

* At Preetz, where his mother was then living.

noted as advantageous. Above his work the Count has written:

> In a soft light, familiar spot,
> Your image smiles a greeting to my heart and eyes;
> And though treacherous speech is silent,
> Still my spirit may enjoy the pleasures of memory.
> The flowery glories of the broad gardens
> The sweet fragrance of your shady groves
> Fancy brings before me in the gloomy winter's night,
> As though under the radiance of a spring morning.

The rest of the space was filled with pomade, soap, Eau de Cologne, and a case worked on cardboard by the young countess, pencils, a mother-of-pearl knife with six blades, etc., etc. And a pretty New Year's card was also laid in the pocket-book.

This letter has again been laid aside for a few days, and I fear you will be impatient, dear little mother, for the certificate. May all be as well with you and the dear sisters as I most heartily wish. Adolf's examination gave me great satisfaction; you soon will have one care less. I quite approve of your not having moved from your house. It is very pleasant in summer, and you will not easily find such a pretty garden elsewhere. Only think, for a single room—in a dear neighborhood to be sure, near the office—without attendance, I pay eight thalers a month; and my comrades all pay more. With wood and lights it mounts up to from 100 to 120 thalers a year. Much love to the dear brothers and sisters. Now adieu, dear mother. Do not forget your

HELMUTH.

RUSKO, NEAR JAROSZYN, September 14th, 1829.
DEAR MOTHER:

First I must crave forgiveness for my long silence. The quantity of business, as well as the many diversions which my stay here brings with it, have been the cause, and now, when I will try to make up for my delay, I can scarcely believe that so much time can have slipped by since I received your letter of July.

I heartily hope that these lines will find you and the others well and happy, all the more because here, in the country, the extraordinarily cold, wet summer has caused an almost epidemic fever.

As far as I am concerned I am in all respects as flourishing as I could wish. In point of money I save enough to dare to hope that by the end of the year, when my present work is done, I may find myself out of debt. This is in itself a great thing, and then Heaven may help me further. With regard to personal comfort, as the most wonderful good fortune would have it, out of thirty-two lots I drew the very one which brought me here to Rusko to the O. family, with whom I made acquaintance at Salzbrunn, and whom I visited here four years since—exactly four years to-morrow—and who have always had such a particular fancy for me that they treat me like a child of their own. This is the third house in which I have been so fortunate as to find such a kind reception; and if it were possible for any place to be the same as home, I might find it here, as before at the Kospoths and the Stemanns.

I was at the Kospoths this summer on August 19th for the Count's birthday. I could only stay a few days, and made a journey of thirty miles [140 English miles], but they appreciated it highly. If I were not in such good quarters here, I would go there to draw out my survey and spend the autumn.

Ever since leaving beautiful Herkow, where I was so hospitably received by the old Starostin, I have been here at Rusko, where I shall remain till the end of October.

If only the old palace there, of the Sapiehas and Piastes, looking out over the endless expanse of black forests, and its great vaulted halls could open, and the rows of portraits of the lords and palatines of Poland look down in amazement on the stranger who had dared to penetrate into those plains where once they ruled, and where now, by some incredible subversion of things, the sovereign is an Elector of Brandenburg, whose Emperor their horsemen had once to release in his own capital—where now neither their name, nor their faith, speech, laws, or manners, survive; while there, where nothing remains of their power but a reflection, or of their greatness but a memory, the eye lingers on a vast heap of ruins—here, to descend to the prose of the present, my residence is a humble dwelling with a shingle roof, surrounded by farm buildings, cottages, and gardens, and enclosed by an oak wood, which has made way for it. But it might be said of this, as of the Greek houses in Constantinople, that they are only built of boards, but conceal within them Asiatic luxury. Here we have pictures, good and bad, antiques and precious chandeliers, crammed into small rooms. Marble tables which once graced vast halls are wedged against narrow windows, and large mirrors hang on ill-painted walls. Amid such things as these lives my host, who, in the Polish revolution, played his part under Kosciusko, and who combines a rooted hatred for the new régime with the greatest kindness to me, its servant. He is far too sensible to be of those who abuse the Government when a wheel comes off, or think it is the king's fault when we get too much rain. But as all intercourse with the Government officials is a grievance to him, and the bad times, high taxes, and new-fangled ways, make him angry, it is his wife who manages all the

complicated affairs of an estate of at least half a
million of Polish gulden, which she does with infinite energy, ability, and shrewdness. A daughter of
about nine, and a niece who is very rich, but unfortunately very ugly, complete the family party with
which I have become completely amalgamated, though
so heterogeneous an item. In fact, I could not more
exactly describe the peculiarities of these good people
than by saying that they—or rather their way of
living and being, are almost exactly the opposite of
mine. In judging of them you must adopt a peculiar, I might say a national standard, otherwise you
will always judge them falsely; and while we regard
them as feather-brained and boastful, they can but
look upon us as excessively pedantic, and even somewhat hypocritical. In forming an estimate of the
young ladies especially, it behoves a man to be on his
guard. Betrayed by their friendliness, and an absence
of formality which surprises a foreigner, a simpleton
might be led to believe that he had but to pursue and
conquer, but he would find it more difficult than with
us, where greater depth of feeling easily comes into
conflict with strictness of manners.

Just as I am about to write you some account of
my mode of life here, I perceive that my rambling pen
has already filled the paper. So you must read the
crossed writing, and at the cost of your eyes learn that
I have almost done my work, and am enjoying a pleasant time of idleness. I am drawing out my maps, and
a few likenesses now and then, and making plans for
buildings which my servant, who is a practised brick-
layer, carries out, while my hostess supplies the materials. I am particularly pleased to be able to do this,
and it is a great convenience to my good friends here,
as craftsmen and artists are very difficult to get and

very dear. The façade of a cellar in the garden looks very fine already, built of broken boulders, on a most elegant design, and soon a bath-house is to be erected of the same material, by the large fish-pond, from a' drawing I am just finishing.

Hunting, fishing—very good—and various calls on and from the neighbors, fill up the time. I have acquired quite a taste here for country management, and I only need an estate to farm it with pleasure.

But all these little employments which occupy my time very pleasantly, look very unimportant on paper —and are also becoming very illegible. Perhaps in the course of the winter I may be able to exchange written for verbal communication. So I conclude, begging you to give my best love to the brothers and sisters, and to remember me with affection. Yours,

HELMUTH.

BERLIN, November 6th, 1829.

I hasten, dear mother, to let you know that I arrived here safe and sound by mail, on Sunday, the 1st of the month. My kind hosts, the O.'s, sent me the first ten miles [about 46 English miles], as far as Posen with their own horses, and supplied me with wine, tea, coffee, roast fowls, hares, ducks, a game pasty, and what not, as though I were starting for the North Pole.

I spent three whole months at Rusko, and went into Silesia once, to the wool fair at Breslau; and if O. had not been able to sell so quickly, I should have flown off for three days into the mountains, which lay before me in a long blue chain. After I had finished my work at Rusko, in spite of the incessantly bad weather, I spent the time in trapping field-fares, threshing, shooting excursions, shaking down the fruit-crop, and such rustic occupations; on wet days we played whist, at which I had to pay a learner's fee, and on fine days I drew every member of the family down to the *struz* or watchman, in his fur coat and red cap, and the housemaid in her very pretty national costume. And every two or three days we were out paying a visit, going to absolution, or mass.

So now I feel quite lonely in the midst of the turmoil of the city, for 200,000 persons cannot make up for two in whom one feels an interest. Happily, my kind hosts will be here in the winter on business, and I shall be glad to see them here. However, to tell the truth, I find the stir and bustle of a town, like my present home, a pleasant change. The theatre especially is a joy to me. And very agreeable it is to meet all my fellow-officers from the various fixed quarters, from the Baltic to Prosna, each one relating his history and adventures in a sort of "Dichtung und Wahrheit," on which the others make their comments with such wit and humor as they have at their command. I am almost the only man who has had even decent quarters.

I have now gone back to my old lodgings at the corner of Grosse Friedrichstrasse and Mohrenstrasse, where I pay, indeed, nine thalers for a single room, but live very comfortably.

Yesterday I again paid fifty good thalers off my tailor's account, and I still have forty thalers, my savings during the summer. Here, saving is out of the question. I wish very much, dear mother, that I may be able to go to you for the new year, to see you and the other dear ones once more. But it could only be for a fortnight at any rate, for I cannot get leave. Much, very much love to the little sisters, and the boys who are with you. I hope, dear mother, that you are as well and happy as I am. For to-day I must close, begging you not to forget your

HELMUTH.

A sorrowful Postscript.—My shirts are in a very melancholy state, and new ones would be highly desirable. But I only wish for three, for in my wandering mode of life more would only be in the way, and be more easily lost. They need be no finer than the last, and I should like the wristbands to be narrower.

BERLIN, January 10th, 1830.

DEAR MOTHER:

Now that I have got into my old life again, I take advantage of the first Sunday morning to announce my arrival here, and send you my hearty thanks for your kind reception, and for your gift which enabled me to make the return journey so quickly and comfortably. When I had done my business in Hamburg, my stay there—alone as I was, and more inclined to look back on my stay with you than forward to the inevitable journey—was so irksome to me, that I was glad when at nine in the evening I found myself in my corner of the coach, between two gentlemen who were as taciturn as I. It was not at all cold, and indeed I had my whole wardrobe on my person. There was a thick fog outside, so nothing kept me from pursuing my own thoughts till we drove into the gates of Berlin. Then I began to feel a little uneasy about my self-granted leave. At Ludwigshut, as luck would have it, I came across the hereditary Grand-Duke, and in the mail office I met the Commandant von Küstrin; I was forced to speak to both, but up till now all is well.

I made inquiry on my way for my purse, but it must have fallen out of my pocket, not on earth, but into the air and on to another planet, for on this, at any rate, no one has seen it. Here I am sitting once more in my snug little blue room at my writing-table, my coffee machine at my elbow, in which, in spite of all the theories I acquired from you, I can never achieve that perfection of concoction which made yours so delicious. Look as I may at the pictures of Lena and Gusta, there is no one here to butter me a roll, and I invariably drop the lower half, which falls, buttered-side down, on the table. But I shall get used to all this. All the morning I am busy; the dinner is a pleasant hour, which I spend in very cheerful company, but the evenings hang fire dreadfully. I miss the comfort and joy of sitting on your sofa, while Lena tells me a story or Augusta makes music, or I chat with you. Neither society nor the theatre can make up for this, and I would give them up gladly if I might only slip over to the yellow drawing-room for a few hours every evening. In fancy I often do so; but then I feel so miserably lonely in my blue one, that I snatch up my sword and cap and rush off to the nearest café, where, after all, I am as lonely as ever, though the place may be crowded with men. If only I had Loui here! for he is like a well-tuned glass harmonica; which ever note you strike it gives out a full chord. But I comfort myself with the worst of all comforts: that it cannot be. With faithful love, your

HELMUTH.

WIERZAKA, NEAR POSEN, June 18th, 1830.
DEAR MOTHER:
In spite of fatigue, work, and change of place, my conscience at last gets the better of my idleness, and reproaches me for not having written to you for so long, and as you do not know where I am, I have even

cut myself off from any news of you.   But I should be only too glad to hear from you once more, and know how you are.   You can easily imagine all the questions which I could ask on the subject, so there is nothing for me to do but to come back at once to myself, and tell you how I have been during the last two months. I would give one of the sequestrated states if everything I want to tell you, and yet more to ask you, were already put on paper.   But as that is impossible, I will try to remember what, during these ten weeks, has seemed to me of any importance, or new or interesting, in the hope that the picture which I shall thus send you from a distance, may interest you for my sake, even though the things it shows you are not important or new or interesting to you.

In May I was sent out to drill the Landwehr recruits for the 8th Landwehr-battalion, at Frankfort.   Here elegant youths with umbrellas, and straw hats, and canes, were put into blue jackets, and so licked into shape that they look now like soldiers, and indeed were hardly to be distinguished from them at the review.   The severity of this paroxysm of drilling is so great that the warrior on his release lies huddled up on his stove-bench in the curliest attitude possible for three days and nights on end, to ease his limbs back into their old joints and hinges after the stretching rack they have endured.   As for myself, for those four weeks, I did not know that life contained anything but dressing, drill, rations, cleaning arms, drill again, inspection, and shouting the word of command. At last, on June 10th, I came home with a consciousness of duty fulfilled and a commendation, and at once set out for Posen.   Tired out as I was, I spent two nights, which I could have wished better employed, in travelling across the sands which Mother Nature has strewn so lavishly over "les terres vastes et sablon-neuses du marquis de Brandebourg," as Voltaire described our country in his rage. When I entered the towered city of Posen, which is full of convents, it was Corpus-Christi day, and hundreds of people, especially country-folks in the old national costume, were following the monstrance borne by the Archbishop in person. Not a Jew would have dared to show himself, though the town swarms with them. As soon as the sacred object came in sight every one fell on his knees and the soldiers presented arms.

There is always something very imposing to me in the Catholic ritual; all the more so because it is in such strong contrast to the indifference which is so often seen among us in matters of religion. I found a visit to the vast and once powerful convent of Owinsk, near Posen, most interesting. I there saw Cistercians, Bernardines, and Sisters of Mercy, who, when the various orders were secularized, were formed into a mixed battalion and shut up here. The rule is extremely severe; twice during the night, even in winter, the poor nuns must turn out to sing for an hour and a half in the choir. Their appearance in the various habits of their orders is very solemn; especially the Cistercians in brown hair-cloth scapularies. It was a strange feeling to me to cross that threshold, over which these poor creatures may never pass out. For them that road leads only to the grave—for us into the world again. We saw the chapel, the parlor with its iron grating, and, to the consternation of the Sisters, we lost our way—three officers—in the cells, affecting ignorance. The good ladies are absolutely uneducated. They do not understand the Latin prayers they chant; but they say that God understands all languages, and so knows what they mean.

From Posen I came on at once to my work, and have put up here with Herr von Treskow at Wierzaka. I have a very friendly host, a good room, an excellent table, a capital glass of wine, a great deal to do, and am perfectly well.

POSEN, June 22nd, 1830.

Before sending this off, I will announce my arrival here, where I must work out my second (and last— here sigh!) section.

My kind host has set out to-day for Karlsbad, and I was very, very near going with him. It was an excellent opportunity, and it cost me much self-denial not to accept his suggestion; but I must repay a sum of eighty thalers which I borrowed last winter, and which I must now scrape together and save. So I gave up the pleasant journey.

FREIBERG-ON-THE-MULDE, July 20th, 1830.

I have already been wandering about for three weeks, dear mother, but though I have very often thought of you, I have never found leisure for writing to you.

To-day nothing shall hinder me from sending you my best wishes and some news of myself. You will have had my enclosure in a letter to my father, sent off on the 30th of last month, and will have learnt from that, that this year's service led me hither through Dresden and the Erzgebirge. So far—*absit omen*—the journey has been most successful, the weather lovely for three weeks on end. I have not once had to unroll my cloak. In the morning, on the stroke of five, I set out on my spirited steed, the servant following on the black horse with a small valise, my cloak, and two bags with maps and dressing-gear. We go on for three —four—five miles [about fourteen to twenty-three

English miles]. If the ride is an extra long one, I halt on the way for five or six hours, and do not proceed till evening, always map in hand. My good beasts eat exactly two full rations each, so, as fodder is very dear, I am almost in the plight of Diomedes, who was eaten by his horses. The day before yesterday I made a very long round. I rode in the morning from Annaberg to Oberwiesenthal, three miles [about fourteen English miles]. To spare the horses I left them there, and went on foot by the new road over the Keilberg, the highest point of the Erzgebirge, where I had work to do, and far down the slope on the other side into Bohemia. By the time I got back I had walked at least three miles [about fourteen English miles] in the hill country, and then rode the three miles back to Annaberg. I got in at seven in the evening, and as I had eaten nothing since five in the morning, you may believe how good the trout tasted. I went through most beautiful country. After visiting some friends in Dresden I rode to Teplitz, by a little known but direct road, saw the battle-field of Kulm, and then proceeded on my way along the lovely Eger valley to Karlsbad. Here I was so lucky as to meet our cousin Moltke, the Russian minister at Karlsruhe. He was to leave two days later, so I spent them with him, and on the 17th he and his wife took me on in a handsome carriage with four horses; our roads lay together for an hour, and I accompanied these friendly connections till my way took me up into the mountains. That evening I was at Schneeberg, at the northern foot of the hills.

To-morrow morning I am going by Tharandt and the valley of Plauen to Dresden, where my major is waiting for me to visit the battle-fields of Kulm, of which I am to do the honors particularly, as to the details of the engagement and the spots to which they refer. To this end I have been obliged thoroughly to study this complicated action and the preliminary movements. I must therefore go across the range again, but shall take another route so as to master it thoroughly.

From Dresden we go to the rendezvous at Bitterfeld, near Halle, where the whole of the General Staff are to meet on August 3rd, and then the real work begins. I enclose you a little flower which I plucked for you on a high cliff of the Erzgebirge, and carried for some time in my hat.

How often I have thought of you while gazing at some fine view; you always so greatly enjoy beautiful scenery. If only you could have seen the lovely valley of Wolkenstein yesterday. The sun set gloriously, and the moon had already risen and was reflected in the roaring torrent; the old castle stood opposite on a high crag. It was so beautiful that I stayed the night there, and scrambled up the height again early this morning. Good-bye for to-day, dear mother; I shall be my own courier as far as Dresden. Now I must survey Freiberg and its old walls and towers. With heartfelt affection, your faithful

HELMUTH.

BERLIN, Christmas Eve, 1830, 7 o'clock.

DEAR MOTHER:

What can I do better than transport myself in fancy to-day, and at this hour, to be with you where so much fun and bustle are no doubt going on. Next to the fact that I cannot be with you, it is a grief to me that I do not know anything about your present home and surroundings; but I can see and hear all the party who are enjoying themselves with and for each other,

over their various little gifts. Neat little handiwork
done by the sisters; good strong shirts, and stockings
with double heels, as if they were meant for Achilles,
from you; tobacco-pouches for the two brothers of the
pen, and strong, useful things from Fritz; a bowl of
punch in prospect, and above all the happiness of being
together are ample reasons for the merriment of the
meeting, and perhaps you are speaking of the absent
—nay, certainly. I fancy I can hear it all.

Yes, I, no doubt, am much quieter here. It is not
possible to pay calls this evening, and even the theatre
allows us to-day to amuse ourselves elsewhere as best
we may for our sixteen groschen. But, just as sometimes one is cross without cause, so to-night, *sans
crime et sans raison*, I am quite content in my own
room and left to my own devices. I really think that
the twinkling of the tapers on your Christmas tree is
shining in on me.

I must tell you that I have already been two months
back in Berlin. I might, to be sure, have told you as
much two months ago, and ought properly to have
done so; but in consideration of my usual punctuality
as a correspondent, and in consideration of the fact
that you have not written to me for four months, I
hope for mercy. One reason really has been that I
constantly expected to be able to give some decisive
news as to peace or war, for that to me is of the most
immediate importance, because in the event of war I
may flatter myself that I should at once be appointed
to the General Staff. I will give you on this subject
not my own opinion, but that of the superior officers
of the Staff: it is that, notwithstanding all the sighing
of second-lieutenants, if the French Government is
strong enough to withstand the pressure of two parties
—Royalists and Republicans alike, both wishing for

war, that they may get the upper hand in the country —peace will be maintained. But whether they will not succeed in striking their citizen-king out of the programme, in setting aside that old chatterbox Lafayette, *le premier radoteur de France*, and Lafitte,* in my opinion is by no means certain, nor is the Revolution of 1830 to be considered as at an end. The Poles, with a discretion which is hardly to be looked for in an insurgent nation, have made no attempt to attack Posen, which is the wisest thing they have done yet. There are about 30,000 men now quartered in that province, but 150,000 could be sent there within three weeks, without withdrawing a single battalion from the Rhine province. Not a State in Europe—unless it may be Austria—can at this moment put as many men into the field as Prussia. Prussia, without doubt or exaggeration, is the only power which, besides having an army well supplied with *matériel* and complete in every detail, is so secure of the feeling of the people that it could conduct a war on the offensive; and since, beyond question, our king at this moment holds the destinies of Europe in his hand, he is all the more to be respected when he, the father of the Empress of Russia and the brother of the Queen of Holland, refused all mediation. A reaction has already begun in Belgium. This is really a revolution in a negative sense. The principles which in France upset the government, in Belgium occupied the throne; and the clergy and nobility, against whom the French rebelled, in Belgium are fighting against freedom and the constitution.

In such a revolution, where hatred and passion unquestionably play a larger part than reason or necessity, it has always been a mystery to me what can have so embittered two nationalities like the Bel-

* Minister under Louis Philippe.

gians and the Dutch, that fifteen years of peace have
failed to amalgamate them; for they have a common
origin and a country in common, and long shared the
same cruel fate. I have sought the explanation in the
history of the two countries, examining it especially
from that point of view; and I have written out what
I fancy I have discovered, in the form of a small
pamphlet which I propose to publish. This work has
taken up a great deal of my time, for as I am at the
office till two in the afternoon, and do not get home
from dinner till four, and am frequently out in the
evening, I have no time but at night; and very often
when you, I hope, are fast asleep, I am worrying myself over their High Mightinesses the States-General;
for, in their pigskin-bound quartos, from which by pref-
erence I derive my facts, I find the record not merely
of all the gallant Netherlanders did during three centuries, but also of all they said, and that is no small
matter. In fact, the trouble has not been light; I have
read above a thousand pages quarto and nearly four
thousand octavo. To establish a single simple fact,
I have often had to turn over whole volumes, and only
that the reader may skip every other sentence, and not
read it after all. However, at the worst I have acquired
a tolerably sound knowledge of the condition and history of a country into which events might easily lead
a Prussian army.

St. Sylvester's Night, 1830, 8 o'clock.

The trumpets and drums of my neighbor's children
drove me out of my entrenchments on Christmas night,
as, of old, the inhabitants of Jericho. I took refuge in
the tent of the Dey of Algiers. Herr Gropius, the
decorative painter, has given us a charming moonlight
view of that pirates' nest painted from nature. But I

will not let the old year set on my delay,* but will wish you all every happiness for the New Year, from the bottom of my heart—the year which will be with us in few hours, and which may have great and important things hidden behind its veil. May it bring war for me, and peace for you! Good-night, dear mother. Adieu. Your

HELMUTH.

BERLIN, January 11th, 1831.

DEAR MOTHER:

I will make my coffee by your recipe, and I have tinkered the big holes in the strainer with some blotting-paper, which is a great improvement. I have got quite into my old groove again. My greatest recreation is the French play, to which I am a subscriber, and so get tickets at half-price. I have also found a very good place to dine at, but on that I spend but little, as a rule; I never breakfast, and often need no supper, as a very good dinner suffices me. I am once more completely fitted out, and by the end of the year hope to have paid all bills. Even at a distance love your

HELMUTH.

BERLIN, February 13th, 1831.

DEAR MOTHER:

It is nearly a month since I last wrote to you, and, as I have still no news from you, I am a prey to every form of anxiety. I know, indeed, that a variety of circumstances and occupations may hinder you from writing, but your last is dated August 8th, of last year, and, as in these six months I have written to you every month regularly, through constant changes of

---

* In the original *Saumseligkeit,* on which the writer remarks—"A happy compound, by which our language combines the ideas of laziness and bliss."

place and occupation, I try to persuade myself that perhaps a letter from you has been lost. But, at any rate, if neither illness nor disaster is the cause of your long silence, I hope, ere long, to be assured of it. I should have many questions to ask, for I have not yet heard a word about your home at Schleswig—but I am hoping for a long letter very soon, and that it will contain full particulars.

I am well. As to my social life, I have been introduced to several family circles which I find pleasant; I often go to the play, and am taking advantage of the last part of my stay in Berlin to enjoy it as frequently as possible. My pamphlet is printed, and published by Mittler, 1831, under the title of "Holland and Belgium in their Reciprocal Relations." It will be issued to the trade to-morrow, in case it should interest any of you. The Chief of the General Staff has brought out some new papers this month on which possibly much may depend.

In a fortnight I am to join my regiment at Magdeburg, unless our stay here is unusually prolonged this year, beyond the 1st of March.

The prospects of war seem increasingly near. The Belgian question becomes so complicated that nothing but a regular European war will cut the Gordian knot at last. This is the more likely, because in these days war and peace and the relations of nations are no longer Cabinet questions; in many countries the people themselves govern the Cabinet, and thus an element is introduced into politics on which it is impossible to reckon.* An elected citizen-king may honestly aim at

---

* This is the first allusion to an idea which, as a General and Field-Marshal, von Moltke again puts forward in the opening sentence of his work "The Franco-German War of 1870–71." (James R. Osgood, McIlvaine & Co., London, 1891.)

preserving the peace of Europe, and yet not be able to guide the people who have appointed him—a farce which, as yesterday's news indicates, is now being performed. And, after all, to be reasonable, must not Louis Philippe naturally prefer to fight Europe with his people, rather than to fight his people with the rest of Europe? But, whatever comes of it, Prussia is armed. She was ready, indeed, before any other State in Europe, and though she did not strike, though it was Prussia who, under such temptations to war, maintained peace in Europe, if she herself should be attacked, she can count on the approval of all, especially of Germany; and public opinion in these days is worth as much as an army.

Here the people are full of new life; the cafés are crowded with inquirers, and it is hard to get hold of a newspaper, particularly a French one. Politics are the theme in every drawing-room, and discussed in the theatres and the beer-shops. Those officers who have the ready money are providing themselves with pack-saddles and field-equipment, awaiting the war—and we who have not, await the war to get the equipment. Councillors and judges are furbishing up their *landwehr* uniforms; only the business men pull long faces.

The night before last tremendous applause broke out at the performance of the "Maid of Orleans," at the passage: "The nation must sacrifice itself for its King!"

The 16th.—Still hoping for a letter. I have kept this back a day or two. This long silence disturbs me greatly. Pray write at last, and do not forget your

HELMUTH.

Letters addressed Berlin will find me wherever I may be.

BERLIN, March 5th, 1831.

DEAR MOTHER:

Right glad was I to have your letter of February 13th, after so long a silence; it arrived soon after I had sent off my last, and I read it with the greatest interest. Thank God that you are all well and cheerful. I delight in transporting myself into your domestic circle, the largest possible in our family. How I wish I could often sit down with you of an evening to chat, or to listen to Gusta's and Loui's music. But the little sketch of your house which you promised me, you forgot to enclose, nor have I any notion in what part of the town or in what street I should find you. And let me know whether you personally prefer Schleswig to Preetz as a residence; as to my sisters I have no doubts; but it is certainly very dear, and you must have many expenses. It must be a great joy to the musical portion of the family that you bought a new grand piano. Then again I should like to know with whom you are intimate, and whether you have met with any one you particularly like. It is a pity you should have no garden—and, by the way, what is become of the cow? But that perhaps is a tender subject with you. Do not be too stay-at-home, but walk out often in the pretty Thiergarten, and avail yourself of the cheerful society of its amusing denizens.

My stay in Berlin has been unexpectedly prolonged. By order from the Cabinet and from the Chief of the General Staff, I and another officer have been appointed to the Survey Office, though my regular service here is at an end, and all the other officers have gone off east and west to their respective garrisons. I have the immediate advantage of drawing twenty thalers additional pay, and we may also regard it as a distinction. I have also been officially asked, whether, in the

4

event of war, I should be inclined to attach myself to the service of the General Staff. So you see how deeply I am interested in these political matters. I am saving at every margin to buy a horse, but where I am to get three from, Heaven alone knows. I may manage to scrape together enough for one. My "Holland and Belgium" has a fair sale. Your booksellers might order it from Mittler; it costs six groschen.

Our court is in mourning for the Duke of Holstein-Gottorp; I am very sorry that he should have died before he could fulfil the expectations which we were justified in forming of him.

We read in the papers here that his Danish Majesty is to grant a constitution, or at least representatives, to your people, in consequence of the disturbances in your province; I fancy that from the point of view of administration these members will find a wide field for improvements.

Farewell, dear mother; by the time I write my next letter, a good deal will have changed perhaps in the world. It is a critical period in small things as well as great, and even my insignificant fate in the world may be decided within a few months. Take care of yourself, and think with affection of your truly loving son
HELMUTH.

DEAR LENA:

I have written off a whole joint of one finger which you will find in the envelope, so you must make the best of a short scrap of a letter this time, in return for your nice long one. But I should like to make it quite beautiful, and to write in verse or in hexameters. This word is derived from *Hexenmeister*, the German for a magician, because good ones are so hard to manage, so I had rather not write them. To make up I enclose the long promised view of Lübeck. The house you see is Miloslav, where I spent this summer; but the town of Lübeck is scarcely visible on account of the rise in the ground, just as in the view on your workbox. When I next go to Schleswig again I will make a point of sketching Lübeck from the side.

All the news you send me of Schleswig and its inhabitants interests me greatly, and not less your account of your own mode of life; I can only beg you to heap coals of fire on my head and put me to shame by writing me a long letter very soon. For the present, good-night, dear Lena; the watchman is very impertinently proclaiming midnight, 180,000 men are snoring all round me, and I have yet to swallow a night-cap of a few dozen Russian words.

Once more, when I really ought to be asleep, I charge you with greeting for Herr and Frau von Stemann, and you must deliver it with special grace, for if I were not half dead with writing I would put in another letter. Good-night.

BERLIN, March 10th, 1831.

DEAR MOTHER:

* * * As to myself, I am now at work in the office of the General Staff, without being attached to it. This much I know: that I and another officer were proposed for it at a council of the Staff officers. So we are regarded as qualified, and that is always the main point. I hope to be ordered this summer to the manœuvres of the General Staff on the Rhine, for the war seems to have come to nothing; indeed, all looks like peace. Then I must have a horse, but do not let that worry you. I have already got half the money, so the other half no doubt will follow. I have deposited sixty thalers in the town savings-bank, and I shall

get fifty thalers in compensation if I am ordered off.
I hope I may soon have good news for you. Adieu,
dear mother. Keep up your health and spirits, and
do not forget your

HELMUTH.

BERLIN, August 7th, 1831.

DEAR MOTHER:

The hope of the expedition to the Rhine, which I
should have liked to announce before, has kept me
from writing to you this long time. But, alas, that
hope seems to have faded. The Chief of the General
Staff cannot possibly quit Berlin at a moment when
the whole world is on fire. The great comet, which
is to be so close to the earth next year that it will
almost run us down, when it gets near enough to
see will certainly keep aloof, in contempt of orders,
to avoid catching Eastern cholera and Western revolution, war, famine, etc., to diffuse in its celestial
rounds.

As regards myself, the doctor has strongly represented to me the necessity of my taking sea baths
again this summer, to prevent a trouble from taking
root which he ascribes to the nerves of the stomach.
I have in fact been confined to my bed, and very
miserable for four weeks. The general, to whom I
really could hardly have applied for leave, sent me
word that no difficulty would be raised in such a case,
but that on the contrary, he insisted on my doing
everything to restore the health so needful to a soldier;
so I shall carry this letter with me to Hamburg. How
sorry I shall be to pass so near you, you may imagine;
but I have only six weeks' leave and must take full
advantage of the baths.

[The end is wanting.]

BERLIN, January 13th, 1832.

DEAR MOTHER:

* * * When I received your letter of December 15th, mine was already gone, and now four weeks have slipped away, during which nothing has hindered my writing but the wish to give you some decided news. But everything goes on so slowly with me that I must wait for that no longer. That I often thought of you and the sisters at such a time as Christmas and the New Year I need not assure you. From the bottom of my heart I wish you all much, much happiness and blessing. And for you, dear little mother, I can only hope that you may live in health and peace and contentment in the quiet comfort of your home at Schleswig, to be the joy of your children for a long time to come. Amen!

A few other matters which I should have been glad to say were settled, are of a literary, or rather of a pecuniary kind. As I was quite unable to pay off a promissory note for a hundred thalers after my journey last autumn, to earn the money I had to call politics to my aid. Then came the protocol of October 15th, laying down the new frontier lines of Holland and Belgium, and within three days a map in revised outline was brought out at the moderate price of three silver-groschen, and copies sent to all the newspapers —nay, and very well spoken of by them all—but without the authors' names. Now these were a couple of officers, sadly hard up, who had executed the work in three days and printed off 5000 copies. Imagine our ill-luck! Almost at the same moment an equally keen speculator brought out just such a map, at just the same price—all wrong, to be sure, for the good man, with the most loyal liberality, makes Holland a present of the whole of Flanders; but what does that matter?

The map goes down with the public. We spent a hundred thalers, and have no idea what the consequences of the competition may be. I think we may be glad if we recover our expenses. We shall probably know the result in a day or two, and if I were not afraid of delaying this letter too long I could send the good or bad news.

Another enterprise has been the printing of a little work I am bringing out on the disastrous state of Poland. One wretch of a bookseller would have nothing to say to it now that Warsaw has fallen; another had no money; however, he proposed to share expenses and profits. The expenses would run to from eighty to a hundred thalers; the profits, with good luck, after paying all cost, to about a hundred and fifty per cent. So this is more risk.*

Meanwhile one pleasant thing has happened to me. The Censor, through whose hands it had passed, expressed himself at a dinner, where an acquaintance of mine chanced to meet him, in the highest terms of praise of the work, which is to be out in about a week. He asked whether any one knew this H. von M., and would not believe that he was only a humble second-lieutenant; he had felt convinced that it was the work of a man with fifty years' experience of the world behind him, and so forth. I will take care that a copy is sent to you.

Of more importance than these is an undertaking I have just begun. It is the translation from the English of a work of nearly 6000 pages, namely, "Gibbon's History of the Decline and Fall of the Roman Empire," in twelve volumes large octavo. The publisher is to

* The work was brought out in 1832 by G. Fincke of Berlin, whose business passed, in 1843, into the hands of F. A. Röse, and was subsequently dispersed among several firms.

give me 500 thalers for this Herculean work * as soon as it is printed, and 250 thalers more when five hundred copies are sold. So I must work for a long time before I earn anything; still, the price is worth the trouble. If no interruption interferes, I hope by diligent labor to have finished it in about a year and a half. I utilize every spare quarter of an hour. The work offers no difficulties whatever; indeed I like it, but it takes up so much time that I hardly have a minute to myself; all the more since I am very busy at the office of the General Staff, where my colleague and I are now drawn into all the duties of the General Staff. However, I am well and content; for after all, work, hope, and health are all that are needful.

So much for myself. But best love to the good little sisters. and Ludwig, who occasionally does me the pleasure of addressing me—an envelope. Always, with faithful love, your

HELMUTH.

BERLIN, April 26th, 1832.

DEAR MOTHER:

In the confident belief that my father will have sent you my letter to him of the 5th, I have postponed answering yours until now. You will have learnt from that letter that I have been appointed to the General Staff. This is quite settled; taking my place is a mere matter of detail, and I shall probably do so in the course of the year—*perhaps* as first-lieutenant.

But the appointment brings with it very serious expenses; in the first place I must have a horse.

---

* This great work of translating Gibbon seems never to have been brought out, though in a letter of April 24, 1833, von Moltke himself says that the first volume is in the press. The translation is at any rate not to be found in the Royal Library at Berlin, nor does the title appear in any catalogues.

Uncle Ballhorn has been so kind as to advance me 200 thalers for immediate outlay, which I am to repay out of the expected profits of my book; but even under the most favorable circumstances this cannot be till next year. I have, however, bought a really capital black horse for those 200 thalers. As horses are always very dear in Berlin, and the prospect of the war has made them dearer, and as in my position I cannot ride a bad one, I had to pay twenty-seven Friedrichs d'or for mine, and the rest of the money went in saddle, bridle, and stable furniture. I might have had a handsomer horse for a little less, but I am quite satisfied now to have chosen the less showy, but, in the opinion of all judges, the sounder beast, and perfectly free from vice. I am obliged to work him very hard on duty, but you may imagine what care I take of him in every other respect. Uncle Ballhorn, who lives but a few doors from me, has lent me a stall in his stable, and I grudge no attention, pains, or expense to keep everything in such a state as to preserve my horse in health and vigor. The great advantage of a good horse is that it costs no more to feed and house than the worst, and the money is only invested, and, barring accident, not lost.

But where is the second horse to come from? That a second is indispensable you will easily believe, when you consider that the journey of the General Staff, though this year it is only to go through Thuringia, involves a ride of sixty miles [280 English miles] and that it is neither customary nor possible to travel without a servant. Occasionally whole days are spent on horseback, and it is not regarded favorably if any order is not carried out at full gallop. One horse cannot suffice for this, and many officers think it scarcely possible to do with two. This is equally true of the manœuvres, and the spring manœuvres begin on May 18th.

For these reasons, dear mother, I am compelled once more to have recourse to your kindness, to beg you, if possible, to help me with 200 thalers. What troubles me is that I should thus again reduce your already narrow income, and it would be a real satisfaction to me if you would allow me to make good the loss in dividends which you will incur, and which I can very well do. But if circumstances forbid your acceding to my request, I shall of course submit, and thank you with sincere affection for all you have already done for me. The loan is not necessary—not indispensably necessary; for if it comes to the worst I must and will purchase on loan, but I shall then buy dear and at a disadvantage, and be hardly pressed to pay. If, however, you think you can grant my request, I shall have the capital once for all, and without special ill-luck cannot be a great loser, while I may make money by it. The first appointment to the Staff leads to considerable outlay, and at the same time to a reduction of pay; the further steps necessitate no further purchases, and bring in better pay and larger allowances. So this certainly is the moment when I most need help, and I hope it will be the last. So, dear mother, I commend my petition to your kindness, and if granting it does not involve you personally in any disadvantageous or unpleasant consequences, I beg you to manage it for me. It is, of course, to be understood that I propose that these 200 thalers should be taken out of your capital, for out of your income it is quite impossible, and I would not accept it. An early decision, at any rate, is of importance to me, since, as I have said, the manœuvres begin at the end of May.

I hope with all my heart that this letter will find you well and happy, and remain, with true affection, your

HELMUTH.

The young officer was consulted by his mother as to his opinion of the love affair of a relation, which seemed likely to lead to an engagement. To this he replied:

BERLIN, May 15th, 1832.

DEAR MOTHER:

* * * As you may suppose I, being insufficiently instructed, and X. being personally unknown to me, I should carefully refrain from any suggestion or advice in such a matter. But, though I should never try to persuade her to the alliance, neither should I advise her to refuse it out of hand. All that I have heard of X. seems to me to indicate a fine character. My personal conviction is that every marriage is a risk which we blindly rush into—for that we should know and judge calmly of the being with whom we join our lot is too much to ask, since we do not love, know, or judge ourselves, and since what we find in married life depends perhaps as much on ourselves as on our partner. If we call only cold reason into council, it is impossible not to see that it is granted to very few men to meet in real life with the ideal of which each certainly dreams once; and even fewer are those who do not wake all the more painfully from that dream which must indeed be the greatest happiness. When feeling is strung to the highest pitch, every inevitable deficiency and every imperfection becomes a discord in the pure harmony, and the higher the expectation, the greater must the disappointment be. This extremely prosaic view is perhaps, nevertheless, the right one, and explains the reason why many *mariages de raison* are happier than those of inclination. * * * In short,

I believe that ecstatic love-making and married happiness are not, to say the least of it, inseparably allied, and that so long as there is no coercion and no evil quality to contend with, sincere, deep, and happy affection may follow on marriage. That X. is a clever man and a rich one is a desirable thing in a secondary degree, but certainly should not influence her decision. This, her own character, and the school in which she has grown up, seem to me in favor of the affair.

I shall be in Berlin till the middle of July; then we move to Erfurt, the rendezvous of the General Staff, whence probably a reconnaissance will be effected of the Main, and as far as Bamberg. This expedition is entirely on horseback, and will take two months. I am ready with two volumes of my work, and shall now discuss the business with my rather dilatory publisher. Farewell for to-day, dear mother. Hoping most sincerely that you are well and happy, I remain, with true affection, your

HELMUTH.

BERLIN, September 28th, 1832.

DEAR MOTHER:

I yesterday received your eagerly-expected letter of the 23rd. It is really shameful that mine to you should have been so late in reaching you. I can only wield the pen with difficulty, as a convalescent; I was thrown, towards the end of the manœuvres, and was rather badly bruised. * * *

I am most anxious to know the results of Wilhelm's examination. What hopes and claims may he not found on such efforts? Would Wilhelm, if he is now more the master of his own time, feel inclined to take part in the translation of Gibbon? He would find the work easy, and perhaps interesting; and, perhaps, too, he might be glad to earn something by such suitable work. If you write to him, pray make the suggestion. I should be very glad, for with so many interruptions for months at a time, I see that I can never finish the work unaided. I am working myself to a wreck over it. Adieu, dear mother, with best love, your

HELMUTH.

BERLIN, November 24th, 1832.

Hearty thanks, dear mother, for your kind letter of the 15th of this month, containing so much good and pleasant news, particularly that Wilhelm and Fritz seem, after such long and earnest efforts, to have gained a better position. If the former, even after passing so well and getting on to the General Staff, still gains no advantage from his appointment (and yet this is said to be the best career of all), it certainly seems to me that with us the requirements are less and the pay more liberal. I read with pleasure that Fritz's modest and conscientious labors are rewarded according to their merit. I remember Major Linde very well, and know how we then esteemed him above most of our teachers, a poor set for the most part. We three eldest must thankfully acknowledge that our efforts are gradually earning for us a better and more independent existence, which we may say without conceit we owe to ourselves next to God, and the help given us by you and my father. And Adolf and Ludwig are in the right road.

As for myself, I am well, and have quite got over my accident. Four of our little corps have already been sent to the Rhine, and I have been for some time in daily expectation of orders to the same effect. Everything now waits on the future; but of that I say nothing, for before these lines reach you everything may be changed.

My daily life is as follows: at seven in the morning I have my breakfast and set to work. Lately I have been very busy with a *précis* of military history, entrusted to me by the General Staff. At nine o'clock, whatever the weather, I mount one of my horses, both very good beasts, and take a brisk ride of a mile or two [from four and a half to nine English miles], and dismount at the office of the General Staff, where I am on duty till two o'clock, and where I read a number of German, English, and French newspapers. Then I go to the café for dinner, and afterwards find another horse waiting for me at my door, and go for a short ride in the Thiergarten. Then I work from four to eight at my translation, and after that usually go into society. If Wilhelm wishes to make an attempt with the work, I should be very glad. I hope to finish the fifth volume this year. I should be extremely pleased if Ludwig could send me soon the sixth; he shall then receive directly the larger half of his pay. Only, if it is inconvenient to him, and he has much other work to do, I will not press him. If I had not to steal the time for my letters, and then were generally already quite tired and sick of writing, I would willingly start a correspondence with him. Adieu for to-day, dear mother. With fond love, thine

HELMUTH.

BERLIN, February 28th, 1833.

DEAR MOTHER:

I received your kind letter of the 23rd, and all the good news it contained, with great joy.

As to me, I am very well. I have been engaged—I may say with business and dissipation alternately—

early and late, for during the carnival pleasure is treated as a serious affair. Almost without wishing it I have been dragged into the vortex of society, from which it is not easy to escape. Various occupations fill each day. I work in the mornings at a criticism of the strategic possibilities of the Thuringian forest or a historical *précis* of the campaign of 1762; the fore-noon is dedicated to office work, in the afternoon every one appears on horseback on the Promenade, and on fine days, such as we are now having, it is brilliant. The fine horses, the crowds of uniforms and equipages, and the close throngs of smartly-dressed and fashion-able women, make this very amusing. After dinner (sometimes, however, I fall asleep over it) I study polit-ical economy, although my own gives me quite enough to do. In the evening the hair-dresser calls and ar-ranges my hair in the most tasteful style; and at eight there is a ball at this prince's or that minister's. I only remain there just as long as I find I have agree-able partners, and often before going to bed I translate a few pages of Gibbon. During the last fortnight I have been to eleven balls, and have danced every dance whilst there, and I find it agrees with me. Last Sun-day evening I was commanded by the king to a *déjeuner dansant*. These parties are small and select, and it is esteemed a distinction to be included. It is a curious fashion; you go at eleven o'clock, dance one waltz, then the gentlemen go into one room and the ladies into another; every one receives a very pretty flower (artificial), leads the lady who has the flower that matches to the table which is decorated with the same flower. The so-called breakfast is really a luncheon, with the usual kickshaws, with turtle-soup, oysters, caviar, paté de foie gras, and other happy results of the cook's art, and suitable drinks. Then all join in a grand Polonaise in the dancing-room, where a formal ball commences, kept up after the candles are lighted till eight o'clock, when the Court goes to the theatre. You can imagine what careful toilets are arranged that they may stand the test of daylight. But these proceedings will soon come to an end; the foreign nobility are already leaving.

To-day four weeks, on March 30th, the word of command will be given, whether I shall be enrolled in the General Staff or not. I may hope in the meantime to send you good news. This promotion brings a fair increase of pay, but it will involve an expensive equipment. The uniform is one of the handsomest and most expensive that we have. It is blue, with a crimson collar and facings embroidered in silver, hat with white feather, sword, silver sash, and epaulettes.

Concerning Gibbon, I wish ardently to be rid of it. I hardly feel justified in spending so much time in a secondary occupation, but necessity forces me to it. I shall soon have finished the sixth volume, that is half of the whole dreadful work, and the first volume is already in print. I shall not undertake such another work again, as I shall not need to, when this is finished. When Ludwig has completed his volume, I hope to send him directly forty thalers in cash, but I think he goes to work too elaborately. A work of nearly 5000 pages cannot be written like a pamphlet. With fond love, yours,

HELMUTH.

BERLIN, April 24th, 1833.

DEAR MOTHER:

These lines have been delayed a long time. You will meanwhile have heard from father the news that I have been promoted, and am now a first-lieutenant.

At present my garrison is in Berlin, but as the next change in the General Staff of an army corps will affect me, my remaining here any longer is uncertain. The garrisons to which I may go are Königsberg, Breslau, Posen, Magdeburg, Münster, or Coblenz. I have gained considerably in salary, for I receive thirty-six thalers, besides ten thalers ration money, as well as cavalry service and three full rations. On the other hand, I must keep a servant and two horses, must live in the dearest garrisons in the kingdom, and have been obliged to newly equip myself in the very handsome, but expensive uniform. The prospect meanwhile is good; and I may hope to be a captain in two years.

How is Ludwig's translation getting on? I expect in a month to have finished the seventh volume, and shall then have reached Ludwig's work. It is terrible work; if Ludwig only has time and inclination to share it! When he has finished his volume two-thirds of the work are done. I also hope to be able to send him his fee directly it is delivered, although I as yet have not received a pfenning. The first volume is in print. Several times, when doing other work, as I have caught sight of the remaining volumes, my heart has sunk. With fond love, yours,

HELMUTH.

BERLIN, July 23rd, 1833.

DEAR MOTHER:

I received your anxiously expected letter of the 18th, together with my sisters' and Ludwig's yesterday; I beg you will excuse me if in the hurry of starting I only answer them summarily to-day, and each kindly share his with the other. Gustchen's betrothal, or imminent betrothal, gives me great pleasure. By this

she secures the best guarantee for a happy future. I
will not deny that I am in favor of *parties de raison;* a
passionate attachment can only decrease.

I beg you to inform Ludwig that concerning the
Gibbon that he has more time than is at all satisfactory. The publisher finds many difficulties in produc-
ing the publication; the chief difficulty was the want
of several thousand thalers ready money in advance.
He has assured me, nevertheless, that now all difficulties have been removed, the printing of the first volume
has begun, and a new volume will appear every month.
But since one must always make a considerable allowance for a publisher's word, the eight volumes will
hardly be out in eight months, and Ludwig can do the
work quite at his leisure. The notes remain untrans-
lated, only where alterations seem necessary; I beg he
will note them, stating the number of the line on a
separate sheet. I have got as far as the 50th chapter
in the middle of the ninth volume. Now there will be
a prolonged interval, but I hope next year, by a last
desperate effort to bring it to a conclusion.

My lovely Italian journey has fallen through; politics interfered in the business, and his Majesty will
confer no permission at the present time, particularly
for that revolutionary country.

It was then proposed I should go to France in order
to attend the manœuvres at Compiègne, St.-Omer, and
Luneville. But they sent a Staff officer, so now I am
going to-day on an official journey to Lausitz, but I
hope that my furlough, with its limitations, will allow
of my visiting the Austrian States. In that case I
shall travel by way of Vienna and Milan. I therefore
beg you will not write to me till I have given you fresh
news, for as yet I can in no way fix dates, where and
when I shall be at any place. Adieu, dear mother;

5

my boxes stand half-packed, the horses saddled.   Good-bye, yours,

HELMUTH V. MOLTKE.

Finished August 9th, 1833.

BERLIN, May 27th, 1834.

DEAR MOTHER:

It is a very long time since I wrote to you, but I have very often thought of you. I am sincerely grieved to hear that you unfortunately are suffering so much. God grant you alleviation and recovery, my kind little mother. I knew you would bear pain with firmness and resignation; it is the peace that comes of a good and clear conscience. It has so often entered my mind that of all benefits early maternal instruction is the greatest and most lasting. The whole character and all that is good in it is built up on this foundation, and since you have brought up eight children to be honorable men, their gratitude and God's blessing must rest on you.

You are so accustomed, dear mother, to seek your own happiness in our welfare, that I trust our dear Guste's marriage will afford you pleasure. How I wish I could be present with you on the occasion, but urgent reasons prevent it. But I hope in the autumn to get a longer furlough and more easily. After such a long separation, I long to see you and my sisters again.

As far as I am personally concerned, I have every reason to be contented—and I am. My position is as pleasant as it could possibly be, my income good, and prospects even better. And for a long time I have been remarkably well. There appears to exist no further trace of my old, deeply-rooted and painful heart-complaint. I acknowledge this gratefully. With sincere love, your

HELMUTH.

BERLIN, June 29th, 1834.

DEAR MOTHER:

Our General-Staff journey is this time towards the Hartz mountains; but the preliminary exercises and the reconnoitring will take me first to Dresden, and from thence I hope to make a trip through the whole of the Erzgebirge, by way of Teplitz and Carlsbad, to Eger.

We set out in the very beginning of July, and only return at the end of August. I should like to have a good account of you, dear mother, before I start. God grant that you may be tolerably well.

As soon as the autumn manœuvres are over (which will be as far off as the middle of September), I have the prospect of being sent on service by my chief to Copenhagen. Now that a steamer goes from Stettin, I can get from this to Copenhagen in two days. Afterwards I go by steamer to Kiel, and expect to be with you in October. I am already greatly rejoicing that I shall see you again after such a long separation.

I shall also be glad to see Augusta keeping her own home, and to make our brother-in-law's acquaintance; are they now at Schleswig or at Kiel? and which is the Burtsche's house?

I have begged my father to pay Ludwig twenty-four thalers, Prussian currency, which will, I hope, be welcome to him. The immediate honorarium (till 500 copies are sold) amounts, as I wrote to him, to 500 thalers; and as there are twelve volumes, this comes to $\frac{500}{12} = 41\frac{2}{3}$ thalers. I have already got to the eleventh volume of this gigantic work; but now it must be stopped for half a year. Farewell, for to-day, dear mother. I pray God every day to keep you in health, and preserve you to us for many long years yet. With truest love, your

HELMUTH.

BERLIN, January 8th, 1835.

DEAR MOTHER:

I write you only a few lines, to thank you affectionately for your kind reception, and to tell you that I got back here safe and sound. As to my further fate, nothing has as yet been heard, and I am still in the same position as before.

My new room is very nice, but even smaller than yours. It faces the same way as your sitting-room, and your star near the * * * * * * sparkles every evening in front of my window, and reminds me of you. Best love and farewell till I have further news. Your

HELMUTH.

BERLIN, February 3rd, 1835.

DEAR MOTHER:

I only yesterday received your dear letter of the 18th of last month, because, by an oversight of the letter-carrier, it was sent back again to Schleswig. Since then you will have heard from my father that, on the very day when you wrote, Sunday, the 18th, I was delightfully surprised by having the Order of St. John conferred on me. The decoration, which is very pretty, is precious to me as a proof of the kind feeling and satisfaction of my superiors. Of all the orders which I could possibly have had, this is by far the most gratifying to me, and in Germany one of the most highly esteemed. And as it is bestowed only on men of noble birth and distinguished family, it is the object of much ambition and no little envy to many. What I am now anxiously waiting for, is to know whether I shall be made captain on March 31st.

Take care of yourself, and spare yourself, dear
mother; you have a strong constitution, but you
should take better care of yourself. Adieu for to-day,
dear mother. You shall soon have a few lines again
from your faithful and loving son

HELMUTH.

BERLIN, March 16th, 1835.

DEAR MOTHER:

Although I have long owed you a letter, I must
postpone sending this for another fortnight, to announce to you at once what the decisive 30th of March
may possibly do for me. Meanwhile, it is a pleasure
to talk with you in fancy. I only hope with all my
heart that you and the others are all well. The New
Year is such a bad time. I have a slight *grippe*, and
hope to be let off with that, but I am struggling with
vague anticipations, which, however, will be certain-
ties by the time you receive these lines. So much at
any rate is certain: that one officer of our little corps
will be sent to Coblenz on the Rhine, and two to
Königsberg in Prussia.

I have begun a lawsuit against my publisher. I
am curious to see whether justice will help me. I
have been most averse to taking this step, and have
at the same time made overtures of peace, and it would
seem that he is inclined to compromise. The day
before yesterday I received a huge document from
Rome. It was my patent from Prince Henry, the
Grand Master of the Order of St. John.

I hardly know what more news to give you but that
my bay is well, and in a race with four other horses,
beat them all. My astronomical knowledge has been
much extended by watching your star, for I never
before observed that all the stars move round in the

heavens. It must now be visible in the evening exactly opposite Ludwig's window—but very high up. I regard it as a lucky star.

The 24th.—The 30th will soon be here. On Monday wish me good luck.

The 30th.—I was made captain to-day. In a few days I shall be able to let you know whether I shall be ordered off anywhere in consequence of this promotion. Adieu for to-day, dear mother. I hasten to send this letter off by to-day's post.

HELMUTH.

BERLIN, April 21st, 1835.

DEAR MOTHER:

For the present I remain in peace here, with the Central General Staff. My chief tells me that the plan with regard to Paris cannot yet be carried out, but "that I am in any case to hold myself in readiness for that post." While I was ill, he rejoiced me by a Royal Cabinet message, of which this is an exact copy:

"With your report, dated January 24th of this year, I received the collected notes of Captain von Moltke of the General Staff, on the Danish land and marine forces. While thanking you for sending them, I regard this very thorough piece of work with much approval.

"(Signed)   FREDERICK WILHELM.

"BERLIN, April 15th, 1835.

"*To Lieutenant-General Krauseneck.*"

As I shall now, for at least a year, remain in my old position, I must now see about replacing my second horse.

With regard to my promotion, four of my seniors in my old regiment are still second-lieutenants. I have passed over their heads, and the whole body of twelve first-lieutenants. Even in the Guards the men who got their commission at the same time with me, are only just made first-lieutenants, and I am perhaps the only captain in the army who entered so late as 1822. Thus I have made good the four years I lost in the Danish service.

As the fruit of my savings I enclose you a scrap of linen; no, to tell the real truth, I stole it. It is a bit of the shirt of a priest who lived 2040 years before the birth of Christ. I know but little else about the good man, and I believe none of his sermons are extant. As, however, he had about 1700 ells of shirting about his body, he will forgive me the theft, no doubt. But is it not really amazing that they should have known how to weave this Byssus 4000 years ago?

In September, the Fifth and Sixth Army Corps are to unite—a fourth of our whole army—for manœuvring in the lovely neighborhood of Liegnitz, at the foot of the Riesengebirge. From thence we shall, no doubt, be sent to the scene of the Russian manœuvres which are to take place at Kalisch, on the Silesian-Polish frontier. Thus we shall not be back in Berlin before the end of October. So I must have good horses. Adieu for to-day, dear mother; I hope this will find you well. With much love, yours, HELMUTH.

BERLIN, June 20th, 1835.

DEAR MOTHER:

Very many thanks for your welcome letter, from which I gather that you have got well through this very bad spring. I hope the tremendous heat which we have had since has not been too much for you, and that your little garden may have brought you some refreshment.

As for myself, I should certainly have written to you sooner, if I had not just now been overwhelmed with business. Immediately after my father's departure, I went on duty for four weeks with the Alexander Regiment of Grenadiers, which is quartered in barracks at the very opposite end of the city. The daily ride through the paved streets in the broiling heat has tanned me quite brown, but also made me quite strong. With this it is the great time for examinations, and within fifteen days I have to examine 143 ensigns and cadets for promotion, and also to finish some writing which has to be done in a hurry. But the more a man has to do the better he does it.

I have also concluded a bargain for a horse. I have bought a second horse for forty louis d'or, so that I have actually one hundred louis d'or in horseflesh in the stable. And they are two very handsome, sound, and capital beasts—*absit omen*, and as a good trooper I spit—few officers in the garrison can show better. Such a horse eats no more than a bad one, and I expect with good usage to get ten or fifteen years' service out of them. I may also observe that they will almost immediately be paid for. I have come to a legal compromise with my publisher, by which he is to pay me the really miserable sum of 166 thalers; but then I am released from finishing or revising the work. Now, as the man is a perfect greyhound for doubling, I am very well content to have got off so well, for only twelve thalers of legal costs. He has already paid me 100 thalers; the sixty-six are to be paid at once. The work is really out of all proportion to the trouble it has given me, and the whole sum is little more than half of what I have had to pay for my grey. In consideration of the superfluous worry, and in obedience to your advice, I am offering myself a pint of Moselle a day this month, and I find myself, on the whole, generally ready for my feed.

Our expedition on horseback will scarcely begin before the middle of July. We have as yet had no further orders, and hardly know more than that it is to be into Silesia, and probably to Liegnitz, Neisse, and the hill country. We are required to be ready to set out at a moment's notice.

Now farewell, dear mother; God keep you well and in good spirits. Take some care of yourself, and do not spare the droschky in this fine weather, but enjoy the beauties of the neighborhood. With best love and attachment, yours,

HELMUTH.

WIEGANDSTHAL, IN THE ISERGEBIRGE,
July 26th, 1835.

DEAR MOTHER:

I have several times already sat down to write to you, but in my present mode of life it is hard to find a quiet moment. But to-day, being Sunday, when you are probably at church and thinking of me, I will make a serious effort, and give you the most immediate news. My duty this time has brought me to the Bohemian frontier and the Riesengebirge. I have had heavy marches, but both my horses, thank God, are well and game. When I arrive at quarters, I have at once to report on the roads we have reconnoitred; by that time I am fearfully hungry and tired, or perhaps have to inspect some old castle, or fortress, or clamber up the hills; and there is little time or strength left for letter writing. But I have thought of you many a time when gazing at a glorious view from a height, and wished that you could be up there too to see it, just for a quarter of an hour.

The finest thing I have yet seen in the course of my journey is the ruin of the old castle of Oybin, near Zwickau, on the Saxon-Bohemian frontier. Never in my life have I seen such an inaccessible hill. Perpendicular cliffs of sandstone, more than 100 feet high on every side, and only one stairway of some hundreds of steps leading into the stronghold. This is almost entirely destroyed, but the chapel remains nearly uninjured; it is in the finest style of Gothic and admirably built. Nothing is gone but the roof and topmost groining, and this is replaced to some extent by the fine light-green birch-trees which have their roots in the old walls. The capitals of the pillars and the arches of the windows are elaborately carved, and being wrought in stone are still perfect. The steps of the altar and confessional, the sacristy, and the cells give a good idea of what it must have been. One wall of this lofty building is very remarkable; it is part of the rock itself, and of course is one with the hill. The body of the church has been hewn out, and outside it a path of about four feet wide divides this wonderful wall from the mass of rock. Thus the whole wall is in one piece. What a labor, before powder was known to blast it! And the view from the castle is even finer than the place itself.

It was very interesting too to see Friedland in Bohemia, Wallenstein's castle. When I arrived the old fortress had been struck by lightning only a few hours before. It had burnt for about an hour, but the fire had been got under and only the roof was destroyed.

The only original portrait extant of that great man is extremely remarkable. As is generally the case, the face is quite unlike the man as one has imagined him. His daughter is wonderfully pretty, but her name was not Thekla, but Katharina; nor did she retire into a convent with Fräulein Neubrunn, but married an Austrian Count. She must be forgiven, since Piccolomini was so far in the wrong that he never existed. I have climbed the heights above beautiful Gorlitz from a point high up, and yesterday early I went up the Tafelfichte. In the evening I rode to the ruins of the old hill fortress of Greiffenstein—splendid! on the top of a cone of basalt. The whole range of the Isergebirge lies below, but the giants which towered up were as usual wrapped in clouds.

You will scarcely find my little town in your geography; it consists of a collection of poor weavers whose golden age is past.

The poor Silesian, with the greatest industry and application, cannot spin the flax which grows at his door as cheaply as the English with their machinery can spin the cotton which they have to procure from another hemisphere. I shall try to give an impetus to trade, by buying at Hirschberg, the chief centre of the Silesian linen industry, a new shirt, as one of mine has been reduced to *charpie* by the long rides. I am already far in among the mountains, but to-day I go even further into Flinsberg, a watering-place in a high mountain valley without an exit. On one side rises the Tafelfichte 3420 feet high, and on the other the Geiersberg, 2343 feet high. The horses are already saddled, so adieu for to-day.

Dear mother, I am likely to take this letter with me to Warmbrunn. At present I am travelling alone and meet my fellow-officers again later on. But I carry small copies of Montaigne and " Childe Harold " in my saddle pocket. Yet I must confess that I do not often want to read, the grand book of nature is spread so wide open here, and is so magnificently and legibly written with mountains, castles and towns, that one's

eyes are not injured as they are with the small type.
I spend all the time I am able to spare in sketching
the lovely castles and their surroundings; perhaps I
may be able some day to show you these pages, they
constitute my diary.

Now, good-night, dear mother, I am thoroughly tired
after a ride to Schweidnitz. I started at six o'clock,
and only got home again at eight o'clock in the evening. God preserve you. With love. Yours,

HELMUTH.

After Captain von Moltke had been at the Royal manœuvres in
Silesia as well as at the Russo-Prussian review at Kalisch, he was ordered to Constantinople, which postponed his expected visit home for
four years. The following letters will offer a welcome supplement to his
famous "Briefe über Zustände und Begebenheiten in der Türkei."
(Letters on affairs and events in Turkey.)

VIENNA, October 15th, 1835.

DEAR MOTHER:

I have not, as you will see by the picture above,*
got very far on my journey, nevertheless I will let you
know from hence that I am well and happy. Unfortunately I have not yet had any news of you, but as
there is a post to-day from Berlin, it may perhaps bring
me something. I sincerely trust that you are satisfied
with your state of health, and that all goes well with
you. I often think of you all so far away.

Not before the 17th of the month could I leave Breslau, as my travelling companion, Herr von Bergh, who
is adjutant in the First Regiment of Guards was prevented coming earlier by official business. I paid a
visit in the meantime to Schloss Briese, not far from
Breslau, where I had quarters during the survey, and
where I was welcomed as an old friend.

* Letter-paper, with a representation of St. Stephen's cathedral.

I arrived here on Saturday, the 10th, at daybreak, and took up my quarters at the "Golden Lamb" in the Jägerzeile. I have already lodged here once before, and my father used also to come to this inn. But since then the little "Lamb" has become an enormous palace, with a fine outlook over the Danube and the bastion towards St. Stephen's.

Vienna is a lovely town just because the streets are irregular, for nothing is more tedious than long, straight streets. The crooked streets have been gradually built as required; such towns have an historical past and appeal to the fancy, whilst those drawn by a ruler are built and regulated by the taste of an individual.

The splendor of the shops is extraordinary, and one is in a state of constant temptation to buy. Every house, besides having a number, has a sign, and these are often so well painted that one stops astonished before them. Some of these sign-boards are by quite well-known masters and worthy to hang in a picture gallery. The "Maid of Honor" stands next to the "White Wolf"; the young "King of Hungary" and the "Archbishop of Cologne" are opposite "Amor" and the "Maid of Orleans."

The centre of the town, the Downing-street of Vienna, is the so-called *Graben*.

You see written on a palace in large characters, "Gunkel." Gunkel is the first notability amongst the clothes manufacturers, otherwise called a tailor. I put myself into his hands for a consultation *en fait de toilette*. After he had looked at my suit critically, Herr von Gunkel wished to know whom I employed. I named Kley in Berlin. "Not bad," said the artist, "but quite a failure!" He wished to see me in dark green, informed me that it was a form of insanity to

wear a white waistcoat, and that the only saving grace
lay in a black cravat.

The driving in the streets is extraordinary. They
are narrow and wonderfully paved, but without a footpath, and the carriages and cabs, instead of going at a
steady trot, drive quite close up to the houses, so that
one really has to take care. No wonder that, having
to give all my attention to this, I am constantly losing
my way in these high, narrow streets. But then I
have only to look up, and as a rule I find old St.
Stephen with his tall spire showing the right way, or
beckoning me to begin my wanderings again, starting
from this sure point. Truly every way leads by St.
Stephen, and every morning I linger a few minutes,
standing under the huge arches and between the
slender, tall pillars that are cut out of beautiful stone.

You may also ascend to the top of the tower; 757
steps lead up to the so-called Starhemberg seat: a little
bench in a niche, from which you can see away over
the vast fen-lands and trace Moravia and Hungary in
the extreme distance. It was here that old Starhemberg sat with an anxious heart, awaiting the continually closer approach of the Turkish forces. The wide
plain was covered with their tents and horses, the
heavy chain, weighing a hundred thousand hundredweight, which now hangs in the imperial arsenal, was
forged in order to bar the Danube. The Austrian
forces were annihilated, the imperial court had fled to
Linz, the State, as usual, was torn by disunion, and
no help to be hoped for. At that time there were no
suburbs outside Vienna, which to-day cover about ten
times the space of the original town. Those same
walls as they now stand, with only a few small out-
works on one side, were the bulwarks of Christendom.
Hunger and sickness had reduced the city to extrem-

ity; it was a matter of days and hours; as the crescent moon shone over St. Stephen's, so Islam would triumph over the capital of the Christian world. How different it might have been in Europe. Sobieski's troopers decided then the fate of the world.

From Starhemberg's seat you may ascend another 100 steps to the top of the tower. From thence you can see the whole of Vienna like a map. The Glacis, which divide the suburbs from the city, and the bastion, make one of the loveliest promenades in the world; the castles and country seats in the neighborhood, the near Kahlengebirge and the distant Carpathians and Alps, which are already covered with snow.

As Bergh has very good introductions, we are usually invited out in the afternoons. To-day we were particularly well received by a Hungarian grandee, who has 50,000 dependents in Croatia, and he placed five different wines before us, all of which he had grown on his estate. We are taking very valuable letters of introduction with us from home to Pesth, Semlin, Bucharest, Constantinople, Smyrna, Athens. As we have introductions everywhere to the ambassadors or the most influential people, these will very substantially assist our proceedings and make the journey as pleasant as it will be useful.

We shall go from this to Presburg early on Sunday, the 18th, and then by steamboat to Pesth, where we remain two days, then to Belgrade and up the Danube to Rustschuk, nearly 200 [936 English] miles from Vienna. We shall be in Rustschuk on the 30th of the month, then go to Prince Ghika at Bucharest, and from thence on horseback with the Tartar to Constantinople.

This is almost the only possible mode of travelling, the best, and absolutely safe; only rather fatiguing, and it will be rather cool on the Balkans. But I shall procure a large sheepskin in Hungary.

I hope, by means of the Embassy, to be able to write to you from Constantinople. I am sorry to say I have had no letter here from you. I beg you will certainly send me a few lines saying how you are, dear mother, also giving me news about my brothers and sisters, and let the letter be (on very thin paper and not crossed) addressed to the *poste restante*, Naples. I expect to reach there in the course of January, and beg you will write some time about Christmas or the New Year, and give me, please God, good news of you all.

I think I shall be in Berlin by March. Affectionate greeting to Adolf, Loui, and my sisters. May you all be well and happy. Now farewell, dear mother. God bless you. With fond love, yours,

HELMUTH.

BUJUKDÉRÉ, NEAR CONSTANTINOPLE,
November 30th, 1835.

DEAR MOTHER:

It is a very long time since I had any news from you. I hope you are well and happy. God guard and keep you! If, as I hope, you get these lines for Christmas, you will at least see I have successfully surmounted several difficulties, that I have kept well, and have been rewarded by a delightful sojourn in an entirely new world.

I only wish you could spend a quarter of an hour here at my window, under which the waves of the Bosphorus splash as clear as crystal, exactly as if I were sitting in the cabin of a man-of-war.*

---

* He is thus represented in a picture which he sent to his mother in a later letter of January 10th, 1837.

Those hills which are so near that one can count the windows in the houses are in another continent—are in Asia. To the right you see in the little green valley a group of gigantic plane-trees; they bear the name of Godfrey of Boullion, for it is supposed that he rested under them when he went as a crusader to Palestine. The old Genoese castle rises up out of that mountain, with the arms of the Italian Republic and the date 1100 over the doorway. On the left you see a lake; it is the Black Sea, the dreaded Pontus Euxinus. Quickly, noiselessly, the light caïques pass by under my window, powerful war-ships anchor close to the houses, and the steamers fly past with waving flags. The extensive burial grounds are really cypress forests. Laurels grow to trees here, and the Italian pines, with their soft, bright green, contrast well with the almost black and motionless cypress trees. Roses are still in bloom in the gardens everywhere, and we have days when it is almost too hot.

When I get back to Berlin I will send you my sketch-book. But I sincerely entreat you to send me news of yourself to Naples; Eduard Ballhorn will take care of it for me. You may imagine how many questions I want to ask you.

On Christmas Eve I shall be with you all in thought, to drink to your health, I hope, either in Athens or in Alexandria. I expect to be in Naples by the middle of January, and shall write to you again from thence.

Good-bye for to-day, dear mother, only keep well and take care of your strength. Lie down and rest a little—you may well do so, for you have worked long enough for us. Once more a thousand greetings. With fond love and thanks, yours,

HELMUTH.

6

P.S.—The rose leaves I am sending you are from Asia, and that you may see that the money has not yet run out, I also enclose a Turkish para.

Your lovely star has lighted me every morning early, when I have ridden out before sunrise.

I must open my letter again to take out the leaves and the para, or else it cannot be fumigated and go with the dispatches from the Embassy. We still have here a few cases of plague, and prudential measures are still in force. As for the rest, nobody thinks about the plague, and there is no more danger than of a tile falling on my head.

To-day we start on an excursion into Asia Minor, and expect to be back in four days, when our rooms will be ready in the Hotel of the Embassy at Pera.

I hope to pay you the promised para personally next year. Adieu, dear mother.

Bujukdéré, December 1st, 1835.

Arnautekioj, near Constantinople,
February 9th, 1836.*

Dear Mother:

I received letters by yesterday's post from Cousin Eduard, but, alas, no enclosures from you, father, or my brothers and sisters, for which I had hoped so much. Meanwhile, Eduard writes in his last account that you are all, thank God, well, and since this is the first news I have had of you, and now only in great haste, for five months, I am naturally much delighted. I trust these lines may also find you in good health and happy.

I do not yet know if my stay here will be prolonged

* In this letter passages occur like the contents of the letters under date of February 9th and 12th, 1836, printed in the "Türkischen Briefe." (Letters from Turkey.)

or not. We are waiting for letters from Berlin by the next post which will decide the matter. It has been most interesting in any case to me to spend the winter in new surroundings.

The Seraskier has been so well satisfied with some small work of mine that he yesterday presented me with a snuff-box set with brilliants, which must be worth, I should think, at least 100 louis d'or, and will cover the expenses of my journey so far. He has also placed at my disposal a horse out of his stable with a handsome bridle and red velvet saddle; it stands in Count Königsmark's * stable at Pera, and I now ride all about the neighborhood. A *sais* is told off to take care of it, and a Kavass, armed with a cutlass, yataghan, and loaded pistols, walks in front of me wherever I go in Constantinople, so that I can scarcely ever be rid of him.

I have been going for some days to the house of a dragoman who is the Seraskier's chief interpreter, and who translates into Turkish whatever I write down in French. Business gets done very slowly here; happily they write less in Turkey than in our country. Writing generally is done here about as fast, and in very much the same way, as ladies' worsted work at home; that is to say, sitting on a sofa with your legs crossed and a long strip of paper on your knees, on which the characters are made with a reed-pen, from right to left. The Armenian with whom I live has a large household, and is reckoned here as a wealthy and important personage. I want for nothing; the table is excellent, and the whole insight into a household on the Turkish plan is extremely amusing. Every other dish is sweet, and besides these, ten dishes of cold *hors d'œuvre* stand on the table, from which every one helps himself as he

* Prussian Ambassador to the Porte.

likes between whiles. There are oysters, shell-fish or caviar, cheese, olives, goat's milk curd, salads, sardines, cray-fish, lobster, peppers, onions, and fruits of various kinds. Coffee is served six or seven times a day in tiny cups. The preparation of it is quite unlike our way of infusing coffee; the grounds are poured into the cup with the liquor and without sugar or milk; but one soon gets used to thinking it very good. Preserves are handed round with it; each one takes a spoonful into his mouth, and then drinks water to wash it down; and every one smokes. I myself can already take a pull with some, though very small satisfaction, at a pipe six feet long, with a large amber mouth-piece and a small red clay bowl. The worst thing is that not a room ever has a stove. People sit—for no one ever thinks of walking for months at a time—wrapped in furs with their legs under them, and scarcely trouble themselves as to whether the doors are open or shut. However, in the middle of the room stands a table covered with a large quilted cloth, and under it a brazier is placed. Every one sits round it to get warm. They get up late, usually not before nine, a good breakfast is served at one, of from five to eight dishes; dinner at seven in the evening, and bed not till one or two in the morning. However, every one is at liberty to please himself. The sitting-room is all sofa, the floor is strewn with rugs, and round the room, close to the wall, runs a deep divan, on which twenty men often sit or recline. Some smoke, others sleep, others again play dominoes, écarté or whist; but for the most part they do nothing and say little. If one is intimate in the house, the ladies will appear, and very pretty they are.

Nothing can be more delightful than the ride by the shore. On the edge of the Bosphorus stands an ancient castle, built by the Turks before the taking of Constantinople. The high white walls with towers and pinnacles twist about so strangely up and down the steep cliffs, that the legend really seems possible which says that Sultan Mahmoud had then planned to form the letters of his name. Shafts of columns, bits of frieze and beautiful carving stick out of the walls of the gigantic towers, which they are built into, as well as grave-stones, bricks, and blocks of stone. Five centuries have hardly effaced any of these footprints, set by Islam on European soil when it first crossed over from Asia. From hence it made its way as far as the Tyrol and Germany, and its followers very nearly succeeded in turning St. Stephen's church in Vienna into a mosque, as they had done at St. Sophia's, where the cross had been adored more than a thousand years.

This old castle is generally the end of my ride. The Bosphorus rushes past it like a great raging river, and hundreds of dolphins leap along, splashing and snorting on the surface. No one is allowed to catch these creatures, which probably feed on the delicious flounders, palamides and gold carp, like the whole population of the capital. The rocky cliffs by the water's edge are overgrown with evergreen cypress, but the shores are edged with an unbroken line of pretty wooden summer residences.

I cross to Pera in a caïque, or ride round in about an hour. The day after to-morrow, being Shrove Tuesday, there is to be a masquerade at the Russian Ambassador's. I have ordered a Slavonian costume from Smyrna, but unluckily it has not yet arrived. I shall have to go disguised as an European after all.

Adieu for to-day, dear mother; in a fortnight or three weeks I can give you further information.

Your ever loving son,

HELMUTH.

SULTAN-HISSAR, March 27th, 1836.

The Pasha of the Dardanelles, to whom I was recommended, has given up to me a pretty little house on the shore, in which I have been living nearly a fortnight. I have a splendid view from my terrace over the Straits, where the great merchant ships, with flags of every nation, are incessantly passing to and fro. Yesterday a fresh southerly breeze brought up a hundred and fifty vessels in half an hour. The Dardanelles is no wider here than a large river, than the Rhine, say, at Cologne, and the ancient castles on the shores give it a quite distinctive appearance. The European shore rises steep and rocky opposite, and the warm evenings and moonlight nights are delicious here. The waves splash under my windows, and toss wildly when the south wind is strong.

I took advantage of the first possible day to make an excursion to the Troad. My little caravan consisted of two Surujee, two armed Kavasses, an interpreter from the Embassy, and myself. When I say that we explored the ruins of Abydos, Dardanus, and Rhoetum, it only means that we saw a few heaps of stones. But even the names here are interesting. Ida was still covered with deep snow, and Scamander—or the Simois—was as full in flood as on the day when so many slain Trojans were cast into its waters. Just beyond the hill-spur of Sigeum are the tombs of Ajax, Achilles, and Patroclus; and a little farther on we came to a flat-topped mound on which, it is said, the proud towers of Pergamon stood of yore. I am sorry that I have never read the Iliad since I was at Hohenfelde.

The country is no more than a wide stretch of desert; very rarely does one come across a squalid village of roofless houses. But there is so much that is new to the foreigner: fields of cotton-trees, herds of camels on the pastures, and above all the view of the islands of the Archipelago. These are made beautiful by the immensely high mountains which crown them. Nearest lay Tenedos, behind which Ulysses concealed the fleet of the Achaians; then Samos, Mytilene, and Imbros, on whose summits the snow lies even in summer. Towards evening we reached a Turkish hamlet; the Aga came out to greet us with the usual words: "May your evening be happy, sir; is your humor good?" and he showed us to a house; the horses, which had come eight miles [thirty-seven English], were led to a stable, and rugs spread for us before the fire. Soon a servant appeared with an enormous wooden tray on his turban, on which supper was served in tin dishes. It consisted as usual of pillaw, mutton, olives, honey and sherbet. Knives and forks there were none, but bowls of water there were, handed round before and after eating.

That there should be no lack of excitement on this day, Nature provided a little earthquake in three shocks. The first was the strongest; every one rushed out-of-doors; this was at five in the afternoon, but I was in the open, and on horseback, so I felt nothing of it. The second shock, however, was at ten o'clock at night; and this again I did not feel, because I was in my first sleep and very tired. But at three in the morning I was roused by being rolled over as I lay on my side on a mat, and all the doors and shutters slammed—there were no glazed windows.

Next morning I visited the ruins of Troas-Alexandra, which was built by Antigonus in the time of Alexander the Great. They are of incredible extent; I rode for above a quarter of a mile [one English mile] along a foundation wall of gigantic blocks of stone,

which may perhaps have carried the city wall. At last
we came to a beautiful ruin in the finest style. This
was the remains of the famous palace of a hundred
gates. Those arches and masses of stone laid together
without mortar may stand another three thousand
years.

There is not a place in the immediate neighborhood
which I have not been to.

PERA, April 6th, 1836.

I cannot possibly add anything more to-day but that
I have returned from my excursion safe and sound,
and to my great delight found a letter awaiting me
from my father, and one from you, dear mother. The
answer shall follow this in about a week, but I will try
how far I can get on before this post goes. Thank
God you all keep so well; thank Lena for her letter,
which gave me much pleasure. I shall still have to
dance the rope for some time yet before I set foot on
firm ground. I have received letters from my chief
in Berlin, desiring me to decide whether I will accept,
under very favorable conditions, a post here for some
length of time, a few years perhaps. The Porte has
asked the King to spare him a few Prussian officers.
I replied that it was not a thing I so particularly
desired that I should ever ask for it; but that if his
Excellency regarded me as especially fitted by my residence here to be of essential use to my fellow-officers,
I would certainly do my utmost to earn his approba-
tion in this position. In short, I declined rather than
pressed it, but the decision lies in my chief's hands,
and that is always best. You will know from Eduard
before I do what is settled.

Adieu for to-day, dear mother; if you saw the long
letters I have already written to-day, you would, I am

sure, excuse me from any more writing. Adieu, with
best love to you all,
                                        HELMUTH.

I have "Lamartine's Travels" with me, and they
interest me greatly. I hope to read them again with
you some day. The olive-spray is from the grave of
Patroclus.

CONSTANTINOPLE, April 28th, 1836.

DEAR MOTHER:

I have nothing new to tell you, but I cannot but
thank you for your dear letter of February 20th, which
gave me great joy. After such a long interval, it is
the greatest comfort to learn from you and from my
father that you are all well.

It is not yet decided whether my stay here will be
considerably prolonged, or whether I may start off
suddenly within a month. My General's orders cannot
reach me yet for three weeks or a month. It is, however, probable that I am fated to remain at Constantinople for some time to come, since I know the country,
and the Seraskier has shown special confidence in me.
A residence here is in many ways extremely interesting, and will no doubt be advantageous from a pecuniary point of view; and yet, when one has been here
some little time, and the charm of novelty has vanished,
one longs ardently for Europe. The company of ten
of my fellow-officers, whose arrival is already expected,
will, of course, make things much pleasanter.

I am still living in the *hôtel* of the Prussian Embassy
at Pera. Life is most monotonous. I get up none too
early, remembering that there are twenty-four hours
in the day. Till breakfast at midday I have work to
do, and that is lucky; afterwards I commonly take a
walk with the younger men about the Embassy. We
loiter into one of the numberless cafés, sit down on low

cane stools, smoke nargilehs or hubble-bubble pipes, look at the vessels passing through the Bosphorus and the dolphins which play about them in hundreds. The circulation of ideas is extremely limited; every one knows beforehand all that his neighbor can know, so when we have told each other whether the wind is from the north or south, or whether Olympus is visible or no, we loiter home again, having accurately ascertained whether it will rain or be fine on the morrow. This is the land of lazy ease, a whole nation in slippers. Towards evening I ride out to the Valley of Sweet Waters; we dine at seven, and what we do for the rest of the evening I really do not know.

The festivities in honor of the wedding of Princess Sonnemond (Sun-moon), or Mihrimah, begin this evening with fire-works on the Bosphorus. There was a little display about four weeks ago inside the factory, by which 180 men were blown to the winds; but it was Kismet—their fate. I hope, dear mother, that a letter from you is on the way, containing good news of you all. I close for to-day, begging you always to remember with affection your truly loving son

HELMUTH.

BUJUKDÉRÉ, July 26th, 1836.

DEAR MOTHER:

Two words to-day, to announce my return from the Dardanelles, where I spent a fortnight. As I must immediately ride out to Pera, and have spent this day, from morning till night, in drawing, it is impossible to write you a real letter. To-day I give in my work, and by next mail I shall have rather more leisure. During my absence at D. I have suffered a good deal from the heat, and yet more from flies, bugs, fleas, and the like; the sea bath, which lay under my windows, was my only salvation. On the return passage, the Turkish steam packet stuck hard and fast just outside the harbor; the Pasha went off in a caïque to the Grand Seignior, and at once sent one out to carry me to land. Meanwhile we toiled all night trying to get afloat, as we were anxious to help the poor English Captain, and the Turks had no idea what to do. All our efforts were in vain, for we had run hard aground, luckily only on sand. By morning a second steamer belonging to the Government, and a great number of men came to our assistance—all in vain. It was not till all the coal and ballast had been taken off and the water let out of the boilers that we got afloat, towed off by the other vessel.

Life is very pleasant here in Bujukdéré; the latest news is that the plague has broken out in the Sultan's Seraglio, so that the good man has had to fly. It is a good thing perhaps, and may lead to stricter measures. Here there is no sickness. As seven weeks have passed since I wrote on June 8th, announcing my longer stay here, I confidently hope to get news of you by next mail. The post communication is so punctual that I can always count on a reply from Berlin in forty-two days, and from Holstein in fifty-two.

As concerns myself, I shall in any case be here for three months, but I hope to go home late in the autumn, and shall go to see you at Schleswig, if only for a few days.

Adieu, dear mother, with much love, your

HELMUTH.

BUJUKDÉRÉ, October 10th, 1836.

DEAR MOTHER:

I cannot possibly allow this mail to go out without writing to you, particularly as your dear letter of

August 17th has been in my hands these three weeks. Thank God it contains good news of you all, and that you yourself are satisfied with your health this summer.

It is not yet decided whether some of our Prussian officers are to come here or no. But they may arrive any day, for they can travel almost as quickly as the answers to our letters. As soon as they arrive I shall apply to be recalled, and can have my orders to that effect in from six to eight weeks. If they do not come after all, I may get away all the sooner; at any rate, I hope to be on my way by the New Year.

At this moment I am very busy with some work which at the same time gives me much pleasure: a survey of the ground on both sides of the Bosphorus. There are many hills to climb, but the trouble is repaid by the most beautiful prospects. We are having lovely autumn weather, and the moist sea air keeps the trees and plants green, though we have had no rain for four months. I rise betimes, and at once let myself drop into the sea—I have taken the opportunity of having about a hundred sea-baths—then I drink my coffee and go to my day's work, either in a sailing boat or a swift row-boat, or, inland, on horseback. Work lasts from nine to ten hours; in the evening I find a capital dinner ready. I have a general pass in Turkish allowing me to inspect every fort and battery; I also have a kavass, a tshaus, a corporal, and as many soldiers as I choose, to escort me and carry my instruments. Since the 1st of the month I have gone over a tract of half a mile in length, by three-quarters in breadth [about two by three English miles], and I intend taking up my quarters for a week or a fortnight in the *Fanar* or light-house at the entrance of the Black Sea, so as not to lose so much time in going to and fro.

I have collected nuts and seeds for you wherever I have been; dates from Smyrna, roses from Olympus, and tamarinds from this place. I hope all may thrive under your lucky hand.

Adieu for to-day, dear mother; I hope soon to have news of you. Till our next happy meeting, with faithful love your

HELMUTH.

BUJUKDÉRÉ, NEAR CONSTANTINOPLE,
November 10th, 1836.

DEAR MOTHER:

I cannot possibly leave your welcome letter of October 5th any longer unanswered, for I have had it now a fortnight already. But the post has been delayed by snow in the Balkans, and only came in last night, bringing me orders to send in two long reports which must go off to-day; so that I have only time to tell you that I am well and hearty, and sincerely hope soon again to have as good news of you as your last letter brought me.

Again I can tell you nothing definite about my stay here, but a crisis is at hand, which must result in a decision.

We are having a really wonderful late autumn. It is as warm as in summer, and all the meadows are green again. Quantities of roses are out in the gardens, and we sit out-of-doors till late in the evening. From my window I have a splendid view of the Bosphorus, and at night it is a beautiful scene, when numbers of fishing-boats shoot about with large fires blazing, to attract and catch the palamides.

With affectionate good wishes, yours,

HELMUTH.

BUJUKDÉRÉ, January 10th, 1837.

DEAR MOTHER:

This very day, when the mail goes out and we are expecting the mail in every hour, I am obliged to go into the city because the Pasha has just sent for me. I hope certainly to get a letter to-day from my Chief, and flatter myself with the hope of news from you. At present I cannot write more than that I am safe and sound, and do not yet know whether I shall be recalled or left here. I would finish this letter next week, for it really contains no news; but as I have written to you regularly once a fortnight for several months, and as the papers are making such an outcry about the plague, I am afraid lest you should be anxious if I delay longer than usual.

We are having a beautiful winter; from one to two degrees of frost, with unbroken fine weather, a blue sky and sunshine. This is advantageous to health, and I am happy to be able to tell you that the pestilence is greatly diminishing; in some places the number of sick has fallen to half; in others there are none.

I enclose you a sketch of my room, made, not too skilfully, by an artist here, and not improved by fumigation round the edges; however, it will give you some idea of my present lodging.*

Good-bye for to-day, dear mother. I will soon write at greater length. I only hope this may find you well, and well armed against your cruel winter. As this letter will reach you not long before your birthday, I heartily wish you joy. God preserve you, dear mother, and you know how truly I mean it. I hope soon to

---

* This drawing (see frontispiece) has happily been preserved. The damage done by piercing the letter for fumigation against the plague has been touched out in the reproduction, and the reader sees the drawing in its original state.

have a letter from you, I have had no news for a long time. All letters come punctually to hand, and the post is as regular as between Berlin and Potsdam. Much love to all our people. Always love your

HELMUTH.

PERA, February 6th, 1837.

DEAR MOTHER:

I must confess that I can no longer remember whether your birthday is on the 2nd, 3rd, or 4th of the month. So, to make sure, I thought of you on each of those days, and prayed Heaven to preserve you for many a year in as much health and happiness as possible. But I beg you will let me know the exact date in your next letter.

You will have learnt from my letter of the 24th of last month * all about the audience granted me by the Sultan, and its consequences. I had a letter not long since from my Chief, by which I am commanded by the King's Majesty to remain for the present where I am. This is certainly not exactly what I wished; however, it has two good aspects: in the first place it shows that I give satisfaction at Berlin; and it is highly advantageous to my pocket.

I have been settled here in Pera for a fortnight, because the Grand Seignior has ordered me to make a plan of Constantinople. Winter had kept away; we could walk out of an evening on the terrace in front of my house without an overcoat, and work was going on famously. Suddenly, four days since, the wind went round to the north, and we are in midwinter. The branches of the old cypresses before my window

* This letter is lost. Compare "Briefe über Zustände und Begebenheiten in der Türkei" (Letters on affairs and events in Turkey), p. 107, et seq.

are bent to the ground with the weight of snow. These cranky old houses rock in the wind as though they must inevitably be blown down, but that Kismet ordains that they shall be burnt down. I look with dismay at the minarets on the Sulimanieh opposite; they are as dry as touchwood and of a giddy height, and the muezzin cries from them through snow and storm that Allah is great; it seems almost impossible that these erections, 100 feet high and only eight feet thick, should remain standing. But they have stood 400 years, and must have seen many another storm. This change of scene is by no means agreeable to me, for I only needed another week to finish my map. At the same time this burst of winter is a great blessing, as it will probably put an end to the plague for this year.

I never could imagine before, why Turks are always represented in furs, or why in the latitude of 40° a fur coat should be an important article of clothing. Now I know better. You should see me here, sitting between a stove and a mangal,* and yet huddled in a large quilted counterpane. The brazier is glowing, the stove does its best, but do what they will the temperature of the room cannot be got above 6.50 degrees of *warmth* (43° Fahr.)—a misnomer indeed—for the snow drifts in on the wind, even on to my writing-table. The houses are built of match-wood, and the invention of putty for window-panes has not yet reached the States of the Sublime Porte. Not a door shuts, and through the seams between the boards, which are a finger's width apart, there comes a current of cold wind which makes the papers dance on the flooring.

How glad I should be to sit for an hour with you on

* A brazier.

the sofa in your warm room, while Lena brought in the great, cold joint, and the tall ale-glasses—I should have plenty to tell you.

The map I have made of this neighborhood has already cost me 100 thalers, but it will in the future be one of the most interesting results of my residence in Turkey. It includes at present the whole Bosphorus from the entrance to the Black Sea, for five miles [about 23 English miles] down towards the Sea of Marmora, and inland for from one to one and a half miles [about four to six English miles] on each side. It includes Bujukdéré, where the ambassadors live; Therapia, where Medea culled her magic herbs; the Cyaneæ, circumnavigated by the Argonauts; Hissar, fortified by the Turkish Sultans; Constantinople, with the walls built by the Greek emperors; and the Seraglio, occupying the site of ancient Byzantium; Pera and Galata founded by the Genoese; Kadikoi, the ancient Chalcedon; the plain of Daoud Pasha, where the Janissaries met, and where they were given the Sandshak Shereef, or the standard of the Prophet, when they were setting forth to conquer Christendom; the aqueducts of Valens and of Sulieman; the last spurs of the Balkans, and the first of the mountains of Bithynia.

Now, dear mother, I must close, begging you to give my love to all the brothers and sisters. Take care of yourself against the cold, keep well, and think lovingly of your

HELMUTH.

7

II.

LETTERS TO HIS BROTHER ADOLF.

1839 to 1871.

ADOLF VON MOLTKE.

ADOLF VON MOLTKE.

ADOLF VON MOLTKE, the Field-Marshal's third brother, born on April 8th, 1804, was in his youth a delicate lad with small features, who grew up under his mother's specially loving care and guidance. His father took less pride in the boy, who was inferior to his elder brothers in physical strength, and only did justice to his remarkable intellectual gifts in later years. Though throughout his life Adolf had to contend with feeble health, he succeeded, by his iron determination and remarkable talents, in attaining a high position in his small native State, which he held for many years.

After studying at the Universities of Kiel and Heidelberg, and passing his examinations brilliantly, he entered on the career of a lawyer, and served, in very critical times, as Councillor to the Chief Court of Justice of Holstein, and in the Chancery Office of Schleswig-Holstein-Lauenburg.

In 1848 the confidence of his fellow-countrymen called him to take part in the government of the united Duchies, as constituted after the armistice of Malmoe. He subsequently filled the post of Administrator to the province of Rantzau, and after the Prussian annexation, he was acting-*Landrath* for the district of Pinneberg. In all these appointments he did excellent work, and did his country various and excellent service. He is remembered there as a clear-sighted and honorable man, who enjoyed the esteem and respect of all. That he was able to work on till the end, he owed largely to the faithful care of his wife, under whose admirable nursing he recovered from repeated attacks of illness which brought him to the verge of the grave. Frau Auguste von Moltke, now living at Creisau, was the daughter of General von Krohn, who distinguished himself as War-Minister in Schleswig-Holstein from 1848 to 1850.

Adolf von Moltke's sufferings increased greatly towards the end of his life. They often compelled him to make a long stay in the south, and it was his elder brother Helmuth who, as usual, assisted him with generous sympathy and affection. Thus, after a residence in Algiers, during the winter of 1866–67, he was enabled to take a leading part, with renewed energy, in the difficult task of governing the Duchies in their new relations to Prussia. But, by the Field-Marshal's advice, he decided, early in 1870, to retire from the service of the State, and to settle at Creisau, which his brother had then just acquired. The brothers were bound by a peculiarly close and affectionate tie of friendship, for they met in a common effort to attain the highest and best; and while Helmuth delighted in Adolf's never-failing humor and versatility, and derived advantage from his legal knowledge, he was always ready to advise and help his younger brother.

It had long been a cherished dream with both to live together on an estate, however small, and gather the family about them. The elder had now gained this hoped-for end, by his brilliant services and the favor of his sovereign; but their desire of living together was not long to be gratified.

In July, 1870, the Field-Marshal was called out to the greatest task of his life; Adolf was again compelled to seek a milder climate, but he could still rejoice in the victorious progress of the German armies, to which he had given two sons, and in his brother's glorious successes. But before the hour of reunion had struck, he had closed his eyes in peace, at Lugano, on April 7th, 1871.

A notice of him published in the *Hamburger Nachrichten*, said: "The whole career of this highly distinguished man may be described as having been animated by unselfish and truly Christian love, and a determination, crowned by brilliant success, to devote his best efforts to the welfare of the State and of the people."

His remains were buried by the side of three of his family who had preceded him to the grave, in the church-yard of Barmstedt, near Rantzau. Among the six survivors who stood by his grave was his brother, the famous Field-Marshal, in simple dignity and deep regret.

"He might die happy, for he knew that you, his children, would be cared for," were his words as he turned away from the little mound, and he faithfully kept his word.

COUNT VON MOLTKE'S
LETTERS TO HIS BROTHER ADOLF.

VIENNA, November 23rd, 1839.

DEAR ADOLF:

I write to you but briefly to-day, dear Adolf, partly because I cannot and must not write much, partly because I now am in hope of seeing you ere long, and reserve a great deal to tell you by word of mouth. The sudden change from a Syrian summer to the late autumn in Germany, the very unhealthy sojourn in quarantine at Orsova, and the results too, no doubt, of great fatigue, brought on a severe attack of low fever. I had to remain three weeks at Pesth, and could hardly drag myself to Vienna, where I had to begin a course of radical treatment. Now I can get up, and out a little, and eat like a wolf; but I must remain here till the middle of December at least, before I am convalescent. At the end of March I shall probably be appointed to an Army corps, and then shall get no further leave. So I had to go this winter, and another reason for it was that I must positively be in Berlin by about the 18th January, and at the end of March.

HELMUTH.

BERLIN, March 31st, 1840.

DEAR ADOLF:

The 30th of March only brought promotion in the General Staff; nothing is altered in my position, and I am now trying to make myself a little at home. I have taken very pleasant lodgings on the Leipziger Platz, close to the Potsdam Gate. This place is no longer the wilderness you saw it, but a Bowling-green * surrounded by railings, with flowering shrubs; and the immediate proximity of the Thiergarten is a decided advantage, especially as I have horses. So I can repeat my invitation to you. You will have a room to yourself, where you can work or be idle undisturbed, and you will find all kinds of mineral waters as good as at the springs. Consider of it, and remember me affectionately.

HELMUTH.

My warmest greetings to your wife.

BERLIN, April 24th, 1840.

DEAR ADOLF:

I received your letter of the 13th with great pleasure, giving us the hope of seeing you in Berlin. I have been promoted, by the King's Order in Council, to the General Staff of the Fourth Army. As this is under the command of H.R.H. Prince Carl of Prussia, I remain in Berlin all the same, draw slightly better pay, and, among other advantages, have a pass into the Court box at the theatre.

I shall probably have to make a tour of inspection of the Landwehr with my illustrious Chief, from the 1st till the 10th of June. So I should be very glad if you could make your visit earlier or later than that

---

* *Sic.* Presumably a grass-plot.

time. My father also proposes to come to stay with me, and if your visits should coincide, it would perhaps be best that my father should go to the Hotel de Prusse in the Leipziger Strasse, and you lodge here with me.

HELMUTH.

BRUNSWICK, August 31st, 1841.

DEAR AUGUSTA:*

You cannot think how much pleasure your kind letter afforded me and the lovely piece of work which you sent to me at Hamburg. The book should properly contain the record of some very remarkable journey, described in an interesting way; for it would be impossible to write anything commonplace on its pages. I had just been wishing for a book with a page for every day of the year; but this is almost too good, and I cannot yet make up my mind to take it into use. How, and through whom, this lovely piece of work came into my hands I have no idea. I stayed but one night at Streit's Hotel, and the parcel was delivered to me there that evening. You possibly have a sprite or fairy at your command, who executes your commissions with such punctuality, and who knew beforehand that I should stop at Streit's, and at no other hotel.

If anything was lacking to your kind letter it was the date—which must not be too strictly insisted on from a lady—to enable me to judge how long Adolf had been taking the waters when he was satisfied with the results. But since he had already received my letter from Heligoland when he wrote, he must have gone through half the course by that time. I only hope that he may go through the sea-bathing with equal success. In Heligoland he must be careful to get

---

* Adolf von Moltke's wife.

lodgings in the Unterland, as they call it, to avoid trying his chest any more by perpetual climbing up steps.

I am wandering in and round the Harz mountains, where the good folks have made so many roads that I cannot come to an end of my survey. The tempting convenience of a railroad brought me over to Brunswick; this evening I return to Harzburg, and by Ilsenburg and Wernigerode to the Ballenstedt Empire, where I shall no doubt meet some of your acquaintance.

You do not mention little Lotte. If she still remembers "Uncle Mond," give her my love. Once more many, many thanks, dear Augusta, for your kind thought. Think always affectionately of your faithful brother-in-law and friend,

HELMUTH MOLTKE.

ROME, March 29th, 1846.

DEAR ADOLF:

I hope the other brothers and sisters have already sent you news of our * arrival here, and of our doings generally.

From a letter which I received yesterday from W. Brockdorff, we learn with regret that the inevitable political squabbles have reacted disadvantageously on your private position in Copenhagen. He thinks you will take long leave of absence. For any man who lives not on his dividends, but on his earnings, health and long life are the chief capital, so I can honestly advise you not to shrink from some small outlay to establish your health and refresh your mind. I should feel inclined to beg you to ask at least six months'

---

* The Field-Marshal had married, on May 24th, 1840, Fräulein Marie Burt; he was now in Rome as Adjutant to Prince Henry of Prussia, who lived there.

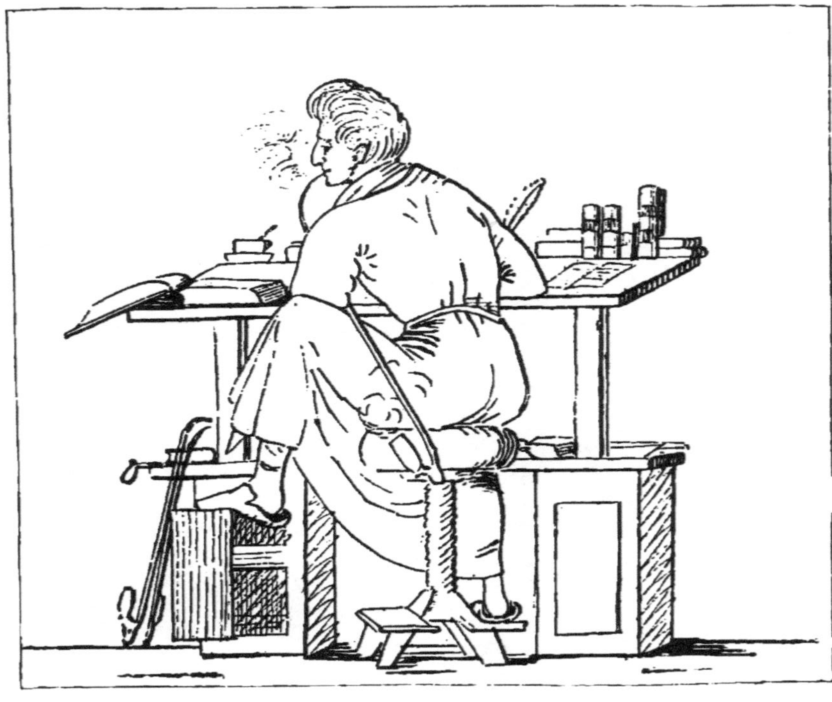

ADOLF VON MOLTKE, A STUDENT.

From a Sketch by his Brother Helmuth, in 1833.

leave and to complete the cure by a visit here. At Kissingen you are already exactly half way to Rome from Copenhagen. Now, Ludwig can tell you that you can get from Rome to Hamburg very comfortably for 150 thalers, or vice versa, and he, travelling with Russian princes and English gentlemen, certainly did not do it cheaply. So if, to please us, you will but extend your journey so far beyond your first destination, I can place 300 thalers, Prussian currency, at your service for that purpose. We are so situated here that a very perceptible surplus remains after paying all expenses, and there could be none which would afford us greater pleasure than seeing you here for a few months. So the cost need not be a serious difficulty.

With regard to the time of year, I can only advise you to set out as late as possible, not before the beginning of August. Then, if you allow a week for the journey, and six weeks for the cure at Kissingen, you will have ended it by the last days of September, when it already begins to get cool. I should advise your going to Heidelberg; from thence you have the railway, and can travel quickly, pleasantly, and cheaply to Basle, and the Swiss frontier. Baden and Freiburg are good places to stop at. At the end of September you have a better chance of a clear atmosphere among the Swiss mountains than even in the middle of the summer. According to your improvement in strength after the course of baths, you might make a walking tour through the Bernese Oberland, and across by Lago Maggiore to Milan, or go by coach to Genoa, by Berne and Geneva. At Genoa go to the Hotel d'Italie, kept by Germans, who will make a bargain for you with a vetturino to carry you to Pisa in a Calescino, or open carriage. The vetturino takes entire charge of you; he provides quarters for the night, breakfast, dinner, and supper, so that you need not speak a word. I advise you to travel by this route, although you could come by steamer, because the drive along the Riviera di Levante is the most beautiful thing you will see in Italy. From Pisa by train to Leghorn, packet to Civita Vecchia, and diligence to Rome. All further details I reserve till a future communication. As soon as you have got down the southern slope of the Alps you will suffer from the heat, even in the beginning of October. But here October is the most delightful month. The first rainfall cools the air, malaria disappears, and fresh verdure decks the Campagna. You may reckon on uninterruptedly fine weather in October and November. If you return in December, *via* Ancona and Venice, you will plunge suddenly from Trieste into the German winter, but then you have a direct and almost unbroken railway journey to Copenhagen.

Five years ago I made the journey from Berlin to Naples, spent four weeks at Baden, and was four months on the road. The cost of that journey was 100 louis d'or (£80), which gives you an approximate idea of things. If you could to some extent break up your household in Copenhagen, and leave your wife and children for so long with her parents, the whole expedition would cost you little, and do you, it is to be hoped, great good. For a man who has had a classical education and is thoroughly acquainted with roman institutions, Rome is still one of the most interesting places in the world; and our temporary residence here gives you the opportunity of enjoying in comfort all that is worth seeing. So take my proposal into consideration, and make us happy by deciding to accept it as soon as possible.

April 4th.—This letter has been kept back longer than it should have been, so it will not reach you for your birthday on the eighth. I add, nevertheless, the heartiest good wishes from both Marie and myself, and wish you for a birthday present a snug appointment before long in Holstein, far from Dano-Germanic broils, a fine official residence with a garden, and a handsome salary.

To-morrow we enter on the Settimana Santa (Holy-week), when there is some fresh ceremonial every day, beginning to-morrow, Palm Sunday, at St. Peter's. On Maunday Thursday the Pope bestows a universal blessing, *urbi et orbi,* from the Loggia; on Sunday the dome of St. Peter's is illuminated, and on Monday there are fire-works from Sant' Angelo. Then the foreigners disperse, Rome is Roman once more, prices go down, and we shall see if we can get a suitable residence, for hitherto we have been living in three rooms which cost ninety thalers a month—on the Corso, it is true, where all the turmoil of the Carnival goes on under our windows. I am at an end of my paper. My best remembrances to Augusta. Yours,

HELMUTH.

COBLENZ, October 30th, 1847.

DEAR ADOLF:

I found your letter of the 4th of this month on my return from a short tour on duty through the Eifel and to Trier. I value a letter from you all the more because I know that you have to take the time for private correspondence from your hours of recreation in the family circle. This letter, also, contains none but good and pleasant news of you and yours. So far, indeed, our paths in life have led us apart, for of all your family I only know your dear wife, since your beautiful eldest child was snatched from you and from us all. If I had remained at Berlin, one of my first excursions would certainly have been to Copenhagen. Even as it is, I do not give up all hope of taking Marie there some day.

I count positively on your visit to us next year, and only beg you to take long enough leave, so that your stay here may not be too strictly limited. You must in any case make an excursion from hence to the Moselle, which, in my opinion, is superior even to the Rhine in beauty. And it will interest you, I am sure, to trace the steps of the greatest nation in history, at Trier. No such important and well-preserved monuments of the Roman period exist anywhere out of Italy as there. We might perhaps make a trip together to Paris or into Switzerland, which Marie has never yet seen. A pair of good horses and a comfortable carriage will take you about the pretty environs of Coblenz, and you shall never hear the little sea-washed country mentioned. You will find our house very comfortable, and arranged for visitors. We are not indeed so happy as to have any children; they are a great blessing, though so often linked with sorrow. I do not know that I used to wish for any other gift of Fortune.

My position in the service is a pleasant one, and promises further advancement. In consequence of my early connection with Prince Henry of Prussia, I have, till my pay is raised to the same amount, a private allowance of 800 thalers; so that I already draw the pay of a colonel in command of a regiment, until I am made Chief of the General Staff of an Army Corps, which must come in the course of a few years, but will involve a change of station. I do not want to rise any higher, and shall then retire. At least that is my intention, unless the proverb comes true for both of us, that the jug that goes often to the well breaks at last. My little wife is my greatest joy. In five years I have rarely seen her sad, and never cross. She has no vagaries, and allows of none in other people. But no one should do her a real wrong, for with the best will in the world she could not forgive it; with all her light-heartedness she has a decided, strong and deep nature, which she would assert under all adverse circumstances. God preserve her from such. But I know what I possess in her. Yours,

HELMUTH.

COBLENZ, January 13th, 1848.

DEAR ADOLF:

* * * As regards the troubles in Holstein, we regard them here from a more German point of view, no doubt. Considering the ultra anti-German policy to which Denmark has adhered for the last fifty years, and the endless obstructions by which it has hampered German efforts towards development, whether as to the Sound dues or the construction of railways, we here can only desire a closer union of the Duchies with the common Fatherland. Nor can there be a more fortunate position than that of a small German nation, with which Prussia and Austria share all its political and military burdens, as you yourself must have observed in Lauenburg. The Sovereign Duchy of Holstein might perfectly subsist without Denmark, but not the kingdom without the Duchy. But for this very reason it seems indispensably necessary to come to an understanding, and this, amid such opposing passions, can hardly be arrived at. All these political dinners, addresses, meetings, and ovations lead to no useful end. But, as it seems to me, what Mephisto

8

says: "It is a law of spirits, that where they get in they must get out again," has its application in this matter of the hereditary rights. It was not the Germans who abrogated the Salic law. Positive rights are on their side; they are fighting for their hereditary dynasty, for legitimate succession, for all which princes so gladly listen to. If the personal union must be maintained, no alternative remains but to retrace the false step taken by one party, and annul the *lex regia*. Whether it is the Prince of Hesse or the Prince of Augustenburg who occupies the Danish throne, is a secondary consideration when the existence of the Danish monarchy is at stake. So I cannot give up my conviction that a closer alliance with Germany is Denmark's best policy.

It is no doubt most unpleasant to stand between the Government and the people under such friction, and greatly to be wished that the present king may reign long enough to calm down excited spirits so far as to effect a union. If his successor should act with less prudence but more decision, matters might be still worse. How glad I should be to exchange views with you on all these things by word of mouth! Yours,

HELMUTH.

BERLIN, July 9th, 1848.

DEAR ADOLF:

The rumor of peace with Denmark is gaining ground, and the necessity for some conclusion is self-evident. What would happen to Holstein if war, whether it came from the East or West, called on Prussia to fight for her own existence and that of Germany? Would she then be in a position to spare a corps of 15,000 of her best troops for what would then be a subordinate end? But alas! I fear that the conditions of this peace will hardly answer to the magnitude of the sacrifice. United Germany has in this matter again left us more or less in the lurch. Prussian commerce and the Military budget have to bear the cost. What would the shriekers in Frankfort say if the union with Schleswig, the abolishment of the Sound dues, and in short all their fairest dreams were not fulfilled? The internal difficulties, the general rebellion of subordinates against orders, of those who own nothing against those who own something, will come to the surface in Holstein as soon as the new organization begins. You, on the spot, will soon be able to see whether you can find an opening suited to your principles, in which you may effect the re-establishment of a legal position. Work in the service of the State will not be very satisfactory, and I can quite understand your repugnance to re-entering it. I, too, should prefer the simplest private life. If we do not have war first, which would change the whole situation, and if we are required to swear a fresh oath to a new constitution, I too shall retire. I could not, indeed, in that case claim a pension after my thirty years' service.—My cherished idea is that by degrees we should gather together on an estate somewhere or other, where each of us should contribute in capital or working power whatever he could bring. I would rather that this possession should be on the beloved soil of Germany. But if matters should become still worse in the home-country, so far as I am concerned I have no objection to the other hemisphere. Still, I cannot conceal from myself the fact that to realize capital at this juncture would entail a loss of perhaps fifty per cent.; and that the ladies, who are always so conservative, would find it hard to make themselves at home among the conditions of a new world. Their disposition binds them still more strongly than us to their native soil, and to tear them from it is a great responsibility. At any rate, however, it seems to me a fortunate thing if your present position enables you now to acquire some knowledge of farm management. The reaction of our unhappy disorders on the hitherto high prices of land cannot be long delayed, and perhaps, in a not very remote future, the moment may come when an estate may be purchased without fear of subsequent loss. Great reforms are to be effected here in official circles. The legislative and Government offices are to be reduced in numbers. The *Landräthe* (country councils) and *Oberpräsidien* are to be abolished; several provinces will be united under the management of Civil-governors, as in Belgium. Prussia has hitherto had an intelligent and honest body of officials, though costly, perhaps, and slow to move. May the new experiment turn out better than the *Gouvernement à bon marché* of our neighbors. The retrospective action of the diminished pensions is a great hardship, since the past state of finances did not require such a measure. They have not yet ventured to give the military profession a shake, because foreign affairs look too threatening; but it will come. Exactly what is meant by "arming the people" I do not understand; I thought we had done so in the fullest sense, in our Landwehr. As I have said, without war the military profession will in the future be but a sorry one. And as I cannot but discern that I am incapable of any greater efficiency in the future than I have hitherto shown, the idea of getting out of it all grows and ripens in me.

I think I wrote to you that I have no intention of settling in Berlin; I hope in a short time to leave this

unsatisfactory place. Perhaps there may be a vacancy
at Magdeburg before long.

Thank God that you are all well at home. I accept
with sincere pleasure the office of godfather to little
Helmuth. God grant that I may be a help to him on
the road over which hangs a darker cloud than ever,
for not even the immediate future can be guessed at
in these days. Your faithful brother

HELMUTH.

BERLIN, August 3rd, 1848.

DEAR ADOLF:

I read your letter of the 30th ult. with the greatest
interest. I think you have done as rightly in joining
in the struggle over the social question as in keeping
out of the political struggle. But will the Duchies be
allowed the liberty of giving themselves, and elaborat-
ing their own constitution? If the Provisional Government should be broken up, and the Holstein troops
disbanded, the constitution would have to be promul-
gated from Copenhagen. Such a peace would be but
a wretched one, but, in the present state of Germany,
how can anything better be aimed at? Never were we
further from a union than now. They will not see
Prussia at their head, and without Prussia nothing can
be accomplished. There is to be a demonstration in
favor of Prussia to-day. I hope that nothing much
may come of it, for all these demonstrations prove
nothing, or very little. Only a small number of persons attend them, and always the same. But popular
feeling is much excited; antagonisms are strongly
pronounced, and the street tumults, which were half
lulled, have broken out again. It is a pity that so
much mud sticks to the tricolor flag, and that it should
be offered by the hands of demagogues. I can give

you no idea of our present situation; we are in the midst of a crisis. But I think that the Frankfort people have given a severe check to the unity by means of union, which is here sincerely hoped for. At any rate, they have done harm to the Schleswig-Holstein business, for Prussia is carrying on the contest there solely in the interest of Germany, and entirely against her own.

Your own position in the Constitutional Assembly will be neither very pleasant nor very lucrative; but I believe that, besides the negative service of taking the place of a revolutionary, you may do very positive good service. A country in the hands of a population who are almost all land-owners, and for the most part well-to-do, must always be a soil on which something can be built up. From some correspondence in the papers, from Kiel, I see, indeed, that our Friends of the people have a branch there.

We read in the papers to-day that Austria is to furnish a contingent to carry on the Danish war. By the time it can come up, the Belt will be frozen over. Germany would rather that, in the event of a war with Russia, Austria should place the 94,000 men in the field, as she is pledged to do as our ally, and of which, in all probability, she would not be able to send out a single man.

Adieu, dear Adolf. Heartily yours, HELMUTH.

The enclosed letter from Colonel Griesheim is somewhat violent, but shows the feeling of the army.

MAGDEBURG, September 9th, 1848.

DEAR ADOLF:

We have not heard from you for a long time, and I address this letter on the chance of it finding you at

Kiel. I do not know whether you have a seat in the Constitutional Assembly, but I see in the paper that you are called as Vice-president of the Provisional Government.

It may be that this Government under Count Moltke is totally impossible in the present excitement. But it fills me with anxiety to think of you in what seems to be such a thoroughly revolutionary, constitution-mongering assembly. I only hope you are not deceiving yourselves in Holstein; I, of course, cannot know what the views of our Government may be. But it will most certainly—I mean the King will—adhere to the armistice as agreed on, whatever they may decide in Frankfort. We have reached the extreme verge of endurance. Both the Ministries, in Frankfort and Berlin, have resigned; but I doubt whether the King will accept the resignation in Berlin. A new Ministry could only be formed from the extreme left; it would only prolong this wretched state of affairs for a few weeks. The time is critical; a breach is almost un-avoidable—a breach with the revolution in Prussia, and with Germany so far as Frankfort is its representa-tive. I believe that the King will dissolve the Cham-bers, and that at Berlin we shall begin again just where we unfortunately left off on the 19th of March. The people must surely be convinced by this time that there is no salvation to be looked for from the party in the *Singakademie*. Strong measures are being taken. The discontent in the army is evidently fanned by the Republicans. They think they will win; very good; we think that we shall. But that it should be supposed in Holstein, that general war will be made for the sake of its petty interests, when matters are so serious all over Europe, is really too much! And what is there that is so atrocious in the armistice? If the laws of the Provisional Government are annulled, so are those of the Danish Government, and, consequently, the annexation of Schleswig too. However, be that as it may, the Prussian army will undoubtedly go back there. You will have no lack of volunteers, and you will see then what you can make of them. *Le remède est pire que le mal!* It will be difficult to make the voice of reason heard above the shrieks of passion, and I should be glad if you were out of it all.

The poor Fatherland! The better sort of the nation are silent, the scum come to the top and govern. They are eager for a reaction which no one wants or wishes for. The immediate future will show whether we can remain in this disgraceful predicament.

For the last fortnight I have been holding a new appointment, and have a great deal to do. That I am glad of; Berlin was almost unendurable. Marie sends her love; she is well, thank God. I must conclude; and, indeed, I know not what more to write. Everything is uncertain, even the immediate future. After the 1st of next month we shall be in a very pretty house in the Domplatz, the best part of the city. When Holstein waxes too hot for you, come to us, wife, children and all; we have plenty of room. The feeling here is very good; they look with contempt on Berlin. It must all end in war; and it is some comfort to think that the first gun-shot will put an end to the part of all these praters. God forgive them for all they have brought on our poor, unfortunate country. Then Prussia will either go under, or come out at the head of Germany, her proper place.

It is interesting to consider the way in which, under the Republic of Paris, they are voting for the censorship of theatres, for a Ministry of Police, the suppression of newspapers and of proclamations on the walls, and for martial law; while under the Monarchy at Berlin, the most unbridled license in every particular is not thought enough.

But enough of these cursed politics. My dear Adolf, my only object is to warn you. A man may be carried away in the midst of such agitation as surrounds you. Schleswig-Holstein has no sympathizers left among the greater number of thinking men in Prussia. Yours,

HELMUTH.

MAGDEBURG, September 21st, 1848.

DEAR ADOLF:

Your letter of the 16th inst. has made it very clear to me how difficult are the conditions under which you are laboring at Kiel, to rescue, in the shipwreck of the times, what may still be saved of order and cohesion. I understand that after the support given by Prussia in the first instance, her apparent sacrifice of the country at last should hardly be approved of. But what events have taken place between the beginning and the end! It was impossible to foresee in March the consequences to which the barricade victories would lead. Affairs at home grew more threatening every day. The power and daring of the democrats increased with every change of Ministers; the newspapers were, and still are, almost exclusively in the service of that party. I need only refer to the Schweidnitz incident. The legal trial by the acting authorities, not the illegal authority of the delegates, has now proved that the military were fully justified. Who could have gathered this from the newspaper reports? And yet this incident formed the basis of

Stein's motion, and Schultze's amendment,* which caused the majority to pass a unanimous vote of censure on the Army, which stands alone spotless and pure, the last and only safeguard of order. The Republic was indeed full-grown; the Assembly had become a Convention. It ruled and governed, it gave the laws and carried them out. The King was practically deposed. The Berlin Bürgerwehr (town militia) endorsed the decision of the Chamber. So much for Berlin. On the day when you wrote the rebellion broke out in Frankfort; there Jordan, Jahn, Gagern, and others have long been on the side of reaction, even Blum and his followers are no longer equal to the times.—Could any rational being believe that Prussia would allow her troops to turn back, would send the Stettin ships within hail of the Copenhagen embargo, and declare war with Sweden and Russia, all because Professor Dahlmann had refused to accept the armistice? He could not even find the men who might have undertaken the measures for carrying out his schemes. This much was certain, the rejection of the armistice meant a breach between Prussia and Germany, the complete destruction of the only thing which could reconcile us to all the evils we have suffered for the past half year—the destruction of the unity of Germany. And for this very reason the left insisted on its rejection. It was contemptible enough, when the

---

* Stein's motion was as follows: "The Minister of War should express himself in an order to the Army, to the effect that the officers were to hold aloof from all reactionary movements, and not only to avoid every kind of conflict with the civil authorities, but to show by their readiness to approach and combine with the citizens that they sincerely desire to co-operate in earnest for the realization of a constitutional legislative body." Schultz's amendment added: "It should also be held a point of honor by those officers who cannot reconcile this to their political convictions, to retire from the army."

Assembly finally came to an opposite determination, and men like Waitz spoke for its rejection and voted for its maintenance—a wide gulf indeed between word and deed. The Poles arrived at Frankfort on Saturday; on Sunday the street-rioting began. It was stopped by the prompt and determined interference of the garrison from Mainz. But I have no doubt that nevertheless the Republic will be proclaimed within the next few days at Baden, and in Thuringia. It will be put down there too. But what a piece of good fortune that in this conjuncture our Army is not on the Schley, but on the Spree. We have now 40,000 men in and round Berlin; there lies the centre of gravity of the German question. Order in Berlin is order throughout the country. A strong Prussian Government, and then German unity can be achieved by Prussia. With all this I will only add that the action of our Government in Holstein may seem hard, unjust, even perfidious, but it was required by superior and higher interests.

Power now lies at Berlin, with a full right to use it. If they fail to do so now, I am ready to set out with you for Adelaide. The next few days must bring great issues.

At the same time I wish with all my heart that your constitution-making may bring peace and blessing to the country. The Danes will no doubt come to their senses; they will not defy Germany a second time when once Germany has settled her own internal affairs; but this will never again be done on the old lines. I could almost believe that men of your stamp and Reventlow's are the only men who could hold the balance between the pretensions of Denmark and Holstein. But if you still have no official employment before the winter, you know you will be welcome here, with your wife and children. We have a fine large house in the best part of the town, and Marie has already thought of everything to make you as comfortable as possible.

As regards my appointment here, I am Chief of the General Staff of the Fourth Army Corps (Province of Saxony). I have plenty to do, for democracy is moving here too. Our neighbors of Altenburg, Reuss-Schleiz-Greizer, Meiningen, and Schwarzburg take care of that. But we step in firmly with our splendid soldiery. The insurgent towns are kept in order by mobilized columns, whole troops of armed citizens and shooting-corps are disarmed, the ringleaders captured, and the rebels plainly taught that the law still has the upper hand. Here in Magdeburg the citizens are well affected. Of course there is a mob, and in these times we may expect an outbreak anywhere. But these are mere trifles; Berlin, that is where the decision rests.

For nearly three months we have been living in the midst of cholera, first at Berlin and then here. Every one has suffered; it is another of the gifts of this year '48, which will long survive in our memory. But Marie is as well and cheerful as ever, thank God. It is really a wonder, with no house to attend to, for we are still living at an inn, alone almost all day, surrounded by scenes of gloom and threatening rumors, she is always equally gay and calm. When I come in, however tired and worried I may be, I find a happy face to greet me. God bless her for it!

Our chief diversion is riding—Marie rides the gray and I the black horse. The bay and the brown one go in harness. In a week we move into our pretty home in the Domplatz, facing due south. We rejoice to think of it. All the furniture is in already. Farewell, dear Adolf, I must close this hasty scrawl. To our next happy meeting ere long. A thousand kind remembrances to your dear wife. Heartily yours,

HELMUTH.

MAGDEBURG, November 17th, 1848.

DEAR ADOLF:

Affairs here have come to a point at which it would be interesting to commit one's thoughts to paper, just to see whether in a few days one might not pass for a prophet, or wonder at one's own blindness. If the outlook were really as bad as the newspapers say, all would now be lost. A cry of indignation—to use the favorite French expression—has gone up from town and country; there is no choice but reaction or anarchy. We are, it is certain, at a serious crisis. It has come to a refusal to pay the taxes. The next step will be red republic. And all this with the full sanction of the press, accompanied by addresses from all parts of the kingdom, and backed up by the bayonets of the armed citizens. In the midst of the storm we are calling out the Landwehr, which is, after all, neither more nor less than the people themselves. There is the whole question in a nutshell. The answer to it will be a crushing defeat for one party or the other.

These are times in which every one must act on his own responsibility. No one need look for instructions from his superiors, and we have ordered out every one of the twelve Landwehr battalions of the province. Only yesterday some of the towns took up arms to prevent the troops marching out, and the railways have refused to convey them. The telegraphs are damaged, and the citizens are offering protection to the recruits if they will refuse to obey the call to arms.

The Republic has been proclaimed in Thuringia, and Dr. Stockmann gives the armed peasants regular pay. The Landwehr arsenals are threatened, some of them already in the hands of the townspeople, and the arms distributed. Good faith, discipline, and order seem now only to be found in the Army and amongst the officials, on whom, of course, the press pours out the vials of its wrath. Through all this tumult the simple words, "To Arms!" will presently sound, and thousands will have to leave house and home to fight against the very principles in favor of which they have just been petitioning, making speeches or applauding them, or perhaps even have taken up arms. It really does seem rather extraordinary.

For all this, I am more hopeful than I have been for the last six months. The state of things has been so insufferable, that one longs for it to be decided—as it must be now, one way or another. I hope to Heaven that reason and right may prevail. The Brandenburg Ministry may be an unpolitical measure, but its resolute attitude makes up for everything. This is the first time since March 18th that we have seen any show of firm determination, and it stirs the hearts of millions. And this time they really are determined— quite determined to face all consequences. There is no doubt but that Berlin will share the fate of Vienna, if there is any rebellion. And this rebellion may be called forth at any moment by the most trivial squabble. Every precaution has been taken, and here in Magdeburg, where enormous stores are collected, and the garrison reduced to two-fifths of its standing in times of peace, we are prepared for the worst. Our splendid Saxons are stationed all the way between Worms and Berlin. We have to help all our neighbors, so that very little is left over for ourselves. But that little we have duly set in motion. Wherever our troops appear, order is at once restored; the well-intentioned come to the fore and the most noisy have vanished. The three bullets in the Prater did not strike Robert Blum alone, but many other people in Germany. However, we are few against many, and no man can answer for the issue. The next few days will be decisive for us. God grant I may soon have good news for you.

The storm at our own doors has necessarily driven the Schleswig-Holstein business into the background. Our papers give us little or no news from that quarter. I should be all the better pleased to hear from you what is going on. I met an officer this evening who had been quartered with Fritz at Apenrade, and who did full justice to him, in spite of his Danish tendencies. That pleased me very much.

I suppose you have sent for your wife and children to Schleswig. I had hoped to go to Itzehoe at Christmas for a week or a fortnight, and we could have fore-gathered there from all quarters, but now nobody can see beyond the next week. Otherwise all is well with us. We have got rid of one enemy, the cholera. It was a wretchedly bad time for me, for I was constantly ill till it went over. It would be terrible to be ill just now. Marie is bright and well, and would storm a barricade at a moment's notice if it were necessary. When you give up your regency, we shall invite you down here. And now, dear Adolf, good-bye. I must make the most of my time, especially to get some sleep, as I am called up twice every night. However, we get accustomed to everything—except to our conquests.

Yours affectionately,

HELMUTH.

MAGDEBURG, July 13th, 1849.

DEAR ADOLF:

The affair at Fridericia is a most painful occurrence, apart from the misery which it must have caused to the sorely stricken families. From a military point of view, it has done little or nothing to alter the situation. The Danes themselves can scarcely think that this victory will enable them to hold the open field outside their fortifications, even for a week. They would most assuredly be utterly beaten by double their numbers of an enemy whose irritation will brook no further delays. If the Schleswig-Holstein troops have suffered severely, the loss on the Danish side has been as great, and they have no doubt retreated to-day into the fortress and on Fühnen.

It is difficult to be quite fair to the vanquished. From my own absolutely impartial point of view, I think one can only admit that the management of the allied troops in Jutland was certainly deplorably bad, and that General Rye might have been defeated weeks ago. How far this delay may have been caused by high political considerations, is not for me to decide; but assuredly no one cursed this policy more heartily than Prittwitz, Hirschfeld, and their troops. That these generals should have purposely withheld their assistance from Bonin, no one can seriously believe. Prittwitz was at four days' march from Fridericia, and was bitterly enough reproached for not being still further off, up in Jutland. Whether Bonin could have been warned sooner, before Rye's embarkation, I do not know. It was in all the papers, and could hardly have led him to adopt other precautions than those he had already taken—to surround the fortress closely, and to keep a vigilant lookout.

The Danish sortie was, strategically speaking, a well-planned operation, and tactically a brilliant passage of arms. There were 14,000 men in the trenches, and 20,000 in the open field. The Holsteiners defended themselves gallantly, but the Danes were braver still in attacking them, and they won. That they did so in spite of a no great superiority in bayonets as attacking intrenchments, and of an artillery that far surpassed theirs in number and calibre, can only be attributed to the suddenness of the attack. But it is difficult to understand how so considerable a body of men could have landed unobserved in the bright moonlight of a short summer night.

But if, from the military point of view, this action of the enemy was a brilliant success, from every other it appears as an unpardonable act of revenge, a senseless cutting down of friend and foe, and a political mistake which is pretty sure to react upon those who committed it.

The unfortunate part of the whole thing is, that it has placed a dangerous weapon in the hands of the ill-disposed, both of those who maliciously accuse Prussia of treachery, and those who are simple enough to believe the accusation. If a truce is now concluded, it certainly will look as if the Cabinet Ministers had purposely sacrificed the Schleswig-Holstein troops, in order to make way for any conditions of peace. Our own troops will be indignant, democracy will gain fresh ground, the south German allies will, if not openly at least secretly, lend a hand to the extravagant schemes of the revolutionary party in Holstein, new volunteer corps will be formed, the credit of the Government immensely lowered, and the first trophy of the attempted union of Germany will be a humiliating downfall.

9

Much as I have wished for a peace with Denmark, I hope that it may not be brought about just yet. The sudden departure of the Danish Ambassador Extraordinary from Berlin, almost leads one to believe that in Copenhagen, too, the democrats are going to overstep all bounds, and that they are making fresh claims, on the strength of a victory that was not really decisive. Her friends in London and St. Petersburg will find that Denmark will refuse any reasonable peace, and public opinion will insist upon a complete occupation of Jutland and a determined attack upon Fridericia (for this has been but feebly carried on hitherto). I must cling to this hope, and wish with all my heart that Denmark may not accept the offer of peace.

My best love to you and yours. Augusta is of course very much excited. I only hope we may soon have better news of poor Krohn. The children are well and blooming. These bad times pass over them and leave no trace; may they soon see better ones. Affectionately yours,

HELMUTH.

MAGDEBURG, August 11th, 1849.

DEAR ADOLF:

We have been expecting you daily and hourly, but at this crisis in your own little Fatherland your time is no doubt fully occupied by serious business; at any rate, I trust you have not been hindered by illness. We leave this place to-morrow at 11.45, and I am writing by the 6 o'clock train this evening, that you may not come to-morrow to find us gone.

Things are quiet enough for the present to permit of my leaving my post for a few weeks. I have much need of rest. We have fixed upon Wangeroog for the baths, though I would rather have gone to Föhr.

However, I do not care to go into Holstein while this absurd outcry about Prussian treachery lasts. I should lose my temper if the public feeling were really such as I must suppose from individual cases, and that would spoil the cure. I should like to have your views upon the subject. It looks as if Holstein were submitting to the inevitable, but *de mauvaise grace,* which will not mend matters. I sincerely hope that you may soon settle down peaceably into your administration of Rantzau.

Our new Cabinet leads me to hope for better things. I cannot quite believe in a war with Austria. It would be like two rivals firing at one another in a powder magazine. Hungary will keep Austria amused for a little while yet, and in Italy peace can only be maintained by force of arms. The latest measure of the central authorities is certainly calculated to revive civil war in Germany, and the second act of the Baden drama might very easily be played in Würtemburg. It seems to me that by seizing on Hohenzollern, Prussia has burned her ships behind her. She must push on the German Cause. Pray Heaven we may only keep the Brandenburg Ministry!—let us have no more weak wise fools! Good-bye, dear Adolf. To our next more agreeable meeting somewhere or other. Affectionately yours,

HELMUTH.

MAGDEBURG, November 12th, 1849.

DEAR ADOLF:

We were heartily glad to find from your letter that you were at last in your country home, and hope that your health may soon be strengthened and improved by congenial occupation. The desperate entanglement of the country's affairs must naturally affect you in your new office, though more indirectly than in the former one, and less so than poor Ludwig, who must really be in a desperate plight.

Here order is gradually being restored. For the town corps to give up their arms is a great step towards a better state of things. I have no doubt that this will shortly be accomplished without any serious hindrance. After that, I may perhaps be able to get leave, though probably for only a very short time. It certainly is not particularly pleasant here for me, public feeling, whether justly or unjustly, being antagonistic. But any change in this respect is not to be thought of for some time to come.

What will come of the Schleswig affair God alone knows. That is the worst business of all, and all the more so that no amount of waiting will help matters; something definite must be done. On the one hand, it is highly improbable that Prussia, after her late bitter experience, will again take up the doubtful cause of the two Duchies at the risk of a European war; on the other, it would be impossible to stand by and see the struggle with Denmark begin afresh, a struggle the result of which would be very uncertain, to say the least of it, even if Prussian officers were allowed to join. Denmark seems bent upon this single combat.

It seems to me that the Government in the Duchies is playing a dangerous game. Prussia is manifestly the only ally they have. Neither Russia nor England will help them, least of all Austria, Bavaria, and the rest, who, though they are taking up their cause both in word and by writing, took care to withdraw their troops first. Democracy is about the worst staff for any one to lean upon, and even that does not seem strong enough in Holstein to affect the attitude of the

Government. However, I am quite willing to admit that the situation there is beyond my comprehension.

We have gone into our winter quarters. There is a beautiful carpet in the drawing-room, and in this splendid autumn weather the sun shines brightly in at the windows. There is no end to the writing I have to do. I should be very glad to read a book once more, but there is no time for anything serious. My Roman map is being engraved on copper by Brose, one of our first engravers, and the King has advanced 700 thalers for it. My General sends his kind regards. He has the goodness to go away now and then, whereby my labors are considerably abridged. My best love to Augusta and the dear children. Let us soon have news of you. Your affectionate

HELMUTH.

MAGDEBURG, January 26th, 1850.

DEAR ADOLF:

We are wondering what will be the result of the royal proposition. I believe that the Government would carry it through if there could be any certainty that it would be adhered to. But that is just what no one does believe, so I suppose that it will come to a *mezzo termine*. I do not believe in a Gerlach Ministry; they would have to make up their minds to treat the dear Berliners to some powder and shot. There may be a modification of the Manteuffel-Brandenburg Ministry, but that would certainly be a great loss, for the system could not well be altered, and they could find no better men to carry it out than those who have brought us safely so far. On the whole, our internal affairs are being put upon a firmer basis, for if the democrats are reduced to passive resistance, they must cease to exist. Action is their real element. If Austria and Prussia could come to a real understanding, the rest would be easy; but I fear that this union only involves the smaller states, and does not affect the really important question at issue between them.

Have you read the pamphlet on "A Review of the Development of Affairs in Germany during the year 1849"? (By Canitz, but the author is not mentioned.) If not, let me recommend it to your notice. Yours affectionately,

HELMUTH.

MAGDEBURG, February 17th, 1850.

Marie sends her best love, and we both hope to have good news of your wife. The abominable weather of the last fortnight has no doubt kept you in-doors. But it must improve soon, and then the country will be charming. These seasonable storms may rage through the high beeches, but I hope they will not damage your roof.

The prospect is certainly very dark. Even though there are fewer actual preparations for war than at this season for the last two years, the whole aspect of affairs is very serious. It is therefore of the first importance, that by the establishment at last of the constitution on a firm basis, the country has undoubtedly gained confidence; more especially as no great results are to be expected from Erfurt. Austria counts for so little as a German power, that we may expect her, in the event of a real union of the States, to try to arrest her non-German interests, even if she had to do so at the point of the sword. There is nothing perhaps to prevent this but the undeniable emptiness of her coffers, and the threatening aspect of affairs in two-thirds of the Austrian dominions, in Italy, Hungary, Bohemia, and Galicia.

Prussia must own that she has not a single friend in all Europe, and must depend entirely on herself. We perhaps still have Louis Napoleon on our side, a man with merely a party at best, and not a nation at his back. In France a bloody conflict seems inevitable, and the issue doubtful. So one does not know whether to count France as friend or foe. Prussia is detested by the democrats of all nations because she is the stronghold of order, while in the eyes of the St. Petersburg and Vienna Cabinets she is revolutionary. She is unpopular in all the family of States, who look on her as self-made and a parvenu, and the small principalities despise her for having fallen from the ranks of the old nobility. So she has no allies, no power of expansion within or without, and has no one to depend on but herself.

Whatever happens, I do not think that that worst of all enemies, democracy, has much chance of success with us. For this time we should stop short at nothing. On the other hand, it is certainly very unfortunate that the struggle in Schleswig seems on the point of breaking out again, and that a not inconsiderable portion of our forces may be involved once more in a fight which, in the absence of a fleet, can, in no conceivable manner, be brought to a satisfactory conclusion. The news that comes in of military treaties with Anhalt, Brunswick, and Mecklenburg in succession, is very encouraging. Were there by the grace of God no King upheld by England, North Germany would soon be united. I shall subscribe at once to the "D. Reform."* My best love to your wife and children. Your brother,

HELMUTH.

* Deutsche Reform.

MAGDEBURG, March 21st, 1850.

DEAR ADOLF:

Our travelling plans may easily be upset by the events that lie hidden in the not very rosy lap of the coming year. It is, however, an immense improvement that we should only have to think of a foreign war. However domineering the tone of the Vienna Cabinet may be, Austria can hardly be in a position to take up arms against the work of German Union. The army in Bohemia is in the most miserable condition, Italy and Bohemia have to be kept in order by a considerable force, and the finances of the Empire give rise to the gravest anxiety. The situation in Russia, who does us all the harm she can in Copenhagen, is yet more serious. Still, if anything could prompt the German races to unite, it would be an attack on the part of Russia. But the real Pandora box of the whole affair is *la belle France* with her recent elections. France has the infinite misfortune to possess three dynasties. Louis Napoleon is apparently sincere in joining the majority against Socialism, but it is only the pressing danger from that quarter which can hold the majority together. As soon as there is any question of a definite and lasting plan of government, the Legitimists and Orleanists will separate themselves from the Bonapartists. An attack from that quarter may occur from one day to another, and will, I am sorry to say, meet with sympathy in South Germany. Bavaria has armed herself, though no one quite sees what for. One thing only is certain, and that is, that her finances are in the worst possible condition. But all the reports in the newspapers about a gathering of the Prussian forces at Erfurt are totally unfounded. Only thirty gendarmes and a few special constables have been sent out, and there is no intention whatever of assembling the troops. Even the first Landwehr regiment, which was stationed in Hamburg under General Döring's orders, has been sent back to the Mecklenburg frontier; from which it may be concluded that our Government has given up all further idea of an armed interference in Danish affairs. It really seems as though Holstein were to be occupied. If the Swedes withdraw now, what will happen in the Schleswig vacuum? Should the Danes advance, it will be impossible to restrain the Holsteiners, and it is very doubtful which is the stronger of the two. The Prussian officers will then be recalled, but at the prospect of a campaign many of them would certainly quit the service in order to stay where they are. Bonin has unquestionably the most to lose, but then he has also the greatest interest in the matter. If his campaign is successful, they will forgive him everything. With Rendsburg and the impassable Eider at his back, he can safely begin operations, and at any rate hold the country round, as far as Flensburg.

Further on than that, the position of Alsen on his flank would make it dangerous for him, but so far he can move freely. The landing of the Danes further to the south might result in the towns on the coast being laid waste, but it would at the same time greatly endanger the troops, who could necessarily only be landed in small numbers. If no split occurs in the ranks of the Holsteiners, they may try to settle the question in a battle. Not that it would probably settle the question. The line of the Eider affords protection to the Holsteiners, for should the enemy cross it, the German armies would be justified in taking serious steps. The Danes will find their protection in Alsen, or in Jutland. It would be unwise of an inferior force to follow them there. Still, it would be of enormous moral value to the Duchies, if they could show that they had the strength as well as the will to protect themselves against the Danes. There is something odious in saying to Holstein: " See how you can fight it out for yourself." But neither Holstein nor Denmark will accept conciliation on the terms which have been offered them. And even the assistance of Prussian troops would not bring matters to a satisfactory conclusion, so long as we have no navy. Besides which, Prussia is just at a most critical point in her own development, and has to hold herself in readiness for a European war at any moment.

Parliament was opened in Erfurt to-day. They will honestly do their best to bring about the union. Should it succeed, the magnetic influence of a united and powerful German State must in a few years, and almost without an effort, bring about what two campaigns failed to effect; the German population of Schleswig will join on rational grounds, against which political formulas are impotent to raise a barrier.

But this union will be opposed not only by the democrats, but by the oligarchy of the small principalities. If the representatives of the people really expressed the popular feeling, both these obstacles would fall to the ground. If there is one point in which Germany was sincere during the struggle of the last few years, it is in her desire for unity; but this desire can make no way against particularism on the one hand and antagonism to social order on the other. I trust that Prussia will keep her word, and go through with the attempt till there is obviously no possibility of success, and then be content to be nothing more than Prussia. There can hardly be any material advantage for Prussia to be got out of the proposed union. As for the small states, the result of the next political convulsion will be either the overthrow of the monarchical principle altogether, or their complete absorption. If Prussia is then still in existence, she will profit by it. Affectionately yours,

HELMUTH.

MAGDEBURG, May 29th, 1850.

DEAR ADOLF:

Under the present circumstances, I do not see much hope for Schleswig-Holstein. It is unfortunate that they could not have come to some conclusion sooner. General von Willisen is unquestionably a most intellectual and capable man, but he is a theorist. He is a better man for you than Bonin, because the Danes always knew that Bonin took his tone from Berlin. Willisen is burning to begin. I do not think that the delegates from Holstein will achieve anything in Copenhagen now, and it will probably come to a conflict in Schleswig. If Willisen keeps his troops together and does not advance beyond Flensburg, so as to avoid having Alsen on his flank, nor permit his forces to be broken up for the protection of the coast line and the towns, the Danes may destroy a few places and carry off some prisoners; but the issue of a regular engagement would then be very doubtful, to say the least of it. Then, too, the matter would assume a totally different aspect if the Duchies actually proved that they could defend themselves. I am only afraid there will be learned manœuvres, and that their attention will be diverted from the chief object in view by the cries of the sufferers. Yours,

HELMUTH.

MAGDEBURG, July 18th, 1850.

DEAR ADOLF:

* * * That is truly a strange peace* which has for its immediate result a fresh outbreak of war. We are unfortunately obliged to confess that it discloses the fact of our having attempted something which we could not carry out. It is true that it only became impossible because one half of our common Fatherland took no part in it, while the other was notoriously against it; true, too, that Prussia saved Holstein in one campaign, screened her in a second, and provided an army for the third. But our present position is nevertheless most distressing, after putting ourselves forward as the champion of Germany. With what bitter feelings our troops will have to withdraw! With party spirit running so high, it will be impossible to prevent a collision between the opposing van-guards, and that will give the signal for a general struggle. The next few days must determine matters. I trust that Willisen will not allow himself to be persuaded to subdivide his troops, nor advance beyond Flensburg, but place himself there on the defensive and collect all his forces to await the attack. The issue then may be very uncertain. Should the Holsteiners be victorious, it would not bring matters to any conclusion, but they would gain an important moral advantage, which would have its weight even with the great foreign Powers. If unhappy Germany can manage to combine to act honestly in concert, Prussia will not be behind-hand. Our troops are stationed close to the Lauenburg frontier, and near the railway. The projected London protocol will hurry on the union, if it is at all possible. It is a painful time.

July 26th.—If it is true that the Danes have spread

* The peace of Berlin, between Prussia and Denmark, July 2nd, 1850.

themselves out from Fehmarn to Tönningen, and this not merely with outposts, while Willisen is stationed in Schleswig, the moment must have come for offensive operations.   If the Danes avoid the attack, he can follow them up as far as Bau, and at least produce a good moral impression.   But perhaps he will confine himself to acting on the defensive, since the Danes would be forced to attack him in order to bring matters to a conclusion.   For their flank position at Alsen is of no use to them, so long as the Holsteiners do not advance beyond Bau.   Willisen's right flank is well protected; and to attack his left, or compel him to move, the Danes must break up their connection.   Things have gone on all right so far, and the maintenance of the armies in their present positions must cost the Danes at least as great sacrifices as the Holsteiners.   It is a pity that the railway from Rendsburg has not been extended to Flensburg.—Everything that the Government there has done or decreed lately is, to me, quite satisfactory.

In Germany, matters look very badly.   That we should be going through a reaction is, to a certain point, not to be regretted.   I cannot resist sending you the accompanying paper, which gives an admirable picture of the two principal aims of Prussia in her German policy.   The effort to gain supremacy, and the exclusion of Austria from Germany if she were strong; compromise and division if she were weak.   In which position we now find ourselves, I leave you to judge. Yours,

HELMUTH.

MAGDEBURG, August 6th, 1850.

DEAR ADOLF:
Since my last letter the first throw has been cast, and to the advantage of Holstein.   That Germany

should look on and take no part is painful and humiliating. I can understand this attitude if some great
end in the world's history were to be gained by it.
But when this end is not attained, not, as it would
seem, even aimed at, the result must be hatred of
Prussia, and contempt for those States which only
raised miserable sums of money by way of help when
soldiers only could be of any use. The Danes have
now gone so far that they must appeal to the German
Confederation to interfere. But where are they to
look for it, at Frankfort, Vienna, or Berlin? The
London protocol may yet perhaps shake us awake in
Germany, but old Barbarossa sleeps soundly in the
Kyffhäuser.

It is so very much easier to criticise than to act,
that one should be shy of expressing an opinion. So
far as can be judged from the meagre reports we have
received, the battle of Idstedt seems to have been lost
for want of a few battalions in the reserve of the centre.
The position was very widely extended; the forces
massed behind the right wing, which was the strongest
part of the position. The intention was to act there
on the offensive; but thus nothing was left for defence
against the attack which the enemy, as might have
been foreseen, directed on the weak left wing. But
how far the Holstein army was from being really beaten
is proved, not only by the great loss among the Danes,
but yet more by their not having taken a step in pursuit.

It does not seem to me likely that General Willisen
will now entrench himself in Rendsburg with his
troops. If he remains there, the Danes also will remain
undivided, and he can neither support Friedrichsort
or protect Kiel. I fancied he might advance on Flem-
hude and Kleine Nordsee, holding the passages over

the Eider and the canal. The Danes must then leave forces in Schleswig, Eckernförde, etc., to cover Rendsburg, and so weaken themselves considerably. It would be very rash to besiege Friedrichsort or march on Kiel so long as an unbeaten army is within an easy march of Gottorp. There is nothing to be done but to attack the army itself, and in its present place it has a strong defensive position, a front to the east and west, according to whether the enemy crosses the Eider above or below it. The railway brings up supplies almost to the spot.

Now or never negotiations must be opened. If the Danes adhere to the insane view of regarding the Germans as insurgents, it must be their task to annihilate these insurgents, and every step they take into Holstein will make this more difficult.

My departure, with that of the black horse, was fixed for yesterday. But so many of my officers have been taken away, that I have first to reorganize my staff. I should also like to see first what is really being done, for it seems that some decision has been arrived at. The tension with Austria increases daily. They are paying us out for what we did *not* do to them in 1848. Still, I do not yet believe in war with Austria. Two great powers can always find a way to an arrangement, at the expense of the weak and presumptuous. The real conflict will, to be sure, be thus only postponed. Besides, Austria has hitherto had the best of this negative attitude. Difficulties will grow to gigantic proportions as soon as she is compelled to act, nay, as soon as she has to put forward a practical programme.

Out of all this confusion I am glad to transport myself into your peaceful home, which, please God, is not endangered. I rejoice that none of Augusta's relatives have suffered this time. I hope too that you will now soon have the horse. I am sending you a perfectly new saddle, an old *Kandare* and a good *Woilach*.

HELMUTH.

MAGDEBURG, November 4th, 1850.

DEAR ADOLF:

Since midday yesterday the peace of Europe no longer depends on the conferences of Ministers, but on the attitude of a patrol party of Hussars. The Prussians and Bavarians must have come into collision in the neighborhood of Saalmünster. A few carbine-shots could easily be fired into the German powder-barrel and blow all the subtleties of politics to the winds. There must be something very perverse about our diplomacy, that every step forward should lead us further into ruin. Soon there will scarcely be any choice but between humiliation and war under very difficult circumstances—a war in which we must keep a front to East, North, and South, and in which we shall not have an ally in the world. Happy is he who in this juncture has not to decide, but only to obey. Two days ago war seemed a certainty. To-day we are doubtful, and every hour which does not bring the order for mobilization makes war less likely. But how we are to get out of all the negotiations already set on foot with anything approaching to honor, I cannot see. The struggle which is dreaded and postponed by all parties must surely break out at the New Year. Griesheim is now Commandant of Coblenz; we shall soon hear something of him.

My General * remembers you with sincere regard, and is always glad to hear of you. There is a great

---

* Lieutenant-General von Hedemann, for a time in command of the Fourth Army Corps.

deal to arrange and prepare here; for, with all the separate dispatches, and forming a corps out of troops thrown together from different provinces, the difficult business of mobilizing an army becomes extremely complicated. I only hope they will not be ordered out till it is quite decided that we are to fight. Demonstrations cost Prussia millions of thalers, and lead to nothing. There is too much talking. Deeds are what are wanted. The Holstein business is still the worst of all. But enough of that. Matters are now so involved that a decision cannot be delayed much longer. Yours,

HELMUTH.

MAGDEBURG, February 25th, 1851.

DEAR ADOLF:

I cannot bear to write of politics; the unworthy part we are being made to play cannot last much longer. As yet, I have never really believed in war; but now I think we must have war within the year. A more disgraceful peace was never signed. And such an army as we had collected! For twenty-four weeks the Fourth Army Corps was mobilized, and brought out of all the garrisons. And such troops! If only Frederick the Great had had such men! Thirty millions (of thalers) are gone for a demonstration, and to accept any and every condition. But the worst Government cannot ruin this nation; Prussia will stand yet at the head of Germany. A union of the *Zollverband* (after the secession of the South Germans) with the *Steuer-verein,** is what I hope for. In Holstein, for the moment, all is lost, but the question must be re-opened. Still, it must be true that a more pitiable nation than the Germans does not exist on earth.

* The toll-union with the tax-union.

10

Mobilization and demobilization have given me much to do, but the result was satisfactory; all that was needed was the will to make use of it, if not, indeed, to make war against all Europe (for our diplomacy had brought us to that), at any rate to negotiate under arms. But we seem to have called out all the strength of the State merely to submit to humiliating conditions. Dissatisfaction is universal and very serious. If victory over Democracy bears such fruit, we had almost better conjure it into life again. But this will not be necessary. 'Yours,

HELMUTH.

MAGDEBURG, December 22nd, 1851.

DEAR ADOLF:

Marie sends you her love. She has some wonderful surprise in store for me for Christmas, and for weeks already she has been burning so to tell it that she has had the greatest difficulty in keeping it to herself. As news for Augusta, tell her that I have got for Marie a dark brown velvet bonnet with camellias, a very handsome, thick Lyons silk dress, *gros grain* with a damask pattern, and a *beige* morning-gown, dark brown, mixed silk and wool. Yours,

HELMUTH.

MAGDEBURG, January 1st, 1852.

DEAR ADOLF:

Marie has had the much talked-of fur waistcoat made for me, and I have given her a beaming lamp, which completely lights up our drawing-room, which is now a picture-gallery. A carpet, double windows, and portières make it a habitable room. I wish you could pay us a few days' visit here. Yours,

HELMUTH.

MAGDEBURG, January 23rd, 1853.

DEAR ADOLF:

The superficial reconciliation of Austria and Prussia might, perhaps, impose on the Copenhagen Government some consideration for the Duchies; though, indeed, it will set no bounds to its revenge on individuals, as its proceedings against poor Krohn show only too plainly. No real help is to be expected, unless from a rising of the German nation, and that would mean a general war, for which Louis Napoleon will probably provide within a few years. His empire assumes more and more of the character of a magnificent swindle. His marriage with this Spaniard completely excludes him from admission into the list of legitimately Royal Families; and the London Stock Exchange, by simply raising the rate of exchange, can overthrow his whole system of finance. The French must soon weary of this adventurer, who will find it harder to remain than to become Emperor. He can scarcely hold his place without some victories, and whether he is himself a general, and that on the pattern of his uncle, remains to be proved. But he must fight and win his own battles, or his General will be Emperor. Affectionately yours,

HELMUTH.

MAGDEBURG, March 4th, 1853.

DEAR ADOLF:

Things look more peaceful on the whole than they have done for long. The Eastern crisis is not, indeed, by any means settled, but it is staved off. What is most important in it is Napoleon's attitude. If war were what he aimed at, he here had a favorable chance of fighting in alliance with England. But he seems really to desire peace. The only question is how long he can preserve it in the face of the people and the army. The commercial treaty, just concluded between Austria and Prussia, is also of great political importance. As neither of these two great German powers has succeeded in seizing the sole supremacy in Germany, they have for a time come to an understanding. This has the great advantage, as regards foreign nations, that one half of Germany will no longer paralyze the other, as was the case during the Holstein business; and it may be hoped that the Confederation will now take somewhat more decisive steps against the pretensions of Denmark. The mischief done cannot, of course, be undone, and Holstein will scarcely yet be induced to join the *Steuerverein.* In this respect the Elbe will still divide that fair land from Germany. Nothing can bring it back, but a general rising of the German nation; but the ravens are still croaking round the Kyffhäuser, and old Barbarossa still sleeps. Yours,

HELMUTH.

MAGDEBURG, June 4th, 1853.

DEAR ADOLF:

It was with sincere sorrow that I received the news of your poor little Frederica's death, dear, sweet child. Augusta too, writes that she accompanied you to the railway, and now, after a short stay together in Ratzeburg, she is snatched from you and your poor stricken wife and us all. God comfort you and preserve the other children, if the dreadful sickness takes a malignant form! But God gives and takes away, and we must be comforted to know that nothing happens but according to his will, however deeply such a dispensation may grieve the parents.

How truly Marie and 'Gusto sympathize with you I need not say. They will both write to Augusta, but

I want to tell you at once how much this unexpected sad news has grieved us all. I can give you no comfort, nor can any one, but only your own religious feeling and trust in God, which will not be shaken but confirmed by misfortune. May God comfort you and help you through the first bitter days! Your affectionate and faithful brother,

HELMUTH.

MAGDEBURG, January 25th, 1854.

DEAR ADOLF:

Political affairs look critical. To me, the German powers seem to be playing a very poor part. Any fresh increase of Russian power is to them evidently a serious peril, and yet they are leaving to the Western powers the task of snatching the chestnuts out of the fire. This will be remembered against us, and will not improve the esteem in which Europe holds us. The Turks seem quite to understand that their religion and existence as a nation are at stake. They are fighting beyond all expectation, and even on the offensive. In pitched battle they would nevertheless be beaten, but it will be difficult to bring them to that. Operations on a grand scale cannot begin there before June. But the smaller Russia's chances are, without the control of the Black Sea, the more likely is it that the struggle will be transferred to a quite different field.

The Czar's decision must be known in the immediate future. To judge from his character, it can hardly be doubtful; though well-informed people believe in a peaceful issue. Affectionately yours,

HELMUTH.

MAGDEBURG, April 6th, 1854.

DEAR ADOLF:

It is greatly to be wished that no large payments should at present be necessary; the low exchange on

paper is of no consequence so long as one is not obliged
to part with it. This crisis cannot last long. The
obstinacy of the Czar has almost succeeded already in
bringing all Europe under one protector. If he goes
on thus the grand coercive measure of the reconstitu-
tion of Poland must be taken into consideration. I
do not believe in the new proposals for peace from St.
Petersburg; it strikes me as a last attempt to gain
over the German powers, more especially Prussia; but
things have gone too far. The assembling of a considerable army on our part appears to me a very likely
event, and the matter must end either by Russia being
thrown back on Asia, or—by a division of Turkey.
The recognition of the equality of Christians and
Mussulmans is practically the dissolution of the Mus-
sulman rule. Affectionately yours,

                                        HELMUTH.

                        MAGDEBURG, October 29th, 1854.

DEAR ADOLF:

What reflex effect the present political situation may
have on the Duchies, it is impossible as yet to foresee.
At any rate, the Western powers perceive what a political blunder it would be to establish a succession in
Denmark which would favor Russia only.

It is said that in return for the active support of the
Western powers afforded to Sweden and Germany, a
division of the kingdom is in prospect. We certainly
shall not engage in any such risks. As it seems to
me, the only conceivable possibility is at an end: a
firm alliance between Austria, Prussia, and the Confederation for the steady maintenance of neutrality
and mediation for peace, or, if this is impossible, for
taking up arms against either the East or the West.
Sebastopol will in all probability fall within a few days.

The town, the docks, arsenals, and fleet will be destroyed, the northern forts not even entered, and the forces withdrawn. Russia will have suffered a great moral defeat and a not less serious material beating. The fleet in the Black Sea cannot be restored under twenty years; the permanent threat to Constantinople is annulled; the Caucasus reinforced for resistance. The Western powers may be all the more content with this result, because, without Austria and Prussia they could hardly aim at any greater issue, and it will be a hard task to fight against Russia and Germany in union. Next spring must bring some decision. Yours,

HELMUTH.

MAGDEBURG, March 5th, 1855.

DEAR ADOLF:

The death of the Czar* is one of those events in which one fancies one sees the direct ruling of Providence. What its outcome may be lies as yet in total darkness; possibly a complete revolution in politics. His last coherent words were spoken to the Empress: "Dites à Fritz que je compte sur lui pour la Russie, et que je lui rappelle les dernières paroles de Papa!"

In response to this appeal, the King has telegraphed to Alexander II., and received a suitable answer.

The Empress's health remains good, and the task of keeping the peace between her two eldest sons will maintain it. The Czar belongs to the moderate German party; Nesselrode, Orlow, and the Grand-Duke Constantine to the extreme Russian war-party. But it is a question whether even the deceased Czar, a man without his match in Europe, was not carried further

* Nicholas I., who died on March 2nd, 1855.

by that party than he wished, and whether the new
Czar will be able to stand against it. Louis Napoleon's
journey to the Crimea, which, improbable as it seemed,
is nevertheless a fact, points to a definite war policy
on the part of France. Matters look badly at Sebastopol. I do not believe in its being taken by storm.
All the courage in the world will not enable a man to
run up a wall. How the question might be settled in
the field is very doubtful, the Allies lacking cavalry;
and the results of a defeat incalculable. Affectionately
yours,

HELMUTH.

MAGDEBURG, July 4th, 1855.

DEAR ADOLF:

Slaughter is still going on in the Crimea, and no one
knows what is the object to be attained. The great
reductions in Austria have brought her practically to
the Prussian standpoint of neutrality. God grant the
German powers may honestly hold together! A force
of 500,000 men ready to fight, whether in the East or
West, are a weight which may, perhaps, save the scale
from turning on the side of a general European war,
of which the first act might be the restoration of
Poland and revolution in Hungary, Italy, and Germany.

I have just made a very interesting tour with the
Crown Prince through the Prussian provinces. The
gigantic work of bridging over the Weichsel [the
Vistula] is really amazing. Five piers, as large as a
village church, support a lattice-work forty feet high,
which from a distance looks like a gasometer. The
open space between the piers, over which the roadway
hangs, is 360 feet. The Nogat is bridged over in the
same way. Wherever we went we found well-pre-

served traces of the powerful rule of the Teutonic Order of Knighthood. There is not in the world such another castle as that of Marienburg, the residence of the Grand Master. In almost every town the castles of the commanders and governors are still to be seen. The original Prussian population, on the other hand, is either extinct, or has migrated. The introduction of Christianity by the Polish Dukes went on from the martyrdom of Saint Adalbert, for two hundred years till the Teutonic Knights were called in. The Order fought for the possession of the country for fifty years, and the primitive race, with its language and monuments, has totally vanished, leaving only a few pots and weapons. The occupation of a tract of country was asserted by the erection of a stronghold, under whose protection German settlements grew up. Only two families—those of Kalnein and Perbandt—can prove their genuine Prussian origin; those of Dohna, Lehndorff, Dönhoff, Waldburg, and others are descended from the Knights. In its prime, the Order was a sovereign power, after Siegfried von Feuchtwangen transferred the residence of the Grand Masters from Venice to Marienburg, and the Kniprode, Jungingen, Aldenburg, and Reuss held sway with a mighty hand, though by dint of constant fighting. The towns which afterwards seceded from the Order bear the stamp of their Hanseatic origin. Dantzig is one of the most beautiful towns I know. It greatly reminds me of Lübeck, but surpasses it in size, beauty, and wealth. The neighborhood is charming; hills from three to five hundred feet high with dense woods, the noble river, the luxuriant lowland and the sea, combine to form a lovely country. I was also much interested in seeing the splendid stud-farm of Trakehnen, and the depots for army remounts at Jurgaitschen, Neuhof, etc. One rarely sees so many fine horses together; at Trakehnen there are above a thousand mares and foals.   Yours,

HELMUTH.

BERLIN, October 27th, 1855.

DEAR ADOLF:

* * * My present address is, Colonel von Moltke, first private Adjutant to his Royal Highness Prince Frederick William of Prussia, Berlin. My young prince is a most amiable and promising youth; and that is the most important point in my position. Otherwise I should not have sought court circles, and often find myself in a difficult position.] I shall see how long I can go on with it.   The journey to Scotland was most interesting.   This evening I have just returned from Letzlingen, where, in two days, we killed above three hundred head of deer and more than a hundred pigs.

A very serious business lies before me, namely, to purchase horses, and then a black, a gray, a red, and a mixed suit, for my travels, for stag-hunting, battue-shooting, and court company.   Affectionately yours,

HELMUTH.

BERLIN,* December 12th, 1855.

DEAR ADOLF:

We are living here in a part of the city of which you can only have seen the first beginnings.   It now contains the finest houses in the town.   Close to us runs the new Schiff-fahrtsgraben (formerly called Schaf-graben), through which the very considerable traffic now passes by water, which formerly went through the town and choked the bridges.   Wide quays planted

* Colonel von Moltke was then living at No. 9/10 Schönebergerstrasse.

with double rows of trees border the canal, forming a very pleasant ride leading by the Thiergarten to Charlottenburg. At the New Year this is a great convenience, and the horses are off the pavement at once.

The war question, I am sorry to say, still remains open this year again. The Russians will not evacuate the Peninsula, and there is no basis for peace negotiations. The Allies are fixed in the Tauric Chersonese, at very close quarters and, as it were, beseiged by Russia. Their position is very strong and hard to take, their supplies are secured by the possession of the harbors of Balaclava and Kamiesh, but they cannot get out. In my opinion there is no alternative left to them but to land again at Eupatoria at the New Year, to win another battle on the Alma, and then take advantage of the victory, whereas they took none of the first, to their very great loss. They can make no terms till they are masters of the Crimea.

It almost looks as if a serious attack was to be attempted in the Gulf of Finland. Of nine army corps the Russians have one in Asia and five in the Crimea. From Finland all the way to Poland they have but three corps, and besides these a considerable force of newly formed troops (Depot battalions and Druschines *). The fitting out of a large number of floating batteries with very long range guns might prove dangerous even to Cronstadt.

The King's last speech proclaimed the maintenance of Prussia's neutrality. Yours,

HELMUTH.

BERLIN, December 12th, 1857.

DEAR ADOLF:

The state of our finance and credit is sufficiently shown by the unshaken currency of German paper.

---

* Or Droojina, Russian Militia.

The Ministry advised the offer of a loan of four millions to the town of Hamburg.   There was a moment's hesitation on the ground of responsibility to the Chambers, and now—Austria is lending it, that Austria who is selling her railways and reducing her army to cover her annual deficit!   This is how we in Germany allow ourselves to be outflanked.

The Danes at this moment have fallen on evil times. The foreign powers seem to have no mind to stand up for them, and if, this time, Austria and Prussia act in concert, they will be wise to join in.   But it is not State prudence which rules at Copenhagen, but party passion.   Yours,

HELMUTH.

BERLIN, December 19th, 1857.

DEAR ADOLF:

With regard to Holstein, I am inclined to think that they must make up their minds to a real concession. Austria and Prussia, and consequently the Confederation, are this time agreed, and in the present aspect of politics, foreign support can scarcely be hoped for against decisive measures on the part of Germany. Even England seems to have got over her complete illusions with regard to this question.   At the same time, the party at the head of affairs in Copenhagen is powerful, popular, and regardless of consequences; so it is impossible to tell what may happen.

With regard to Austria's financial aid to Hamburg, matters are as follows: The circulation of all Government paper money is there compulsory; bullion is therefore lying perfectly idle in the bank, and it is quite legitimate business to draw out 600,000 florins interest per annum.   The credit of Austrian paper will, however, not be improved by it.   With us, on the contrary, the bank is obliged to keep an equivalent in silver of one third of all the paper in circulation. For the four millions ready cash, sent to Hamburg, twelve millions of paper should have been withdrawn, which seemed a risk in the crisis which affected Prussia as well. For Hamburg this business is still a doubtful success. It is an open question, whether the reckless operations are not too extensive to be met even by this loan. In 1854, Hamburg's import and export amounted to three hundred millions, I believe, and in 1856 to six hundred millions. The possible losses attending the issue of a ten million loan, as well as the interest, must be borne by the Senate, and eventually by the tax-payers. Thus the whole population is called upon to pay, to save their great merchants from possible bankruptcy. The great money crisis has, however, one good result in the general fall of prices. This is already felt, and I hope will continue. The value of money has risen, and as this is a fixed amount, which cannot be increased at will (the substitute not having proved satisfactory), more commodities can be purchased for the same money. The good harvest has also helped. Rye, which formerly cost fifty-six, nay, even sixty, can to-day be purchased at thirty-eight.

There is no doubt about a real and steady improvement in the King's health. The marriage of the young Prince Frederick William, whom I shall probably accompany on his visit to England, has been postponed till January 25th of next year, so the Prince of Prussia may possibly be able to be present at the ceremony. It is, however, quite impossible to foresee as yet whether the King will then be in a condition to resume government, with all its burdens, excitement, and anxiety. I have not seen his Majesty since the morning of the 7th of November, when he was taken ill. All business, so far, has been withheld from him, but he has seen many of the persons who are in his confidence, from whom he heard of the death of General Reyher, of Rauch the scupltor, and other events that have happened during his illness. He principally occupies himself with his favorite study, plans for buildings. Stüler, Humboldt, Groeben, Dohna, Kleist, and others have seen him. The last-named tells me that he has changed but little.

The task of the Prince of Prussia is one of infinite difficulty; having to carry on the Government on the lines hitherto laid down and with the instruments at hand, so that in many instances he is probably forced to renounce his own principles. The self-denial and tact displayed by him are generally admired, but all the freshness of a new Government has been wanting. A definite scheme is most desirable, but if the King should not fully recover under the Queen's most loving and skilful care, it is an extremely delicate business.

As to myself, I have been appointed "to undertake the business of the Chief of the General Staff of the Army," since the death of my honored predecessor. As this position is properly that of a General of Division, and I hold only the rank of Major-General, this appointment can only be temporary. I still wear the scarlet collar of the Infantry uniform; my salary too is 800 thalers less than that due to the position in the Staff. Otherwise, I have all the functions and attributes of the Chief; an official residence, general orders, and so forth. My force consists of 64 men, among them 50 of the so-called "Grand," but in reality very small, General Staff, and the Staffs of the nine army corps and eighteen divisions. The funds appropriated to the department amount to 26,000 thalers for general purposes, over which I have full control, out of which I have to pay for the trigonometrical and topographical survey of the country. In this I have at my command a corps of 30 officers, drawn from the army; I have also 10,000 thalers for travelling expenses. At the beginning I was obliged to work very hard in order to acquaint myself with the duties of my office; with the business and the *personnel*. This last is of great importance, not only for the good of the corps itself, but especially for that of the Army. Yours,

HELMUTH.

No date.   (July, 1859.)

DEAR ADOLF:

So peace is concluded between the two Catholic Emperors. The long and short of it is, Austria would rather give up Lombardy than see Prussia at the head of Germany.

Indeed, Germany came very near establishing the dangerous precedent of a real unification. Revolutionary despotism and reactionary conservatism have an equal interest in preventing this. The 2nd of December gave up its programme, and Francis Joseph a province, in order to establish an Italian Federation after the fashion of the German Confederation, and this at the moment when the conviction was stronger than ever, that the German Confederation was a hindrance in time of peace and a menace in war. The future will show whether the Italian Federation is anything but a way of leaving the question open. The Austrian Emperor, as member of two such Confederations, may get entangled in some curious complications.

Germany, unhappy Germany, has exhibited to the world the miserable spectacle of individual interests triumphing over strongly roused national feeling. Whose fault is this?

If Austria had wanted us for an ally, she might have had us long ago. She wanted us as vassals, unconditionally, and without any return; nay, without any security that she would not make peace at the very moment when we had declared war.

No wonder that it was insisted that we could not enter on a war in defence of misgovernment in Italy, the Concordat and the police system, when it must necessarily begin with an attack on the French in France. What were we to tell the people that the war was for? It would be calling the people rather than the army of France out to fight. We—Germany was neither attacked nor threatened in any way. Not even an army of observation was sent out against us. Could anything be said in a war-manifesto, but that war was entered on to avert a possible future danger, that it was war against the lasting strength of the most powerful State in the world, which threatened our existence? The attitude of Prussia and Germany made it possible for Austria to assemble her entire army in Italy, though she declared, on the "Bundestag," her willingness to do even more than she was pledged to as an allied power. Was that army not enough to defend her interests in Italy? Excepting half of her Twelfth Corps in Galicia, two cavalry corps and the Reserves, her whole army was concentrated in Italy, and practically nothing left for Germany. Hence the haughty demeanor of the diplomates, and the reference to Olmutz.

But the contrary view has found some supporters. Prussia's very existence is endangered by any war with one of her great neighbors. We have no allies. England has no army, and the Russian forces are 400 miles [about 1872 English miles] from the Rhine frontier. Aid from Russia could only arrive when all is over. No ally could do us the service which Austria does us—not for love of us—by engaging 200,000 French at a seat of war 100 miles [about 468 English miles] away. We do not want to fight for Austria, but against her, solely for our own interests. Russia is less able to interfere with us in this matter than she ever has been, or perhaps will be again. England, which absolutely needs a strong continental power, will declare herself as soon as we act.

We had to choose between these two views. A difficult choice. It was made. The mobilization of six corps was ordered, and the order for mobilizing the remaining three was drawn out. Their transportation by railway was fully prepared for, the troops were *en route* for the different points whence they were to start. The transport was to begin on the 15th of this month. The rolling stock was collected from all the railways of the country on the three lines. Any one who knows the organization of the Prussian army and Landwehr, knows that we cannot dawdle with it; when once it is assembled it must proceed to action.

Neither the battle of Solferino, nor even the armistice, made any change in the plans which the Prussian Government had decided upon. Prince Windischgrätz declared on the 8th July that the Emperor would not yield one foot of territory, not one single prerogative in Italy; and yet on the 7th the armistice had already been concluded " to facilitate negotiations."

Austria was convinced that Prussia was intent on war, that the advance of 400,000 Germans would force the Emperor Napoleon to withdraw a considerable part of his army from Italy to France, and that thus Prussia might conquer his provinces of Lombardy and

11

Piedmont; but she was also aware of the motion made in the German Diet on July 4th,* and—peace was concluded.

Prussia missed a great opportunity. Only four weeks ago we might have placed ourselves at the head of all Germany. It has been very shrewdly remarked that Prussia proposed as a condition of her taking action, that which appears to be the natural *consequence* of her action. In doing so she exposed herself to danger, but great historical transformations cannot be effected without danger.

Now we are left entirely to ourselves, and I am convinced that we shall prepare for coming events with all possible care and diligence. But that our situation will soon be more favorable in a political and military sense than in the immediate past, I very much doubt.

A bold resolution can only be the act of one man. At a meeting of many the *pros* and *cons* of a matter are always discussed with so many good and indisputable arguments on each side that one nullifies the other. Every definite proposal is met by the most incontestable difficulties, negative views prevail, and all meet on the neutral ground of inaction. It needs a Frederick the Great to take no advice and to act solely on his own responsibility.

Until after the Prussian question has been studied, an interval of quietude has set in, contrary to all expectation, and I hope to be able to visit Gastein next month for a much-needed course of waters. Marie, of course, goes with me. Afterwards, in September, we want to make a trip to the high Alps. Yours,

HELMUTH.

* On the 4th of July the Prussian envoy proposed in the General Assembly that his king should be entrusted with the supreme command of the German allied armies in the war then impending.

BERLIN, January 2nd, 1860.

DEAR ADOLF:

I am pretty well, but just at present have a great deal to do as President of the Coast Fortification Commission, the representatives of the Maritime States being invited to meet here on the 9th of the month. Whether Hanover will join is very doubtful, and this throws many difficulties in our way.

The meeting of the two Houses on the 12th of this month is anticipated with some interest. The Bills for the Regulation of the Land Tax and Military Reform are measures of the highest importance. Affectionately yours,

HELMUTH.

BERLIN, December 19th, 1861.

DEAR ADOLF:

I have nothing new to tell you of this tedious Europe. Count Rantzau, formerly Provost of the Monastery in Uetersen, who is now living in Berlin, having accepted office in the Ministry of Foreign Affairs, asked after you most kindly. I have before me the Memoirs of the Prince of Nöer. I have not yet read them, but they are received with general disapprobation throughout Germany. The reduction of the army in France has come to nothing. M. Fould must see where he can get the money. The general armament continues. Our elections have turned out very badly; it is not impossible that Waldeck may become President of the Lower House. The members, who cannot see that Prussia is at present the sole guarantee for the peace of Europe against the superior force of France, will move the reduction of the present standing army. This will be rejected, and it may lead to the dissolution of the Diet. England is on the point of war with the Yankees (*sic*), and Russia in the middle of a terrible crisis, between a dissatisfied and plundered nobility and a populace suddenly freed, and impossible to educate. There seems to be a change for the better in Hungary, their intoxication is going off; but the state of finances and of Venice will paralyze any action beyond the frontier for some time to come. Your brother,

HELMUTH.

LONDON, December 22nd, 1861.

DEAR ADOLF:

I answered your letter of the 30th of last month immediately after its receipt in Berlin, but as the mail leaves only once for Madeira, that is the day after to-morrow, I fear you will receive this letter and my first at the same time. According to the Postal Guide, the steamer arrives at your island on the 1st of January next, so I wish you a happy and healthy New Year with all my heart. The same mail will, no doubt, bring you a letter from Augusta, with good news from Rantzau, and thus convey the best possible New Year's present to yourself and your wife. Christmas Eve you will spend in fancy with the children, who this time have only their grandmother to give them Christmas-boxes.

The sudden and totally unexpected death of Prince Albert has no less unexpectedly brought me to England. The Crown Prince wished me to accompany him; to-morrow, Monday, 23rd, the elaborate funeral ceremonies for the Royal Consort will be held in St. George's Chapel, Windsor. The whole solemnity will occupy only two hours, and take place within the wide precincts of this magnificent royal castle, the procession passing from one wing to the other across the courtyard. All mourners and their suites are to wear black evening dress; but otherwise the traditional ceremony and splendor will be observed. The express train leaves here for Windsor at 10 o'clock and returns at 2 o'clock; at seven we shall be at Dover, toss on the channel all night, rush through Cologne on Christmas Eve, and arrive in Berlin early on the 25th.

The Queen has been removed to Osborne, and will not be present at the funeral. It is a well-know fact that the death of her aged mother affected her so much as to make her seem unconscious of all about her. No one knows how she will bear this terrible blow. The Prince, a handsome, prudent, and intelligent man, had reached only the age of forty-two. Their family life was an exemplary one, in every respect, and especially gratifying in such a high position. Now the Queen must decide on war or peace without his advice; and to add to her troubles, Lord Palmerston is said to be ill. Though it seems to be bad policy for America to make war upon England, I doubt whether the Washington Government is strong enough to deliver up Mr. Slidell, etc.,* in the face of the democratic outcry.

And this is what England demands, neither more nor less, and anything short of this means war, and the consequences are incalculable. If the decisions in New York were founded on political considerations, it might be supposed that the Republic wishes to indemnify itself for the almost inevitable loss of the South by trying for Canada. Reinforcements will be sent thither in a few days. This is a serious matter enough for us Prussians. At a time when Russia and

---

* Messrs. Slidell and Mason, the two Confederate representatives, had been forcibly taken from the English mail steamer *Trent*, while on the way from Havana to St. Thomas, by the American man-of-war, *San Jacinto*.

Austria are crippled by internal troubles and England engaged in a war on the other side of the ocean, France has only Prussia to contend with in her endeavors to rule and bully Europe. Perhaps the very fact that she is called upon to decide in matters of such grave importance will rouse the British Queen from the depth of her sorrow.

Here in London we are having continuous fog, a thermometer at four degrees above freezing-point (centigrade) and a biting east wind, which appears to be even less agreeable on this island than on the Continent. With all the boasted comfort, we can never find a warm room. Between an open grate and sash windows, it is impossible to obtain a steady temperature of fifteen degrees (54° Fahr.) from morning till night. Though I skip luncheon, I have had my fill of the heavy food for a fortnight in advance, and I am very glad our stay is limited to four days only. To-day, Sunday, the official ennui is prevailing, and I will content myself with going to Westminster Abbey, and gazing at the Houses of Parliament from the outside.

Yesterday I went to Sydenham; I am vexed you did not visit the Crystal Palace, it is far more remarkable than is generally supposed; more especially it contains specimens of architectural styles such as are not to be seen elsewhere.

One must travel to Nuremburg and York, to Granada, Egypt, Greece, and Ethiopia to see what is here collected under one roof. But what is the good of beautiful scenery without blue heavens? The most forlorn moor looks more beautiful in a rosy sunset than the Isle of Wight in a fog,—and that is the secret of the charm of the Roman Campagna, which in itself is not much more beautiful than the marshes at Uetersen. Your descriptions of Madeira have evoked in myself and Marie a craving for southern climes—*Veder Napoli e poi morire*, they say, and really there is some truth in the proverb, for one who has seen Italy can never be entirely unhappy afterwards. Even on a foggy Sunday in London one may transport one's self in mind to the scenery of mountain and sea, with that tropical wealth of color, which now greets your eyes. And yet, perhaps, you are thinking with longing for the gray north; for friends, and not scenery, are most dear to the heart, after all. Your brother,

HELMUTH.

BERLIN, March 19th, 1862.

DEAR ADOLF:

Your letter of the 3rd of this month arrived here on the 16th. Communication between us and the Island, at a distance of 600 to 700 miles,* is both certain and rapid, since your letter made, on the average, fifty miles [German] a day; but it certainly is not frequent. As, strange to say, there is no direct communication with the Portuguese mother-country, you will have to proceed pretty far along the Meridian of Faroe, and approach the Equator within one-third of its distance from the Pole, almost to the tropic of Cancer; the near proximity of the tropics and the Sahara will make themselves felt even as early as April. The sea, however, will temper the heat, and the Canary Isles may prove very interesting. I expect you will have to spend a few days there waiting for the steamer. Your letter arrived here just one day after Guste, Ernestine, and Frederike had left; we read it in all possible haste, and sent it after them; for this reason I have quite forgotten if you go to Cadiz first, or, as I imagine, to

* Madeira, about 2800 to 3200 English miles.

Gibraltar direct.   I should prefer the latter route, and I enjoy picturing you as you enter between the "Pillars of Hercules."   To the right, in the far distance, the Atlas Mountains, to the left the flat coast of Europe, and, towering up, the mighty rock of Gibraltar.   This Gebel-al-Tarik, the Mountain of Tarik—the Omayad caliph—has on its western slope the smiling city, with green trees and gardens; from the rocky galleries towards the desolate, sandy isthmus on the north, British cannon threaten orthodox Spain; on the east the rock is a precipice, several thousand feet high, perfectly inaccessible, almost bare of even a green blade, and grimly fine as it plunges into the dark-blue, almost unfathomable waters, which here join the Atlantic.   On this rock the Saracens still maintained a footing, when Christian intolerance drove from European soil a nation of several millions, far more cultured than their conquerors, who injured themselves most, and soon sank into indolence, barbarism, and the Inquisition.   The Arabs took their latch-keys with them; their beautiful ballads to this day sing of the valley of Granada, and the splendor of Seville, and they confidently trust that Allah will reinstate them there at some future time.

You can observe a true picture of the domestic life of this remarkable people in Seville by entering the court-yards of some of the houses; the Alcazar retains its splendor in spite of the addition of the lions of Leon, the towers of Castile, and the additions made by Charles V.

* * * An excursion to Arles, Nimes, and Avignon, from Marseilles would be easier, because entirely by railway; it would give you an idea of the character of Provence, and enable you to see the important Roman remains.

If, as I believe, the steamers between Toulon and Genoa do not touch at Nice, I would suggest that you should go to Nice by land; do not miss the Corniche, at any rate. You can hire a Vetturino and a two-wheeled Calescino to carry you to Voltri, but strike a bargain with him before leaving, in the presence of the hotel-keeper. The Vetturino generally undertakes to provide food, and thus you get on very comfortably. The *caparra*, or earnest-money, which the driver hands over to the traveller, must always be insisted on. The Riviera di Levante, the coast from Genoa to Lucca, is still more beautiful, as far as La Spezzia (Porto Venere) at least. Beyond that, your purse, the weather, and the time at your disposal must decide at what point you will turn off to the left.

The news of the "identical notes," issued by all German cabinets against Prussia, has probably penetrated to Madeira. Nevertheless, an understanding has been effected just at this moment between Berlin and Vienna in relation to the Hesse question, though the law of election has not been touched upon; but Austria has given in to our views in other respects, not without some sacrifice of its former standpoint. The Elector, however, seems not disinclined to allow the Confederation to collapse altogether.

The Denmark troubles have assumed a worse aspect; the Danish "rump parliament," from which the two German members have just been expelled, rules the country to the Eider line. This must finally lead to a breach, however unwilling we may be. It is open defiance.

Add to this that we have just passed through a Ministerial crisis. The Liberals, who had expressly declared their intention of forcing out the Liberal Ministers, have attacked the most liberal member of the Cabinet, Herr von Patow, on a question of expenditure in such a way that he has sent in his resignation. The King, instead of accepting the resignation, dissolved the Diet and adjourned the Upper House. It appears, however, that four of the Ministers insisted upon resigning unless a certain programme of government was accepted, which the other three Ministers opposed. So we have had a dissolution of Parliament and a Ministerial crisis all at the same time.

Patow, Bernuth, Auerswald, and Pückler have left office, Von der Heydt, Roon, and Bernstorff remain; Prince Hohenlohe, the President of the Upper House, Count Lippe, Von Jagow, Count Itzenplitz, and Mühler are the new members.

Nobody knows as yet on what lines this new Ministry will proceed. The right will probably gain some ground. But then the newly elected chamber may tend more to the left. Affectionately yours,

HELMUTH.

BERLIN, December 15th, 1862.

DEAR ADOLF:

To-day Madame von Krohn handed me a letter from your wife, that had been enclosed in one to her; without date (all women seem to be averse to dating their letters), but for which I nevertheless thank her very much; we gather from it, to our great joy, that your stay on the magical Isle in the Atlantic is attended by constant improvement, both in your health and hers. The more beneficial the Madeira climate proves to you, the more desirable it seems to prolong your stay. If you go a few floors higher in this palace of nature, you will be somewhat out of the oppressive heat, though it may interfere with your fishing. An officer who went with his wife to Italy, in order to save her lungs, met with four degrees of frost in Verona, where there was no way of warming the rooms. In Paris the Emperor goes skating with his wife, and even at Cannes the prevalent temperature is that of an Arctic landscape.

According to the advice of our physicians, even a six months' stay in the tropics does not suffice really to cure a deeply-rooted disease, though it may do much towards mitigating it. It would therefore be well now to consider the possibility of your prolonging your stay in Madeira for a whole year. There is yet time to obtain leave of absence, and to make the necessary arrangements at Rantzau, where everything, by the way, goes on as usual. As no heavy travelling expenses have this time to be taken into account, 200 thalers per month will probably suffice.

On your return in the spring of 1863, I hope thoroughly cured, you will be sure to find your office in good working order, and take it up yourself with renewed strength. Then you can linger a few months on your return journey with recovered health and make use of the time to visit the most interesting parts of Southern Europe.

You need not get frightened at the prospect of such a long absence. To me the matter offers no serious objections. The children are as well cared for as you could wish, the Government can hardly refuse you leave, as you supply a substitute. At any rate, I beg of you to give it due consideration, and if you can make up your mind to it, take the necessary steps at once.

Here for some days we have had such biting east winds, that even sound lungs feel it; but the thermometer shows only six to seven degrees of frost, and no snow, I am sorry to say.

We have seen the sun to-day for the first time for several weeks, and already the spiral line of its course is high enough for it to shine over the neighboring roofs, into my beautiful south rooms, warming them perceptibly already at midday. I always hail this transition to summer with joy, for I only live in summer, and then only in the evening when I go out riding. I detest the cold, especially in-doors.

Yesterday I attended the opening of the chamber in the cold chapel of the castle, and in the cold White Hall. I observed some curious people on that occasion, a number of very young men and some suspiciously black beards. There were also a few figures reminding one of Bassermann. And these are the men expected by the people to govern the country better than the king.

It is generally supposed that the reformers will go cautiously at first and not string the bow too tightly. Cordially your brother,

HELMUTH.

BERLIN, January 20th, 1864.

DEAR ADOLF:

We are all glad that you stood the continuous biting cold so well of the last three weeks. A thaw with westerly winds has set in here to-day, but, in spite of the abhorrence of the cold acquired in the somewhat debilitating south, I pray to God for only two weeks more of frosty weather, so the unhappy German conflict, in which we have been entangled, may be quickly and radically ended. The troops will have hard times, in consequence of the slow transport service, but we do our best to make them comfortable with blankets and hot beer.

German affairs are indeed not unlike those of a

lunatic asylum. We had to prepare against the most monstrous possibilities, and had to take measures against them. No one knows whither we are drifting with demagogism, imbecility, and arrogance. But as Austria and Prussia have now joined hands not only as to the German question, but also as to its consequences, the chief danger is for the present averted. I am so overwhelmed with work that I cannot add a word save my affectionate regards to you and yours.

HELMUTH.

BERLIN, January 29th, 1864.

DEAR ADOLF:

As far as I can see, the final throw will be cast within a week's time. If there is still more frost, things can be managed without too great a sacrifice; and then there is a probability that a decisive settlement of the Danish question may be arrived at. After that we have got to deal with the minor States of Germany, which will give us plenty to do.

Prussia and Austria for the present proceed strictly within the lines of the treaties, in order to avert, if possible, a European conflagration. An encounter with the Danes can hardly be avoided, unless they retreat at the last moment to their islands, abandoning all their material of war, which would be the least desirable thing of all. When the question is finally settled, we can but offer Denmark "personal union," demanding in return full rights for the Duchies, or at least their entire independence; and material guarantees for good behavior in the occupation of some fortified place, a standing German force, a war indemnity, etc.

Russia will certainly declare herself against the Duke, and never since that Empire has existed in

Europe has it been in a position to throw such direct and powerful influence into the political scale; and this in spite of the Polish insurrection, or rather in consequence of it. This would complete the confusion in Germany, and the three northern powers might make war on South Germany and France. In short, no statesman, perhaps, can see beyond the next few weeks, much less I. I hope for a victory to improve the aspect of affairs, both abroad and at home. The mere advance of so important a body of troops as the Prussian-Austrian army will support law and order, even in Holstein. We are willing to spare the irritated sensitiveness of the minor States and their Commissaries, but everything has a limit. If the Grand Duke of Oldenburg closes his principality of Eutin by shutting the gate at Schwartau, this is an eccentricity which can only happen in Germany. But when the minor States challenge Europe to war on their own responsibility, leaving Austria and Prussia to fight it out for them, strong measures must be taken.

Wherever we turn things look serious enough; we can only wait for what comes next. Your brother,

HELMUTH.

APENRADE, August 1st, 1864.

* * * The preliminary peace has to-day been signed in Vienna. Cession of the three Duchies, occupation of Jutland until peace is ratified, and if, against all expectations, this should not be effected, the armistice to continue for twelve weeks at any rate, that is, until the navigation is closed. So this war is ended, with as much success as could be expected. Now comes the second act, the German question, for which we have shed our soldiers' blood and spent millions. A

prolonged sequestration will, I suppose, precede the final settlement. The Great Powers who have conquered the country will surely keep a hold on it until matters are arranged. The Duchies will probably have to take upon themselves not only part of the Danish National Debt, but also something like twenty millions of war costs. It is only fair that they should pay something for their liberation. As a necessary consequence, all officials must be released from their oaths of allegiance, and for the present fulfil their duties as representatives of Prussia and Austria. So I believe that your own position will be all you could wish.

Poor Denmark! poor king! The founder of a new dynasty, who begins his reign by losing one-half of the realm! Sweeping reductions are inevitable in the army and navy, in the court and administration; indeed, it is doubtful if this State can continue to exist as an independent kingdom. We have even smaller ones in Germany, but they exist only by the support of Austria and Prussia. If they should forget that, and try now to exist independently of the two Powers, they would soon find out their mistake. The fall of Rendsburg * should prove a lesson to them.

Hitherto they have seemed to fear the democracy of their own countries and capitals more than the great German Powers. Herr von Beust talks as if he intended to declare war against us ere long.

I do not forget, however, that new complications may arise at any moment. We have treated with a

* Rendsburg is a city in Holstein and was formerly a fortified place. After the Schleswig-Holstein troubles of 1848 it was occupied by the Prussians and Austrians for a time and later on turned over to the Danes, who promptly razed the fortifications, ransacked the magazines, and carried off the entire implements of war, the property of the Duchies, to Copenhagen.—H. F.

king and a Government, who may to-morrow cease to exist, when the conditions are know in Copenhagen. We cannot but await the next news with much anxiety. From what we hear, the Queen and General Hausen are the only men of them all. The entire army is assembled on the Island of Fühnen. Only the guards, few in number, are stationed on the Isle of Zeeland, together with a strong body of militia. We learnt what these are in 1848.

HELMUTH.

BERLIN, June 24th, 1865.

DEAR ADOLF:

* * * The question of the Duchies is coming to a crisis, the consequences of which cannot be foreseen. The only thing perfectly clear to me is, that Prussia, for reasons of domestic and foreign policy, cannot afford to give up possession. The decision of the delegates is quite a secondary consideration. We cannot be converted by criticism when it is conceived in a retrograde spirit, and for this reason the representatives should never have been asked, the assembly never have been called. Assemblies are the mere tools of individual intriguers, and a useless or dangerous plaything where political necessity alone can decide. It could, at most, be out of consideration for the Emperor Napoleon. But in that case his style of doing things should be adopted—first seize the country and afterwards ask how they like it. To effect this there are only two alternatives: either to indemnify the part owner or to make war upon him (or make him declare war against you). The first would involve a cession of Prussian territory, and this has hitherto been absolutely rejected by the King; the other course, therefore, is not impossible, and its consequences are incal-

culable, as the whole of Europe must of necessity take sides, however unwilling some of the States might be, since France is engaged in Algiers, Mexico, and perchance in North America, Russia has enough to do at home, and England is as powerless on the Continent as she is presuming.

I still hope that an understanding may be come to which will lead the way to a reconciliation between the two German Powers. The peace of Europe would thus be secured and all interests served—but those of the Wurzburgers. We all send our best love.

HELMUTH.

BERLIN, May 26th, 1866.

DEAR ADOLF:

I take advantage of a few free moments to answer your letter of the 16th, and to thank you for your expressions of sympathy.

These are indeed serious times. War is inevitable. I do not think that it is in the power of man to prevent it.

The destiny of Germany is now to be decided. The passion of the Germans for separation, observed by Tacitus, necessitates decision by force of arms. We never have had a Louis XI., who crushed the power of his vassals in France just at the right moment. It may be true, as the Austrian newspapers assert, that the juxtaposition of two great powers in Germany is an impossibility. One of the two must fall. The struggle will be terrific. Austria has made greater preparations than ever before, and we too are ready to put our whole force into the field. It seems as though Germany must pay her neighbors, right and left, with provinces.

12

I doubt whether the minor States, which are so eagerly stirring up the blaze, will fare better under the sole authority of the victor than under the fluctuating influence of the two great Powers.

It cannot be denied that the attitude of the people of Holstein has done much to bring on the present crisis. If Prussia should be worsted, then the Holsteiners may see their wish of forming a petty State fulfilled on condition of their taking over a debt of ninety millions. But then they will have no Prussia, which alone guarantees the existence of the Northern small States. Austria will not burn her fingers for the Holsteiners, and the German Confederation, which never did anything in its life, will do even less when it is dead.

Fifty years of peace have shown that union can never be achieved by means of a peaceful understanding; the German mind is too unpractical and too easily carried away by phrases. If it is God's will that Prussia should solve the problem, the general European situation is not unfavorable.

We have no friends in Germany. The confederation has become Austria's tool, the decisions of the majority are the echo of the Vienna Cabinet. Yet this, and even the European Conferences, and above all the resolutions of Unions and Corporations, are mere cobwebs, and can no longer stop the rolling stone. Austria has never yet prepared for war without striking; she is not rich enough to disarm before some success. In Italy, no Government would be strong enough to suppress the enthusiasm of the nation. We ourselves have not desired this war, but we accept it with calm confidence. God grant us victory—for with Prussia Germany would fall. With hearty greetings,

HELMUTH.

BERLIN, January 28th, 1867.

DEAR ADOLF:

* * * On the whole an understanding between the States has been arrived at, which enables us to lay before Parliament, when it meets on the 24th of the month, a definite programme. But there still remain many points for final settlement, especially in the important question of military help. For the minor States have had soldiers so cheaply that to make the show which Prussia has shared with them for the last fifty years their forces must be doubled or quadrupled. Now it is impossible to increase the taxation of these States suddenly and to a proportionate amount. The decree of annexation was formally proclaimed in Holstein on the 24th of last month, as I presume you will have heard even in Africa. The recruiting is going on quietly. In Hanover and Frankfort very serious disturbances occurred when the older men were called out to muster, no doubt in consequence of some prompting from outside; but a fortnight later they were called out again, and order secured by a body of troops. Several hundred of the refractory were removed from the place and sent out for eight weeks' drill, which very much astonished them, but the lesson was effectual.

We are here in the midst of the carnival; every evening something or other takes place, and at 10 o'clock at night, when one is thinking of bed, we have to proceed to Court, concert, or soirée. Servants and horses get no rest before 1 A.M., and to work as usual in the morning. This is bad for the health.

February 13th.—We were getting rather uneasy, as a fortnight had passed since your departure by steamer, and yet no news of you; to-day Guste, however, sends on from Ratzeburg a long letter from Fritz. He does

not appear to be overpleased with the expedition on
the whole; still, his letter is full of good lodgings,
agreeable hosts, sun, air, and ocean, eighteen degrees
of warmth, good breakfasts, blossoming roses, arau-
carias, palms, and oranges—in short, of the various
elements of which pleasant winter quarters may consist.

To me, at any rate, among gray fogs, dripping
gutters, and long evenings, such a glimpse into the
sunny South is a smiling picture. The swarms of
naked beggar boys would not trouble me very much.
Misery, with us, hides itself in ill-ventilated hovels
where it is not seen; and hunger and cold mean death.
In the South, the poorest has the sun to warm him,
and the sea and banana trees allow nobody to starve.
On the whole, we hope the stay in Algiers will give
you much pleasure.

Yesterday the Reichstag elections took place, and
we are very curious to know the result of these direct
elections. The returns have so far come in from a few
districts only. In Sonderburg Ahlemann (a Dane) has
been elected; at Neustadt, Bockelmann, against Ober-
präsident Scheel, defeated. Pastor Schrader was
elected in two places; I do not know anything about
him. But a small number of votes have been regis-
tered in Holstein. I am standing for this district
against Herr Wiggers, and congratulate the city of
Berlin if I am defeated. The "City of Intellect"
chooses a Mecklenburger as its representative.
Schleiden is returned for Oldesloe, Baudissin-Fried-
richshof for Rendsburg, Baudissin for Eckernförde,
Councillor Jensen for Glückstadt, Staatsrath Franke
for Tondern, and Doctor Goldenbaum for Bergedorf.
According to the newspapers, just come to hand, Bismarck, Roon, myself, Falckenstein, Steinmetz, and

Herwarth are defeated in the six divisions of Berlin, and as many democrats elected. The masses are blind, and woe to the State and society, where they obtain supremacy. Perhaps the rural districts have done better; the returns are not yet in.

HELMUTH.

BERLIN, March 10th, 1867.

DEAR ADOLF:

The debates in the Reichstag take up a great deal of time, but are interesting in the highest degree since the preliminaries and elections are at last ended.

There are indeed some very talented men in this assembly, before whom conventional speechifying, talk for the sake of talking, comes to nothing.

But it seems as though even superior minds brought with them only their narrower views of life from the minor States.

Councillor Franke, in his attack on the election of the Alsen representative Ahlemann, exhibited much ill-feeling towards the Danes, but found no echo among the members. Twesten, too, looks at European affairs only with the eyes of a Schleswig-Holsteiner. Herr Meyer (from Hamburg) failed to impress the House by his high-sounding phrases, and the Catholic parson Michaelis, not *à Kempis* but of Kempen in Silesia, who damned the whole business on church principles and gave us a sort of Capuchin sermon,* at once became a standing joke.

Warnstedt has as yet made no speech, but Münchausen has spoken on the side of King George, attacking Prussia all round. Personally, the man made a good impression upon me. He spoke quietly and with dig-

---

* Referring no doubt to that of the Capuchin monk in Schiller's Wallenstein.—H. F.

nity, though he was conscious of very general disapprobation. I have also listened with great interest to Waldeck, who attacks the Government programme from his own standpoint, which is opposed to particularism, and is liberal, almost republican.

The assembly listened to the speeches of Braun (of Saxony), Miquel-Osnabrück, and Wagner, for the motion, in perfect silence, and Bismarck twice replied in a really statesmanlike speech. I am collecting the short-hand reports; it is a pity that none of your papers report the Reichstag meetings; it will be worth your while to read the speeches later.

By the time the general discussion had lasted two days, I was convinced that the rejection of the Constitution-Bill is an impossibility. All the opposition can do is to fight over the separate clauses; they cannot ruin the whole thing, so they will try to damage it in detail.

If the day had but twenty-four hours more! To-day we have sat from ten to three; at present there is a divisional meeting, and the regular work of the office to be attended to. Besides all this, I am very busy editing a history of the last campaign, which is soon to appear.

I hope to be able to complete the family tree in all its details. The sheet of paper is as large as a tablecloth, for the living generation alone boasts of a hundred members. If I ever succeed in acquiring landed property, I will have it set out on stucco. It ought, I think, to spur on our posterity to be worthy of their ancestors.

HELMUTH.

May, 1867.

DEAR ADOLF:

The Reichstag will probably close on Tuesday next. I have no doubts of a satisfactory result. After that the Prussian Diet meets; happily I have nothing to do with that.

The Luxemburg question will hardly lead to war just at present. Louis Napoleon must be aware that he is not prepared for it; but he cannot say so to his vain Frenchmen; public opinion is much excited in Paris, fomented by party spirit, and an explosion is not impossible. Nothing could be better for us than that war, which is bound to come, should be declared at once, while Austria is, in all probability, engaged in the East. She has 30,000 troops at this moment assembled at Semlin, but whether it is against their fellow Croats, or the Servians, nobody knows as yet. We count on seeing you on your return trip; within six weeks the situation will be clearer. With affectionate regard,

HELMUTH.

BERLIN, November 29th, 1867.

DEAR ADOLF:

I am sorry that you have not been a candidate for election to the Reichstag or Diet. The Duchies are represented by uncommonly queer specimens; it would be an injustice to judge the country by their hopeless incapacity. Franke is the only man who speaks to the point, without empty phrases, though he is hostile to the Government. None of the others have succeeded in holding the attention of the House for five minutes. You will not find these remarks in the short-hand reports, for one half of the speeches are delivered for the benefit of the short-hand writers only. If it will interest you, I will send you the report of this year's proceedings, as well as the second part of the account of the campaign. You will have received the first part. I will also send you the maps of the battle-fields. Your brother, HELMUTH.

BERLIN, January 24th, 1868.

DEAR ADOLF:

A great deal is being done to relieve the famine in Prussia; aid comes from all parts of Germany, and even from abroad. For all that, the detestable climate of this country, blessed as it is with such excellent soil, cannot be changed.

Here the entire husbandry must be finished in a few months. When we begin ploughing in Silesia * the Prussian farmer must have done his sowing. This involves an immense stock of horses, etc., and many hands, which are not to be had. Remission of taxes and donations of money are hazardous remedies; employment of the needy the only effectual help. This will now be offered in abundance on road and railway making, but the weather hinders the beginning.

Things are far worse in Algeria, where the Emperor offers the ridiculous sum of half a million of francs [about £19,800, or $96,000]. But I cannot believe that the domestic difficulties of France will insure peace. On the other hand, he will only play the *va banque* of war when he sees no other way of holding on. A better guarantee lies in the fact that France alone is too weak, and Austria not ready.

The *Zoll parlament* [commission on import duties] meets in March, and will show if the German nation is willing to make use of the opportunity of effecting the union, which Providence offers every few hundred years, and for which everybody is shouting, singing, and dining; but which, after all, is never quite to the pattern set up by each German race as distinct from every other. Such a union can never be effected but

---

* Meanwhile the Field-Marshal had acquired the estate of Creisau, near Schweidnitz.

by coercion; we shall have to fight for it sooner or later.

We had a pretty fair harvest in Silesia, plenty of straw—which I wanted badly, as I am obliged to buy 1000 thalers worth of artificial manure—but less grain. I still have two thousand bushels of wheat on hand; good property at the rate of four thalers per bushel. I shall have to build in spring. The buildings are entirely of stone, but the house has only a shingle roof, and the roof-tree is rotting. Besides, I am going to lay out a park, in which bridges must be built, roads made, and 10,000 trees planted. I shall not live to walk in their shade, but there are some fine old oaks already. I rejoice every day to see the sun rising higher over the roofs; we may hope for summer again some day. We both send hearty greetings.

HELMUTH.

BERLIN, December 24th, 1868.

DEAR ADOLF:

Our dear Marie died this afternoon at 3 o'clock, after sixteen days of severe illness, but a short and painless death-struggle. A dreadful fever snatched her from us after all means of medical skill and careful nursing had been exhausted. Several days ago, while yet fully conscious, she took leave of us, and prayed for us in her worst delirium. I cannot desire her to awake again. She has led a life of rare happiness and escaped the sadness of old age. Her open, true, and pious character made her beloved by everybody, and her death has caused much grief.

Jeanette* arrived this morning. Guste has devoted herself to nursing. They are both a great comfort to me. Your brother, HELMUTH.

* Baroness von Brockdorff, Frau von Moltke's sister.

BERLIN, December 30th, 1868.

DEAR AUGUSTE:

I thank you affectionately for your kind sympathy in my bitter grief. Those who knew Marie can feel the greatness of my loss and the emptiness of my life. Nothing more beautiful can be imagined than she looked after all was over, and the sweet and tranquil look on her face. She seemed to be only asleep. She is now in her coffin in the little Catholic Chapel at Creisau, surrounded with innumerable wreaths of flowers and palms. The Mayors and head-men on the property begged to be allowed to carry the coffin. The little church was strewn with green fir branches, and many wept bitterly. They all had loved their young and beautiful mistress. I hope in the spring to finish a little vault for Marie and myself; I had always thought Marie would do this for me. The mausoleum will be erected on the top of a small wooded hill near the house, from whence there is a wide and beautiful view of the estate and mountains. I hope to make the spot so attractive that every one may be tempted to linger there.

With most affectionate greetings to Adolf and the girls. Your desolate brother-in-law,   HELMUTH.

BERLIN, January 9th, 1869.

DEAR AUGUSTE:

I thank you again and again for your kind sympathy in my affliction. You knew Marie well enough to estimate the depth of my sorrow. It still seems like a dreadful dream to think of her being torn away from such blooming, vigorous life.

Our relatives have done everything to lighten my

burden as far as outward matters are concerned. Jeanette is still here, and life goes on as usual. Fritz and Guste will do me the great favor of sacrificing their home in Lübeck, to which they are so much attached, and coming to live with me. This I regard as a great kindness. As the King has been graciously pleased to appoint Henry to be my second Adjutant, I have those about me who were in loving intimacy with Marie. I shall presently send a few trinkets which belonged to her; accept them as a remembrance. I have reserved a keepsake for your daughter Marie, her godchild, till her confirmation. I beg of you to remember kindly your faithful brother-in-law,

HELMUTH.

CREISAU, August 29th, 1869.

DEAR ADOLF:

At your next visit here you will find that great progress has been made in Creisau. The first-floor rooms are now very pretty and ready for the reception of guests. The entrance-room on the ground-floor, which is hung with granite-marble paper, forms a tastefully arranged hall in its simplicity; the large buffet appears to great advantage opposite the front door. The house, on the whole, is furnished, and that very considerable expense is at an end. In the autumn we must proceed again with the bridges and road-making.

The landscape gardener was here yesterday. He has reserved for me, at Breslau, a number of conifers, which are to be planted out round the chapel and in front of the future burial-place. But the man says the Steinberg must be supplied with water, as otherwise the plantation will not thrive. How the water is to be raised thirty feet is now the question; it will certainly cost a great deal. The rock is to be blasted this week, so as to give the side of the hill on which the chapel stands a more rugged appearance. The gardener comes next week to plant the pine trees, as August is the best time for setting them out. The third year's income of the estate will thus be spent.

The harvest is almost in, except the second crop of hay and the potatoes. Now we must prepare for next year. Horses and men are all busy, so I had to get strange workmen for the Steinberg job.

Grapes and greengages have also come in, but the greater part of the vines will, I fear, not ripen. We only had about a dozen peaches. The pelargonium beds in front of the house are splendid, and the Ricinus has grown to a height of $9\frac{1}{2}$ feet.

After you left us at Dresden, where it was really wintry, we had no sunshine after the first day throughout the whole journey of inspection, but we never got a wetting.

From Stolpen we made delightful excursions into the ravines of the Saxon Switzerland, and the whole party assembled every evening in the best spirits. They ran especially high over a monster stirrup cup at Grossenhayn, where the Crown Prince was then still visiting us. From thence I came here with Henry by railway, in lovely weather, the day before yesterday, and ever since we have had beautiful sunshine and few gnats, and are driving out as usual in the carriage.

As I am to attend the King to Pomerania and Prussia, I shall set out for Berlin on the 2nd or 3rd of September, but hope to be able to spend the latter half of the month here, and October. Then I have to arrange a harvest festival for the people, and a shooting-party for the neighbors. Your brother

HELMUTH.

CREISAU, October 28th, 1869.

DEAR ADOLF:

Many thanks for your kind letter of the 25th, which found me still here in Creisau, where I have been detained by all sorts of business. A great deal has been done since you left; the house is completely set up, the chapel surrounded with a garden planted with above a thousand conifers, and a good path made up to it. In front there is a terrace, the whole slope is covered with turf, and a fountain made to which nothing is wanting but the water—the principal thing, to be sure. A large American fire-hose refused to work, so I am having a force pump put up with iron pipes. We are also building a bridge 28 feet long and $8\frac{1}{2}$ feet high over the Peile on the way to Wierischau and regulating the course of the stream, which otherwise washes away my land every year. The banks are already laid with fascines in several places, and the rifts filled up with earth. The whole income from the estate for the year has been laid out on it. For some days the snow on the hills has been coming lower and lower, and to-day, even on the plain, the sun lights up a perfectly wintry landscape, with green trees. I must now return to Berlin to-morrow, whither Guste first, and then Fritz, have gone before me to settle in winter quarters.

I see from your letter how hard it has been to you to resign your post.

You have served the cause of your little Fatherland with faithful devotion and acknowledged merit, and have risen to a distinguished position in very difficult times. It is no wonder that you cling to the soil with all the fibres of your being. But you were serving a losing cause, to the very last moment; or at least circumstances took a different course from that which you expected and intended; this and your health closed the higher career to which your talents entitled you. Nevertheless, it must be confessed that the new Government has behaved liberally to the Holstein officials. The lack of professional occupations will, of course, bring with it a sense of idleness, and if you can reconcile it with your health and financial means I would not advise you to give it up, although, I must confess, that I am very happy in my freedom. I have banked up and trenched here like a day-laborer, and I could certainly find suitable employment for you in the field of literature.

As soon as I am at Berlin I will inquire about the Supreme Court and the principles on which pensions are granted, and let you know at once.

BERLIN, July 18th, 1870.

DEAR ADOLF:

How things have changed in the few days since my journey! The desperate adventurer of Boulogne is setting two nations at each other to save his dynastic interests if possible. Never was a war more justly undertaken than this on our side, so we hope for God's aid. But His ways are not our ways, and He attains His ends in the evolution of the world, even by lost campaigns. Still we hope for the best; the political situation is favorable, for we have ground for assuming that, for the present, we have no second foe in our rear. So I can nowhere await events in greater quiet and security than at Creisau. News, official or private, reaches Schweidnitz as quickly and surely as Berlin. * * *

It is a fortunate circumstance for Helmuth that he will now be an officer at once, and while still young be engaged in a war, for which we elders had to wait forty years. * * *

Beg Fritz to tell Ernst and August,* that I will take them both in the baggage-train. The saddle-horses and four carriage-horses must for the present remain at Creisau, for everything here is full to overflowing; the men may then come up with the horses in ten or twelve days, and will get their first orders. August may bring the 200 thalers which are in the fire-proof safe, my dressing-gown and slippers, and some of the linen. Plain clothes may remain there. It is to be hoped that the harvest will be got in quickly, we shall want it; it has failed entirely in Northern France. Few, probably, of the laborers will be called out; they are for the most part old cripples, but the inspector will have to go; he certainly is still bound to serve. I am glad that you can already extend your walk as far as to the chapel; if the bailiff has no pressing work on hand, get him to make a bench on the lower terrace.

Much love to you all. I hope you will find a real home at Creisau.

HELMUTH.

FERRIERES, September 21st, 1870.

Ferrières is a château three miles [more than fourteen English miles] east of Paris, furnished with royal magnificence, the creation of the fifth great power in Europe, the apotheosis of Mammon. Here Rothschild received the Emperor Louis Napoleon; as Count Molé once entertained Louis XIV., so in our time did the parvenu of wealth entertain the parvenu of power. Official newspapers of the time mention a shooting

* Two servants.

party, at which the Emperor brought down the strangest game; among other things a parrot which shrieked "Vive l'Empereur" as it fell. Now the whole nation is shrieking "A bas l'Empereur," and Ferrières is the head-quarters of his enemy, who, after besieging Metz and Strasburg, has now to embrace what Victor Hugo calls the Sacred Capital in arms of iron. Paris has, since yesterday, been completely invested on all sides, and we live in hourly expectation of hearing how the hundred thousand Gardes-Mobiles, of which the papers speak, will take this embrace. The last French corps left intact, the Fourteenth, did in fact oppose the advance from the south, but was driven back yesterday behind the forts, losing seven guns. The Fifth Army Corps, at the head of our advancing forces, had some fighting on the 17th, 18th, and 19th, and I will not send off this letter till I have news of Helmuth.

La France, "qui est plus forte que jamais," even under these circumstances, talks big, as usual. Any army in the field has ceased to exist, but they still have M. Rochefort, *professeur de barricades*, and *la poitrine des patriotes invincibles*. Nevertheless, La République made her appearance here at head-quarters yesterday in the person of M. Jules Favre.

September 22nd, evening.—I have just heard that Helmuth is well and unhurt. He is now quartered at Versailles, and will have time and leisure to write to you and describe the most splendid palace in the world. I will go over there one day soon.

Wilhelm sends no news of himself, but the 17th Dragoons has, to my knowledge, not yet met the enemy; whether it had been sent to the siege of Toul, or is quartered in Rheims to keep the Francvoleurs in order, I do not know.

I have to-day a letter from Geheimrath von Frankenberg, who has been to see you at Creisau. The kind old fellow sends me an ivy leaf from the chapel. Oh, if only Marie had lived to see these times! But I believe that departed souls do not lose their cognizance of earthly things, and that her patriotic heart sympathizes with us all.

We have now had several days of the loveliest autumn weather, and I hope that, after the dreadful rains in Silesia, you are having the same. But it is very cool in the rooms to the north. Dear Adolf, I wish you could spend the winter somewhere in a warmer climate with your family. If possible I would join you, for such a campaign tries the strength severely when a man has sixty years on his shoulders, as I have. But I cherish a private hope that I may be shooting hares at Creisau by the end of October.

M. Favre has not yet come out from Paris again, and as he quite lately declared that not an inch of French ground, not a stone of a French fortress should be surrendered, and as, besides this, the Parisians have, throughout the campaign, read news only of victories, they must be somewhat surprised to hear quite different proposals on a sudden. I should not be at all astonished to hear that they had murdered him. A red Republic is a far greater danger to the République of honest people than the hostile army can be; and this perhaps will be appealed to, to maintain social order in the Capital of Civilization. After 2000 Gardes-Mobiles had given up 300 bad guns the Prussians were very well received, and Sèvres begged for a garrison.

In Paris gas-lighting ceases from to-day, and water is only to be had at fixed hours; all the railways are interrupted. The Bois de Boulogne is full of beasts
13

for slaughter, and from our position at Meudon and St.-Cloud we could fire upon them at any moment. The promenades of the beau and the demi-monde have ceased, and the Parisians have to-day had no milk in their coffee. How long they can hold out remains to be seen. Henry, of course, is flourishing; he has all the pleasant part of the campaign. He dines royally, and has a capital grand piano at his service in the evening.

If Guste only takes care to keep the rooms warm, I think it must be delightful now at Creisau, where the leaves are turning red and yellow. The rain we have had will have been good for the turf and plantations, and I hope that everything is green about the chapel. I am glad that Wilhelm the gardener has remained; in spite of Fritz's recommendation, I should have been sorry to spare the gardener where so many great sacrifices were made. August and Ernst are quite well. One of the young horses has a very bad throat, but I have put a horse into harness—one of about ten thousand taken at Sedan—who goes very well, so I take a drive every day in the pleasant sunshine.

I only hope that it is as fine with you since the harvest is over. But there is always something to do in the country, and Geheimrath Gellhorn never likes to spare the farm-horses.

This is the fourth letter I have written; the one lost perhaps may be found again; one mail was certainly interrupted at Verdun, and will perhaps be published in *Figaro*, so that you will read your letters after all. Do get "Kladderadatsch"; it is extremely amusing just now, and I figure largely in it. To conclude, my affectionate greeting to the girls, to the Gellhorns, Reichenbachs, and all friends.

HELMUTH.

VERSAILLES, October 12th, 1870.

DEAR ADOLF:

Your letter of the 4th of this month came safely to hand, but I would not write till Helmuth was released from his very exposed outpost close to the Seine, at Meudon, just outside Paris.

Yesterday he marched in at the head of his regiment, and the tallest man in it, and will be here for a fortnight. The King at once asked his name. He is very well, and looks splendid with his iron cross. He enjoyed a capital breakfast with me most uncommonly, after having had to remain unrelieved at his post for three days.

We are in the unpleasant predicament of having to allow ourselves to be fired at without replying, for our 4-pounders are of no avail against the 74-pounders of the forts. The siege-train, above 100,000 hundredweight, cannot be brought up very fast by the only line which has but just been restored. If any movement is seen, even of the smallest group of men, the forts fire their gigantic shot to a distance of 6000, 7000, nay, from Mont Valérien, 8000 paces, with great precision. It is great waste of ammunition, when you consider that firing one shot costs 93 thalers. As chance will have it, a shell hits sometimes, and we thus lose about a dozen men daily, besides others killed by chassepôts at from 1000 to 1500 paces.

This of course has not the smallest influence on the outcome of the campaign. Nothing makes Paris so furious as our attempting nothing. Victor Hugo writes: "Nous avons cru voir arriver Arminius et nous ne voyons que Schinderhannes."

At the same time, now that we must limit ourselves to investing the city, we have entered on a very tiresome stage of waiting. Starving-out is a slow process, as Metz shows, but it leads to the end. Every sortie hitherto has been repulsed. Nor are we altogether idle in the open country. The hopes of Paris are centred on the Army of the Loire, which was said to be really advancing. Well, this army was yesterday broken up, and Orleans is occupied by us. To-day we shall be on the other side of the river, which, as is well known, no hostile force has ever crossed before. The Government in Tours must find another abiding-place.

Will this unhappy country discern at last that it is conquered, that its condition is worse every day? But I have no doubt that news of a victory is even now being published. It is certainly noteworthy that the *Gaulois*, instead of a leader full of lies, published a letter from a French officer who has the courage to tell the French the truth. You will see it in an early number of our Berlin papers. The situation cannot be more accurately depicted than it is by this intelligent and well-informed soldier.

That a grand sortie from Metz was again repulsed on the 9th you will have learnt before this can reach you. Matters cannot go on so there much longer. It is a hard trial of patience for the besiegers; harder still for the besieged. The persistency and endurance of the French must be acknowledged; it is partly the result of its seeming to them quite incomprehensible that they can be defeated; and yet the superiority of the Germans has been proved in every fight, even when the French had the advantage in numbers, as on the 10th of August, and here outside Paris. The whole operations of the invasion could not, of course, be carried on without a decided numerical superiority on our side—the simultaneous investment of Metz, siege of Strasburg, and march on Paris. The Emperor's foolish advisers, praters in the Chamber, and heroes on paper, should have begun by ascertaining what was the true significance of United Germany.

The Republican authorities in Paris dare not put the question to the country. In the snuff-box of an emissary a decree was found, signed by Favre and Gambetta, which prohibits the election of a constitutional assembly, fixed for the 16th of the month by their colleague Crémieux, and blaming his prejudiced proceeding with terrified caution. Thus there is no prospect of any constituted authority in France with which any serious negotiations may be opened. It is indeed reprobate conduct to deceive the nation by persistent lies as to the state of the country. If Paris holds out till the stores of food are really exhausted, the situation may become frightful to think of. Even if peace should be concluded and traffic fully restored, how can supplies for two million souls be thrown in, even with our best efforts to help? The environs of the huge city have been cleared of food for ten miles round [about forty-seven English miles], and the railways have all been broken up in places by the Franctireurs. It would take months to repair them where they have been blown up. The only road which we have so far been able to re-open we use for our own supplies. It is frightful to see the havoc made by the mob in power, and laughable too. In the fine roads which lead to the capital, the pavement has been torn up and trenches dug across, but then we drive at the side on the wide avenues. The noble oaks and chestnuts have been dragged away to form abattis, the tall arches of the viaduct lie in ruins in the river-bed. These barricades would have had some sense if they had been defended, but the Francvoleurs have all made off, and their devastations checked our advance guard but a few hours, and the army not a single day in its advance. We everywhere found our pontoon bridges laid by the side of the ruins of the solid masonry which the French had blown up, and which it will cost the country millions to restore. The villages about Paris consist for the most part of delightful villas and châteaux. The residents were compelled to turn out, and those who would not go had their houses set fire to. The soldier, of course, forces a door when he finds it locked, the cellar to find food and wine, the cupboard for a cloth or a plate. So in many places the havoc is serious, while order reigns wherever the inhabitants have resisted this tyranny, or where officers of higher rank are in possession of the quarters. Here in Versailles, for instance, you might think that perfect peace reigned if it were not for the roar of cannon from Paris. All the shops are open, and French industry already can show different portions of the Prussian uniform for sale. Jewellers and watchmakers are not afraid to display their costly wares. Orders from headquarters are stuck up at the street corners forbidding any one to ride on the footway, or to smoke in the galleries, and in the fields the farmer ploughs and sows without a fear that his horses will be seized. The requisitions and billets are, no doubt, a heavy burden, and every one wishes for a speedy end of all these calamities.

I not least; and I often long for the restful silence of the Chapel hill. News from that peaceful home comes like a gleam of sunshine in the endless stir and agitation, and painful expectancy in which we live here.

It is a pity that you should have to leave Creisau and disperse to the various ends of the earth; but it must be cold now at the foot of the Eule, and it seems to me that you should remain till about the end of

November in our warm, sunny quarters at Berlin, where there is so much that is interesting to see, for Augusta and the girls both. The whole house is entirely at Guste's disposal, for Henry and I are not likely to return soon. There, too, you have all the earliest news. If fortune favors us, you can remain there till the troops march in. Thus, it seems to me, you should postpone your move to Lübeck definitely till next autumn.

When you have spent the winter in Switzerland, Creisau is really lovely in the spring, and everything will be ready for your reception there. Double windows and heating apparatus make the house habitable quite early, and we go thither as soon as may be from Berlin. I must now conclude with affectionate greetings to all relatives, and our friendly neighbors.

HELMUTH.

VERSAILLES, October 27th, 1870.

It was with great pleasure and sincere gratitude that I received the good wishes from home: Adolf's letter closed with the wish, "May Bazaine celebrate the 26th by the surrender of Metz."

So it has come to pass: the capitulation—but for some quite unforeseen accident—is to be accomplished at 5 o'clock to-day.

Before these lines can reach you, the telegraph will have announced the great news, and 101 guns from the Lustgarten will proclaim it to Berlin. A hundred and fifty thousand more Frenchmen will be made prisoners, and the strong fortress of Metz falls into our hands. Nothing of the kind has been seen in the world since the Babylonish captivity. We need an army now to guard our 300,000 prisoners.

France has no longer an army, and yet we must wait till the Parisians, who are raving in delirium, give up this hopeless resistance. I should not wish to be in a hurry to adopt the last cruel alternative of a regular bombardment.

The sorties, so far, have been wrecked on our outposts; they have never got so far as our main positions. But pursuit on our part is out of the question, and we are losing men daily from the fire from the forts, which fire haphazard, with an incredible waste of ammunition, at a range of 8000 paces, above three-quarters of a mile [about three miles and a half English]. Every shot costs 6 thalers [about 13s.], the great marine steel shells as much as 93 thalers [about £10]; and with from sixty to a hundred rounds they kill three, five, to twenty of our men, as chance may direct. Part of our lines lie within range of infantry fire, and we are careful to take off our caps before peeping over the top of a wall or a breastwork. Every attempt at relief from outside has been defeated and dispersed, but the Government still spurs on the hapless population in the provinces, by lying reports and patriotic bombast, to make fresh efforts, which have to be suppressed by the destruction of whole towns. The audacity of the Franctireurs must be punished by severe reprisals, and the war is assuming a horrible aspect. It is bad enough when armies have to tear each other to pieces; but to set nations against each other is not an advance, but a lapse into barbarism. How little a rising of the masses, even of so brave a race as this, can do against a small but disciplined force should be seen with all its consequences by our liberals, who preach the arming of the people.

So long as there is no real authority in France, recognized by the nation, we have no alternative but to continue the devastation of war to a still increasing extent.

New clouds are forming on the political horizon in consequence of attempts at mediation. It is incredible, but true, that Count von Beust has not profited by his recent defeat, but persists in playing with fire. He had better beware, for we are in a position to turn play into earnest. But he will no doubt think better of it.

The 17th Regiment of Dragoons was fired at by volunteers on its return to St. Quentin and thirty-five men were wounded. Wilhelm is now before Mézières, of which the siege was begun yesterday.

Helmuth has been feeding up here for the last fortnight, and is now at the outposts; he came here yesterday on leave by special command from the King. I went out to see him to-day, with Henry, to take him some food, wine, and cigars; he is perfectly well. Henry has been promoted and transferred to the 60th Regiment, where he is soon to have a company; till then he remains with me.

You no doubt are by this time all in Berlin, where it is at any rate less raw than at Creisau. The winter here too has set in early, and the trees are almost bare of leaves already. Happily our men are all under roofs, excepting the outposts; there is no lack of firewood, and the food is excellent.

I hope you are all comfortably lodged, Adolf especially, on the sunny side of the house. The situation may quite possibly be clearer within the next few weeks, and before you set out.

I believe that almost the safest plan is that, as before, no one should sleep in the house; the sheep dogs will keep guard. I fancy you will remain quietly at Berlin through November; there is no severe cold before Christmas.

It is quite true that the étapes at Stenay allowed themselves to be surprised—a company and a half—not from Mézières, but from Montmédy. Destruction of telegraphs, removal of rails, and disasters on the line are constantly going on, with consequent shooting of the guilty and levying of fines from the nearest villages. In reply to a private inquiry in Guste's letter, I will give Henry his brother John's gold watch at Christmas; it goes capitally; I always meant him to have it after my death.

Count Brockdorf has been taken prisoner, and carried beyond Orleans to the south of France. From what Colonel Wright, the commander of his regiment, writes to me, he is well treated. No prisoners have as yet been exchanged, and no exception can be made in favor of an individual. Peace, it is to be hoped, will soon release all. I beg Guste to say this to Frau von Bülow, who wrote to me. Count B. is engaged to her granddaughter Loën.

October 28th, eight in the morning.—A telegram just come from Metz; the fortress has capitulated—three Marshals, 6000 officers; in all 173,000 men prisoners, only 16,000 sick.

HELMUTH.

VERSAILLES, November 23rd, 1870.

DEAR ADOLF:

Sister Augusta writes that you are to set out about the 28th of the month. This may perhaps reach you before you start. I have not written for some time.

When one has lived for months haunted day and night by one single idea, it becomes a perfect torment, and yet it is difficult to shake it off. After Sedan and Metz it may have seemed to you in Berlin that all was over; but we have been having a very anxious time.

The greater part of our forces are detained round Paris, and the obstinate endurance of Bazaine's army —though he is now proclaimed a traitor—hindered the earlier advance of fresh troops. Meanwhile, the terrorism of the Provisional Government has contrived to work on all the good and bad qualities of the French nation—their patriotism and courage, their conceit and ignorance. Surrounded as we are by hostile bands of armed men, within the circle we have had to face desperate sorties, and treachery and surprises from without.

Now, when the whole French army has migrated, as prisoners, to Germany, there are more men under arms in France than at the beginning of the war. Belgium, England, and America supply them with weapons in abundance, and if a million were brought in to-day, within a few days we should have a million more Frenchmen to deal with, for the terrorists drag every man, up to the age of forty-six, from house and farm, from home and family, to follow the flag. That such a mode of warfare is an atrocity to the country, and inflicting its deepest wounds, is the last thing that troubles them; their first object is to secure their own power in such a way that the nation dares not question its legality. It cannot be too often repeated that we have granted full liberty of voting—the freest election, indeed, that France has ever known—even in the districts we occupy, even without an armistice and unconditionally. From the standpoint of common humanity it can only be wished that proof should be afforded that the firm determination of a whole nation can make it impossible to conquer them, that an army of the population, a "Volksheer," such as our liberals insist upon, is sufficient to protect it. The German standpoint is indeed opposed to this; and we hope to prove that the rising of a nation, even with inexhaustible resources and such patriotism as the French, cannot hold its own against a brave and disciplined army; and the cosmopolitan and philanthropist may comfort themselves for it, in the case of a recklessly provoked attack and war.

Now we have assembled our forces and accept the challenge. Something definite will probably have occurred by the time this letter reaches you. But only merciless severity will enable us to gain our ends. Fouqué tells of a knight who went about to defend and help, but every one fled before him, because, wherever he appeared, great misfortunes were sure to follow. And so it is here with the towns and their protectors, the National Guard and the Volunteers. The inhabitants of a fortress cannot complain; but when a town is nearly destroyed in the fruitless efforts of its defenders to hold it against the enemy, as was the case with Châteaubun and others, it is barbarity on the part of those protectors. Those towns which are so lucky as to have none are very well off. We have restored the railways and canals in Rheims, in order to convey coal to 40,000 factory hands; the vintage, which is very abundant, has been gathered safely, and the champagne trade is in full swing. Here in Versailles all the shops are open, the market overflowing with provisions, and the farmers ploughing in the fields. Beyond our outposts, however, lies a wilderness, created by the French themselves, of deserted houses, ruined villas, burnt palaces, and hewn-down forests. But the great fact is that an armed crowd is very far from being an army, and it is brutal to lead such men into battle. The war is ever growing more bitter and hateful. No one could long more for peace than I do, but I would never agree to a peace which, after such sacrifices, failed to insure the existence of Germany.

Much depends, however, on Germany herself. The debates in the Reichstag will be very interesting when the subject of South Germany comes under discussion.

I have only good news to give you of our relatives. Wilhelm and his squadron have at length joined the regiment, and are stationed to-day in the neighborhood of Chartres. Helmuth is with the outposts near Paris, but will be relieved in a day or two. Henry and I look him up from time to time and take him some provisions. I beg that Augusta will not worry herself about any small outlay; we have all we require; I have saved and laid by sufficient for the young generation, and we old people need not stint ourselves.

It does not matter that you should have been unable to hear beforehand of a *pension* in Switzerland. Switzerland is so thoroughly arranged for the reception of visitors, that one can always find suitable quarters. I can recommend Beaurivage—not in but below Lausanne on the lake—and more particularly the Hotel du Parc at Lugano. The journey may be a little longer, but think of German comforts under an Italian sky! It is worth much to be so near the enchanting lakes of Lombardy.

It is useless to make any plans for the future, but I hope that when the war is over, the King will allow me to rest for a while.

Henry has just returned from the outposts, having seen Helmuth, well and cheerful, engaged upon the trenches.

HELMUTH.

VERSAILLES, December 22nd, 1870.

DEAR ADOLF:

I received a postcard from Wilhelm dated the 17th. He writes from Ouzouer, near Châteaudun, and says,

"We have been fighting every day since the 2nd of December, with the exception of two days of rest. The cold in the bivouacs was really frightful. I am glad to say, however, that I am quite well, thank Heaven. The ground is so soft now, that it is almost impossible to get along; indeed, some of the horses stuck fast and had to be shot. The poor beasts are of course worn out in consequence, particularly as food is scarce. But mine are all well except the mare, which had to be shot."

His mare, the beautiful one I gave him at Nicolsburg, had to be left behind ill at Rambouillet. Well, the great thing is that the rider himself has remained unharmed. The 4th Division of Cavalry has performed wonders throughout the first half of December. Gambetta says, in some correspondence which has been captured and was certainly not arranged for the public eye, "Nous n'avions que la 17 et la 22 division devant nous, tout au plus 60,000; nous avions 200,000 et nous ne pouvions pas avancer." The truth is, General Chanzy was driven back in great disorder beyond Le Mans, and is now probably gathering the fragments of his army together in the entrenched camp at Conlie, where, for the present, we do not intend to follow him. Wilhelm will, therefore, in all probability, have a longer rest in the neighborhood of Chartres. The troops have much need of rest.

Yesterday, with great expenditure of material, the French made another unsuccessful attempt to break out. Like hens who proclaim by their cackling that they have laid an egg, the Parisians announced their intentions by a furious cannonade from all the forts. In the morning, a movement of the troops against the position of the Fourth and Fifth Corps was at once seen to mean hostilities. The preceding evening, our reserves had already been ordered to the real point of attack on the north-east. There, three whole French divisions began the attack, and were driven in at every point. By the evening we had retaken every outpost, even the most exposed, and now I am curious to see the next victorious bulletin from Paris.

Helmuth has been stationed at the outposts for the last ten days, and I have driven out several times to take him provisions. Yesterday, the forts threw 300 shells of the heaviest calibre into the ground occupied by the Fifth Corps alone; the result was one wounded fusilier. These people appear to derive a special pleasure from making a great deal of noise from behind a safe shelter, or else they must want to get rid of some of their ammunition.

I have no news yet from Helmuth, but should have heard, had anything happened to him.

However, he must be relieved one of these days, and then he can come here for a rest.

The universal longing for this terrible war to end, makes those at home forget that it has only been going on for five months. They hope everything from a bombardment of Paris. That this has not yet been done, they attribute to a delicate consideration for the Parisians, if not to the influence of personages in high places, while we only think of what is most possible and practical from a military point of view.

I have had this verse sent me by three separate persons:

> Guter Moltke gehst so stumm
> Immer um das Ding herum;
> Bester Moltke, sei nicht bumm,
> Mach' doch endlich Bum, Bum, Bum.[1]

---

* Good Moltke, you always go about things so quietly. Worthy Moltke, don't be stupid; do at last go bom, bom, bom.

What it means to attack a fortress in which an army lies ready to defend it might have been learned from Sebastopol; Sebastopol only became a fortress during the siege, all the materials could be brought up by sea, the preparations lasted ten months; the first storming cost 10,000, the second 13,000 men.

To bombard Paris, we should first have to hold the forts. Nothing has been omitted towards the employment of this forcible measure, but I look for far greater results from a slower but surer agent—hunger.

We know that for weeks, only a few gas lamps have been burned in Paris, that, in spite of the unusually early and severe winter, scarcely any of the houses are heated, as there is an absolute dearth of coal. A letter from General B. to his wife, which was captured from a balloon, gives the following prices—a pound of butter 20 francs, a fowl 20 francs; une dinde, non truffée, bien entendu, 60 to 70 francs. He describes a charming little supper: " herring with mustard sauce; then a delicious little filet de bœuf dont on faisait fête. Paul, le cuisinier avait fait des bassesses pour l'avoir, il a promis au boucher M. et Madame M. un sauf conduit pour un des forts, pour tâcher de voir les Prussiens."

These confidential communications between man and wife do more to show us the real state of affairs than any amount of newspaper reports, which always exaggerate on one side or the other. Famine is not yet within their walls, but its forerunner, high prices, is. The Rothschilds and Pereires can still get their " dindon truffé," the lowest classes are paid and fed by the Government, but the entire middle class has long been starving. Such a condition of things cannot continue for any length of time. It is true that this is assuming that we shall beat all the armies that are continually being freshly collected against us. But only the Advocates' reign of terror can succeed in getting such armies together—badly organized, without trains for supplies, and exposed to the inclemency of the weather; even without ambulances or surgeons. However patriotic and brave they may be, these unhappy creatures are incapable of contending against our well-organized, gallant troops. The hardships in the bivouacs are decimating them mercilessly, and the wounded lie by hundreds by the wayside, wholly uncared for till they are found by our ambulances, on whom the French fire. The Franctireurs are the terror of all the villages, on which they bring ruin.

But enough of these horrors! God grant a speedy and satisfactory issue to it all—and of that I have no doubts. If I am spared till the end of this war, I should like to go straight to Gastein. When the daily strain on the nerves is removed, they break down, and Gastein has been specially recommended to me for the winter. From thence I could easily reach Riva by way of the Brenner Pass, and we might perhaps meet. I hope that your girls are good climbers, and have at least gone as far as the little Protestant (Calvinist) chapel on the way to Glion, from which you have such a magnificent view of the Lake, the Rhone valley, and the Dent du Midi. Augusta is probably unequal to the climbing, but the road is quite level all the way to the Château of Chillon. Give them all my best love. I wish you all possible enjoyment of that delightful place. I hope you took maps of France with you, and that you have subscribed for the German papers. There is nothing to be got out of the French ones, while our official reports are always to be relied upon. With best wishes. Your brother,   HELMUTH.

14

VERSAILLES, February 3rd, 1871.

Who would have thought, dear Adolf, that you in Switzerland would find yourself, so to speak, at the seat of war, and yet I suppose that by this time the greater part of what was Bourbaki's army has sought refuge in this neutral territory—thus relieving us of the trouble of guarding them. You will have learned from the papers that a three weeks' armistice has been proclaimed. We occupy all the forts, and Paris itself is now merely the great prison in which we guard the captive army. No armed Frenchman may leave it, nor one of us go in.

Meanwhile we are turning the ramparts and the guns of the forts on the town, and if the truce does not end in peace, we have it in our power to reduce the proudest city in the world to a rubbish heap, besides once more stopping the supplies, which are now allowed. As all the French armies are now defeated, and we occupy a third of the whole country, we might expect to see some signs of yielding; but the French are so entirely under the dominion of tall talk, that one can answer for nothing. A dozen violent orators could persuade the whole National Assembly to the most extravagant measures. Gambetta's last edict is a proof of this, wherein, in opposition to his colleague Favre, he harps on the old string about the foreign barbarians and war *à outrance*. If only the rest of the wandering members of the Government join him, we shall soon have two governing bodies, and then twenty—which means none at all. In fact, the country is threatened with anarchy. We must therefore be fully prepared for a continuation of the war, and the exasperation of our men—already bad enough—will rise to a frightful pitch.

Henry will have told your wife that things are not nearly so bad at Nanteuil. "A rough and bloody trade is war." Fancy that Helmuth arrived with his company after a long march, foot-sore, hungry, and frozen. He had the good luck to find quarters in a beautiful villa. After a time the provision column arrived, and nothing was wanting but a fire at which to dry and warm themselves, and cook. Wood there was in plenty, but the rich proprietor had influence in high places, and had obtained an order that not a tree should be felled. Could one take it ill of the men that they cut up a few arm-chairs and pianinos?

My health keeps up wonderfully; however, when the strain is over I suppose I shall have to hurry to Gastein. I have my game of whist now every evening, since things are quieter than during the first half of the campaign. It has a very soothing effect before going to bed. Henry sends his love to you and yours, as does your brother

HELMUTH.

VERSAILLES, March 4th, 1871.

DEAR ADOLF:

I safely received your letter of the 19th from Clarens, but there was so much business on hand at the moment—some of it of a very difficult nature—and the situation was altogether so uncertain and strained, that I could not make up my mind to answer. Since then the preliminary peace has been ratified, but in such hot haste that our troops could only spend twice twenty-four hours in Paris. However, it was sufficient to have performed an *acte de presence*. The King's Regiment, which had taken a prominent part in the siege, and had been brought by rail from Orleans, only had time to join in the parade yesterday at Longchamp in the Bois de Boulogne. Helmuth is well. We only saw one another in the distance; his battalion is to be quartered here to-day. Wilhelm marched to-day to Rouen from near Lisieux, on the left bank of the Seine. You have every reason to be proud of both your boys. They have behaved well; and by the mercy of God have remained unhurt all through this bloody war, though placed in the exposed positions that usually fall to the lot of the younger officers. Henry is very well, and extremely popular with all his fellow-soldiers. He acts as my adjutant and looks after my housekeeping and accounts.

The definite conclusion of peace cannot be expected for about two months. Till then we shall continue to occupy the whole country east of the Seine and the forts round Paris. At present we can only discharge the Landwehr, and still retain half a million of soldiers in the country.

The Emperor remains with the army for a fortnight longer, in order to review the troops. He has to be in Berlin for the opening of his first Reichstag. I trust that the Commander-in-chief may not have to stay behind, but that I too may return to Berlin about the 18th of the month. I am put up for election for the districts of Haidekrug and Cleve-Geldern. The Reichstag and the return of the troops will probably keep me in Berlin till the summer, before I can go to my beloved Creisau, where I would wish to spend the few remaining days of my life. I cannot thank God enough that I have been spared to see the end of this great world-historical war. "The Lord's strength is in the weak." But I shall only really rejoice over our success when everything is over. How often it has seemed as if all were going well (as at Metz and Sedan), when suddenly something has occurred to open up the whole question afresh. We are having the most delightful spring weather, like early May at home. The little shrubs are growing green already, and I dare say that in a fortnight the cherry trees will be in blossom. And then the wonderful surroundings of the splendid capital! but covered, alas, with the remains of burnt dwellings, ruins, and hewn-down woods. But the people are already beginning to build it up again, and the wealth of the land is such that all traces of the calamities of this war will have disappeared in a few years, if they can only get a strong Government. But I do not see how any government is possible—and particularly in France—if there is to be full freedom of speech and of the press. The greatest danger now of every country lies, I suppose, in Socialism. The relations that are springing up with Austria I consider very good. Like Austria formerly, France will of course snort for revenge, but when she recovers her strength she is more likely to turn against England than against the mighty Central Power that has been formed in Europe. England will then reap the fruits of her short-sighted policy.

On the 15th of April I removed to the new headquarters for the General Staff, for the furnishing of which his Majesty has granted 12,000 thalers more; there will be plenty of room there, and I hope that you will spend the time between your return and your final establishment in Lübeck with me. I must close with best love.

HELMUTH.

FERRIERES, March 11th, 1871.

DEAR ADOLF:

I hope that you arrived safely at Arco.

The entry of the victorious army into Berlin will

take place in the first days of May, and you can be present at it; I think Ludwig will probably come too. I see, indeed, by the papers that you are standing for the 6th Holstein district against a Herr Jenssen. Should you win, you would then have to be in Berlin by the beginning of April (after a fortnight's leave, to be obtained from the President), and you could stay with me.

After to-day's conferences, I consider the last important differences as to the interpretation of the preliminary treaties to be removed, and am much relieved. Till now I have had no real satisfaction in the whole business.

I hope you had a really pleasant trip on the Lake of Como, the finest of them all, I think. How the girls must have enjoyed the oranges; what we get here are unripe stuff, but the second year's fruit is excellent.

I suppose you saw the very interesting town of Trent on the way home. I advise you to make a tour from Botzen (splendid Dolomites in the distance) to Meran —at Sterzing you will find good quarters for the night at the Elephant Hotel—then over the Brenner, spending a few days at Innsbruck (Castle Amras).

Your letter of the 2nd from Lugano (is it not lovely?) reached me while I was still at Versailles. I hope that you approve of the conditions of peace. Belfort is quite French.

You were very lucky in your journey over the Simplon. Did you notice the gigantic ivy on Isola Bella?

The Fifth Corps will leave no permanent contingent in France. It will be sent home after the peace has been definitely concluded, and the first milliard paid. You will then most likely see Helmuth in the summer at Creisau, as Leignitz is so near.

As far as our news goes, all our family are well and hearty—Helmuth on the march to Dijon. Henry joins me in love to you and yours.

HELMUTH.

BERLIN, March 21st, 1871.

DEAR ADOLF:

We regret to find from sister Augusta's letter of the 17th that illness still detains you at Lugano. Fortunately you have comfortable quarters there, and I beg you most earnestly not to hurry your departure. Even if you receive a mandate to the Reichstag, which opens to-day, I do not advise you to come before the Easter recess, which will fall early. It is sufficient if you inform the President that you have fallen ill on the journey. Here we have frost and ice at night and fires in the day-time. After having had some warm days, we have a touch of winter again, which no doubt reaches beyond the Alps; but there it is sure to turn mild and fine again soon.

Henry and I have returned safe and sound, but the peace is hardly yet to be trusted. As you must have seen from the papers, Paris is at this moment entirely in the hands of the insurgents. If the Government does not soon get the upper hand with them, and if it is true that the troops of the line are fraternizing with the rebels, France will fall a victim to anarchy. As yet they have not been able to take the matter from the right side. As far as we are concerned, the Assemblée Nationale is official France. It is the most freely elected assembly that ever was elected. The rural population and the landed proprietors are amply represented. If they give in to the Paris mob and foreign agitators, they betray their country, and only another military dictatorship could restore France to what she was. Meanwhile we remain there with 600,000 men, and only send the Landwehr home. Yesterday, fifty-six years ago, Napoleon I. landed in France from Elba; it would have been like his nephew, if under the existing circumstances, he too had performed an *acte de presence.* He, however, landed yesterday at Dover.

God be with you and restore you to health, dear Adolf. My best love to Augusta and the girls. Do not miss seeing Villa Carlotta (Sommariva).

HELMUTH.

BERLIN, March 31st, 1871.

DEAR ADOLF:

Till I received your letter of the 28th, it was not possible to give you any direct news. A fortnight ago I telegraphed to you at Arco that Jenssen had triumphed by a small majority. I thought you would be glad to know as soon as possible how you stood. Now you can at least wait in peace on the other side of the Alps till the warm weather comes, and I assure you it is abominable here. I am only sorry that your reason for a lengthened stay at Lugano should be such an unpleasant one; however, as soon as you are a little stronger you will be able to enjoy the beauty of the home journey all the more. Only do not move till you are really convalescent. We shall be delighted to receive you at the General Staff, but I hardly think I shall be able to move in before the beginning of May. The offices are nearly all removed, but the Chief's residence is not ready yet. When we shall get our troops home, it is impossible to say. The Guards and the Fifth Corps were already on their way back, when they all had to halt, and only the Landwehr was sent home. It is a great trial for us as well as France, to have 600,000 men stationed there. But with the deplorable weakness of the Government one must be prepared for everything; at any rate she has no credit, and no one will lend her the sum, without which we will not leave, so long as Paris does not surrender. On this account we have consented that 80,000 men should assemble at Versailles. But that little chattering Thiers still thinks that by proclamations and phrases, and without shedding of blood, he can reform those ruffians who have declared the Assemblée Nationale to be dissolved, have impeached its members, and threaten shortly to drive them out of Versailles. The man's vanity will not permit him to transfer the power which he does not know how to use into the hands of a capable general, without which measure there is no depending on the troops. Thus it is when dilettanti come into power. Only a dictator can bring the affairs of France to a satisfactory issue, and he would have to begin with wholesale slaughter in Paris. If no dictator can be found, civil war and anarchy are inevitable. We all send our love, and wish you a speedy convalescence, and fine weather. More details later on. HELMUTH.

(Last letter to his brother, who died at Lugano on April 7th.)

CREISAU, September 15th, 1871.

DEAR AUGUSTA:

* * * How often we recall Adolf's last visit here, and how much he enjoyed it. Altogether, it is very consoling that the evening of his completely spent life should have been so peaceful. He must have been satisfied and happy, not only with the results of the great events he was still spared to see, but particularly with the conduct of his two sons, who, by God's grace, were preserved from all harm. To expire so peacefully, surrounded by his loved ones, was indeed an

enviable end, such as one could only wish for after a long career like his, in which every duty was faithfully performed. We all send our best love, and I remain with the most heartfelt wishes, yours,

HELMUTH MOLTKE.

BERLIN, August 5th, 1874.

DEAR AUGUSTA:

It was a comfort to me to see the body of my brother Fritz once more yesterday morning; his face was so composed and peaceful, with the look of an honest man. He died in his sleep, as it would seem, like his brother Adolf, without a struggle. During his last illness, he begged me to attend to the carrying out of his last will. I have opened it in the presence of our relatives, and have acted on his instructions.

HELMUTH.

BERLIN, December 26th, 1874.

Many thanks, dear Augusta, for the very excellent portrait of my brother Adolf, with his familiar but suffering expression. It recalled him to me most vividly. I have only loving recollections of him; no discord ever marred the harmony of our relations; one could not help being fond of him. I have obtained a very good enlarged picture of my brother Fritz, and one of Marie too. They have all gone before me, because, I suppose, God was satisfied with them, and their life's work was accomplished. Yours,

HELMUTH.

BERLIN, December 7th, 1875.

Herewith, dear Augusta, I send the children the ten thalers they wished for. I possess only two pairs of boots, and all the clothing we could spare has already been given away here, where the distress is so much greater and assumes a far more terrible aspect than in the country. The demands upon those who have anything to give away are proportionately greater.

I try to the best of my ability to help the people on my estate by arrangements for the general benefit of all. Small gifts to individuals are very apt to go to the wrong person, and to relieve them of the duty laid on them by God of providing for their own families by harder work and greater economy. Poverty and distress are necessary elements in the scheme of life, —what would become of the whole social system if this stern necessity did not force men to think and work. We all send our love, and wish you a happy Christmas.

HELMUTH.

BERLIN, November 16th, 1890.

DEAR AUGUSTA:

Many thanks for the picture of my dear mother. By a curious chance the enclosed letter came into my hands at the same time, containing a touching trait of her kindness of heart.* Pray return this letter, for I

* EPPENDORF, November 12th, 1890.

HOCHGEBORNER COUNT:

Just now, when every heart is rejoicing over your Excellency's ninetieth birthday, I was reading a little memoir to my grandfather. In this it is stated that Moltke's parents were living in 1807 at Augustenhof. By my grandfather's desire I take the liberty of relating a little incident that occurred at that time.

My grandfather, Frd. Th. Mau, was born at Augustenhof on August 3rd, 1806, where his father farmed the dairy of the estate. At the New Year 1807 the farm buildings and a barn were burnt down. It was at first supposed that this had resulted from some carelessness of my great-grandmother's, in melting down lard (twenty-four pigs had been slaughtered the day before); it turned out, however, that the fire was the work of a malicious workman. My great-grandfather lost heavily—almost every-

should like to give my sister Lena the pleasure of seeing it. Lena and you are the only two survivors who knew my mother. I sent a hearty reply to my unknown octogenarian foster-brother. With renewed thanks, your old brother-in-law,

HELMUTH.

thing—in this fire; but the kindness of your Excellency's father helped him up again. He remitted half the rent and the value of the burnt corn. My great-grandmother fell very ill in consequence of the fright, and was unable to nurse my grandfather, a very delicate infant only a few months old. Here, too, the great kindness of your Excellency's mother came to the rescue; she herself nursed him for three months, and so saved his life. The sponsors named on his certificate of baptism are Major Frd. Victor von Moltke and Bernhard Paschen.

My grandfather has often related this incident, and now, in his 85th year, is a strong, sturdy old man, who, with his whole family, esteems himself happy to thank your Excellency once more for all the kindness which your Excellency's late lamented parents showed to him and his parents.

CHARLOTTE MARTENS.

III.

LETTERS TO HIS BROTHER LUDWIG.

1828 to 1888.

LUDWIG VON MOLTKE.

LUDWIG VON MOLTKE.

LUDWIG VON MOLTKE, the Field-Marshal's fourth brother,
was born in 1805. The circumstance of his parents being
obliged to change their place of residence several times during his boyhood may, perhaps, be the reason why, as a lad of
fourteen, he was sent to the house of a connection, Herr Ballhorn (Privy War-Councillor), to attend the Friedrich-Wilhelm's
Gymnasium, or College. Frau Ballhorn, his father's sister, did
her best, by faithful care, to fill the place of his mother, and
her gentle loving-kindness won his affections and undying rev-
erence and gratitude.

At the age of seventeen, Ludwig was confirmed in the
Church of the Trinity, by Friedrich Schleiermacher. The
teaching of this illustrious man had a decisive influence on
his subsequent development. In 1826, he left the college with
excellent testimonials of ability, and went to study law at the
universities of Kiel and Heidelberg. Of the many incitements
to study which both towns afforded to his natural aptitude for
learning and art, the strongest was that exerted by Professor
Thibaut, of Heidelberg. This distinguished jurist not only
assisted the young son of the Muses in his studies, but invited
him to his house, where Ludwig's remarkable musical talent
was encouraged and cultivated by the practice of classical
works. After passing a brilliant examination at Kiel in 1831,
he worked for some years in Schleswig, first in the Landes-
gericht, and then under the Government. At this time he
became engaged to Fräulein Marie von Krogh (spoken of in
the letters as Mie), the daughter of Geheimrath von Krogh;*
they were married in 1838. In 1841, having an official appointment (as *Amtmann*, or governor), at Fehmarn, he moved
to Burg, where he lived for eight years in the quiet exercise of

* Ober-Forst and Jägermeister.

his functions, to his own advantage and that of the little island he governed. There two sons and four daughters were born; both the boys unfortunately died young.

The disorders of the years 1848–50 made his duties more difficult; he held himself bound by his oath of allegiance, and maintained his post in the face of the rebellious population of the Duchies. He was therefore called away from Fehmarn in 1850, and only reinstated in office in 1853, as council (Rath) to the Lauenburg Government at Ratzeburg. This position he still held in 1864, and continued in it after the little province had become part of the kingdom of Prussia, till he retired, in 1868, from failing health. He now devoted his leisure to renewed study, but more especially to music, for which he had a passion. Numerous compositions were the outcome of these hours, as delightful to others as to himself.

As he grew old, he suffered much loss in his family circle. In 1866 he lost his wife, his worthy match in her high-minded views and superior gifts of mind. Two daughters died of lingering consumption; another left her home as a happy wife, and yet another as maid of honor; so that one alone remained with her father. But his firm faith triumphed over these and other trials. When he closed his eyes in eternal peace on August 22nd, 1889, his children could say that his course on earth had left a track of light; it was not, indeed, glorious with immortal fame, like that of his greater brother, but bright with the honor, respect, and love of all who had known him.

Though a stern sense of duty and unmovable loyalty were the foundations of his character, their transfer to the Prussian sovereign was made easier to him by the part he played in the resuscitation of his native country during the wars of 1866 and 1870–71. As a patriot, he rejoiced in the glory of United Germany; as a man, in the successes which the nation so largely owed to the brother he ardently admired and loved. He was so much accustomed to make way for him in all humility and modesty, that this slight sketch of his life would have seemed to him too insignificant, as to subject and matter, to find a place in a volume dedicated to the splendid career of his brother.

LETTERS TO HIS BROTHER LUDWIG.

OELS, August 24th (1828).

DEAR LUDWIG:

Although you say at the end of your letter that you have changed more than the world about you, it seems to me that you are in many respects just what you always were. For one thing, that you still think of me with affection, and again in your steadfast bent towards the study of *Jus*, to which, however, something must be jus' wanting when a man has to study it for its own sake, as has been your case for so many years. You yourself know how much more interesting learning becomes to us by application to the real circumstances of life, and I dare wager that you would study criminal law with far greater zeal if you were sure that, within a year, you could apply it to having a man broken on the wheel or beheaded. It also seems to me that in my beloved native land, of which I cannot help being fond, abstract learning is much less highly valued than practical skill, knowledge, and judgment; and as I credit you with these, even more

15

than with learning, I should almost advise you to try
your fortune here. I know, of course, that Ithaca is
fairer than any other land; but I can honestly say that
I would not go back to my old position for any consideration, and have never yet regretted making the
move hither. So far as I can gather, there are here
capital prospects for a man who, having studied law,
has taken up some special subject—forest-law, for instance. But, of course, an examination is insisted on,
dear Loui. And you must not give up the fiddle and
the piano; how much I should like to hear you play
again. I am now quite well-to-do; we might live
very comfortably together in Frankfort or Berlin. I
have to spend some months in each of those places. I
have a great dislike to Berlin; how much I should
prefer to settle in Frankfort, where I have lived so
pleasantly these last few years. But it lasts for only
four months, during which I can only study and ride.
It is not easy to be known in society there.

Here I am going on very well. My hosts are kindness itself. I do not know whether it is sheer vanity
which makes the society of superior people so attractive to me. This much is certain, that nowhere can
less arrogance be seen than here, and that people are
more than commonly courteous when they have a historical past and a splendid name. The Kospoths are
connected with all the princes and magnates in the
country. The day before yesterday we went to a harvest home with some of their relatives, and we danced
in the barn and had great fun. That I am happy you
may be sure, as I have been writing verses. I will
send them to you all hot, as they have just flowed
from my pen, as soon as I have told you that the
young countess left home yesterday with her friend, a
girl of whom she is very fond, that she is to be back

to-day, and that we have often swung them together
in the same swing.

Räthsel.

Ein Bild des Lebens ist's, des regen Lebens,
Das aufwärts bald uns treibt und wieder abwärts strebt,
Das wie des Herzens Hoffen, wie unstätes Sehnen
Jetzt sinkt, jetzt steigt und schwindelnd hoch uns hebt.
Es trägt Euch unter Blüthenzweige.   Staunend
Schaut über Wald und Flur der Blick. — Es schwebt
Auf Sturmesschwingen fort. — Doch in dem Augenblicke,
Wo Ihr am höchsten steht, zieht's wieder Euch zurücke.
Und wie ein rastlos Herz durch Freude, Hoffnung, Bangen
Führt's doch am Ende nur, von wo Ihr ausgegangen.

Dort sah ich jüngst zwei liebliche Gestalten,
Sie waren ineinander eng verschlungen.
Die Arme auf der luft'gen Bahn umrungen,
Schien eine stets die andere zu halten.

Ein leichter Nachen trug sie auf den Wogen
Mit flatternden Gewändern, wall'nden Haaren;
Und wenn es nicht zwei holde Engel waren,
So hatten Engelsbande sicher sie umzogen.

Durch die Orangenreihen blick' ich wieder,
Der Himmel hüllt uns rings in Wolkenschleier.
„Sie sind getrennt schon!“ rauscht der Pappeln Wehn,
Aus blauen Augen fallen Thränen nieder,
Ein Strahl nur aus des Abendrothes Feier
Scheint mir ein Bild von bald'gem Wiedersehn.*

* The verses are a transparent enigma as follows:

An image this of life, uncertain life
Tossing us skywards and then downwards tending—
Of hope, of varying hope and fond desire,
Which drags us down or lifts to giddy heights.—
It leads you into leafy shades.   Amazed
The eye looks down on wood and plain.   Aloft
Upon the pinions of the storm you fly
Till, at the highest, suddenly cast down.
Or, like a restless heart, you are led on,
Through joy, hope, fear—to end where you began.

But lately two fair forms I there beheld
Clinging together in a close embrace.

I must now tell you of a terrible adventure which befell me. Lately, as I was coming home, my servant made the preposterous demand that a wagon with a fine team of oxen should get out of his road. The beasts were not at all inclined to accede to so monstrous a request, and the amiable brutes ran at him with such effect that the paper on my plane table, which my valiant henchman very cleverly used as a buckler in this tilting bout, was accurately divided into two triangles, making two drawings instead of one; the compass was a ruin, and the work, which was almost finished, had to be copied all over again. For a week I have done nothing but plan roads, build houses, and plant trees without end.

Now adieu, dear Loui.

BERLIN, November —th, 1828.

Your welcome letter, dear Ludwig, reached me at Briese, where my stay was prolonged till my return to Berlin. Well written as it is, and full of interest, I cannot be wholly convinced, by the reasons you adduce, that it is better for you not to come here. It almost reminds me of what Falstaff says of reason and

> Their arms entwined, each seemed the other's guide
> And partner as they went their merry way.
> A fragile bark bore them across the waves
> With flutt'ring robes and loosely streaming hair;
> And if they were not angels, as they seemed,
> Angelic love had surely linked their hearts.
>
> I look again beyond the orange grove,
> Clouds gather round us now and shroud the sky;
> "Alas for they must part!" the poplars wail.
> From those blue eyes the heavy tear-drops fall;
> Yet, from the sunset glow, a radiance smiles
> The promise that they soon shall meet again.

blackberries.* However, I cannot try to persuade you to take a step where, as I cannot deny, there are so many difficulties in the way; and the man who fails of the fortune he has run after is certainly ten times more disappointed than he who waits for it to come to him.

In spite of your contentment under the rule of the Skjoldings, I perceive by your sighing that you are not quite happy about its legal institutions. "Law and rights are inherited like hereditary disease; they are handed down from generation to generation and silently spread from place to place." But if Lübeck law and Danish law, and Christian V.'s law and Waldemar's law, and Jutland law, and Heaven knows what other law, are equally law, your hair will stand on end with law.

However, dear Ludwig, if you think that by strenuous industry you can have done with work in a few years and then be free to do what you will, believe me, you will lose the enjoyment of those years only to buy a few others when you are past enjoyment. Do not rush into extremes. Between Gaius and the pandects play a few of Rode's variations, and if possible turn the pandects into rhyme. For you seem fully to have recognized how imperatively and seriously necessary it is that we should make our own way in life. The time soon passes during which a man looks out on life as a landscape, and a fair one, where all that is loveliest, though unseen, lies, he knows, behind the mist which still veils it. But to cross it he must choose a road; and once started, no return, no deviation is possible. Onwards, then, and God grant that our ways may sometimes run so near that from time to time we may clasp hands.

* "If reasons where as plentiful as blackberries, I would give no man a reason upon compulsion."—F., "King Henry IV.," Part I.

I often go to the play. I saw yesterday a performance of Don Giovanni; only think, for the first time. Fancy yourself in the splendid opera-house. Not a seat is vacant, not even the last seats to close the gangways. Spontini, the king of harmony, appears in the conductor's chair, his hair elaborately curled; he looks about him, sees all in perfect order, raises the ivory wand, and the grand overture bursts out—now a broad stream flowing on, solemn and calm, then swelling and rising to a torrent which only such an orchestra can give out, then thundering like a cataract which sweeps everything before it. The overture is loudly applauded, Apollo and his companions aloft express their approval, and Wauer comes forward as Leporello. Blume presently follows, elect by nature to play Don Juan, with Madame Schütz, who puts enough passion at any rate into the part of Donna Anna. Bader is the Ottavio, so you may imagine the divine duet " Dein Gatte wird Vater dir auch sein." The queenly Milder, as Elvira, joined her voice to the other two in the incomparable trio of Masks, and to crown all, Schätzel was the Zerlina. You will have read of her in the papers. I like her better than Sontag. In short, it was admirable throughout down to Gern (junior) as the Sbirro, and Blume had to reappear and bow to the shouting crowd after the devil had fetched him away.

You would find Berlin much altered if you could see it. The amount of building is incredible; I will take you through long streets and squares, till you will hardly be able to guess where you are. I greatly miss the society which I so thoroughly enjoyed during the last two years of my stay in Frankfort. Perhaps, too, because I there played a more important part, for *qui brille au second rang s'eclipse au premier.* I do not frequent Court circles; I never did but from vanity, to feel that I had been there; now I am wiser, and so more contented.

P.S.—November 15th.—Apropos, go out to Nienhof one day, with Wilhelm or Adolf; you will be affectionately received and make some very pleasant acquaintance. The society of the landed aristocracy of Holstein is, I think, the pleasantest to be had there. Our nearest neighbor was a Count Reichenbach, the owner of the hereditary estates of Goschütz. He had there an admirable Kapellmeister and some excellent musicians; he made all his household employés, vassals, etc., practice as an orchestra, and often performed operas in a magnificent music-room. I have heard the Berggeist there and Jessonda.* The part of Jessonda was sung by a Countess Götzen, who had such a voice as is rarely heard.

I must now close, for I am quite stupefied with much writing. Adieu, dear Ludwig. Yours,

HELMUTH.

No date (Early in March, 1829).

Vom Opfer der Atriben im gülb'nen Opernsaal
Eil' ich zu beinen Freuben, bu ftilles Rosenthal.

(From the sacrifice of the Atrides in the gilded opera-house I fly to thy delights, peaceful vale of roses.) Or, though not to the poetical land of the vine and the troubadour, to my own snug little room, where I try to conjure up such poetical ideas as a second lieutenant can invent without the aid of wine. Now let me tell you what has happened to me since I received your letter this afternoon. After seeing five acts of a French play in less than two hours, I hurried off to B.'s to give as little offence as possible by my late

---

* Operas by Spohr.

appearance. However, I was there early enough to arrive before the play began, and to see " Trau, schau, wem!" a piece in which I myself rehearsed any number of times some years ago, which fate has condemned me to see on every amateur stage, and which I could repeat by heart backwards. The piece plays at least two hours; the interval is still going on; and how long the second piece will play Thalia only knows, and she may have my place to see it. I have got myself into my sky-blue dressing-gown, and am munching a crust of bread and butter with a sigh of relief. I had no mind to be verse-making there, I can tell you.

How much more delightful is the society of your thoughts; and I thank you sincerely, dear Loui, for writing to me so unreservedly, irrespective of our difference in age or of the bent which education and circumstances have necessarily given our characters. This, however, only refers to you. As I had no education but thrashing, I have had no chance of forming a character. I am often painfully conscious of it. This want of self-reliance and constant reference to the opinions of others, even the preponderance of reason over inclination, often give me moral depressions, such as others feel from opposite causes. They were in such a hurry to efface every prominent characteristic, every peculiarity, as they would have nipped betimes every shoot of a yew-hedge, that the result was weakness of character, the most fatal of all.

And this is associated with an innate element of sensitiveness, of scorn of the ignoble, nay of pride, which has often carried the frail vessel out on to stormy waters, where it has obeyed the caprice of the waves rather than the compass; it is the most reckless rider that ever spurred a weary steed to a daring leap, and then fallen shattered by its collapse; it is the fire of an air balloon, that one moment carries it to the clouds, only to fall into unknown depths.

If there is anything complimentary to myself in this, it is not meant so. How I envy almost every other man!—sometimes for their very faults, for their sternness, indifference, and rectitude—and this brings me back to you.

That you should get plenty of amusement out of society in the midst of your studies, which I know you steadily pursue, I think quite right. You yourself objected to Chesterfield, of whom I know a little, on the ground that he is principally useful where he is least used. In my experience, flattery is always well received when it comes from the heart; if it does not, it must at least be ingenious. Dullards and lovers are content with good intentions, coquettes insist on the performance. The worst to deal with are *passées* beauties, but one takes care not to get into that dilemma. But flattery may also be one reason why such simple men are often successful in society. I am reminded of some lines by one of my comrades.

> Da tritt ein alberner Junge mit vielem Lärmen ein,
> Die Andern verstummen Alle, man hört nur ihn allein.
> Er faselt von seiner Stute und vom Trakehner Hengst,
> Und wie er mit einer Kugel zwei Hasen schoß unlängst.
> Er sprengte im letzten Jahre zweimal im Bade die Bank,
> Sein Vater hat zwei Majorate und liegt gefährlich krank.
> Da wenden die Augen der Damen' sich schmachtend nach ihm um:
> Er erbt zwei Majorate, und ist so göttlich dumm!

I am now reading, with the greatest pleasure, Heine's "Reisebilder," of which I told you. They are quite admirable, and full of wit and talent. It is a great pity that the author's individuality is not more pleasantly revealed, for his utter atheism and equal vanity and discontent are unmistakable.

28th.—I am just setting out for Frankfort; a case with almost all my possessions is already gone, and I no longer feel at home in my little room. So my thoughts have gone before me, and that makes letter-writing difficult. I am very glad to go back to Frankfort, partly because I am known there, partly because the spring is very pleasant there in the midst of endless orchards, partly, too, because it is again a change. At the end of May I shall be out on survey again, either at Posen, or in Swedish Pomerania. I am travelling to Frankfort, *extra post*, with Studnitz, but it is very difficult to get there; the mail from Breslau was upset five times on its last journey. The snow is still five feet deep, and I only pray that the Oder will wait till I am safe in Frankfort before it carries away the bridges.

Now, adieu, dear Ludwig; I wish that, instead of writing, we could for once have a good talk. Till then, however, do not forget this, the only way of communicating with me; and though it is sad to have to transmit one's thoughts by panting horses instead of winged words, not to get an answer till you have forgotten the question, and still more, to speak of past and present when the writer's present must be the recipient's past—in spite of all this, and the fact that this transmission of ideas costs six silver groschen for freight, it is the only means of communication, so I beg you make diligent use of it. Farewell, dear Ludwig, so arrange your life in Kiel that your good spirits, industry, conscience, and verse-making go hand in hand. If you go home, greet them all from your very loving brother,

HELMUTH.

BERLIN, January 13th, 1830.

DEAR LUDWIG:

It is certainly a bad business to be compelled to finish a piece of work within a fixed and limited time; and I need not say so to you who, by Michaelmas, neither sooner nor later, must not only have amassed a considerable quantum of legal knowledge, but have so pigeon-holed and ticketed it as to be able to bring out and display the required article at any moment, were it the oldest stock in the shop. Thus, and perhaps worse, is it with my letter, which shall be written to-day, neither sooner nor later, though not a single pen will mark, and my thoughts will wander from the matter in hand, as I am interrupted every instant.

* * * It does one good every two or three years to feel once more that there is such a place as home; although, to tell the truth, the story of little Töffel always recurs to my mind; for some folks can never quite forget the old Töffel, however hard the new Töffel may try to improve on him.

Here is something that occurred to me in the coach, but the person who speaks is by no means to be identified with the author. You must find out for yourself who it is.

Ihr tabelt mich, daß ich oft störrisch schweige,
Der glatten Welt die düst're Stirne zeige,
Daß ich nicht so, nicht tief genug, mich neige.
Den dürft'gen Scherz, Ihr wollt's, soll ich belachen,
Soll, welche Qual, wohl selber Späße machen,
Wenn mir der Sinn so voll von ander'n Sachen!
Und Ihr habt Recht! Man wird es bitter tabeln,
Daß ich das Flache, Niedrige nicht abeln,
Daß ich wie And're oft nicht benken kann,
Daß ich der Tonkunst göttlich hohes Walten
Zu hoch für seichten Spott wie Lob zu halten
Mich dreist erkühnt. — Wahr ist's, ich hab's gethan!
Allein, ich wollte Niemand damit kränken,
Kann dieses Herz nicht immer klüglich lenken.

Und wie sie hart dagegen auch verfahren,
Das inn're Heiligthum, ich will's bewahren.
Glückselig wohl, wenn sich ein Wesen findet,
Das mich versteht, das eng sich mir verbindet.
Und kann's nicht sein — o laßt mit mir vergeh'n,
Was außer mir doch Keiner mag versteh'n.

Farewell, dear Loui, remember me kindly in your thoughts, and when you have time and inclination write to me from your cozy room, among your books under the lamplight.   With sincere affection, yours,

HELMUTH.

BERLIN, March 7th, 1831.

DEAR LUDWIG:

I received the few lines from you enclosed in, or rather enclosing, mother's letter, and read them with much pleasure. It is a sad pity that we are each stuck so fast to our respective little clods, and that the ideas which arise so easily in familiar intercourse have first to be painfully put into words, and then still more painfully, not to say illegibly, committed to paper. How I should enjoy such a chat with you one evening, as we had last winter in Kiel, but, for the present, that is out of the question.   As regards myself, I am saving up the proceeds from my scribbling to buy a horse in case of war. As I ought—supposing I am on the General Staff—to have five, I leave it to Heaven to discover where they are to come from.   Even in peace I require three, and I have only written enough for half a horse as yet.

It amuses me very much, when any little articles of mine are in the magazines, to watch the faces of the readers at Stehely's. They would hardly recognize your obedient servant in the worthy author, for these children of my fancy, or rather of my necessity, are all running about the world unfathered. If peace continues in this beautiful world, I shall *camminare nel giardino dell' Europa* and see Rome and Naples—that I am determined on.

You, I suppose, are preparing yourself with all your might for the perillous risks of a Danish examination. In this respect, his Danish Majesty is much to be envied. As the duties there of the County Court and the Government often fall to the share of one person in the shape of some "right honorable" (*sic*) magistrate's secretary; as the State pays its servants so incredibly little, and yet—by reason of the competition —may require of them such an enormous amount of talent and knowledge, it ought properly to have nothing but Cannings and Pitts for its assessors and referendaries. I hope with all my heart you may get through this purgatory quickly and successfully. I have been wandering about here for the last week in the character of a royal, Prussian, exceedingly lengthy topographer, with another officer, the only examples of our species. The office being broken up, all my colleagues have returned to their garrisons, and my friends being thus scattered to the four winds from Nimmersatt to Trier, I find myself almost reduced to my own agreeable society, which, between ourselves, I could wish were more agreeable.

One of the greatest pleasures of Berlin is the Museum, which has only been opened since you left. I would spend an hour there daily, if I had not to be at the office of the General Staff every day till 2 o'clock. I shall not describe the outside of this magnificent building; it has been lithographed, engraved, painted on tea-trays and embroidered in beads, till one could fill the entire Museum with good and bad pictures of itself. Should you, however, as an uninitiated person, care to glance into this palace full of the wonders of ancient and modern art, let me invite you to mount the broad flight of stone steps to the gigantic colonnade, where the first thing you will notice is the change in the appearance of the Lustgarten. This square, where the recruits used to stand in long rows balancing themselves on one leg, is now laid out in regular grass-plots, surrounded by iron railings and wire-fencing, and intersected by broad paved walks. In the middle stands the fountain, from which an immense jet of water, driven by a forcing-engine at the Werder Works, is to spring. At the foot of the steps is the pedestal for a colossal vase twenty-four feet in diameter, made of a single block of stone. It is the largest known, and a machine worked by steam has been cutting it for two years. The long rows of poplars were dug up in the winter and planted in a thick group in front of the cathedral, in order to hide that hideous building, which looks more like a Casino than a church. Even old Dessauer marched over one fine night from the Lustgarten to the Wilhelmsplatz. The other brave generals must have been much surprised next morning to find a sixth in their party, and that the inventor of the iron ramrod, whose patent was fifty years older than their own. How particularly embarrassing for poor Schwerin to be standing there, in such an exceedingly unorthodox costume, his pigtail all untied, sandals instead of gaiters, and no trousers at all. But the old Field-Marshal still holds the flag in his hand, as he did when he so gallantly stormed the Austrian batteries, and when only the fourth bullet that struck him brought him to a stand-still—or rather to a lie-still—but could not make him yield.

But I forgot that I had left you standing at the door.

It is by such a flight of steps and through such rows

of pillars that one ought to enter a hall like the one
before us.   It is of the height of two stories, and finally
rises above the building in a splendid cupola.   Floor
and walls are of cement, inlaid with mosaic.   Half-way
up, a gallery runs round it, supported on pillars of
yellow marble.   The light falls from above upon a
great circle of antiques, which had lodged till now
under the ruins of the Camp Vaccino, in half-buried
baths, or at the bottom of the Tiber; for Mother Earth
was the Museum in which these art treasures sought
refuge from Vandalism till they awoke once more to
the light of day in these wonderful halls.   Meanwhile
these high and mighty Olympian dignitaries had
suffered severe losses in the matter of their divine
arms and legs during their 2000 years' incognito underground, and it was highly necessary to set them on a
modern footing by supplying them with the missing
noses, ears, fingers, and so forth.   And Kronos, the
mighty monarch, even after being repaired, is but an
emigrant reinstated in his titles; for what relation
indeed can there be between these old gods and the
new world which wonders at them?   The crowd sees
little beyond the hewn stone, looks up in the catalogues
the sum paid for it, and cannot for the life of it understand how they came to put those beautiful smooth
feet and arms on the yellow, mouldering torsos.   On
the other hand, if Aphrodite were to meet one of our
charming Berlin ladies with gigot sleeves that make
her double her width, and stays that cut her in half,
her hair dressed à la chinoise, her boas, shawls, etc.,
would she not say like the Indian when he first saw a
European, "Is that all you?"   In our law-abiding
country, Pan would be carried off to Strausburg for
a vagabond, or made to enlist in the Landwehr as of
doubtful origin, and Diana arrested in any forest for

infringing the game laws. What with duties and the excise, Bacchus has almost become a stranger with us, or has, at least, been brought into disrepute by the dreadful productions of "Mont vert" on the Oder. Though his cult is still kept up, his most ardent worshippers come, all too frequently, in collision with the police, long scores, watchmen, and other calamities. Even Ceres has been brought so low by the existing corn prices, and particularly the malt-tax, that if the potato crops did not make up for everything she would get no credit anywhere, not even with Privy Councillor Thaer * at Möglin. Our young people know more of the Messenger of the gods than is good for them, but he may consider himself lucky to have found such a comfortable berth here, for, under the existing postal system, Herr von Nagler would never have entrusted even the most unimportant office to his care.—I would gladly have taken you up to see the pictures, which interest me still more, but we must leave that for another time. Good-bye.

HELMUTH.

BERLIN, January 12th, 1832.

DEAR LUDWIG:

Many thanks for your letter of the 9th, which I received to-day; but first of all, let me congratulate you heartily on your accession to office and dignity. Though it is no doubt most ungenerous of the State to ask you to give your services for nothing, it must always count for something that you should be able to advance in your profession without leaving home. I hope that you may speedily be chosen councillor, for your King perhaps pays better for advice than for work.

---

* Thaer, a celebrated agriculturist, who had a model farm at Möglin, near Wrietzen.

With regard to my translation of Gibbon, I have a proposal to make to you: that you should share the trouble and the proceeds of it, always supposing that your new circumstances leave you any time over for your own occupations, and that you care to employ it in such work. In the event of your accepting, I must first remark that the work is not of my choosing, but was formally offered me by Fincke, the publisher, who wrote to me, after I had sent him the two first chapters as sample translations: "My offer is based on opinion that it is of more importance to you to produce a work which will further the interests of learning than to receive a large sum for it. If the book is to find readers, the chief points to be considered are a low price, an attractive appearance, and the speedy publication of the entire work. Under these circumstances, and after the most careful calculations, I find that I am in a position to offer you the sum of 500 thalers when the book comes out, and a further sum of 250 thalers after the sale of 500 copies, which sum, as I am well aware, is not in any way equivalent to the magnitude of the labor."

The chief drawback to our both doing it would be, that the publisher objects to a translation by two people, as interfering with the unity of the style. This would, no doubt, be difficult to achieve by two writers, but not, I think, impossible, and for the following reason. Gibbon's style is of that nature that one's best plan is to render it literally, even to the division of paragraphs. The striking affinity between the English and German languages makes this quite feasible, and thus the two parts of the translation will be very similar, because, to express myself mathematically, two quantities that are equal to a third are also equal to one another. To make this similarity quite

16

perfect, we should only have to agree upon certain details. For instance, Gibbon employs an overflow of adjectives, the outcome, as I take it, of a profound knowledge of his sources. From these he derives the characters of the persons he refers to, but this is not evident in his text, and as all the readers of Gibbon have not Gibbon's learning, the epithets are often unfamiliar, and seem contradictory, and rather weaken the effect than otherwise. Such adjectives I have taken the liberty of omitting altogether, and in fact, have made it a general rule not to translate anything which appears obscure or doubtful. In conclusion, such frequently recurring terms as officer, lieutenant, company, when alluding to the Romans, must be translated by "Befehlshaber, Legat," etc., and the English measurements and currency done into German. In this way I think there will be no visible difference in our work.

Now as to the disadvantages of the undertaking, they are firstly, secondly, and thirdly—the loss of time. With the magnitude of the task always confronting me, I have translated hitherto (since the New Year twelve chapters, over 600 pages) with a certain nervous rapidity, and have arrived at the conclusion that by exerting the utmost diligence and speed—unfortunately more than is prudent—a volume may be finished every four weeks (I of course take into consideration that one has other business to attend to), which would bring the work to an end, supposing it were possible to continue at that rate, in a year. As to difficulties, to be frank, I have so far met with none. Although my whole acquaintance with the English language was gained by a four months' course of lessons and the reading of a few novels, I translate more easily from the English than the French, which I think I know pretty well. The relationship between the two languages assists one so much, that one need hardly read the sentences through, the German ending fits on so easily to the English beginning. I might almost say that with the translation it is more important to know your German thoroughly than to literally understand the English (I mean, one must have the construction, turns and idioms of the German language at one's fingers' ends). As to the English, I am convinced, from what I saw when we were together, that you know ten times more of it than I do, which is neither meant as a compliment to you, nor can be, after what I have already said.

The translations which I have to refer to are one by Wenk, 1788, continued by Schrieber, and one by C. W. v. R., 1789. A complete translation of the whole work does not exist. The latter serves me as a dictionary. It is a literal translation of the words in their original sequence, and therefore very convenient for my purpose, but otherwise unintelligible. The other is a freer and better translation, but the German is often very bad and the style always clumsy. However, it must not be forgotten that, in fifty years, the constant development of the language would be sure to make a German book sound awkward and unfamiliar.

Any other difficulties, drawbacks, or "buts," I am happy to say, I have not found. Should these not frighten you away, you can take for your share, whichever part interests you most. I should be very pleased if you happened to choose the part relating to the laws, as that would present great difficulties to me, which I should probably be unable to overcome without assistance. All the books, the original and the translations, that you cannot get where you are, I can send you; and at the same time a chapter or two of my own translation, because similarity is more important than superiority. From what the publisher promises, you will see that the pay for each part would be about sixty thalers, which might after all be an inducement to you, as you are making nothing at present. If all turns out well, let us follow in the train of the Goths and Vandals and fix a rendezvous in ancient Roma, who after her "Decline and Fall" still is the queen of the world (*sic*). My longing to go there increases with every chapter, and I shall not rest until I have made that journey.

Two free copies of my "Internal Condition of Poland" have been sent off to-day to the booksellers in Kiel and Schleswig, from whom you can get them.

Good-bye, dear Ludwig. Think over my proposal and tell me what you decide. I should be very glad to come into communication with you by these means, and to have your assistance in a work that is almost too much for me. Yours,

HELMUTH.

The following letters only begin again after his return from Turkey.

BERLIN, April 8th, 1840.

DEAR LUDWIG:

The changes in the army, of the 30th, have not resulted in my having to leave Berlin, so I have made myself a little more at home. I now repeat my invitation to you to spend a few weeks here. My apartment is one of the pleasantest in Berlin, and you shall have your own room and a separate entrance. In front of your window you have the beautiful "bowling green" with flowering shrubs, into which they have converted the Leipziger Platz since you were here. The Potsdamer Thor is only fifty paces off, and the really much improved Thiergarten, which is decking itself with green for your reception, is in the immediate neighborhood. If the weather is bad there is a riding-school just at the back of the house; and if it is fine, you can have capital Arabs and ride out. Fifteen cabs stand ready under your windows from morning till night, in case you prefer to drive, and at the Struve Establishment you can get every kind of mineral water just as good as at its own source. The Royal Library is open to you, and there are theatres and concerts in plenty.

I shall probably be put upon the General Staff of the Fourth Army Corps one of these days. Prince Carl of Prussia, who is at the head of it, lives here in Berlin. Yours,

HELMUTH.

My address is: Leipziger Platz, No. 15; it is in the Fürstenberg Riding School, ground floor, right-hand side.

BERLIN, March 19th, 1842.

DEAR LUDWIG:

Although I am looking forward to seeing you soon here, I cannot put off thanking you for your kind letter of the 8th. I am extremely pleased to hear that you like your official post. I understand it perfectly and envy you for it, for that is one of the chief conditions of happiness. How I should like to see you established some day in one of the old castles—Cismar or Travendahl, with Mie,* the picture of a *dame chatelaine*, and the little ones, whether boys or girls. We poor military men never have such prospects. I could sing with the Jubel lieutenant:

> "For twenty years of thrashing empty straw,
> I have earned 17 thalers, 25 groschen." †

---

* Pet name in the family for Marie, née v. Krogh, Ludwig von Moltke's wife.

† So hab' ich zwanzig Jahre leeres Stroh gedroschen
Für 17 thaler 25 groschen.

How gladly would I settle myself under your jurisdiction on a little farm, at Stocksee or some such little estate. But these are dreams that one puts off and puts off, till suddenly there is an end of all things. We are carried along by the force of circumstances; we think that we drive, and we find that we are driven.

It surely is not right of you to put away all thought of poetry for years to come. For poetry is only possible "while the world is seen through an airy veil— when every bud conceals a wonder, and every vale is filled with blossom, when we have nought and yet enough—we thirst for truth, yet delight in illusion." *

But illusion passes away and truth becomes sterner, till at last one becomes so sensible that one ends by throwing all one's youthful enthusiasms overboard as mere moonshine. My translations are purely matter of fact; all that is necessary is knowledge of one's own language. As translations yours are inferior to mine, but as poetical conceptions they stand immeasurably higher. They may not be true to the original, but are always works of art, and certainly deserve to be added to and given to the. public.

However, the technical difficulties in the way of translating from English into German are great, and in the case of Byron often insurmountable. This lies in a certain deficiency of beauty in the English language, which, however, becomes of advantage to it in its predominance of monosyllabic words (some Frenchman has called English *le chinois européen*). It is generally impossible to reproduce in a German line of five or six

---

* Wenn Nebel noch die Welt verhüllen,
Die Knospe Wunder noch verspricht,
Wenn man die tausend Blumen bricht
Die jedes Thal uns reichlich füllen:
Dann hat man nichts und doch genug,
Den Durst nach Wahrheit und die Lust am Trug.

words, the sense of an English one of double or three times that number.

I am looking forward with great pleasure to the approaching family congress. Only once before in our lives, at Eutin, have we all met together—as we can never do again, one of us having been already called away. We cut our names in a beech, which I could find again at any moment. God grant nothing may come between. I received a letter from my father a little while ago, in which he tells me he had been threatened with a stroke. He had to be bled at once, but seems to have quite recovered. Yours,

HELMUTH.

BERLIN, December 9th, 1842.

DEAR LUDWIG:

You have our deepest sympathy in the severe loss which you and your dear good wife have sustained. Only time can soften the first bitterness of your grief. May the rest of the children soon recover. * * *

My father complains very much in his last letter about his rheumatism. When he was here in Berlin, he was so well and in such good spirits that we were delighted. I very much hope that he will come to us next year on a long visit. We get on with him capitally, especially Marie, who has the charming quality of never taking anything amiss, as it never occurs to her that any one should suspect her of wishing them ill. Marie is a wonderful little woman. It is impossible not to get on with her; she is perfectly tempered (*sic*), and fits into her new circumstances admirably. She has been presented at Court by a lady of high rank, and made her *début* in society yesterday. It is too early to say whether she will please; at all events, she is very elegant. Her equable good humor is inexhaustible. Though you are in grief, dear Ludwig, it will please you, I am sure, to know that we are happy.

If your business permits of it, you really ought, for your poor wife's sake, to come to us this winter. I could send a carriage and horses to meet you at the Mecklenburg frontier. Do not hesitate to bring the children with you, we have room for you all; and think what a pleasure it would be to us. In faithful affection, yours,

HELMUTH.

BERLIN, April 13th, 1844.

DEAR LUDWIG:

This year we have a grand Review at Halle, so that I cannot get away till October. After last year's experiences, I dare not go to the Baltic or the North Sea for baths at that season, and that is why I thought of Nice, where I could bathe in the winter. Another plan was to go to England in October, where one can still take sea baths, especially in the Isle of Wight. We should take that opportunity of seeing London and something of old England. I cannot say yet which of these plans, or indeed, if either of them can be carried out, and I find it very hard to choose between the palm groves of Aquitaine and the art treasures of Britain. Marie would probably prefer England, and of course we could only make this expensive journey so long as there are no children, who would either have to be left behind, or make it still more expensive for us. One can always manage to get to the South, and I think we might some day go together to Switzerland, and to the orange gardens of the West. Next year we shall be able to travel by rail from my door to Zurich, into the heart of the Swiss Alps. Even now, one can go in a single day from here to Zwickau by Leipzig and Altenburg, a distance of fifty miles [about 234 English miles], for a few thalers. In three years there will, in all probability, be an unbroken line of railway from Kiel by Hamburg, Berlin, Frankfort, Breslau, Brünn, Vienna, Triest, Venice, Milan. This is no chimerical prospect; the line is partly finished, partly in process of construction. Ninety miles [about 421 English miles] of it can already be used. That is what we are doing in Germany. While the French Chambers are still engaged in discussing the matter, we have paid down three hundred miles of railway, and are working at two hundred more.

Amongst the latter is the Hamburg-Berlin line, to whose board of directors I belong. The greatest difficulty that we have still to contend with is the Danish Government. It wants to force us into keeping along the Elbe and through Lauenburg, which would cost us two million thalers more than the route we had chosen by Schwarzenbeck. There is some talk of a deputation to Copenhagen, in which I am to take part, but the matter may yet be settled by diplomacy. Meanwhile we have begun the line in Heaven's name, and intend it to be finished in 1846. We shall look forward to a visit from you then, if not sooner.

I wish you could spend a few weeks with us at some time. I am sure you would like our house. The balcony is a great comfort. The bushes are beginning to sprout, the fat chestnut buds are opening, and in a week the fruit trees will be in blossom. Does the sun ever shine where you are? I cannot imagine Fehmarn, except with the foaming waves beating against it, and wrapt in a cloud of hail and sleet. And yet I can quite well believe that you can be very happy there, and I would change places with you without a moment's hesitation. It must be a great pleasure to you to have your island in such good order, to make roads, administer justice, and ride about the country hunting foxes. I suppose it is not always the same as on that day, when we had to hold on to the bathing-machine as we were going down to the water. When the limes are in blossom in Burg, and the sun sinks into the sea, your island kingdom no doubt looks quite pleasant, and at any rate your home affords you all the comfort that the country cannot.

The want of literary or artistic intercourse must be a great privation. Have you not even a book-society for getting new things? I must buy Herodotus—a pity I did not have him with me in Asia. In that respect, I was in the same position on the banks of the Euphrates as you are on the shores of the Baltic. You ask about my literary productions. Besides a few contributions to the *Allgemeine Zeitung*, I have written an article upon railways, and have just finished a description of the Russo-Turkish War of 1828. The manuscript has been submitted for approval. But it is very difficult to find a publisher for military works. They have such a small circle of readers, and are so expensive on account of the necessary maps which accompany them, that one gets very little for them. If I make a tour in the autumn, I shall, no doubt, gather materials for a short book. Travelling always rouses my desire for writing, which is apt to slumber in every-day life. Affectionately yours, HELMUTH.

BERLIN, December 25th, 1844.

DEAR LUDWIG:

I received yesterday your pleasant letter of the 18th, so it is but fitting that I should to-night—in spite of the echoes of Christmas revelry—send good wishes for your birthday, and a post-horn full of good news to the sea-washed town which you and yours seem to have grown to, as a snail grows to his shell. That is, in fact, a good thing; and I understand it in you, since you have there found suitable employment, and wield your ruling trident with success over the Obotrites who inhabit your island. But Mie, I should have thought, would have climbed now and again to the highest summit of the island, to gaze at the beech groves on the mainland, her soul " seeking her native land." But a wife's native land is home; *ou est-ou mieux qu'au sein de sa famille.* I believe, too, that in time one ceases to be sea-sick when the island rocks in a violent storm. Besides, there is every likelihood of Fehmarn being frozen in this winter, so that you will easily skate across to your nearest neighbors on the mainland—Ehlersdorf, Cismar, and so on. I am glad that the mild climate of Fehmarn should have tempted some families thither from Holstein—besides the young preachers, who, like iron, pervade all nature, even to meteoric stones—to establish themselves under your sceptre, for I had been wishing you had some society. If, after all, you would like to exchange your governor-ship for the post of Major in the Royal General Staff of Prussia, cedo Major*em*—which means I will give you my place and take yours, all the more readily because you will ere long be enthroned no doubt at Travendahl, Gottorp, or some other castle in pretty Holstein, where you will like yourself exceedingly. I should like to take you round my room to see all my Christmas boxes; there is not a more splendid sight in the two hemispheres. * * * (He here enumerates several presents, and gives a description of the opera-house at Berlin, then just re-built and re-opened.)

BERLIN, February 5th, 1845.

DEAR LUDWIG:

Capital news from you has just reached us. A Moltke at last! How the old father will triumph! But not even for the christening can he travel in this severe weather, and for the summer he has unfortunately planned a long tour to Marseilles and Nice. A thousand congratulations to you and Mie. We shall all of us certainly take to our hearts this single man-child of our numerous race, and help him forward in life to the best of our power. I have none but good news. * * * Affectionately yours,

HELMUTH.

BERLIN, May 30th, 1845.

DEAR LUDWIG:

It was with sincere sympathy that we received to-day the news of your little son's death. It seems as though our name and race were not to be perpetuated. How truly we feel for your grief and poor Mie's! Adolf's lot, indeed, to lose a child at the age of seven, must be a harder one. God keep your girls. You tell me that Mie is to spend the summer at Nyegaard and Wedelsborg with the little girls. Then, instead of remaining all the time alone and lonely in dismal Fehmarn, I have a plan to propose to you. An opportunity seems to offer for your making a journey to Rome, at no cost, and I hope pleasantly. The case is ·this: The Adjutant of Prince Henry of Prussia, the King's uncle, who has been living in Rome these thirty years, has died suddenly in consequence of a fall out of a carriage. I am one of the candidates proposed to the Prince to fill the vacant post of Adjutant, and as I have excellent recommendations, it is possible, even fairly probable, that I shall be appointed. The names are already sent in; the decision must come in about three weeks, and if I am selected I must set out in the beginning of July. I propose to make the journey by sending on my own horses and carriage as far as Dresden by easy stages, so as to accustom them to the work. I shall follow in a few days by railway. From Dresden, where the country is pretty, I shall go on, eight to ten miles a day [from about thirty-seven to forty-six miles English], by Prague, Linz, Gmünden, Gastein, over the Alps, through Lombardy, to Venice, Perugia, and Rome. This will take about six weeks, but it is the pleasantest way of travelling. You can stop where you please, and take a day's rest at the finest points—and there are many on this journey.

Now I offer you with all my heart a seat in my carriage; we will occupy the box-seat in turns; it is very comfortable, and you have the best view from it. My journey will be paid for, so that it will not cost either of us anything. The return journey will take you three weeks *viâ* Ancona, and by steamboat to Triest. Then sixty miles [about 280 English miles] by railway through Vienna to Olmütz and Hohenmauth; by railway again from Dresden to Magdeburg, and from thence by steamer to Hamburg.

By my calculations this excursion cannot cost you more than 100 thalers, which you would consume at home in three months. But if the whole undertaking seems too much for you, you can make St. Mark's on the little square at Venice the goal of your journey, or stop on a snowy peak of the Alps, or wherever else you may be attacked by home-sickness. After all, the whole scheme is quite uncertain. If nothing should come of it, stay with us in Berlin till we go to Ems, and we will set you down at Ilmenau, where you can spend a few weeks at the waters, in the mountain air.

At any rate, it is necessary that you should forthwith get three months' leave. When you have got that and are once out of your island and at Kiel, the rest will come of itself, with the help of steam and good horses, by beautiful roads and through exquisite country. The season is not, to be sure, the best for Italy, but the mountain torrents and Alps will refresh us on the way. The whole journey will to me be doubly interesting if you share it, and it will never probably be made so easy to you again.

And now, dear Ludwig, in anticipation of many an If and But, and much, certainly well-founded, hesitancy, I would only make one remark from my own practical experience. If a man cannot make a plunge when a great decision has to be taken, never in this world will he achieve anything. We will make Mie umpire to decide whether you are to accept this offer or no. But settle it at once, and let me know your decision soon, if possible in favor of it. The exact day of departure cannot of course be fixed, but you must be free by the beginning of July. If it should be postponed for a few days, you can remain here, or else you may spare yourself the long round by Berlin. Steamers start from Hamburg every evening at six, and reach Magdeburg in thirty-six hours; and from thence it is no further to Dresden than to Berlin. But that we will discuss more fully when we are agreed as to the main point. Think of the Hesperides, of Venice the Queen of the Sea, of eternal Rome! And so I end. Your faithful brother,

HELMUTH.

BERLIN, June 12th, 1845.

DEAR LUDWIG:

As yet no decision. This to begin with.

With what joy I learned from your letter of the 5th

that you decided promptly and rightly. Although no answer has come from Rome, nor could have come, I write these few lines in case—so that the time may not seem too long to you, and that everything may be ready as far as possible.

The matter must at this moment be lying before the Prince for decision. Whether he will make any further inquiries I do not know; but I should think not. My Prince wrote the strongest recommendations to his uncle, whom he visited not long since in Rome; not, it is true, till a few days after an autograph letter from the King had mentioned the names. I only hope the old gentleman has not been in too great a hurry to decide, so that my testimonial may have reached him in time. If he selects me, I shall be fearfully busy. I must stow all my possessions somewhere, give up my quarters, fit myself out, arrange my money-matters, pay no end of visits and make several introductions, pack up, treat with express-agents, and what not. And I hope to get it all done in a week, although I can make no definite arrangements in this uncertainty. During that week the horses must go to Dresden by easy stages and get into practice; after that they can make long journeys of from seven to twelve miles a day [about thirty-two to fifty-six English miles]. We shall overtake them in one day by railway to Dresden. If, on the other hand, the decision is not in my favor, a possibility which must be considered, I have made no fixed plan. I should propose to meet you in Berlin, which you can reach by steamer (of the Seehandlungs Dampfschiff Co., Potsdam); they start at five in the morning four times a week—for eight thalers. We will at any rate make a tour in the mountains. This we will settle when we meet.

Adieu, dear Ludwig. I thank Mie for deciding so

kindly, and wish her a very pleasant stay with her family. Marie is as glad as I am that we have persuaded you to come to Rome with us. Affectionately yours,

HELMUTH.

BERLIN, July 2nd, 1845.

And still no decision.

You must certainly have expected it this time, dear Ludwig, and I hardly like to write to you as I cannot yet announce it. Still, none is better than a rejection; *dum spiro spero.*

God only knows why. Whether the old Prince has been making further inquiries at Berlin before making up his mind; if so, the suspense may last till the end of this month again. Take patience—as we must too. * * * At any rate, if the decision is in our favor I will write two days running, in case a letter should be lost. I would not leave you without any news at all, though I am, in fact, only writing to say that I have nothing to write.

Adieu, dear Ludwig. Marie sends her best remembrances; I hope to have good news for you soon. Affectionately yours,

HELMUTH.

BERLIN, July 27th, 1845.

MY DEAR LUDWIG:

Still no answer. Again my letter begins with these words. As I now learn, the names did not reach Rome till the beginning of this month. If Prince Henry takes as long to think about it, it may be some time yet before anything is settled. As the King is now gone to the Rhine, it is hardly possible that anything can be done for the next fortnight, and I can no longer postpone Marie's journey to Ems. I have arranged to have any news that comes forwarded immediately by Coblenz. If I should be ordered off, I shall leave Marie at Ems to finish her course of waters, and also leave the carriage and horses; I shall hurry back to Berlin to settle everything. You shall at once be informed.

It was said a little while since that the Prince would not appoint any married adjutant; however, this seems to be unfounded, and the matter is just where it was eight weeks ago. My father has again paid us a visit here of three days. He was very ailing when he arrived, but soon got better, and was much pleased. Adieu, dear Ludwig, only do not lose patience. Affectionately yours,

HELMUTH.

COBLENZ, September 2nd, 1845.

DEAR LUDWIG:

And still nothing settled!

I cannot bear to write any more since all my letters have the same weariful beginning. You have spent the whole summer in uncomfortable suspense, and all alone too; I only hope that when the answer comes at last it may be favorable.

If we set out later than October, the tour through the Alps will certainly have lost much of its interest. But Rome is Rome, even in the winter, for no snow lies on its venerable face.

It is lucky that I did not stay waiting in Berlin any longer. Marie has happily got through her course of waters at Ems, and can remain there for the second part of the treatment. We are very well; between the two courses we are making a delightful excursion to the Aar Valley and the Rhine, and are now going up the river by Rüdesheim to Bad Langen-Schwalbach, in the Duchy of Nassau, where we shall stay a fortnight. Your brother,

HELMUTH.

17

BERLIN, October 25th, 1845.

DEAR LUDWIG:

On my arrival here to-day I found the news of my father's death. From all the late reports it was only to be expected, and after such long suffering could only be desired. Nevertheless the fact is a shock. I also found here your kind letter of the 25th, and read the details of my father's sufferings with an aching heart. How long and terrible was the struggle of that strong constitution! But life had now so few pleasures for him; even travelling had lost its charm—God grant him rest and peace!

My news, dear Ludwig, is that I have to-day received my appointment to Rome. Unfortunately you have waited the whole summer alone, and now, when your family are about you again, you say you have lost the wish to travel. Nevertheless, I hope you will not leave me to go alone. At any rate, I will wait for you here three weeks, which will give you time to apply to Copenhagen for an extension of leave. I have not yet really had time to think about anything. I shall probably travel in my own carriage, but posting, which will shorten the journey considerably. I only give you immediate notice, so that, if you have not altogether given it up, you may take the necessary steps in time. Let me hear soon whether or no you will give me this great pleasure; then, as soon as I have recovered myself and considered the subject more fully, I will furnish you with particulars. Marie and I send our best love to Mie. It will be hard on us to give up all our belongings, perhaps for years. To be sure, we see everything to-day through a shroud. Affectionately yours,

HELMUTH.

BERLIN, November 7th, 1845.

DEAR LUDWIG:

Twelve days have already gone by since I wrote to you, on the 26th, that we are going to Rome, and expect you to come with us. As, however, no letter from you has reached us till now, we count on the best, namely, that you yourself will make your appearance immediately. We can but repeat, Marie and I, our pressing invitation, and hope to see you here as soon as possible, for we shall be ready to start in three or four days; but we are no less ready to postpone our departure for even more days if you are waiting for an answer from Copenhagen.

Pardon these hasty lines. An auction is going on in the next room of all our pretty things. Away at any loss! is the motto. How gladly we would hand over many things to Mie for her house if the carriage were possible. A thousand greetings to the dear sister-in-law; she will certainly urge you to go; she is unselfish enough. Adieu, dear Ludwig. Let us hear of you soon—or rather let us see you. Yours,

HELMUTH.

BERLIN, Wednesday, November 12th, 1845.

DEAR LUDWIG:

The three weeks since I wrote to you on the 26th ult. are nearly spent, and if, as I expect, the King gives me my orders to-morrow, I can no longer put off my journey.

It is possible that I may not receive my dismissal this week, but it is also possible that I——

As I am in the act of writing, a messenger has come in to require my attendance to-day at noon. So I shall leave this on Friday, 14th, for Leipzig direct, where I shall find the carriage and horses, and go on by railway, on Saturday, to Werdau. From thence I drive in three days to Nuremberg, where I shall put up at the Rothen Ross. We shall be there till Tuesday, the 18th.

If you go by railway from Kiel to Hamburg, from thence by steamer to Magdeburg, and by railway from Magdeburg to Werdau *viâ* Leipzig and Altenburg, and take the mail on to Nuremberg, it will take you exactly three times twenty-four hours. This letter will reach you on Saturday, the 15th, so you can join us on Thursday, at Nuremberg. At any rate, you can still overtake us even later, by posting to Munich, railway from Donauwörth. However, I hope that, even while I am writing, you are already on your way. If you should reach Berlin after we have started, it will be quite easy for you to catch us up at Nuremberg, since we shall travel not more than seven or eight miles a day, and the mail goes twenty miles a day. I know not what else to add, and shall be truly grieved if you let this good opportunity slip, and deprive us of the pleasure of your company, without some very good reason. A thousand greetings to Mie. Adieu. Your faithful brother,

HELMUTH.

ROME, April 2nd, 1846.

DEAR LUDWIG:

After your letter from Venice had reassured us as to your having happily escaped the brigands of the Marches of Ancona, we heard from Guste and then from you, from Fehmarn, that you had arrived at home safe and sound. I am truly glad that your stay in Rome should have left you some interesting reminiscences. We ourselves were not really in a position to receive you as we could have wished; we, too, were strangers, and not sufficiently settled. Your successor will find things more comfortable. Your departure has left a great gap; and in many a delightful drive we exclaim: "If only Loui were with us!" Two things especially, I particularly wish that you could have seen. One is the Columbarium by the Porta Latina. How kindly was death in those days! The Columbarium, which was only discovered ten years since, is a little room elegantly decorated with stucco and frescoes. From the roof a six-branched lamp hangs from a bronze chain, and all round there are little niches in the walls, in which stand urns, still containing the bones of the dead. Graceful altars, mosaics, and sculpture are not lacking, and thus a man could collect the ashes of all those he loved, divested of all that is repulsive, in a little hall, till he himself was deposited there. Then the god of the poppy wreath and the inverted torch was still extant, the graver brother of smiling sleep; not the skeleton with a scythe, and the fires of purgatory in the background. Then, too, an oak or two did not matter, while to us they are a store of wood to warm us thriftily for a whole winter.

The second and more splendid excursion is to the top of the dome of St. Peter's. Close to the tomb of the Stuarts you enter a passage, leading through the tremendous side wall into a sort of spiral way; it goes up and up a gently inclined plane, and after a long but easy ascent, you come out in the open air on a rocky platform, at about the height of Monte Mario. To the right you see the hut of a mountaineer, or watchman, close to which a shoot of water, as thick as your arm, springs out and fills an ancient sarcophagus. Behind you, stand strange peaks of rock, which, when seen from the other side, appear as gigantic statues of the Apostles; and at the other end of the plateau—or, to be accurate, the roof of the church, covered with flags of travertin—a rotunda rises before you, as large as the Pantheon, but much higher. You go in through a door, and a fearful gulf lies before you. Far below glitters the gilt cross on the top of the bronze balda-chino, which itself is higher than the Schloss at Berlin. There are swarms down there of tiny dwarfs, and a distant chant falls, as an echo, on your ear. In the furthest depth of the abyss a white-haired old man is kneeling with clasped hands in front of the shrine, surrounded with lamps, which contains the bones of the most militant of the Apostles. You involuntarily draw back to the wall side of the ledge, five feet wide, below which no holdfast is visible. Remove one of these huge blocks of stone, and all the rest will fall in ruins on to the marble floor of the church. But I will not make you giddy, for we have yet to climb up to another similar ledge at the top of the drum, where the hemispherical dome begins. There it is wiser to look up than down. The whole vast vault is lined with myriads of stones forming a mosaic; the saints and martyrs in the lowest row; then the Apostles, with Christ in the middle; above these, angels and cheru-bim; and at the very centre God the Father looking down from above, but somewhat indistinct, and only to be seen by an effort. All these pictures, which, from the floor, are of life size, are in fact colossal; a little angel supporting a garland of flowers might unhesitatingly take his place on the right wing of the body-guard of the 1st Regiment. Above 300 steps lead up between the double shell of the cupola to the gallery at the foot of the lantern, and seventy more bring you to the very top, exactly over the high altar.

If the tower of St. Michael's Church were placed below you, you would not notice it, for it would be beneath your feet.

Mount a metal ladder of about thirty rungs, and you find yourself in the ball. Though it will hold eighteen men, they are in anything rather than a comfortable position, and you are glad to find yourself outside again, whence you have a glorious view. Rome lies before you like a map in relief, with all its churches, palaces, walls, and towers; the eye follows the windings of the Tiber for a long distance, under the Milvian Bridge, past the Castle of St. Angelo, and away to the shimmering streak which is the Mediterranean. A broad green plain spreads out to the steep limestone wall of the Sabine Hills, from whose rifts the Anio bursts forth, visible amid the shining walls of Tivoli. The volcanic slopes of the Alban Hills rise in rounded outline, and the villas of Tusculum and Albano and old Algidus are clearly seen. The rows of tombs intersect the plain, indicating the lines of the ancient roads, and the giant arches of the aqueducts are seen for miles, as far as mountains. But now I will restore you safe and sound to your wife on the level soil of Fehmarn.

I will try to procure the books you mention; but it is almost as difficult here as on your island. Meanwhile I am studying Niebuhr's Roman History, which, with the sharpest scalpel of criticism, cuts away the flesh of legend and poetry and lays bare the skeleton of truth. Numa and his Egeria, Romulus even, are myths; Porsenna, like Hercules, an aggregation of fabulous tales; Horatius Cocles and the rest, mere inventions; nay, Peter himself was never in Rome. What is to become of Egeria's grotto, and Nero's tomb, and the Tarpeian rock, which, indeed, we had to pay half a paul to see? This is "the thirst for truth and delight in illusion." *L'histoire c'est une fable convenue*, but to dispute it is like disputing dogma. You destroy something, but can put nothing better in its place. So I went again yesterday to the fountain of Egeria, and persist in believing that good King Numa studied law-giving there. At the same time, I may observe that when you and I were together we failed, in some incomprehensible way, to find the beautiful Nympheum, though it is quite near, only somewhat closer to the city. It is a lovely cave, out of which springs a thread of lukewarm, slightly acid water, and in the background a horrible reclining figure has been placed, instead of each one being left to imagine the Nymph as beautiful as he may.

All our things, plate, etc., arrived safely soon after your departure. As yet all our search has failed to discover a suitable residence. My Prince was very glad to hear that you had reached home safely. He has suffered much this spring from podagra and chiragra.

My plane-table too has arrived, and I am hard at work mapping the environs of Rome. Nearly two square miles [about nine square miles English] are already done, but I have nine such sheets to prepare, and shall have to work at them for a very long time, more especially as in summer the heat is too great for such work. I wander up hill and down dale in enormously high boots, against thorns and snakes, and meet with no interference but occasionally from sheep-dogs or herds of oxen, over a circuit of a mile and a half already [nearly seven miles English]. Of course I hunt diligently after old walls, tombs, and basalt pavements, and rejoice whenever I can include some ancient name, such as Fidenae, Autumnae, Villa Liviae, Ad Gallinas, and the like.

I have begged Adolf to extend his journey beyond the baths, as far as this, and I hope that you will have encouraged him by your example. Nay, more, we are half hoping for the Burts; for there is no miracle so great that it may not occur in Rome.

Now adieu, dear Ludwig. Marie sends her affectionate greetings with mine to your dear wife and the sweet children. With sincere affection and attachment, yours,

HELMUTH.

COBLENZ, July 12th, 1847.

DEAR LUDWIG:

* * * With us, all is well and happy. I returned yesterday from a journey through the Rhine provinces. It was the first anniversary of Prince Henry's death, and thus the end, for me, of a very busy year, during which I travelled about 2000 miles [above 9300 miles English]. The last journey, with my commanding general, was interesting, and led through old Roman settlements; Colonna, Agrippina, Aquisgranum, Moguntiacum, Augusta Trevirorum, and others, where magnificent remains still exist. Near Trier, at Igel, there is a splendid family tomb, with sculpture and an inscription. At Trier the King is having the old basilica of Constantine restored; an amphitheatre has been dug out; the baths, the palace of Constantine the Great, the aqueducts, etc., remain almost half complete. Castell, a Roman Castrum, is beautifully situated on a rocky promontory on the Saar. There, too, lies Johann von Lützelburg, the blind King of Bohemia, who was killed at the battle of Crecy. But here at Confluentes, is best of all. Adieu, dear Ludwig, for to-day, and much love to you and your absent ones. Yours,

HELMUTH.

COBLENZ, November 14th, 1847.

DEAR LUDWIG:

I am busy getting my Roman map copied out, and arranging a sort of guide to the Campagna, in the style of Westphal's,* only I hope a little less dry. How splendidly you could help me, with your knowledge of the ancient classics. Unfortunately, I must put it all aside at present, for my whole time is occupied by a very dry and extensive official task: the working out of a new plan for the mobilization of our Army Corps. It is besides much more difficult to procure the necessary materials here than in Berlin. A physical geographical introduction to it lies ready. Then I intended to begin on the walks in the environs, after the manner of the Florentine letters, only keeping more closely to a definite purpose. Unfortunately I have to content myself with translations. My aim is to connect existing remains with historical events. These can, therefore, only be given in the briefest form, and the places must form the connecting links in the chain of events. With best love, yours,

HELMUTH.

MAGDEBURG, September 27th, 1849.

DEAR LUDWIG:

I do not know if you are aware that Adolf has been very seriously ill. His post in Berlin, though not an official one, brought a great deal of agitating work in its train. His lively interest in his little native land, so natural considering the important position he occupied there, and finally the confidence reposed in him by all parties, drew him into a most busy life. Besides

---

* J. H. Westphal: The Roman Campagna. Topographical and antiquarian aspect. Berlin, 1829.

which he took no care of himself; so one night, on rising from his writing-table at three o'clock, he had a sort of hemorrhage. He had to be bled considerably, and a subsequent relapse has made the matter very serious. Professor Langenbeck was his doctor, and cousin Eduard nursed him faithfully till Augusta could be fetched. Now he is happily so far better that he can leave Berlin and withdraw from the political turmoil.

I know too little of the complicated state of affairs to be able to offer you advice in your present difficult position, but I will not conceal my opinion that, with all possible caution, you must nevertheless submit to the Government. Should certain ill-disposed persons succeed in stirring up the ignorant masses about it, the worst they could do would be to turn you out of your post by force till order was restored. An opposite course of action would enable you to hold your position up to that point, but you would run the risk of losing your place altogether by a legal decision. Whatever may be thought of the unfortunate occurrences in the Duchies, I still think that a Schleswig official can recognize the present Government as his lawful authority. The appeal made by the Government to the consciences of every Schleswig official, and thus to each individual's idea of justice, is certainly a very unwise and rash proceeding. Liliencron has already sent in a petition to the Government to repair the mischief they have thus set on foot by some steps in the other direction, and it is to be hoped that something of that kind may be done.

Men who have some knowledge of the matter tell me that affairs in Schleswig may be brought to a satisfactory conclusion. The chief thing is to get over a few difficult months. Prussia's threat to withdraw from the whole business may probably lead the Great Powers to speak a serious word to the refractory island folk.

I have a general feeling that things will improve. The pendulum movement of the democratic revolution is over, I fancy; it is becoming stationary once more; still, it is not impossible that, following the natural laws of gravity, it may now deviate to the other side. Democracy is played out for the present, though no doubt other great struggles are impending. "There will be an age of heroes after the age of shouters and writers."

The groundwork of the great movement in Germany is the undeniable desire for unity, and if the Cabinets will not adopt the only possible way to this end— which is now offered them, let them call it absorption into Prussia or what they like—the struggle may doubtless break out again at some future time. But order will certainly be restored in the immediate future, for as it has been very properly observed, liberty has sometimes come of order, but order was never the outcome of liberty. Though indeed, if we do not keep wide awake, order will not be of very long duration.

The transactions in our Chambers show some signs that the people are awakening to a better consciousness. God preserve to us the much-despised Branden-burg-Manteuffel Ministry; they have saved us all.

To descend from great things to small, let me only tell you that Marie and I spent four weeks at Wangerooge for the sea-bathing. I should like to have gone to Föhr, but the nonsense about Prussian treachery kept me away. It did us both a great deal of good, and we needed it. There is as much to do as ever, but we are beginning to see daylight at last.

Our Landwehr is returning, and the country thereby relieved of a heavy burden.

When will the time come again for a pleasant visit to us? Should you be forced, against all expectations, to leave your little island, do not forget that Magdeburg is very easy to get at. A thousand kind messages from Marie to yourself, your wife, and all the children. Most affectionately yours,

HELMUTH.

MAGDEBURG, January 15th, 1850.

DEAR LUDWIG:

I took my wife to see her parents, with whom we spent a very merry Christmas. But I had to be here again on the 4th, so that unfortunately it was impossible to go farther than Neumünster, Rantzau, and Uetersen. I wished very much to visit both you and Fritz. We have not met since we were in Rome. Those were other days! We grow so serious and so prosaic under the inevitable yoke of business. You have the additional weight of hopeless political entanglements, and yet I see from a letter to Augusta that you can still turn your mind to literature. If you will send me your translation of "Marino Faliero," I will see if I cannot find a publisher for you. Of course it would have been easier if you had written "Three Questions" or "Revelations," or something of the sort, that is much more attractive nowadays than Byron or Moore. That reminds me we ought some day to collect the poems that we have translated from time to time. I enclose one or two as dried rose-leaves from warmer days. To translate the whole of Moore is certainly a frightful thought. I cannot even try to pick out the good poems from the mass of inferior ones. * * *

Rantzau was doubly interesting to me on this journey. A recollection of my earliest youth attached
itself to the pointed tower at Barmstedt, to the drawbridge over the castle moat, and to a large garden,
where we plotted with some naughty boarders at Pastor
Wilke's (for it is forty years ago) to steal some plums.
It was dark when I arrived at Elmshorn by train, and
having no luggage I hurried off on foot. After losing
my way completely in the deep snow, I came at last
through a splendid beech wood to a drawbridge. In
the castle court I was met by two gigantic white figures, which turned out afterwards to be snow men, and
I got quite a shock when the tower clock just over my
head struck eight. I felt quite nervous as I entered
the house, but found Adolf and Augusta having tea.
He is much better than I had feared. It is a great
pity that his convalescence should fall in the winter
time; he is not allowed to go out at all, which would
make the soundest person ill.

At Itzehoe, I heard a very pretty little composition
of yours, to a song of Geibel's, I fancy; in short, it
seems that Melpomene and Euterpe have disembarked
at Heiligenhafen. They certainly have not come to
Magdeburg.

It is always expressly stated on our theatre-bills that
the building is heated, otherwise nobody would know
it. One freezes mentally and bodily. If I had not the
immense cathedral in front of my windows, there
would be nothing here to indicate the presence of a
higher culture.

What is going to happen in Holstein? I cannot
think that it will come to blows again, although General Bonin, with his 30,000 men and 80 guns, would be
pleased to have another word with the Danes. The
Swedes have certainly no desire to delay any longer,

but the question is how General Halm is to put his
hand between hammer and anvil. If he leaves the
field open to the contending parties, it is very doubtful
which would come off victorious. If it were the Holsteiners, they would march into Jutland, but that
would by no means end the matter. If the Holsteiners
should be beaten, they would cross the Eider, and find
a strong support in Rendsburg, and a still stronger in
the population of the country, which, after all, is part
of the German Confederation, and cannot be overrun
by the Danes without further ado. Thus nothing will
be conclusive one way or another. This can only be
achieved by diplomatic means, and notwithstanding
all that is sure to be said to the contrary, the matter
must be taken in hand by a superior Power. But this
Power must be stronger than the local Government.
In any case a weak government is infinitely worse
than a tyrannical one.

The year has only dawned as yet, and no one
knows what the first spring morning may bring with
it. A powerful Austrian army is standing at our frontier, and we—receive assurances of good-will. To the
Triple Alliance, at least two kings are wanting. Hohenzollern is a possession *in partibus infidelium*, and
Baden does not know how to get rid of that ill weed
Democracy, except by throwing it into her own fields,
where it frequently falls on well-tilled ground. In
Berlin there was a Ministerial crisis over the Proposi-
tions, and, after these were safely passed, a Constitution, of which they do not yet know whether it will
work, and which costs, to begin with, fifty millions
(according to Beckerath, however, only the ridicu-
lously small sum of forty-nine millions). I may observe incidentally that all Government shares and
paper have fallen about 25 per cent., so the conquests

may easily cost us a few hundred millions. The railways are paying nothing, and the share-holders would really not be to blame if they went over to the opposition.

It is some comfort when, in spite of all the endeavors of the enlightened disciples of progress, the old-domestic Court of Justice, parental rule, and much-abused beneficient legislation, remain intact at home. Mie probably thinks the same. Remember me most kindly to her. How I should like to see your little troop of daughters (though little only as compared to the family of Danaos, King of Argos), for "Hannemusse" must have grown a stately maiden since the days in which she turned away with a "Boo" from my beard, and called out for "Roast hare!" in her sleep. But my paper and your patience have come to an end. Affectionately yours,

HELMUTH.

I forget if I wrote to you that my ten square miles round Rome are being engraved by one of the first engravers in Berlin—Brose. The King has advanced 750 thalers, but it will take two years to do. I hope it will be a fine work, and you shall have one of the first copies. I began a guide to the Campagna, but had, of course, to put it aside. I should like to show you what is finished.

MAGDEBURG, April 21st, 1851.

. DEAR LUDWIG:

I was called away from the seaside last year by the preparations for war, just as I was about to cross over to England. We saw the chalk cliffs gleaming in the sun, and could have been at the other side within three hours. It is impossible to say whether I shall be able to make up for it this autumn; who can make plans nowadays six months in advance? We are very far indeed from rest as yet. The humiliation to Prussia is too great for the situation to remain very long as it is. Everywhere victorious with her arms, and beaten at every point in diplomacy—it is very deeply felt here. Yours affectionately,

HELMUTH.

MAGDEBURG, December 14th, 1851.

DEAR LUDWIG:

Herewith I send you a copy of my Roman map—at least the two sheets that have been completed as yet—and the materials for a guide through that part of the Campagna contained on the map.* These last are, it is true, only fragments, but being in the shafts all day and every day as I am, I find it impossible to carry out the work. Reumont is to be Chargé d'Affaires in Florence, and is leaving Rome, so that he cannot undertake to assist me in it. I leave it to you to decide, from the present specimen, whether you care to continue the historical researches, though it is of course uncertain if anything will ever come of the whole thing. Unfortunately, the map has been reduced to a very small scale, and to go through all the annals of antiquity and the Middle Ages, merely to determine what occurred on such and such a small spot, however remarkable, would be a labor, having for its only reward the interest of the work. In case you would like to occupy your present leisure with it, I have added the two sheets belonging to Westphal's guide. The cathedral library will no doubt supply you with all the classical writers. Niebuhr's Roman History is, I think, absolutely necessary to a right understanding

* We know that this guide was never finished from G. von Bunsen's published "Wanderungen um Rom. Aus Graf Moltke's handschriftlichen Aufzeichnungen" (Wanderings round Rome; from Count Moltke's manuscript notes.

18

of the facts contained in the classics.   But even if you would rather devote yourself to Melpomene than to Clio, it will interest you to see the map, as you have been in Rome.   In the opinion of competent judges, the engraving is so beautiful that you would not easily find anything more perfect in its way.   I hope the whole map may be ready to appear at the beginning of next year, and I shall then lay a copy of it before His Majesty the King, whose munificence has made it possible to bring out so costly an edition.   Every sheet costs the firm 1500 thalers to engrave.   The scale of measurement has not yet been put in.   But on the main roads you will find the milestones indicated by M. 1, M. 2, etc.   These are always 2000 paces, or $\frac{1}{5}$ of a geographical mile (15 to the degree *).   The sheet for the south is not nearly finished yet; particularly the markings of eminences in the gardens to the west and south of Rome have to be deepened, and many corrections still to be made.   Your faithful brother,

HELMUTH.

MAGDEBURG, January 7th, 1852.

DEAR LUDWIG:

Here you have the necessary scale of measurements for the Roman map to $\frac{1}{25000}$ of the real distances; in explanation I make the following remark.   The unit of measurement is the ruthe or perch † of the Rhine provinces: 2000 to one Prussian mile, which is only shorter than the geographical mile ($\frac{1}{15}$ of a degree of latitude) by one perch, therefore almost identical.   The perch is divided into 10 decimal feet, the foot into 10

---

* This is a little less than the old Prussian mile; as 985 to 1000, or 4·611 English miles (Meyer's Lexicon).

† The scale is set out to three standards :— $\frac{1}{4}$ mile Prussian; 1 mile Roman; 8 stadia of 250 paces = $\frac{1}{25000}$.

decimal inches, so there are 100 inches to a perch. Thus the mile contains $100 \times 2000 = 200{,}000$ inches.

As the map is drawn to a scale of one twenty-five thousandth, there must be $\frac{200000}{25}$ inches, or eight decimal inches to the mile.

The old Roman mile is very nearly the same as the modern Roman one, the former having $75\frac{4}{10}$ and the latter $74\frac{1}{2}$ *toises,** a difference of about four paces.

When there is any mention of the Roman *passus* it always means a double pace, the movement of both the right and left foot being considered as one step. Therefore 1000 Roman *passus* make 2000 Prussian paces.

The stadium is $\frac{1}{8}$ of a Roman mile, therefore 250 modern paces. In this way, the ancient measurements will agree with those on my map, only it must always be noted whether the starting-point is one of the older gates, or one of those in Aurelian's Wall. For instance, the miles on the Flaminian Way are counted from the old Flaminian Gate, which stood near the foot of the Capitoline Hill, whereas Porta del Popolo was a mile away from this gate. This would place the Allia River at a distance of 10 millia (10,000 Roman paces.)

In the same way the old road to the east is reckoned, not from the Porta Pia or Salara, but from the old Porta Collatina, which stood where you will find a large earthwork marked, behind Maria Maggiore.

What is your objection to the style of my guide? Surely it can be well and carefully and interestingly done in that form. Often when I have come upon a heap of ruins I have thought, What may not have happened here! what events are connected with these remains! The guide-book form has just that advantage over a scientific inquiry, that the latter drags the

* Or fathom of 1·829 mètres.

reader mercilessly through dreary wastes of minute
dissertation, while the former strolls pleasantly with
him through the country, remarking only what is
grand, attractive, and noteworthy. If you are interested in the work, I advise you, wherever you find
anything in the classics which relates to the places, to
write it down very briefly in separate paragraphs like
those I sent you; but always in distinct notes. They
are the stones with which to build up the whole later
on. They will be sure to find a place; for instance,
the graceful epigram on Nero's golden house, though
it belongs to Rome—which will not be touched upon,
there being so many learned works upon it—may be
quite appropriately brought in at Veii. Another visit
to Rome would really be necessary before the final
arrangement, in order to refresh one's impressions on
the spot, to add some picturesque touches and round
off the whole work. And that is not so impossible.
Should my circumstances allow me a little leisure, I
mean to study the history of the Middle Ages as connected with Rome. Ranke's admirable History of the
Popes will be a guide and gives the authorities.

As I have remarked in my introduction, legends will
not be excluded. That will not hinder us from glanc-
ing behind the scenes and showing the groundwork of
truth. And so I always come back to Niebuhr, though
Schlegel scoffs at him.

Am Wafferfall von Tibur
Steht der große Niebuhr,
Um römifche Gefchichten
Auf feine Art zu blchten ;
Lateinifch und etrurifch
Warb friefifch und niebuhrifch.

I will only mention the marching of the Plebs to the
Mons sacer, a proceeding which remains perfectly in-

comprehensible and senseless without the key which Niebuhr gives to it.   Your brother,

HELMUTH.

MAGDEBURG, March 23rd, 1852.

DEAR LUDWIG:

Reumont has proposed to me to apply to Dr. Emil Braun in Rome, who will write a brief article to accompany my map.   I do not quite know what to do about it, as I know nothing of Braun's style.   I am in daily expectation that the engraving will be finished, and shall then go to Berlin, to lay a copy before the King, who has taken a great interest in it.   I shall take the opportunity of speaking to Professor Gerhard, and it may probably be necessary to send Braun what I have already done.   As you are not likely to be using the MS. now, I will ask you to send it back—only the MS. sheets—but I hope that you will not deprive me of the results of your excursions in the classics, even if they do not strictly refer to the map.   There will always be a place for anything interesting or piquant. Whether the whole thing will come to anything I greatly doubt; perhaps when I am gone to my rest. At present I can get nothing done, and may be glad if I get through each day's business.   Affectionately yours,

HELMUTH.

MAGDEBURG, November 17th, 1852.

DEAR LUDWIG:

We found it most refreshing to spend a week once more in Berlin.   I went there about my Roman map, which is finished at last, and I laid a copy of it before the King.   I am daily expecting a number of presentation copies, and hope to be able to send one with these lines to you, and one for Professor Forchhammer in Kiel, who sent me his survey of Troas. The engraving has turned out very beautiful, and the King, whose memory for places is incredible, kept me nearly an hour in his private room questioning me on the details. On the other hand, my manuscript, which I sent three months ago to Alexander von Humboldt, seems hopelessly lost. It never reached him, and all inquiries of the post have been without result. The orderly who sent the packet off is dead, so there is little prospect of getting it back.

I am reading Ritter's Geography of Palestine, and specially of Jerusalem. It is a favorite scheme of mine to go there some day and make a plan of those most interesting places. Yours,

HELMUTH.

MAGDEBURG, February 24th, 1853.

DEAR LUDWIG:

The lost child has been found. After all researches at the post-office had been unavailing and we had given up hope, Humboldt writes me a day or two ago, that the manuscript is with him. The celebrated author of " Kosmos " give as his excuse, " *quand on fait vieux, on devient d'abord sourd et puis imbécile.*" However, I am very glad to know that the work is safe, but there is small hope of my continuing it—perhaps in my old age. Yours,

HELMUTH.

MAGDEBURG, June 5th, 1853.

DEAR LUDWIG:

Early this morning we received the sad news that Adolf's gentle, good little daughter Friederike had followed the sister who died a while ago to the grave.

Adolf writes in unutterable grief and distress, and when I remember how cheerful and happy he was a short time ago at your house, it warns me of the instability of all human happiness. The deep religious feeling of both Adolf and his wife is their only comfort. God help them over the first sad days, and preserve the rest of the children, for with the delicacy of the boys and the terrible malignity of the disease, there is ground enough for anxiety. Yours,

HELMUTH.

MAGDEBURG, December 23rd, 1853.

DEAR LUDWIG:

* * * I am so busy just now that I cannot even read my newspaper every day, although the Russo-Turkish affair is of the deepest interest to me. I think the most Christian Czar *has got in a scrape,** which he wishes he were out of again. If he is not master of the Black Sea, he will not so easily cross the Balkans. The campaign has cost him one year and 100,000 men, which he cannot bring back. He cannot take possession of anything either, for with the most passionate desire for peace, Europe would never permit him to have Constantinople, and all the rest is not worth the cost. The decision of the question is all the more likely to be transferred from the Danube to the Rhine, and to Italy, which would result in some rather curious complications. Then, in the general struggle, the Danish question would at once be brought up for discussion, for our little neighbor's insolent scorn and thirst for revenge cannot be allowed to continue, unless Germany first goes to the bottom. You are lucky to be out of all the coming worry. Yours,

HELMUTH.

* In English in the original.

BERLIN, March 16th, 1856.

DEAR LUDWIG:

The detestable, cold east wind that has been tormenting us for the last fortnight is making everybody ill, and reminds one forcibly of the statement that Germany is really habitable only as far as Heidelberg. Even Tacitus says: "Who would leave Attica, Italy, or Africa to dwell in these horrible forests and deadly swamps—unless it were his native land!" The Ratzeburg Lake has one advantage over the country round Berlin—it is not dusty; but it is just as cold and windy. I am curious to know if it is any better on the Rhine. When you visit us again, dear Ludwig, you will find us in a beautiful large city, which has sprung up since you were last here. The Landwehr Canal, otherwise the Schafgraben, has been transformed into a gently winding, navigable stream, with broad avenues and magnificent houses on each bank. This is our nearest driving and riding road, running close behind the Thiergarten, and the old pheasantry, now the Zoological Gardens, and into the Charlottenburg road. Extensive cherry plantations give shade to the neighboring fields, and cover the worst of the sandy wastes. Over everything rises the mighty cupola of the Palace, and the numberless high and pointed spires of newly-built churches have quite altered the view of the city from a distance. Then there are the factories, with their steam shafts, gigantic barracks, railway stations, and isolation prisons outside the gates, not to mention gasometers, water-works, and granite footways; in fact, Berlin has become a beautiful city, and well worth the trouble of another visit.

If you can read anything but official documents, let me recommend Droysen's "History of Prussian Politics." Its interest is not confined to Prussia. I am just now reading Riehl's " Naturgeschichte des Volkes." Yours,

HELMUTH.

BERLIN, October 13th, 1858.

DEAR LUDWIG:

We—Marie and I—are now settled in our comfortable winter quarters, and are only waiting for friends and relations to come and take possession of the numerous guest-chambers. Perhaps you may some day make up your mind to the half-day's journey, and make Mie and one or other of the daughters acquainted with Berlin.

You have, perhaps, already heard that I was definitely appointed Chief of the General Staff at the close of this year's manœuvres. The appointment came sooner than I could have expected, as it is really the office of a Lieutenant-General.

Marie sends her best love. We made a very charming summer excursion into the Salzburg Alps. Excepting that we very nearly broke our necks, it was really delightful. For the manœuvres, too, and up till the last few days during my official journey with the staff, we had such fine weather that my overcoat was simply so much unnecessary ballast. Whether the fine weather has disappeared because the comet is no longer visible, or *vice versa*, can only be decided when we know if the yellow fever has left Lisbon because the Archbishop has returned, or the Archbishop returned because the yellow fever has disappeared. How is the hunting getting on? I wish you bad luck in it! Affectionately yours,

HELMUTH.

BERLIN, February 10th, 1859.

DEAR LUDWIG:

The forty-four pound roebuck of your shooting came safely to hand, and was warmly welcomed by Marie and me. We have hung it in the cool larder, and it will make a capital foundation to some unavoidable dinners and supper-parties. The *appetit savant* of our guests will appreciate it, and we beg to offer our very best thanks for the handsome present, only wishing we could invite you all to partake of it.

Please tell Mie that there is no reasonable excuse for war, except at the outside that *la France s'ennuye.* But the unreasonable will sometimes occur, and the matter looks mad enough. I do not, however, believe that it will come to an outbreak just yet; the Emperor is too wise to sail *contre vent et courants* as long as he has any choice in the matter. But perhaps he no longer has. *Il fourra dans un guépier.*

My tendency to giddiness which you have no doubt detected in these hurriedly written lines is slowly decreasing. But my recovery is retarded by the almost uninterrupted writing of the last weeks, and by the many social engagements which in my position we cannot altogether avoid, and which interfere seriously with my night's rest. I must close, therefore, thanking you once more. Who would think, to look at the ·Schmielau Moor, that it bore such fruits as well as bilberries. Most affectionately,

HELMUTH.

WILDBAD GASTEIN, 29th August, 1859.

DEAR LUDWIG:

* * * Bad-Gastein lies in a deep valley, and yet it is as high as the Brockenhaus, 3000 feet above the sea. The mountains which enclose the valley and rise to a

height of 10,000 feet, covered with perpetual snow, form, strictly speaking, the backbone of old Dame Europe. They belong to the great chain of Alps that stretches from Switzerland to the Balkans. To the north and south long valleys run parallel to it from west to east. They are wide and cultivated; considerable rivers traverse the beds of these valleys; in them lie the principal connecting roads, and they are full of the towns and villages.

The valleys running from north to south are of a very different character, being narrow, wild, and lonely; the waters of the glaciers rush down them in foaming torrents and thundering water-falls. The Gastein valley is one of these.

It has three very distinct basins, whose almost leve' plains, now alive with meadows, fields and Alpine huts, once formed large lakes. The outflow of the waters was hindered by rocky dams, probably deposited there by land-slips. In the course of thousands of years 'the Gastein torrent succeeded in forcing an outlet, and now casts itself over these three shelves in a series of superb water-falls.

A day or two ago we made an excursion to the upper one of these three lake basins, the so-called " wet field " (Nassfeld), a meadow apparently without any opening, and surrounded by mountains 10,000 feet high. Owing to this year's continuous heat, the snow has disappeared even from the highest peaks. But in the depressions between them lie a few glaciers stretching their arms far down into the valley. Their sea-blue coloring makes them easily distinguishable from the snow. The glaciers, as you know, are perpetually moving downwards towards the valley. They push huge rocks and masses of stone before them, threatening the most beautiful pastures and the dwellings of man with destruction. But the lower they slide the stronger is the effect of the sun's heat, the sources of the torrents are more numerous, and the water-falls become grander. The heat which dries up the rivulets of the plains, fills the banks of the mountain streams. The plain of the " wet field," which is about a mile long by half a mile wide [German], forms a delightful enclosed meadow, covered with sweet-smelling Alpine herbs. In the spring the matchless blue of the gentian is the prevailing color, and the low bushes of Alpine rose which clothe the rocky walls are in full bloom. In this remote solitude there are but three human habitations; a deep and solemn silence is its characteristic feature. Only the cow-bells sound faintly from the meadow, and the brook flows peacefully as yet across the valley. But as it leaves the plain it leaps thundering into a frightful abyss, the "Bärenfall," while by its side a considerable stream glides noiselessly over 400 feet of smooth red rock, forming the Schleierfall, and arrives at the bottom in the finest spray. They have succeeded, by blasting the rocks, in making a steep bridle-path along the course of the torrent, leading in many places across bridges. You often hear the water roaring far down below, but the deep abyss hides it from sight. For above a mile the river forms a succession of water-falls, which only cease when it reaches the middle basin. Here again it has to turn mill-wheels, hammer out iron, and wash gold; then it hurries murmuring through the plain as if it were going to slip quietly out, never dreaming what a terrible catastrophe awaits it before it reaches the lowest valley—a series of falls in close succession of 630 feet altogether. By the side of these falls lies Wildbad Gastein.

My bedroom in the Imperial Badeschloss is immediately beside the water-fall, and in spite of the double windows you might imagine yourself in the cabin of a steamer. People with weak nerves have great difficulty in accustoming themselves to the constant roar. Part of the water resolves itself into a cloud of mist rising into the air, and the bridge, which spans the fall in one bold arch, is covered in with a glass roof, enabling one to cross without getting wet. The whole stream forms a snowy mass of foam between its dark, rocky banks clothed with pine-trees. Here from several openings, the beneficent spring gushes out in great abundance with a temperature of 39° Reaumur [about 120° Fahrenheit].

Now, as the heat of the earth is known to increase one degree for every 100 feet, and the temperature of spring water is about 7° Reaumur [about 47° F.] on the surface, it follows that this thermal spring must rise from a depth of at least 3200 feet. It has to cool for twenty-four hours before it reaches the proper bath temperature. The water is crystal clear; no chemical analysis has succeeded in discovering the smallest trace of organic matter, and however long it is left standing no sediment ever forms in it. Its reviving effect is shown, for instance, on completely faded flowers, which when placed in it regain their bloom, as I myself have proved. In the great open bath the white earthenware tiles appear to be sky-blue, but it is only the color of the water. The baths are very comfortable. The first few knocked me up very much, now they are doing me good, but one has to be very careful with them and can easily overdo it.

Gastein has been known and used as a bath for thirteen hundred years, and yet, till within a few decades, the place consisted merely of a dozen wooden houses built in the style of the country. With a varying scale of size and ornamentation, this style retains its peculiar characteristics all over the Alps. The plentiful forests provide the material in the shape of tree-trunks, which, laid one upon the other and dove-tailed together at the corners, form the walls. The roof, too, is of wood. As there is no iron it has to be made flat, or the shingles lying one above another would slip off. They are held together with laths, which are kept down with heavy stones in case of storm. On account of the almost daily rains, the roof has to pro-ject far beyond the walls of the house, and at the same time it covers the gallery, which the want of open ground renders necessary for drying purposes. The result is a warm and comfortable house, and even the poorest hut has an appearance of trim neatness. This rises to actual elegance in the Bernese Oberland, par-ticularly in the fine carvings of the galleries in front of every story on the best side of the house. In the more wealthy houses these galleries run round the whole house. The poorer people regard the winter store of wood, which is piled up to the roof on the weather side, as a protection, though of course an ever decreasing one. On the opposite side the roof is pro-longed almost to the ground, and shelters the cattle. On the other hand, the fodder is kept in innumerable little huts on the spot where it is cut. These huts are built exactly like the houses, entirely of wood, with flat projecting roofs held down by great stones and walls of tree-stems. Hundreds of them stand in the valleys and on the pastures on the mountain slopes, where they are scarcely visible to the naked eye.

What has arisen naturally and as the result of necessity has always a greater charm than the outcome of mere caprice. The crooked road formed by the exigencies of the ground is more attractive than one that is made straight with line and rule; the really national costume more beautiful than the levelling black coat. The Austrian uniform is white because the Moravian, Bohemian, and Austrian sheep are white; that of the frontier is brown, because the wool there comes from brown sheep. The hussars wear their becoming uniform because no button-holes can be made in sheepskin, so cords have to be sewn on. Laced boots, bare knees and short leather breeches are the right thing for the continuous exertion of the mountaineer, and, with the pointed gray hat, adorned with the chamois tuft, constitute the handsome costume of the Tyrolese. The Italian does not put on his round jacket, but carries it hung over his shoulder, because his climate permits of it. So, too, the styles of architecture are determined by local conditions, and each is perfectly distinct from the other. The moment you leave the Alps for Germany, stone architecture at once begins, with towers, gables, and oriels, cozy seats in the deep window bays, vaulted halls, stone steps, and often quaint additions, terraces, and balconies.

As you go farther north romance dies out. No beauty of landscape suggests it, and the most urgent necessity—shelter from the rude climate—is the first consideration. The unsightly bricks do not permit of such ornamentation as masonry. Everything is reduced to what is absolutely necessary, and so the hideous square building arises, affording the largest amount of room with the least expenditure of time. The roof is made high and pointed to keep off the weight of snow, and finally straw comes in place of stone, and the beasts of the fields shelter under the same roof with the human beings. On the Rhine, the Siebengebirge marks a very distinct boundary between

the Franconian and the Saxon style of architecture.
What a difference between Coblenz and Cologne!

But I am in Gastein. Here stone palaces are rising
all round the water-fall, and have nearly driven out
the wooden houses; for the luxury of the capital has
been transplanted into the solitude of these Highlands.
It makes a very pretty picture. The handsome, white-
washed houses, the rocky declivities thick with black
pine, the tender green of the meadows, and the silvery
foaming river, make up a most picturesque view.
From my window I can see the greater part of the
lowest shelf of the valley. On both sides rise the rocky
walls 7000 feet high, clothed at their foot with pine
forests, further up with pale green pastures, with here
and there a shepherd's hut, and above all, the bare
summits of the mountains. The bed of the valley,
which is about four miles long, and half a mile wide,
is entirely filled up by the most splendid meadows,
some farms, and numberless hay-sheds. At a distance
of a mile [about $4\frac{7}{10}$ miles English] rises the slender
and elegant white tower of the market town of Hof-
gastein, but behind that again, the bare peaks of the
Tännengebirge shut in the view.

This beautiful valley seems to be secluded from the
rest of the world, and without any opening. Only a
grim ravine, the so-called Klamm, leads down to the
broad valley of Salzach. The ruins of an old castle
look like the bar that closed this exit, and, no doubt,
it kept it barred for many a long day. But the long-
suffering torrent manages to slip through, and escapes
by one last desperate leap into freedom, which forms
the wonderful water-fall, where it finally emerges.
The road, which has been made with great trouble and
ingenuity, follows it with less precipitancy.

We found some very sociable people here, but they

are leaving just as we were getting to know them.
We leave here to-morrow for Meran, travelling slowly
through the beautiful highlands of Steiermark and the
Tyrol. The doctor makes a great point of his patients
not returning to business immediately after treatment.
I have ordered my Staff to Treves for the 1st of Octo-
ber. The autumn manœuvres start from thence, and
I expect to be in Berlin again by the middle of October.
Good-bye, dear Ludwig. Marie joins me in love to
you and yours. As writing is a great effort to me, you
will do me a kindness by giving the others news of us.
Very affectionately yours,

HELMUTH.

BERLIN, November 18th, 1860.

DEAR, GOOD LOUIS:

I have long wanted to write to you, particularly to
congratulate you on your appointment as Kammerherr.
I only returned to Berlin a few days ago, after having been constantly absent and on my travels since the
1st of May. Our last excursion was to Masuren, on
the Russian frontier,—no great pleasure at this time
of year. On the other side of the Vistula everything
was buried in snow.

During the last few days of our stay in Gastein, we
went for a walk every evening on the only road which
connects this rocky nook with Europe, and inspected
the travellers who arrived by the mail.

I have all sorts of committees to attend, which
greatly occupy my time. In the evening I am so tired
that I get Marie to read me the lightest literature,
mostly English books by Dickens, such as "Household
Words," which contains some very pretty things.

I must confine the political information which Mie
asks of me to the remark that one still has more

19

chances by betting on peace, rather than on war; for no one so easily makes up his mind to stake much, if not all. But I may be mistaken even in this, so I prefer to prophesy nothing. Most affectionately yours,

HELMUTH.

BERLIN, April 23rd, 1864.

DEAR LUDWIG:

I take the opportunity of little Rose's birthday, not only to wish her every happiness, but to give you news of us after a long interval.

The strain of anxious expectancy of the last weeks has been lifted by the events of the 18th.* But apart from the mourning into which thousands of families have been thrown by the loss of relatives, feeling as to the issue must differ widely in the families round you, so many of whom are bound to Denmark by the closest ties.

The enthusiasm with which that little country fights for its cause, the endurance and devotion with which the army held its position at Düppel, must excite the admiration even of their opponents. Their troops suffered indescribably, far more than ours, which had the initiative of attack, and which, being superior in number, could relieve each other in the arduous task. But were the Danish authorities, in their insular security, justified in demanding such sacrifices? Was it even a just cause for which they demanded them?

I think it may be asserted that for several centuries, and particularly since the accession of Christian VII., Denmark has claimed a position amongst the European powers, not based on her own nationality, which she has only been able to maintain to the injury of another and greater power; and this is at length obliged to

* Storming of Düppel.

defend itself. Even the strongest can only permit himself to be insulted by a weaker foe up to a certain point. The Germans in the Duchies could have lived long and happily under the sceptre of a Danish king, but it was impossible that they should submit for any length of time to the decisions of the majority in a Danish parliament. From the moment when Prussia and Austria ceased to paralyze one another, as they did in the last Danish war, the Government in Copenhagen could no longer hope to assert her pretensions single-handed. It is true that divisions still exist in Germany, but the Würzburg governments go as much too far in their demands as they are behindhand with the means to carry them through. It has been known for weeks in Copenhagen that direct help was not to be expected from abroad, either from France, England, or Sweden. In spite of all the advantages of their position and entrenchments, the Danish forces were at last obliged to yield to an opponent not only twice as strong, but better drilled, armed, and equipped. And yet an assembly of lawyers, newspaper men, and chamber orators decreed resistance to the death.

The Danish press is abominable. Were it really the voice of the Danish people, one could have no pity for them. Even in these last days it decried even the military honor of those who have defeated them in every engagement. They are accused of theft, incendiarism, treachery, and cowardice. They say that the Prussians have to be forced into fighting by abuse and blows, that they must be called off from Austria because they will not bite; and the greatest absurdities besides. For instance, about the battle of Eritsoe, between Austria and Prussia, in which, "according to the probably exaggerated account of the inhabitants," 3000 men fell, "the loss at any rate was very great."

And the President of the Ministry and Bishop Monrad communicate these maunderings of some obscure reporter as facts to astonished Europe, add official footnotes, and the *Times* dishes up such nonsense to its readers.

I suppose there are hardly any such good-natured souls as our soldiers. No sooner is the last shot fired than the tall Westphalians begin, like nursemaids, to carry the Danish and their own wounded to the nearest hospital, where they all receive the same careful attention. Henry describes these scenes in his letters. The Danes go on shooting till our men are close upon them, then throw away their arms, ask for quarter, and get it. In each fight there were 20, 50, 100, and on the 18th, 3145 [prisoners]. These crowds, numbering now more than 5000 men, are treated in Prussian fortresses like Prussian soldiers. In the hospitals, particularly in the really luxurious one belonging to the Knights of St. John, Danish officers and common soldiers lay side by side with the Prussians.

Altogether it would hardly have been possible to show more humanity than has been done in this war, though it certainly entailed indescribable privations and sufferings on the troops.

The bombardment of Sonderburg was inevitable. The Danes know best what military value this part of their fortified position has for them. The summons to evacuate the fortress occurred ten days before, in the shape of a few shells which were thrown in, but was not followed up by any further cannonade. The townspeople left then, but subsequently returned.

The Danes are so obstinate that it will need a second decisive blow to bring the military part of the question to an end. The difficulty is how to get at them. What diplomacy will make of it then, God alone knows.

Would that in Denmark too the Conservation element could emancipate itself from the nightmare of the prevailing Democracy. A Denmark which should refuse to exist at the expense of Germany would at once be Germany's most natural ally. I believe firmly that Sweden is far more dangerous than Germany to Denmark's independent nationality. The assembling of the troops at Schonen, too late to be of any use to Denmark, is more menacing probably to her than to us.

But enough of war and politics.

Best love to Mie and your daughters, especially to the Rosebud, and may it open sweetly in the warm spring sunshine. Your faithful brother,

HELMUTH.

BERLIN, September 9th, 1866.

DEAR LUDWIG:

I have just received your sad news of the death of your excellent wife. I can well imagine the deep grief in your family. Mie leaves behind her the love and respect of all who knew her. Her even temper and kindly disposition, her faithful performance of duty, her rule in the household, and unremitting care for her children, can never be replaced. You will miss her grievously. Who would have thought that her old mother would outlive her; it will be a great blow to her. Still, by God's mercy, many members of our family are still with us, though at a great age; some of us must soon meet on the other side. For to-day accept this expression of my most heartfelt sympathy. If we can be of the slightest use or assistance to you, you may count upon your brother,

HELMUTH.

BERLIN, April 14th, 1867.

DEAR LUDWIG:

* * * I want so much to get away and look at an estate in Lausitz which has been recommended to me by a competent and disinterested judge as a very advantageous bargain. But there is still the Reichstag, though it probably closes the day after to-morrow; then till the 20th a Commission on the plans for the naval harbor, then the wedding of the Count of Flanders—(not to mention my own silver wedding,—is it possible?), at which I have been appointed to wait on the King of the Belgians. Then there is Louis Napoleon with his lunatic Frenchmen, and finally the continuous rain which is making me quite ill. On this prospective estate there is an enormous castle, in which Augustine the Strong stayed when he journeyed to Warsaw, and wild deer, and black game, and fishing. It would be charming if we could all retire from public life and go to live there altogether.

I have asked Fritz often enough to leave his goods and chattels quietly in Flensburg, and only look after a house when he returns. If I make this purchase, he and Guste would at once have a place to live in rent free, and, what is most important for him, congenial occupation. For so long as I cannot be there myself for any length of time, some trustworthy person would have to be always on the spot. Most affectionately,

HELMUTH.

CHRISTMAS EVE, 1868.

DEAR LUDWIG:

This afternoon at three o'clock our beloved Marie' departed this life. Her beautiful features still bear the impress of the noble, upright, and faithful spirit which endeared her to all who knew her. No care, no medical skill could save her; a terrible fever snatched her away. The continual alternations of hope and despair broke us down at last. Only yesterday evening, while she slept for seven hours, we still had confident hopes. This morning dreadful palpitation of the heart set in, accompanied by delirium. She had a presentiment of death much sooner than this, took leave of us and prayed in a low voice for us all. To-day during the most violent fever of delirium her looks and trembling movements expressed her thoughts. After a short, slight convulsion, she then fell asleep to wake in a better world, from which I would not recall her. Guste has in her quiet way performed wonders. Your brother,

HELMUTH.

BERLIN, 26th December, 1868.

DEAR LUDWIG:

The others have no doubt told you of the course and end of the terrible illness which for sixteen days kept us constantly alternating between hope and fear, and exhausted all our strength.

Gently and painlessly Marie fell asleep on Christmas Eve, a few hours before the distribution of the Christmas presents to the servants, which she had arranged herself. Her countenance, like the most beautiful marble bust, expressed the quiet resignation, the resolute strength of her character. Decomposition set in very rapidly, and the coffin has already had to be closed to-day.

The service will be performed here on Monday at three o'clock, and on the same evening the body will be removed to Creisau, whither I accompany it.

You and your children will be able to appreciate the

loss I have sustained, for you knew Marie's worth.
Your brother,

HELMUTH.

BERLIN, January 23rd, 1869.

DEAR LUDWIG:

It is with much concern that I hear from your yesterday's letter of Guste's illness; God forbid it shall
be that terrible rheumatic fever. I fear that she is feeling the after effect of her severe spell of sick-nursing,
when for sixteen nights she got no rest. I too felt
some of these after effects, but it seems to have gone
over now. I hope that Jeanette, who left this morning, will write us a few lines this evening. Your
brother,

HELMUTH.

BERLIN, March 22nd, 1872.

DEAR LUDWIG:

All the letters and even the excellent southern fruit
came safely to hand, after a few wanderings, and
pleased us very much, especially Hanne's letter written
in such a firm hand, and the pretty little sketch of the
Ufergebirge. It is to be hoped that by God's help she
may be completely restored to health, but I think you
will have to entertain the idea of spending next winter
too in the warm south, if the cure is to be thorough.
In that case it is not worth while to make the long
journey back just for the few months of real summer
that we have in the north, and you would do better to
avoid the heat, in Switzerland, by going to Glion, 1000
feet above Montreux, or to the Upper Engadine, 5000
feet above the sea.

You still have to claim 1500 thalers from me. Instead of this sum, however, as it is the Emperor's birthday, I want to make you a present of 21,000 thalers,

with the interest from the past New Year. I have a hundred shares in the Central Bodencredit, at 200 thalers—nominally 20,000 thalers, put by for you in a special money-box, which you can fetch or send for here at any time. The shares, which are above par, yield an annual dividend of 1000 thalers. This amounts to 250 thalers for the first quarter, and on the 1st of July 300 thalers will fall due, which you can dispose of as you please—either have sent to you or use in some other manner.

With a fixed increase of 1000 thalers to your income, I hope you may be free of care.

When Hanne is a little stronger you can make some charming excursions from Nervi to the Riviera. I have a lively recollection of Rapollo. The road to it lies through a tunnel, with a magnificent view looking back upon "Genova la superba." I have never seen such splendid breakers as there and at Chiavari. La Spezzia, and Porto Venere, both quite near, are said to be particularly beautiful.

At Creisau we are building and planting busily. You will find it greatly changed when you come again. With best wishes, your affectionate brother,

HELMUTH.

ROME, April 20th, 1876.

DEAR LUDWIG:

For a fortnight we have been housed on the Capitoline, the most famous of the Seven Hills of Eternal Rome, where once stood the temple of Jupiter Stator, now the Caffarelli Palace. It is now thirty years since you accompanied us here, and much has changed since then. Almost the whole of the old Forum has been dug out, the lava pavement of the Via Triumphalis has been uncovered, and the marble flooring of the temple, from which rise the shafts of granite pillars, some entire almost to the capital, but most of them merely stumps. It is not beautiful, but very interesting. Still more important excavations have been carried out on the Palatine, which I overlook from my windows, where even the foundations of the *Roma quadrata* of Romulus have become visible, made of blocks of tufa put together without any mortar. But the wide Campagna beyond, as far as the Albanian Hills, the mighty arches of the Aqueducts, the straight line of the Via Appia with the ruins of Cæcilia Metella's tomb, and away over the Viaduct to Arrina—all this has remained unchanged.

And so, too, the self-same Pope is there who was chosen in 1846, only that he has moved out of the Quirinal to self-inflicted imprisonment in the Vatican —a prison, to be sure, which has not its like in the world.

I remember so well how stately Count Ferretti, on whom the Holy Ghost had laid the choice of the Conclave, drove in Benvenuto Cellini's golden coach through the densely-crowded streets from the Quirinal to St. Peter's. How enthusiastically he was greeted then! He was expected to create the "unità d'Italia." But the union of the Italian principalities under the dominion of Rome could only be accomplished by means of revolution, by the revolt of the people against their rulers, the driving out of the foreign despots—in short, by those violent convulsions which were reserved for later times. And how could a Pope approve of all this? His liberal politics were soon converted into the very opposite; he was called Pio Nono the Second, and he had to fly to Gaeta till the reaction of 1850 restored him to Rome, where, however, he was only able to govern under the protection of French bayonets, and by proclaiming a state of siege. And yet this remarkable old man has carried the claims made by Gregory VII. and Innocent III. to temporal power further than any Pope before him, in numerous Concordats, in the Encyclical, and finally in the dogma of Infallibility. But at the very moment when Papacy has in theory reached the highest point of its power, its worldly supremacy breaks down. Victor Emmanuel had already put himself at the head of the national movement, when the victories of the German army forced France, for her own safety, to deprive the Pope of his last support, thereby opening the gates of Rome to the Piedmontese King. And now, in the Quirinal, within the old Wall of Aurelian, sits the Imperator who governs from Etna to the Alps, and exactly opposite, on the Janiculus, is a prisoner who claims the sovereignty of the world, a monarch without a realm, yet exercising an enormous influence in both hemispheres. The nearer to Rome, the more the nimbus of the Roman Church vanishes; still, she has on her side the women of all Catholic and even of some Protestant countries, with emotion, imagination, and narrowness, all mighty factors. No external power can prevail against the Papacy; it has weathered worse storms than these.

The result in Rome of the revulsion in politics is that one sees fewer priests than formerly, rather fewer beggars, and a great many more soldiers. The great Easter festivals of the Church have not taken place, nor the Miserere in the Sistine Chapel, the Benediction from the Lateran, and the illumination of the dome of St. Peter's. The temporal power now has to provide *panem et circenses*, and the twenty-six hundredth birthday of the city is to be celebrated to-day by an illumination of the Colosseum, but it is blowing and raining as if we were in the dear old Fatherland. The day after to-morrow we go a little farther south, to Naples, after having been entertained nearly three weeks in the kindest manner by the Keudells. Every morning we visited the endless treasures of Rome, and drove every afternoon in the Campagna. My stay here has done me great good, and my asthmatic affection is much relieved.

I wanted to have sent you this letter, dear Ludwig, before leaving Rome, of which you no doubt retain a lively recollection, although your stay there was unfortunately so short. From Naples we shall turn slowly homewards, making perhaps a short halt in Switzerland, to wait and see if it is not going to be spring at last. I shall then go straight to Creisau, and hope that you will come to fetch your little daughter Hanne, who will hardly be able to leave Goerbersdorf sooner than that. In the meantime much love from your affectionate brother,

HELMUTH.

BERLIN, September 15th, 1876.

DEAR LUDWIG:

I was delighted to find from your letter of the 1st, that you were enjoying yourselves in Creisau. But if so, why do you want to leave again so soon? You ·might at least stay till the 2nd of October, and put off your visit to Dresden till after the ceremony at Parchim.*

I think it would be most fitting for you to return thanks for me to the Grand Duke, the town, and all concerned, and especially to the committee. Three or four of the giants,† from Wilhelm to Ludwig, will cer-

* Unveiling of a statue of the Field-Marshal.
† The Field-Marshal's four nephews, his brother Adolf's sons.

tainly be present, and will represent the name grandly.
Yours affectionately,

HELMUTH.

CREISAU, October 7th, 1876.

DEAR LUDWIG:

I read your description of the ceremony with the
greatest interest, and Ludwig, who arrived unexpectedly yesterday, was able to give further details and
brought cuttings from the newspapers. It really
seems to have been a success, but I was very glad to
be able to look on from the safe shelter of Creisau.
For many a one now sleeping under the green sod in
France did more than we who survive; and even to
some of us, public opinion is most unjust. I will mention only Manteuffel, who, in spite of the greatest and
most successful achievements, is one of the most unpopular men in Germany.

However, I shall be obliged to go to Parchim in the
late autumn, in order to thank my native countrymen
in person.

I regret that you should not be in Creisau, which is
delightful just now, with 16° of heat [about 60° F.]
and bright sunshine. The pine-apple house is ready,
and the plants bought, and in three years' time my
successors will be able to eat the fruit. The fountains
play in two of the basins, but there is still a good deal
to be done. In the evening I go out shooting with
Ludwig and the gamekeeper.

Hares are scarce this year; all the March broods
have been destroyed. Yesterday the keeper shot a
roebuck and a pheasant. But it is a pleasure only to
watch the ways of the animal world in the silence of
the falling darkness, and in these surroundings of
woods and hills. During the day there is much to be

done, and the day is over, and it is time for the game of whist, before one has fairly looked round. With my best thanks for having undertaken the journey to Parchim. Your brother,

HELMUTH.

CREISAU, October 27th, 1876.

DEAR LUDWIG:

What a pity that you were not here for the shooting on the 24th. It was a sunny, beautiful day, and the view from the different points most wonderful. The principal guns were Bethusy and his nephew Reinhold, Count Harrach, Herr von Salisch, Count Perponcher from Neudorf, the Lieres, Zedlitzes, and Websky. But we only killed fifty hares and one deer. However, Mamsell [the housekeeper] had prepared a delicious dinner—but I will not pain you by mentioning more of the menu than mock turtle, pâté de foie gras, carp in aspic, and venison, which I shot myself a week before, at sixty-one paces at full gallop. I think the poor beast must have been predestinated.

When you come next year, you will find the orchard house finished and 400 plants bearing fruit; and two fountains splashing in front of the veranda and the elm trees. The water has been conducted into the kitchen garden and the hot-houses, so that it is no longer necessary to drag every watering-can full up from the Peile. In the garden round the little house on the hill, into which Aunt Augusta is going to remove presently, we have planted a nursery of more than 5000 little oaks. Besides which, a road will be made this autumn through the orchard, and the long copse, so that we can drive three quarters of a mile [more than three miles English] through a park. There are more than a hundred magnificent oaks in the farthest wood, which will then be seen to advantage.

On the Chapel hill all the birches—the ill weeds of the forest—will be rooted out in three years. So you see there is much work to be superintended; the rooms are good and comfortably heated, and we have lovely sunshine again to-day after a few days of fog. I cannot therefore make up my mind to return to Berlin. I dare say the Reichstag can do without me at first.

* * * On the 26th the regimental band came over from Schweidnitz, followed by the school-children, under the command of the master, and then the Sisters marched up with their little troop. They were all taken into the great hall, where Mamsell had provided mountains of bread and butter, and two barrels of beer, so that all of them, even down to the babies, went on their homeward way satisfied and rejoicing.

. With the pile of letters I still have to answer, I must close here with best love from us all. Yours,

HELMUTH.

BERLIN, July 8th, 1879.

DEAR LUDWIG:

I have just arrived here from Creisau, and must send little Hanne my most affectionate good wishes for her birthday to-day. I hope that she has recovered from her late indisposition, and that you and Friederike may have a very pleasant day.

I came here to stand by my party during the third reading of the important Duty and Tax Bill, as a single vote sometimes turns the scale. I hope, however, that after the long discussions that have gone before, the final business may not last very long, and I shall be able to return soon to Creisau.

It is very charming in the country, and when you come you will find much that is new; all the plantations especially have grown immensely. The agricultural year, it is true, has closed very badly, with a considerable deficit instead of a surplus. Now, however, the management is in the hands of Ludwig and a capable, or at any rate honest, steward.

The young crops are looking very well, and promise a rich harvest, if we could only have some warm, dry weather. The violent rains have flooded the Peile till all the meadows are under water. However welcome the overflowing of this little Silesian Nile may be in the spring, it is equally disastrous at the time of the hay harvest. Everything is encrusted with a fine gray slime, and the greater part of the abundant hay had to be thrown away. The continuous damp is of course most beneficial to the young trees in the plantations, and they are a mass of fresh green foliage. With best love to you all,

HELMUTH.

BERLIN, April 12th, 1882.

DEAR LUDWIG:

This is indeed delightful news. If, as we will hope, all your daughters are equally generously remembered —for which, may God reward good old Count Wedell —they will all be provided for.

And now you can take things a little more easily in your old days. I had made up my mind to that myself, but one has to bring much resolution to bear upon it; the abominable habit of economy sticks so firmly that it is difficult to get rid of. When, however, all those belonging to us are provided for, it is really a duty to think of ourselves.

In a day or two I leave with Helmuth Moltke for

Zurich, and go from thence to Ragatz; a few baths there would do you too a great deal of good. With congratulations and best wishes, your brother,

HELMUTH.

CREISAU, May 30th, 1884.

DEAR LUDWIG:

If you wish to see Creisau in full beauty, you ought to come soon. The foliage is magnificent; not a cockchafer or a caterpillar has touched it. The meadows are covered with a first cutting of hay, and it is to be carried to-morrow. The hawthorn is in full blossom, and a thousand buds are opening on the rose-trees by the chapel. And none of you are here to whom to show all this splendor! My wine-cellar is well filled, and four carriage horses are there for driving out. We all send love, and are looking forward with much pleasure to your arrival with Röschen in a few days.

HELMUTH.

CREISAU, October 29th, 1884.

DEAR LUDWIG:

My sincerest thanks to you and Röschen for your good wishes for my birthday No. 85. Your tasteful present arrived punctually in time for the shooting on the 23rd, and met with the unqualified approval of the twenty guests at table. I was most fortunate in having chosen for the shooting the one perfectly fine sunny day we have had, and the landscape glowed in all the beauty of blue hills and the autumn tints of the woods. One hundred and seventy fine hares, four deer, two snipe, and one owl were brought home. The pheasants were not to be driven out of the thick cover, and, con-

20

trary to all expectations, only four were shot, of which two were sent to Uetersen and two to you.

The next day I had to go to Berlin, but only stayed one day, and so kept my birthday in the railway carriage; but I spent the evening with relations in Saarau, to which I branched off from Königszelt. I returned here in the midst of storm and rain the day before yesterday, and found a pile of telegrams and letters, at the answering of which Helmuth and I, *viribus unitis*, have had to work for two days.

We two are now reigning here in solitary splendor in our roomy castle.

Now that yesterday's election battle is over, I hope we may soon learn something of the result; I hope you will carry Bismarck through. Here, in the country, we do not, as you might suppose, choose a farmer, but —in our wisdom—a chimney sweep. He is said to be a great orator, and can make the voters believe all sorts of things. I am curious to see if my friends in Litthau want to have me again. Printed papers have been sent to me in which they say that, though I am in other respects really quite a good man, I am of no use as a Member because I vote for the corn and timber duties—certainly the chief articles of commerce in Memel. For all that, an unknown lady of that province has sent me a pair of knitted woolen gloves, and if the ladies are on my side there is still hope for me. With best love, your brother,

HELMUTH.

SAN REMO, March 24th, 1885.

DEAR LUDWIG:

Affectionate greetings to you from the edge of the Ligurian sea-board, of which you must have pleasing recollections from the time of your stay at Nervi! It is certainly a delusion when we think in Germany that there is no winter here. Even to-day I feel colder than in Berlin. Out-of-doors and walking it is delightful, but in the rooms a temperature of $+12°$ Reaumur is most unsatisfactory. The sun is always bright and the sky clear, but the east wind is peculiarly cold and piercing. But that will soon change. Not only the almond and apricot but pear and cherry trees are in full blossom, and the orange and citron trees full of hanging fruit. I am living in the house of a German medical man, Dr. Goltz. From our windows we look down upon the deep blue sea, and the promenade is delightful along the thousand feet and more of stone terrace, planted with palms, and the breakers come plunging in below. At the other side stand the palatial hotels, in an almost unbroken row. On a calm day it is delightful to walk or sit there and listen to the murmur of the waves, the tranquil breathing of the slumbering sea. At other times they beat fiercely against the rocky shore, sending the foam flying up over the Molo.

We were very quiet for the first week. We are very comfortable, and have made excursions into the immediate neighborhood. Ingeniously constructed roads lead through the olive woods and up the hills to Madonna della Guardia and della Costa, while others run along the shore between countless villas. The violets are over, but the roses are on the point of opening, and will afford a most lovely sight. The orange trees, too, are beginning to blossom, a sign that the fruit is ripe. And yet I am looking forward to a German spring which, when it does come, is far more beautiful than it ever is here. All these gray olives and holm oaks are not to be compared with a green meadow and the first tender leaves of the beech woods.

I expect to reach Creisau in May, and hope then to see you and Röschen again. Till then good-bye. Your brother,

HELMUTH.

NERVI, April 17th, 1885.

DEAR LUDWIG:

To-day I send you a friendly greeting from this well-remembered place—what a pity that you should not be here too! I dare say that you too lived in the Hotel Victoria, near the shore, where, in the wing which was probably built afterwards, I have a charming apartment with a view over the palm and orange trees to the sea. The railroad, which has of course been constructed since you were here, and runs between Genoa and La Spezzia, piercing the promontories with eighty tunnels, has no doubt brought many changes to Nervi, but the delightful footpath along the sea-shore past the old Saracen tower was certainly there in your time. Protected at the back by high walls, you have before you the endless expanse of the sea. I can sit there for hours watching the play of the waves. The long dark blue roller comes rushing along, "ever coming and ever fleeing," and then with flying white mane it casts itself upon the low crags, and writhes foaming between the rifts in the rocks. The Italians call these waves *cavallos*, in remembrance most likely of the steeds of Hephæstos. I am sure you often visited the Villa Gropallo with its great garden, where fresh blossoms are breaking out beside the ripe fruit on the orange and lemon trees.

I find it warmer here than on the Ponente. Nervi has this peculiarity, that no gorge opens down from the mountains; the bay is enclosed in an unbroken wall of hills, and receives only the south wind with open arms. The grand promontory of Portofino wards off the terrible east wind. With this configuration of the land it is impossible that there should be any promenades unless you were to climb up to Sant' Ilario. It is all shut in by houses and walls; but the walk by the sea makes up for everything.

What a really enchanting land this Italy is! As long as it was the wrestling ground of Germans and French its poet might well say, "Deh! Fosse tu piu forte, o meno bell' almeno!" (Röschen will correct this line); but now she too has got her " unità." Every creature begs here; the children hold out their hands with a "Moriamo di fame," but they dance merrily away if they fail to get anything. The mass of the population lives under heavy burdens, but life is not so bitterly earnest here as at home; even the poorest need not freeze to death or starve. There sits a young fellow on the cliff smoking his *lancietta*, "cool to his inmost heart." He catches a fish, buys a handful of roast chestnuts at the next street corner, and is supplied with food for the day. The rest of his time he spends at the boccia or in lazy contemplation. Wherever there is a little pool or brook or some rainwater, there the women of Nervi assemble with the most animated conversation to wash the "gleaming garments," with which, to dry them, they adorn even the windows of the palaces. But you find good-humor everywhere.

I intend to make one more short excursion to Santa Margarita and Rapallo, in the Levante, then to stay in Cadenabbia, on the Lake of Como, till it is spring in Germany. Then indeed it is more beautiful in our beech woods than here, and I shall take it as a peculiar favor from God if I am permitted to see the awakening of Nature in my own home for the eighty-fifth time. With best love, your brother,   HELMUTH.

BERLIN, May 24th, 1888.

DEAR LUDWIG:

* * * I regard it as a special mercy of God each time that I live to see a new spring. When a man has outlived his three-score and ten years, he can only pray that the Lord will take him mercifully to Himself, without too much suffering and infirmity. True it is that "Death is never a welcome guest," still I have no wish to live through the next few years; a bad time is coming for Germany, and I unfortunately cannot seclude myself in peace. *Beatus ille qui procul negotiis*, is not vouchsafed to me; I may yet have to swear allegiance to a fifth King of Prussia.

I have just returned from the grand wedding at Charlottenberg;* the papers will give you full descriptions. The bride, with the crown on her head and covered with the Crown jewels, looked charming. In the midst of all the splendor the Empress Augusta was brought in, in her wheel-chair, all in black, without any kind of ornament. The tears came into my eyes as her grandchildren knelt before her to kiss her hand. Then the Emperor came in, his tall, noble figure unbowed, greeting the company with a kindly smile. Only his eyes to me looked sunken, and his breathing was rapid and very painful. It is heart-breaking to see him struggling with inexhaustible patience and sweetness against his cruel fate; one foot on the throne and the other in the grave.

My home party send affectionate messages to you and Rose, your faithful nurse. And so God bless you. Your feeble old brother,

HELMUTH.

---

* Prince Henry of Prussia, son of the Emperor Frederick, was married on this day to Irene, Princess of Hesse.

INDEX.

DATE INDEX TO LETTERS.

THE END.